WHISPER OF
SHADOWS
AND SNAKES

J.S. BURNS

ISBN: 978-1-7643376-2-5 (Paperback)

ISBN:978-1-922854-23-0 (Ebook)

Published by J.S. Burns

www.jsburnsauthor.com

Cover design by Jake Burns

Interior formatting by Jake Burns

Edited by Kristy Martin and Chloe Cran

This is a work of fiction. Names, characters, places, and incidents are products of the author's imagination or are used fictitiously. Any resemblance to actual persons, living or dead, or actual events is purely coincidental.

CONTENTS

DEDICATION

For Simba.

You sat by my side hour after hour, word after word as I wrote this story.

It breaks my heart that you aren't here to see it through to the end.

I did it buddy.

This one's for you.

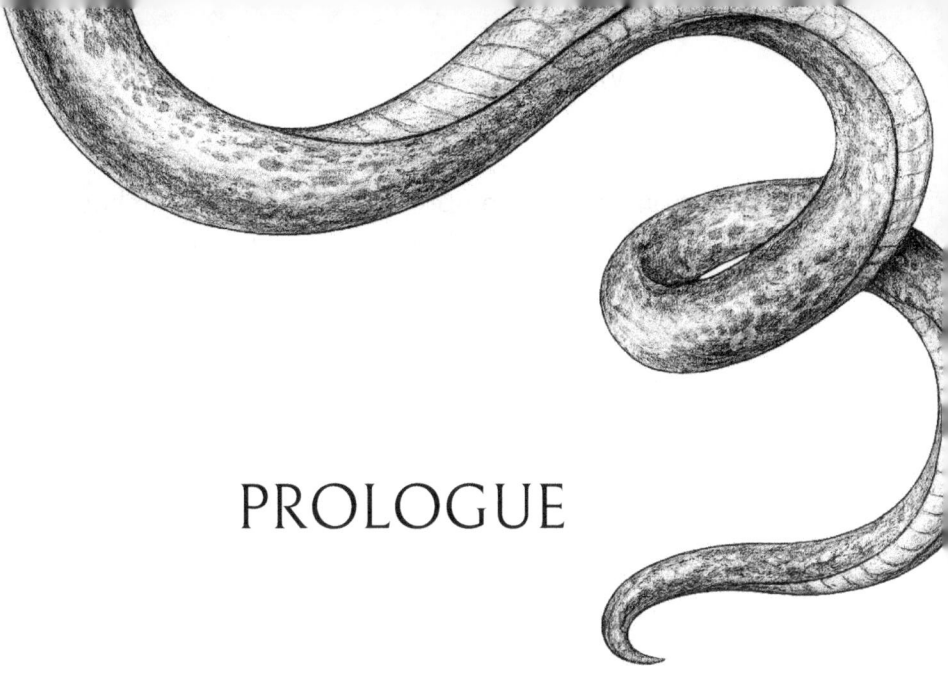

PROLOGUE

Two dark smudges detached themselves from the shelter of a low-lying bush. They moved as one through the night, melting into the shadows and disappearing through the rough landscape, only to appear several metres closer to the tall, proud walls made of crumbling stone. The figures crouched, taking shelter amongst some prickly shrubs. Overhead, the full moon peeked out from the cloud that had been concealing it, bathing the ancient walls in silver light.

A cool breeze rustled through the star-shaped leaves of the surrounding maple trees. Shadows stretched from the lone building that sat hunched behind the stone walls, its façade cracked and dilapidated, scars from a battle fought lifetimes ago. The shattered windows that pockmarked the front of the fortified building were empty aside from a few dusty cobwebs.

The bright red roof had faded over time to a dull pink, and many of the tiles had broken or fallen off, darkness gaping from the now-empty holes. Mountains arched over the building, their peaks reaching up to pierce the dark sky.

The watery moonlight washed over the silent landscape, giving form to the shadowy figures crouched within the tangled shrubs. There were two men, clothed entirely in black. The taller man straightened slightly, reaching his arms over his head. As he stretched, his sleeves pulled back from his wrists, revealing swirls of dark ink tattooed against his pale skin.

A shiver travelled down his spine as he tried to ignore the eerie silence of the surrounding countryside. Besides the lone building sitting ominously before him, housed behind its protective walls, the two men had encountered only the twisted maple trees that grew at the foot of the surrounding mountains.

The moonlight sparked against metal as the man shifted, revealing a razor-sharp blade strapped across his back. Subconsciously, the man's fingers tightened the leather straps that ran diagonally down his chest, holding the weapon in place. Upon his face, he wore a carved mask, painted the same inky black as his clothes. It was simple in its design, with delicate strands of silver paint embellishing the eye sockets. Small horns protruded from the forehead of the mask and a grinning mouth adorned the bottom, where a set of tusks jutted from the painted lips.

The man took a deep breath, clenching his jaw in discomfort as even the brisk night air was made stuffy by his mask. He hadn't chosen to wear the face-covering out of a love for its design or in the hope it would strike fear into his targets with its inhuman features. He wore it for one reason only: to conceal his identity from prying eyes.

The tall man's companion was the complete opposite: short and solid. He wore the same tight, dark clothes as the other man, but a flabby gut and poor posture made him seem almost comical. The shorter man's mask was plain in comparison to his companion's, only covering the bottom half of his face. His eyes had a tired, dull look, like the very thought of not being in bed was draining. He would have been immediately dismissed as a threat if not for the lethal-looking bow and arrows slung over his round shoulders.

A cloud engulfed the moon, and darkness fell over the two men. They sprang into action, leaving behind the shelter of the prickly shrubs and darting silently to the base of the wall. The taller man ran his hands across the wall's surface and, quickly finding a handhold, he began to haul himself upwards. He was strong, as was evident from the rippling muscles outlined beneath his skin-tight clothing as he climbed, scaling the wall in a matter of seconds, his movements supple and precise.

Crouching at the top of the wall, he looked down to see his companion struggling, barely a metre from the ground.

'Hurry up,' he muttered impatiently. His voice was low and enticing.

The short man stared at him venomously and continued up the wall, his breathing quickly becoming more laboured. Throwing his head to the sky, the tall man, Kisho, whispered a curse beneath his breath. Reaching up, he removed the mask covering his face and took in a mouthful of the cold air. Moonlight pierced through the billowing clouds and illuminated his shockingly youthful features. He was young—barely a man. Icy blue eyes quickly scanned their surroundings, taking note of the small, square courtyard nestled within the four stone walls.

Kisho's gaze darted amongst the deep shadows blanketing the paved garden that was barricaded from the outside world. He frowned. The only structure within the walls was the rundown building with the faded red roof built against the back of the courtyard, close to the imposing mountains.

Sighing and revelling in the unobstructed fresh air filling his lungs, Kisho rolled his shoulders, running a hand through his hair. He could see no one; however, he didn't relax, a feeling of unease prickling beneath his skin as the silent shadows beckoned from the inside of the rough walls.

He, unlike his unwanted partner on this mission, knew what their purpose was. He served Azrael, a ruthless, power-hungry warlord who would stop at nothing to fulfil his dark wishes. The warlord surrounded himself with allies known only as the Dark Council. Not many people scared Kisho, but his skin prickled every time he thought about the evil, twisted beings that made up the council. They hovered around the warlord, murmuring in his ear, planting thoughts of power, violence, and domination.

But the warlord's army would not be enough; he needed a weapon. And so Kisho had been summoned, which in turn led him on his search for a school hidden away in a small pocket of the world. Protected by mountains and miles of rough, unpopulated land, the school took in orphans and runaways and gave them a home. Many of the students were trained in self-defence and combat, and the warlord himself had once been a student there—before he was driven out for the murder of one of his classmates.

Hidden in the school was the weapon: an amulet that the Dark Council had traced through ancient legend, predicting its immense power to control the four elements of nature. Kisho had been told that there were several outposts dotted around the base of the mountains, serving as watchtowers of sorts, allowing the school that was hidden high amongst the rocky peaks to be warned of any potential intruders. But it didn't make sense to Kisho— surely this wasn't one of the outposts. It looked so rundown and overgrown, like no one had set foot in it for centuries.

Looks can be deceiving, thought Kisho, and he hoped that he was right. The warlord had made it clear that if he was to fail, he would never see the dawn break over a new day.

The short man hauled himself up onto the wall with a sigh of relief. 'You took your time,' hissed Kisho, annoyed. 'We can't get spotted or it will be over for both of us.'

'Whatever,' replied the short man, his voice gravelly and punctuated by heavy breathing. 'This place is deserted. I—'

There was a low whistle followed by a solid thump, and an arrow appeared buried in the short man's throat. His eyes widened in shock as his hands rose to grip the arrow now embedded in his neck. He grappled at it weakly before his eyes glazed over and he slumped forward, lifeless.

Kisho launched himself sideways just as two more arrows whistled past his head, clattering harmlessly into the wall where he had stood moments before. His legs bunched underneath him as he spun around, his sharp eyes catching the shadowy figure across the courtyard. The attacker was already nocking another arrow to their bow. In one fluid motion, Kisho threw himself forward, tumbling off the wall and into the darkness below, landing hard on all fours.

He bit back a hiss of pain and was immediately on his feet, sprinting across the cobblestones towards the opposite side of the courtyard where the shadowy figure had been. Ivy snaked out of the wild gardens, threatening to trip him as he dodged around the clinging fronds. His breath came in even, controlled bursts as he gathered himself for the confrontation ahead.

Metal flashed in the air above him, causing Kisho to leap forwards, colliding with a large fern as he rolled over and onto his knees, drawing his sword. He desperately slashed upwards just as his opponent dived on him again, their swords meeting in a savage clash, the sound cleaving through the silent night.

His attacker was dressed similarly to him—in skin-tight, flexible clothing and a cloth mask that covered the bottom half of his face. Kisho roughly twisted his blade to the left, forcing his opponent to stumble back a step. A curse escaped his lips as he felt the cool breeze on his face, and he realised he had left his own mask atop the wall where the short man had been shot. Adjusting the tight grip on his sword, he lowered himself into a crouch, ready for the next attack.

Kisho's opponent's eyes slid past him to look over his shoulder before focusing back on him. The moment had only lasted a split second, but that split second had been a mistake. The hair on the back of Kisho's neck stood up, and he desperately lunged sideways while hurling his sword at his attacker. He heard a grunt of pain followed by another whistle as an arrow once again missed its mark and clattered onto the overgrown flagstones that covered the courtyard floor.

Kisho glanced backwards just long enough to see that his aim had been true as he watched his attacker pry the blade out of his leg with a spurt of blood. Swiftly, Kisho turned and hurled himself over a garden bed and into a thick mass of jumbled ivy and overgrown hedging.

Steadying his breathing and forcing his trembling limbs into obedience, Kisho shrunk further into the jungle of tangled, dense bushes, treading carefully to remain silent amongst the brittle fronds. Through the branches and vines around him, he could see his opponent limping towards where he had disappeared, growing ever closer.

Kisho retreated stealthily until his back hit the rough bricks of the courtyard wall. He had nowhere else to go. He bit back a curse as the archer swung himself down from the wall above and landed with a thump next to the man who was now bleeding heavily from his leg. Both of Kisho's assailants were male and very clearly skilled in combat, judging from how close he had just come to being shot with an arrow. As the archer moved closer, Kisho noticed that he wore identical clothing to the man with the sword.

Clearly some sort of uniform, thought Kisho, his interest piqued as the two men stalked ever closer to his hiding spot.

Kisho closed his eyes and steadied his breathing. Focusing on the cool night air on his skin, the sound of the leaves rustling softly in the breeze, the crunch of footsteps getting closer. He felt power awaken within him, swelling with each deep, deliberate breath. He dived deep into that feeling of power, caressed it in his mind, and delved into the warm feeling it awakened inside him. His skin began to tingle, goosebumps racing across his body as a feeling of intense ecstasy rushed through his veins, causing him to almost gasp out loud in pleasure. His head and shoulders arched back and with an intense rush, he disappeared, his clothes crumpling to the ground.

As the waves of pleasure subsided and the swell of power returned to a dull glow inside Kisho's body, he opened his eyes. The world had faded to blurry shapes, enveloped in a bluish tinge. His vision had decreased dramatically; however, as he breathed in, he was bombarded with an entirely new sense.

Smell.

His forked tongue darted out of his mouth, and instantly an image appeared in his mind, painting the landscape before him. The two assailants were still stalking towards him, their bodies appearing as a dull orange glow, indicating their body heat and separating them from the hazy mess of plants and clothing surrounding his long, serpentine body.

Slowly, Kisho slithered forwards, his tongue continuing to dart in and out of his mouth, painting an image of his surroundings. He was an obsidian viper; one bite from his fangs and a man would be dead in seconds. Kisho slunk out from the shelter of his crumpled clothes and circled to the left, taking a wide arc around his two stalkers, branches and leaves brushing silently against his black scaled skin.

He remembered the first time he had shifted; he had been a young child. The viper had been his first transformation, and the rush of endorphins and nausea from shrinking down to the size of a snake had been too much for him. He had instantly lost hold of the shift and grown straight back into his human body, vomiting profusely all over himself and refusing to ever shift again. Time had passed since then, and that small child had grown—and had lots of time to practise.

Muscles coiled and uncoiled as Kisho slunk up behind his two unsuspecting victims. One final flick of his tongue

WHISPER OF SHADOWS AND SNAKES

showed him the location of his targets. His snake body rippled, drawing in power as he retracted into himself, ready to strike. With a rush of energy, he launched forwards, fangs snapping out as he latched himself onto the first man's leg, venom pumping into his victim's veins. Thick blood welled in his mouth as he drew back, lashing his body sideways and lunging again, deadly liquid flowing freely from his mouth as he struck a second time, burying himself into the archer's ankle.

As quickly as he struck, he forced his body backwards, retreating into the thick undergrowth. His snake form did not have very good hearing, but he waited silently as the muffled cries from his prey slowly subsided. Once again, he steadied his breathing, focusing on that power inside him, willing it to flow through his veins, filling up his body. With a rush of power and pleasure, his midnight black scales rippled and his body exploded upwards, cracking into the branches of the bush above him.

Twigs scraped against his skin as he felt the familiar, nauseating rush of growing from a few inches to six feet tall. The black scales swirled and thinned, forming intricately detailed tattoos inked onto his pale skin. Kisho hissed as the cool night breeze bit into his naked body. He glanced down to where a tattoo of a large snake wrapped down his right arm. The ink itself was still twisting and forming as it slowly settled into its final resting place, the serpent's head becoming still on the back of his hand.

Kisho gingerly stepped out from the shrubs, wincing as his bare feet caught in the prickly undergrowth and sharp branches scraped against his stomach and thighs. As he emerged from the tangled mess of bushes, his ears picked up sharp, shallow breathing. Cautiously, Kisho walked over to his two attackers, both crumpled on the ground. One laid limply on his side, but the other, his bow and arrow still clenched in his hand, was on his back, his breath coming in ragged gulps.

His eyes rolled to the side as Kisho knelt next to him. He scanned Kisho's body from top to toe, taking in the multitude of animals inked across his naked skin. 'Who—who are you?' he managed to gasp out as spasms wracked his body.

Kisho held his arms out, a cocky smirk pulling at his lips. 'Me?' He paused for a moment, faltering, shadows flickering in his eyes.

Letting his arms drop back to his sides, Kisho stood, his muscles moving seamlessly beneath his skin. Under his breath, he muttered, 'I'm nobody.'

His blue eyes flickered back towards the man as one last spasm rocked his body, foam forming at his mouth before silence fell. Blank eyes staring at the full moon far above.

With a sigh, Kisho reached down and started undressing the man. 'Sorry,' he muttered. 'But what better way to sneak into somewhere secret than right under everyone's noses?'

Moments later, Kisho was dressed as his assailant, bow and arrows slung across his shoulder, mask in place over the bottom half of his face—concealing his features. He dragged the bodies into the bushes, and after a few seconds' hesitation, returned to the corner of the courtyard where he had shifted. He reached down into his pile of clothes and withdrew his sword, adding it to the assortment of weapons strapped across his back. Straightening his shoulders, Kisho took a deep breath and set out across the courtyard, moving steadily towards the mountains looming overhead.

Two hours later, Kisho hauled his body up over a cliff face, sprawling face-down on the soft grass atop the rocks. Sweat ran down his back and his slow, steady breaths had given way to loud gasps as he sucked air into his lungs. Groaning, he balled his spasming fingers into fists and pushed himself upwards, his arms shaking with the effort. Cursing himself for not shifting into an owl and flying up the cliff, Kisho rolled his shoulders and stretched out his legs before taking stock of his surroundings.

He was perched on the edge of a lush, sprawling valley, hidden among the mountain peaks. Colossal maple trees filled the gorge, forming a natural barrier between the top of the mountains and the basin floor. Between the intertwined branches, numerous lights twinkled—the only sign of human habitation. *The school,* Kisho thought, anticipation fluttering in his stomach as he smoothed down his unfamiliar clothing. *Hopefully this disguise works.*

He gazed around the mountain top, marvelling at how well hidden the school was. It felt completely isolated, cut off from the rest of the world far below. The mountains around him formed a natural valley, roughly oval in shape, as if a giant had picked up a spoon and taken a huge scoop out of the rocky summit.

He was perched atop the peaks at the southern end of the basin, and in the distance, at the opposite end of the school, the moonlight glimmered off a vast stretch of water. Begrudgingly, Kisho shook his head. Whoever had decided to hide the school here atop the mountains had been smart. It would be almost impossible to launch an attack on the valley—and so easy to defend against any enemies.

Kisho's power stirred and he felt a pull in his gut, beckoning him forward and down towards the lush trees.

Magic calling to magic—a quiet whispering voice.

Stretching out the last of his cramped muscles from the arduous climb, Kisho launched himself forward, following the unfamiliar pull that urged him onwards. As he plunged into the dense undergrowth, he realised he was not alone; figures flickered at the edge of his vision, other people dressed similarly to him moving among the trees. Silently, he flitted from shadow to shadow, the thick grass masking his footsteps as he slunk deeper into the forest.

Torches rose from the ground at intervals throughout the valley, flames lighting the twisting paths throughout the rough tree trunks. As Kisho stalked through the flickering firelight, the canopy above him caught his eye, and he stopped dead in his tracks.

Perched above him, spread amongst the solid branches of the large maples, were tree houses. Each immense tree easily housed a handful of the wooden structures, many of which were camouflaged by the thick foliage, making it difficult to see just how many tree houses there were.

Footsteps crunched through the leaf litter close to Kisho, and he quickly ducked into the shadows behind one of the maples just as a woman stepped into view. She was elderly, her brown hair streaked with grey and her face stern as she stalked through the night. She wore identical clothing to Kisho's stolen garments and carried a lethal-looking blade in her hand. The woman's eyes flicked back and forth as she moved through the winding paths within the forest.

Some sort of teacher, maybe? Kisho thought as he eased out of his hiding place, taking care to move in the opposite direction to the one the woman had gone in. No need to attract any unwanted attention. Not when he was this close.

The whispering voice urging him forward grew louder and louder as he made his way swiftly through the valley, his power churning inside of him and becoming impossible to ignore. Sweat trickled down his brow as he pushed himself faster, his movements becoming more reckless the closer he got to the source of magic.

Abruptly, the trees around him ended and a small grassy field spread out before Kisho, bordered on the opposite side by a grove of bamboo. Peeking above the thin trunks was what appeared to be some sort of roof. Magic and power now throbbed in his head, making it almost impossible to concentrate as it pulled him forward. He stumbled into the field, the moon sliding out from the clouds and bathing Kisho in silver light. He froze, crouching down to the ground, desperately trying to block out the incessant voice in his head that urged him onwards. Slowly, he began to move forward, low to the ground, easing himself across the exposed strip of grass.

A high-pitched giggle sounded from behind him. Kisho bristled and spun around, pulling a dagger from his boot. His keen eyes could see nothing, but another giggle to his left had him swiftly spinning, hurling the dagger in the direction of the noise. Grass rustled, and the dagger thumped harmlessly into the earth.

Suddenly, tiny hands shot out of the grass around Kisho's feet and latched onto his legs, clawing at his skin through his pants. Panic surged through his body, and Kisho fell backwards, more hands grasping at his body and pulling him tight against the earth.

Arms wrapped around his head, holding it in place as a creature emerged from the undergrowth and stepped into view. It was humanoid but tiny, barely ten inches tall. Its skin was a translucent blue, with eyes black as night taking up most of its tiny head. It giggled again, baring its razor-sharp teeth. The grass parted, and more of the creatures revealed themselves, holding Kisho down as he struggled and kicked.

'What do you want, sprite?' Kisho snapped, naming the creature.

The sprite crouched on Kisho's chest, slicing a thin line down his cheek with its sharp nails. It raised its blood-soaked finger to the moon, breathing in the scent of magic in his blood.

'We've never tasted one of your kind before,' it crooned, still examining his blood. 'Magic may be gone from this world, but it lingers in your veins, boy.'

The small creatures around Kisho started hissing in excitement, jostling each other to move closer to their leader. 'What are you, hmmm?' mused the sprite, its long tongue snaking out of its mouth to slurp the blood off its finger.

The sprite gasped loudly, and its eyes rolled back in its skull as the blood reached its lips. Its body spasmed, and colours rippled through its translucent skin before it fell forward with a hiss. Slowly, the sprite opened its eyes and locked onto Kisho's panicked gaze.

'So much pain,' it whispered. 'So much regret. What did I see, boy? Hmmm. I saw fire—a ritual? Tattoos inked onto your skin. Others with the same markings, but different. Then nothing but death. Blood and darkness and fear. Fear as you ran, as you did nothing.' The sprite turned to its waiting companions. 'It's been a long time since we've feasted on human flesh, but The Mother has gifted us tonight.'

The waiting sprites giggled maniacally and closed in on the trapped boy.

At the mention of The Mother, the primordial source of all magical creatures, fear and adrenaline shot into Kisho, and with an almighty pull, he wrenched himself free of the small hands that had been holding him. Blood flowed where the fingers had been embedded in his skin. He rolled to the side, ripping another dagger from its sheath on his leg and slashing at the advancing sprites. They screamed as he carved them open, black blood spurting onto the grass. Quickly, Kisho launched himself to his feet as more and more sprites clawed up his legs, trying to drag him backwards. He twisted and hacked with his dagger, panic taking over as he fought to stay upright, to keep moving forward.

Hands were now digging into his back as creatures weighed him down, dragging him to his knees. His dagger was wrenched from his hands, and his face was slammed into the ground, dirt filling his mouth, making it impossible to breathe. Dread flooded his mind as Kisho desperately thrashed in the grass, ripping the small creatures from his body and clawing his way towards the bamboo grove.

Suddenly, darkness washed over the field and silence abruptly fell. Kisho launched himself upright. The moon had vanished behind a cloud, and the sprites had gone, too. With no hands holding him down, Kisho tore across the field, only stopping once he reached the shadows of the bamboo grove. Breathing heavily, he turned back, wiping blood off the slice down his cheek just as the moon re-appeared from behind the cloud. Instantly, sprites rose from the grass, their depthless black eyes piercing into Kisho's.

One of the sprites limped forward, a massive gash down its leg. 'I have tasted your blood, boy,' it hissed. 'I have seen your past, your shame, your fear. All of it.' It glanced at the moon. 'We may be slaves to the moonlight, but we are many. We are spread far and wide throughout the land, and now that we have had a taste of your magic blood ...' The sprite trailed off threateningly and sank back into the grass, its brethren swiftly disappearing in its wake.

Kisho spun on his heel, shouldering his way through the bamboo before he doubled over, vomiting into the grass. He shuddered uncontrollably, blood oozing from a multitude of scratches across his body. Memories flickered through his mind, thoughts and feelings he had forced himself to forget, recollections the sprite now shared from drinking his blood. Biting his lip and forcing his panic down, he hauled himself upright, head throbbing as he stumbled blindly forward through the bamboo. Barely aware of the magic pulling him deeper into the night.

It wasn't long before Kisho stood in front of a plain door on a small wooden building. It was perched within a rocky hollow, surrounded on all sides by the tall bamboo shoots, cut off from the rest of the valley. His magic throbbed in his veins, urging him forwards, screaming at him to open the door and step through the threshold. The building was nothing special: a curved, emerald green tiled roof, sculptures of cranes perched on each corner of the green tiles. Steeling himself, Kisho pushed open the door and slipped inside.

Instantly, the voice pulling him forward and the magic raging in his blood went silent. Kisho let out a long breath, his head clearing and his mind quieting, allowing him time to concentrate. It was dark on the other side of the door.

He reached out to the wall to guide himself, pausing only briefly for his eyes to adjust to the dim light before he breezed silently down a short corridor. There were no doorways opening off of the hallway, nowhere else for Kisho to turn, and so he continued, reaching a long staircase. Unease prickled in his gut as he climbed the stairs, his heartbeat picking up speed the further he slunk into the unknown. To ease his mind, Kisho drew his sword, clenching the hilt in a vice-like grip.

Suddenly, Kisho reached the top of the stairs and lost contact with the wall. Sensing open space around him, he quickly retreated half a step, eyes straining to make out his surroundings. The room before him was made predominantly of wood, with high vaulted ceilings and minimal furniture. A large, four-poster bed stood against one wall and bookshelves lined another, filled with a haphazard assortment of books and ornaments. The only light came from the opposite corner of the room.

Kisho frowned and made his way forward, slipping silently over the wooden floorboards. The back of his neck prickled as he moved closer to the light, but he ignored the feeling and continued onwards. Kisho's breath caught in his throat as he drew alongside the light source. Sitting upon a wooden bench was the amulet, the source of the soft glow.

The amulet itself was beautiful. It looked to be made from a material Kisho had never seen before, pale in colour and perfectly smooth, save for the intricately carved design that spiralled around the outside of the circular pendant. The centre of the amulet flowered into a group of crystals, all emitting a soft white light. A leather strap, plain in comparison to the gem, looped through a hole at the top of the amulet. Power pulsed from the object, rattling through Kisho's body, begging him to draw closer. Smiling to himself, Kisho reached for the treasure just as candlelight blinked into existence behind him.

Startled, Kisho spun around, bringing his sword up and moving into a well-practised defensive stance.

Standing in the middle of the room was a short old man. His hair grew in white tufts around his ears, and he was clothed in a loose nightgown. His long beard brushed along the ground and flowed in a gentle breeze. Kisho noticed the movement and his eyes flicked to the left, seeing an open window. He stepped back ever-so-slightly. All he needed was the amulet, and he could make a run for it. A flash of light caught Kisho's eye, and he adjusted the grip on his sword as he noticed the old man had placed the candle on the ground and drawn a long, slender blade.

The short man twisted the blade slightly, catching the candlelight and blinding Kisho, forcing him to turn his head. As he did, the old man struck, covering the distance between them with blinding speed, taking Kisho by surprise. Desperately, Kisho blocked the man's attack, sparks flying off their swords as they clashed together. The old man effortlessly forced Kisho to backpedal with a flurry of quick stabs with his sword. Kisho barely managed to evade each thrust that was thrown at him. His mind reeled;

the skills his attacker possessed had completely thrown Kisho.

He needed to gain the upper hand, or he risked losing his life.

Kisho lunged forward, savagely bringing his sword down for a killing blow. His opponent twisted to the side, his dexterity completely at odds with his age. Moving in one fluid movement, the old man swung his sword low and then quickly changed direction, slamming the pommel up under Kisho's jaw. Bright light flashed behind Kisho's eyes as he fell backwards onto the floor.

Blood filled his mouth, and he spat it onto the wooden floorboards as he scrabbled backwards, bumping into the wall behind him. His eyesight cleared, only for him to see the old man looming over him, sword raised above his head. It had been a long time since anyone had bested Kisho, and never had it been an old man. But he possessed speed and skill that clearly outmatched Kisho's own.

'Who are you?' Kisho asked through clenched teeth as he delved into his power, willing a transformation to come over him.

'I am the principal of this school,' the old man answered with a smile, 'and I am the last face you are going to see.'

'I doubt that,' Kisho said through a smirk as his power surged outwards, engulfing his body, the wolf inked onto his left bicep beginning to tingle and grow.

Just as Kisho closed his eyes, ready to lose himself in the shift, his power vanished. It was as if a hand had clamped down on a flame, extinguishing it. He gasped as his magic sucked back into that small part of him, leaving him vulnerable and still human. His senses reeling, Kisho opened his eyes to see the old man's sword swinging towards his throat.

Kisho dropped his own sword and lunged forward onto his knees, feeling pain on the back of his shoulders as metal sliced through his flesh.

'Who are—How did you do that?' Kisho stammered, warm blood dripping down his shoulders and pooling around his hands. 'What did you do to me?!'

'You think you're the only one with magic, boy?' sneered the man. 'You think you can come in here and take the treasure I have been guarding for over a thousand years?'

Kisho felt cool metal press against the side of his face.

'I know your kind,' the old man paused. 'That is, I used to know your kind. I thought you were all wiped out, but clearly, you managed to run away. And you still live in fear, covering your face with a mask.'

Anger blistered through Kisho's body as he started trembling.

'I didn't run.'

'What was that, boy?' The blade pressed deeper into Kisho's cheek. 'You'll have to speak up.'

'I said,' Kisho growled, spitting more blood out of his mouth, 'I did not run!'

Kisho lunged upwards and grabbed the man's long beard in both his hands, wrenching it with all his strength, causing the old man to tumble sideways. Kisho rolled forward, hissing as his damaged shoulders slammed into the hard floor. The damper on his magic lifted as the old man lost control, falling onto his side.

Kisho staggered forwards, pain flashing through his body as he slammed against the wall next to where the amulet sat. He heard a door open behind him and footsteps thud into the room. Impulsively, Kisho's hand shot out and clasped the amulet tightly.

A concussive wave of power exploded from the treasure, blasting Kisho against the opposite wall of the room. Bright green lightning flashed through the sky outside the window, followed by an earth-rattling *boom*, causing Kisho to grasp his ears and double over as the whole mountain shook. Leaves rained down from the great trees outside as the blast echoed through the valley, shattering the glass window and knocking over the bookshelves lining the wall of the wooden room.

Minutes passed as the whole world shook.

Eventually, the shuddering stopped and the dust began to settle. Kisho unfurled himself from the tight ball he had collapsed into, his whole-body thudding and aching with the blast of power. He blinked open his eyes to see the old man had climbed to his feet, rage twisting his face as he advanced a step towards him.

Kisho's eyes flicked to the doorway to see that a new presence had entered the room—a young woman. She was tall, her height giving her an imposing appearance. Ashen hair framed her face, the strands almost translucent.

Her skin was white as snow and her eyes were pale, the only colour coming from small flecks of gold hidden in their cold depths. Shock radiated from her as she glanced back and forth between the old man and Kisho.

'Ash,' the old man said without taking his eyes of Kisho. 'It is time. The descendants of The Four have been called. Everything has been put into motion.'

The woman, Ash, cupped her mouth with her hand, tears forming in her eyes. 'No—no, you're wrong. I won't let this happen.' Her lips pressed into a thin line. 'I'm not ready.'

The old man's expression softened as he took a small step towards Ash. 'You have heard the whisper of shadows, seen the darkness growing. It is time.' He paused. 'Remember who you are. It is a powerful thing to have faith in yourself.'

He turned towards Kisho, who had slowly been easing his way towards the shattered window. 'You are made of magic, boy. You would have sensed the shadows whispering, the earth changing, old creatures stirring in their slumber.'

As the old man talked, figures rushed into the room behind Ash, outnumbering Kisho ten to one. Looking at the newcomers, he recognised the stern old lady who had passed him earlier in the night. Her companions were all dressed similarly and carrying an assortment of weapons. Kisho swore to himself. This was supposed to be an undercover mission. Silent and quick, in and out. He had no idea what the old man was babbling about or who or what Ash was, but he needed an escape. The amulet in his hand sent a burst of power up his arm as if reminding him of the magic he possessed.

Kisho straightened, stepping into the moonlight cast through the open window, his long shadow falling over the old man in the centre of the room.

'Which element do you prefer?' Kisho mused, holding up the amulet in the moonlight. He inspected the designs wrapping around the crystal centre, frowning as he noticed a small chunk of crystal seemed to be missing. 'Fire, water, wind, or earth?'

'No!' Ash gasped as the old man sprinted forwards, so fast he was barely a blur.

Kisho smiled savagely and held the amulet before him, palm out, delving into the power throbbing up his arm. The crystals in the centre of the treasure turned a bright orange, illuminating the old man barely five steps from him. With a grimace, Kisho released the power of the amulet and fire erupted from his palm, engulfing the old man in blistering heat and scorching flames.

Fire lashed through the room, eagerly eating into the wooden surfaces, the air crackling with the heat from the inferno. Kisho cut off the stream of power flowing from the amulet and, without a second thought, spun on his heel and leapt out the open window. There was a loud explosion behind him and sparks erupted at his back as he vaulted through the window frame, illuminated from behind by a wall of hungry flames.

He landed hard on the grass outside and was instantly on his feet, legs pumping as he sprinted through the darkness, branches whipping at his face. Shouts echoed through the valley, and he heard voices startlingly close behind him.

Kisho risked a glance over his shoulder and saw Ash barely ten steps behind him, her face a picture of hatred. He snapped his head back around, dodging under a low-hanging branch and leaping over a small stream, his breath coming in ragged gasps. The use of his power and the fighting all night had drained him.

He slipped the amulet over his neck and pushed himself onwards, sweat running freely down his back, mingling with the blood from his wounds. He just had to make it to freedom.

His mask had concealed his identity; once he escaped, no one would know who he was.

The sky lightened as Kisho climbed the steep terrain at the edge of the valley, blood-red bursting across the clouds as the sun rose. As he vaulted up and over a particularly large part of the cliff face, a hand roughly grabbed his boot, pulling him down. He turned to see Ash desperately clinging to him, a snarl fixed to her face, wind whipping her hair into a halo around her head. In the distance, Kisho could see a raging inferno surrounding the wooden building. People swarmed the flames, trying desperately to extinguish them.

'There is nowhere for you to run!' Ash yelled. 'Above you is a sheer drop down the side of the mountain.'

Kisho twisted his foot out of her grasp and slammed his heel into her face, sending her tumbling a few feet down the slope. Without so much as a pause, Kisho's trembling arms hauled him upwards again as he forced himself further up the mountain, his body silhouetted by the blood-red sky.

With one monumental push, Kisho's fatigued body crested the last outcropping of rock edging the valley. He now stood on a narrow precipice; behind him was the valley and, barely ten steps in front of him, the mountain fell away to the world below. A sheer drop.

Ash scrambled onto the ridge behind him, staggering to her feet, her breathing hard as she drew her blade. Cold wind whipped at the both of them, biting into their exposed skin. Kisho studied the woman. Something was off about her, her silver hair, her angular features. She moved with the silent grace of a predator as she stalked towards him. Framed against the ruby sky, she looked entirely not human.

'I told you,' she hissed. 'There is nowhere for you to go.'

Kisho glanced at the drop behind him, reaching up to ensure the amulet was fastened securely around his neck. He took a deep steadying breath, rallying the last of his strength.

He locked eyes with Ash, a smirk tugging at his lips. 'That's where you're wrong.'

Kisho took one last breath and launched himself backwards off the cliff, sailing into the pre-dawn air.

Power exploded through his body, ecstasy flooding through his veins as he shifted. He revelled in the high of the transformation, the pure, undiluted energy flowing through him. Within seconds, his clothes fell away and his wings opened, snow white feathers catching the wind. He soared upwards, the amulet heavy around his neck as he circled back, already high above the mountain peaks.

His owl eyes easily picked out Ash standing on the mountain top below him, her mouth gaped open in shock. He let loose a savage shriek and tucked in his wings, plummeting past her and down the side of the mountain, disappearing into the thick clouds.

And into the untamed world below.

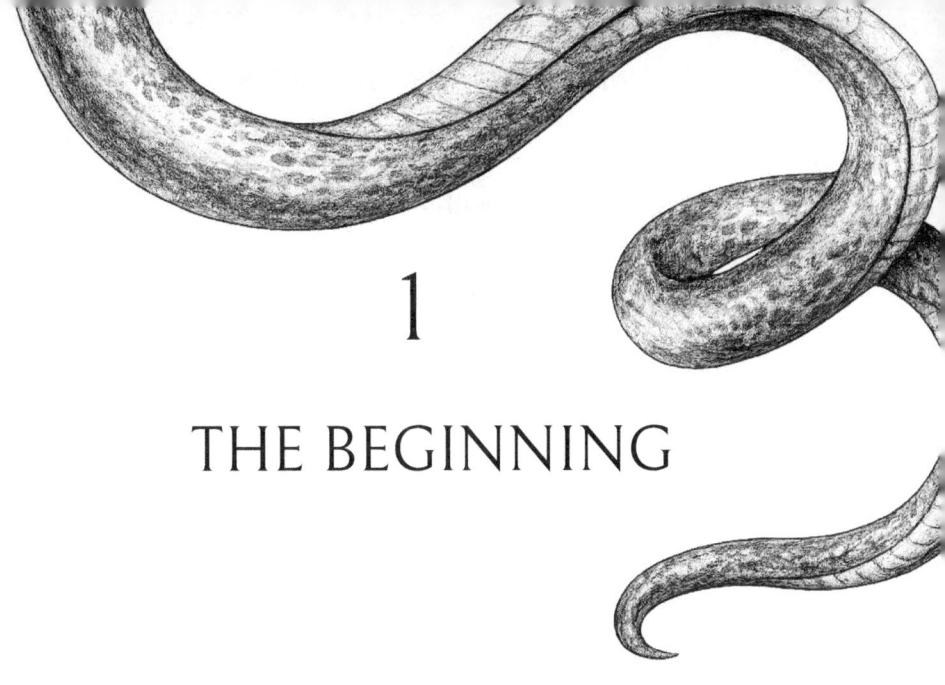

1

THE BEGINNING

Brrring, brrring, brrring!

The last period at River View High was finally over. It was Friday, and the students were excited about a couple of days off school. Everywhere, children joked and laughed as they swarmed out of the main building. The mood was infectious as parents stood chatting in groups, enjoying the light summer breeze and greeting their kids with smiles and hugs.

Alek and Benny were among the last to emerge from the school. Benny was average height with long, messy black hair and brown eyes. He had a very short temper; he was stubborn and the type of person who was always getting into trouble. Alek was the opposite. He was tall, smart, and liked to keep to himself. He had a pale complexion, sandy blonde hair, and bright blue eyes. The two boys had met twelve years ago in first grade. Benny had gotten into a fight with another boy over whose turn it was to play in the sandpit. Alek, seeing the argument, had rushed over and diffused the situation, calming Benny down in the process. The two boys balanced each other out, their opposing personalities creating an unlikely but strong friendship.

Alek wasn't usually the type to find himself in trouble but, more often than not, he was dragged into a myriad of situations by Benny. Circumstances that Benny usually relied on Alek to get them out of.

Not that either of them complained. They were both in their final year of school, despite Alek celebrating his eighteenth birthday a few months prior, and they were nervous about the years to come and how their friendship would continue when they didn't spend every day together. So, for now, they were inseparable, enjoying all of the messes Benny managed to get them into.

Alek breathed in the fresh air and grinned at Benny. 'Only two weeks left of term, then summer break!'

Benny snorted, flicking his hair out of his eyes. 'Yeah, but that just means two weeks to start and finish the five hundred assignments I have.'

'And once again, it's your own fault that you haven't started them!' Alek said, turning to walk backwards so he could face his friend. 'I offered to help you, but you get nothing from me now.'

'Oh, come on man, seriously?' the darker-haired boy pouted, shoving his hands into his pockets.

'Yes, seriously,' Alek mimicked sternly. 'And—' He stopped short, noticing a mischievous gleam in his friend's brown eyes. 'Benny, what are—'

Alek's words were cut short as he slammed back-first into someone behind him, knocking them both to the ground. Benny burst out laughing, doubling over in hysterics. Alek rolled over on the ground, mumbling apologies as he climbed to his feet, turning to see who he had knocked over.

He felt blood rush to his face as he took in the person climbing to their feet before him. She had long brunette hair and a tan, toned body. Alek watched awkwardly as she gracefully rose to her feet with an ease that made him look like a bumbling child.

Benny's hand clapped down onto his friend's shoulder. 'Honestly, Alek, you need to watch where you're going, running down my poor cousin like that.'

Alek shuffled his feet in embarrassment. 'Sarah, I'm sorry … I didn't mean to.'

Sarah's face broke into a wide grin. 'Alek, honestly, it's fine!' Her gaze turned to Benny, and her eyes narrowed. 'You, on the other hand, are a right asshole. You knew perfectly well Alek was going to run into me!'

'What—me?' Benny asked, feigning innocence. 'Why on earth would I want to give myself the pleasure of watching two of my favourite classmates run into each other?'

Sarah rolled her eyes but grinned. Benny's temper did not run in the family. 'Anyway, I was coming over because gymnastics practice was cancelled today, so I thought I'd walk to the party with you guys.'

Alek groaned, slouching his shoulders as anxiety stabbed through his stomach. 'I forgot about the stupid party.'

Sarah was popular. She always had been, even when Benny had introduced them soon after they became friends. *She is kind of beautiful, I guess,* Alek thought begrudgingly, looking at her warm smile and the way her green eyes sparkled in the sun. There had been plenty of times when Sarah had tagged along with the two boys over the years, and Alek had formed an unlikely friendship with the popular girl.

Alek was insanely jealous of the ease with which she managed to fit in at any social event, winning people over with her confidence and bubbly personality. A skill he definitely did not possess. He saw her more as a sister, though. She had always been kind to Alek, taking him under her wing at the numerous parties she dragged him and Benny along to and making sure Alek was okay.

'Oh, come on, buddy, it'll be fun!' Benny said, snapping Alek out of his thoughts.

Alek ran his hands through his curly hair, enjoying the feel of the wind tickling his skin as he clamped down on his anxious thoughts. 'You know the only reason I'm going is because you made me promise I would, and I don't want to walk home alone.'

Benny threw his arms around both his friends' shoulders, leading them towards the exit of the school.

'Well, Sarah, you're always welcome. Especially when that troll you call a boyfriend isn't hanging around you.'

'Troll, hey?' a new voice said from behind them.

Benny's shoulders tensed as he turned to take in the large muscular frame of the boy walking towards them. 'Hello, Christopher. I presume you'll be joining us?'

'Chris!' Sarah exclaimed happily, throwing herself into his arms and giving him a passionate kiss.

Benny and Alek rolled their eyes at each other. Sarah and Chris were the 'it' couple of the school. Sarah was head of the gymnastics squad, and Chris was in every sporting team the school had. Despite their stereotypical high school romance, the pair had been dating steadily for three years now and had no intention of slowing down once school ended.

Alek glanced away from the loved-up couple. He wouldn't be surprised in the slightest if they were still happily together in fifty years' time, married and with an army of grandchildren.

'Well, of course I will be, Benjamin,' Chris replied with a wink. 'I can't trust you two boys to walk her to the party safely. She needs a man like me.'

Sarah rolled her eyes. 'Oh, right, because I need a big strong maaaan to walk me to a party. What, you think I can't look after myself just because I'm a girl?!'

Alek bit back a smirk. Sarah may look like she just stepped off the front page of a fashion magazine, but she was tougher than anyone he knew. She had always stood up for what she believed was right, no matter the consequences.

Chris snorted, laughter bubbling from his throat. 'Oh, please. You and I both know you'd be the one protecting me!'

'That's more like it,' Sarah said smugly, patting her boyfriend on the arm.

'You two are gross,' Benny said, turning away with a sigh.

'Let's get this over with.'

****

Six hours later, Alek regretted his choice to come to the party. He reached up and unhooked half of the buttons on the front of his white school uniform shirt, trying to get some air in the overstuffed house. Sweaty bodies bumped and ground against him as he made his way through the loungeroom, searching for his friends. He'd had a little to drink, but nowhere near enough to feel comfortable surrounded by so many people.

Loud music thudded through the house, pounding in his head and making it difficult to concentrate. When he and his friends had first arrived at the party, Alek was in awe of the house. It was huge—bigger than any house he had ever lived in. Floor-to-ceiling windows bordered the living areas, and perfectly manicured gardens spread out around the building with two pools nestled into the tropical-style landscaping.

But now, all Alek wanted was out. He shoved his way past a few knots of people, briefly noticing Chris and Sarah playing spin the bottle with a few very obviously drunk classmates. Alek shook his head, pushed his way past some guys swaying to the music, and wrenched open the glass sliding door, taking a long breath as crisp night air smacked against his clammy skin.

He closed his eyes, enjoying the feeling of the air as he left behind the thick, claustrophobic atmosphere inside the house. It was darker outside, the only light coming from the illuminated pools. Alek wandered out further, searching for Benny, already formulating an excuse to leave the party early. If he didn't find him in the next few minutes, he was going to bail without saying goodbye.

Examining his surroundings, Alek noticed a group of Benny's other friends hanging around by one of the pools. Taking a breath, Alek walked over, blushing as he realised the whole group had been swimming and were now wearing only wet underwear that clung to their bodies.

'Hey,' Alek said to the closest guy, doing his best to ignore the boy's lack of clothes. 'Have any of you seen Benny?'

The boy turned to Alek, the pool light casting shadows across his athletic body. 'Yeah, dude. He's up on the roof.'

Alek risked a glance down at the boy's figure, noticing how low his underwear hung on his hips. 'Thanks,' he mumbled, beginning to turn away.

A strong hand clasped his upper arm, and he turned to see the boy had taken a step away from his friends. His dark eyes now raked up and down Alek's body.

'Why don't you come for a swim?' the boy asked, his voice low and alluring as he hooked one thumb into the waistband of his underwear, causing them to ride dangerously low.

Blood rushed through Alek's body and he bit his lip, his gaze flicking towards the pool and the boy before him. The boy was illuminated by the rippling blue light from below the surface of the water. His heartbeat thumped in his chest as he allowed himself to be led into the shadows of the garden towards the further end of the pool, his breath coming in shallow gasps as he stood at the edge of the water.

'I don't know if—' Alek started but was quickly cut off as the other boy slipped his underwear off, his muscular body painted in flowing shadows from the pool behind him. Without hesitating, the boy's fingers reached forward and began to unbutton the rest of Alek's shirt.

Alek's eyes quickly darted down over the boy's body, heat rising in his blood, painting his face scarlet, and he felt fingers brush against his stomach, causing goose bumps to spread across his skin. As the fingers slipped down, curling under the waist band of his pants, Alek threw his head back, forcing cool air into his lungs. Through his wild, half-focused eyes, he picked out a lone figure sitting on the roof a few metres away, partly obscured by the array of palm trees and tropical plants surrounding the pools.

With a start, Alek recognised Benny, and clarity rushed back into him. He pulled the other boy's hands from his pants and took a shaking step back. 'I'm—I—sorry, but I can't,' he stammered, avoiding the boy's gaze.

'Hey, man,' the other boy said, holding up his hands, palms out. 'It's cool. I just thought you were into it, that's all.'

Alek shook his head, hurriedly stepping back as the other boy slipped into the clear water. Alek stumbled back through the dark towards the house, his heartbeat still thundering in his chest. What had he been about to do? Guilt prickled at the back of his neck as a shiver passed down his spine. His mouth dry, he made his way around the side of the house to a ladder. Grasping the rough, wooden rungs in his hands, he rested his head against the wall.

The coolness from the bricks soaked into the skin of his forehead, easing his mind as he forced deep breaths of the night air into his lungs. Around here at the side of the house, the party was muted. The loud music a dull thud, the voices of drunk teenagers a quiet hum. The breeze blew around his body as he trembled, his mind in disarray over what he had almost done. Leaves from the palm trees around him whispered together in the wind as Alek threw his head back, looking to the stars for answers.

What did I just do? he thought, searching the sky. *I must be more drunk than I thought. That's the reasonable explanation. He was a good-looking guy; anyone would go for that.*

The stars blinked down at him, offering no answers to the turmoil in his mind. Unsure of how he felt, Alek shoved his emotions down, hauling himself up the ladder and onto the top of the house. He risked a glance down to the ground below and instantly regretted it, his head spinning at the elevated height. Quickly stepping away from the edge of the roof, Alek carefully made his way across to where Benny was sitting, settling down next to his friend with a groan.

'Showing your age, groaning like that, old man,' Benny teased, bumping his shoulder against Alek's.

'Oh, whatever—I'm barely a year older than you,' Alek grumbled, looking below them to the pools and breathing out a sigh of relief to see that the events of the last five minutes had happened out of view of Benny on the roof.

'Go swimming?' Benny asked quietly gazing out at the sky.

Alek's eyes snapped to his friend's face, studying those uninterested brown eyes, searching for the reason behind the casual remark. Panic started to swell in Alek's chest. Maybe Benny had seen? How would he explain what happened?

'Um, no?' Alek said, feigning indifference. 'Why do you ask?'

Benny shrugged, and Alek's shoulders sagged as he realised his friend wasn't really invested in the conversation, just making small talk. 'Your shirt is unbuttoned, so I figured you'd taken it off to go swimming or something.' He turned to look at Alek, a twinkle in his eye. 'Or you were with a girl.'

'Screw off,' Alek gasped, shoving Benny sideways as the boy chuckled to himself.

Alek rolled his eyes and drew his knees up to his chest as he looked out at the view before them. His gaze roamed around the city lights in the distance, the skyscrapers and streetlights causing the night sky to glow. But his eyes were drawn to the massive patch of darkness in the middle of the city lights—the Old Town.

The town, River View, had originally been built within a massive basin in the surrounding landscape. This was before the ground became too marshy and swampy to live on, causing the government to move the city to the edges of the crater, surrounding the remnants of the original town.

The city modernised and expanded, high above the old forgotten buildings left to rot in the bottom of the crater. A large suspension bridge had been built across the centre of the basin, creating ease of access from the north side of the new city to the south. However, the bridge only catered for vehicles, not pedestrians. The Old Town was left, unchecked, and forgotten by all except for the gangs and homeless people that had nowhere else to go, creating a cesspool of crime and violence.

There had been many news reports about the dangers of going down into Old Town, and his mother had told him that if she ever found out he had gone there, he would be grounded for life. No one in their right minds ever visited the ghostly town. Even the police had cancelled all patrols after several officers never returned from the shadowy streets.

Benny and he had joked about venturing into the mysterious, decrepit maze of buildings a few times, but they'd never been serious. Instead, they had stood on the edge of the crater, Alek lost in his thoughts as he wondered what the people living down there had done to deserve such a life.

Alek lifted his eyes, looking instead towards the south side of the city, imagining he could see his own home nestled amongst the rows of indistinguishable suburban houses. His small house looked nothing like the mansion he was currently at, with its landscaped gardens and designer furniture. *But that's the north side for you*, Alek thought to himself with a pang of jealousy. *Streets of rich people trying to one-up their neighbours with their flashy cars and fancy homes.*

'What're you doing up here, anyway?' Alek asked, tearing his gaze away from the distant lights.

Benny took a while to answer, and when he did, his voice was hesitant. 'I don't know, man. I just feel like our lives are about to change, you know?' He paused, brushing his long, dark hair back from his face. 'Like, we're about to graduate school. We might move away and not see each other as much, and we haven't really done anything.'

'What do you mean, "we haven't done anything"?' Alek asked, tilting his head. 'What on earth do you want to do?'

'Nothing! I mean, I don't know.' Benny sighed. 'We used to always get up to stuff when we were younger. Go on adventures, break the rules, get in trouble. And now, I feel like all we do is the same thing every day. Get up, go to school, come to a party, and then go home to bed, only to do it all again.'

'Yeah, but those adventures were like sneaking out of the house to go get ice cream when we weren't supposed to because we were twelve,' Alek pointed out. 'Or that one time Sarah marched us off to a protest because the school canned the funding for her gymnastics team.' Alek grinned at the memory. Sarah had barged into his house, where he and Benny had been getting ready for a sleepover, and demanded they come with her immediately. The two boys had been dragged through the city to the school with no explanation and had hand-painted signs shoved into their hands.

Sarah had rallied together half of the school, and the protest lasted a good part of the weekend before the principal finally gave into Sarah's demands and re-instated the gymnastics team. The rally had been born from Sarah's selfish feelings of betrayal, but in using her outrage to create the protest, she had brought together a myriad of students who would never normally be seen together.

Sometimes, Alek wished he had her determination. Once she put her mind to something, nothing was going to stop her. She felt things in such a different way to him, and she poured her feelings into whatever scheme her brain cooked up. Alek, on the other hand, preferred to wallow in his emotions and shortcomings.

Benny dragged his hands down his face with a sigh. 'Look, I don't really know what I'm trying to say, okay, dude? Only that I feel like we need one last grand adventure before everything changes and we never get to see each other again.'

Alek elbowed his friend in the ribs. 'Bastard. I don't know what your plans are, but I plan on seeing you every day for a long time still.'

Benny snorted. 'Don't make fun of me. You know what I mean.'

Alek began to speak when there was a colossal crash and bright green lightning splintered across the sky. Both boys jumped violently as a loud rumble shook the world. The trees around them quivered, and the house beneath them rattled viciously, causing them to slip a few metres towards the edge of the roof. Shrieks and screams came from the party below them as the power flickered and went out, casting the surrounding city into shadow.

Minutes later, the shaking stopped and the lights turned back on, revealing frightened teenagers huddled together in the backyard, looking around with bewildered expressions on their faces.

'What the hell was that?' Benny asked, his panicked gaze mimicking Alek's own. 'We never have earthquakes here.'

'We should go,' Alek said, climbing to his feet. 'It's getting late anyway. Let's go find your cousin.'

'Benny?' Sarah's voice floated up from below them. 'Alek?'

Benny barked a laugh. 'Speak of the devil. Up here, Sarah!'

Sarah popped out from underneath the shelter of the roof, glaring up at the two boys. 'I have been looking for you two everywhere. I want to go home; I don't know what the heck that was, but it's ruined my party mood and I'm ready for bed.'

Chris chuckled, walking up behind Sarah. 'Come on, guys.

If we start walking now, we should get home before midnight.'

'Great,' Benny muttered to Alek. 'The last thing I feel like doing is walking all the way to the other side of the city in the middle of the night.'

Alek shrugged. 'You just said you wanted an adventure. Now, come on.'

****

Barely twenty minutes later, Benny and Alek were both struggling to hide their heavy breathing. Alek looked to his right, trying to find anything to distract himself from the long walk ahead. The earthquake had caused little havoc throughout the streets. If it wasn't for the leaves and branches on the ground or the small cracks in the earth,

15

Alek would have convinced himself he had imagined the whole thing.

He and his friends walked along a shadowy boardwalk that bordered the Old Town, the earth quickly dropping off into the crater barely two metres from his feet. They had left behind the huge mansions of the north side of the city and were currently trudging through a small thicket of twisted, stunted trees. The winding boardwalk hugged the edge of the crater, leading them steadily homeward. Alek peered into the darkness blanketing the Old Town, imagining he could see the gangs of criminals prowling around the deserted streets under the cover of night. Lost in his thoughts, Alek didn't realise the others had stopped, and he collided into Benny with a loud thud.

'Watch it!' Benny snapped, clearly frustrated with the hourlong walk ahead of them.

'Sorry, sorry,' Alek muttered, looking at Sarah and Chris. 'Why are we stopping?'

'You know,' Sarah said, biting her bottom lip, 'we have to walk all the way around the crater to get home … but we could just cut straight through the middle.'

Benny stiffened. 'You want to go through there?' He pointed to the Old Town.

Alek swallowed a lump of fear that had risen unwillingly from his chest as he looked at the shocked expression on his friend's face. This was too much, even for Benny, who was usually down for anything. A cold sweat broke out across the back of Alek's neck as he pictured the danger they could be in if they were caught amongst the ruined buildings.

'Well, it's better than walking for hours!' Sarah argued, stepping up to Benny's face. 'The Old Town is, like, the size of three football fields. It would be so much faster to just cut straight across the middle instead of walking all the way around the outside!'

'Don't get in my face, Sarah,' Benny snarled, his hands curling into fists. 'This is the stupidest idea I have ever heard; you'll get us all killed if we go through there! Do you not remember the news reports about those police officers that disappeared? Do you want that to be us as well?' Benny turned his narrowed eyes to Alek. 'Do you agree with my idiotic cousin?'

Sarah crossed her arms and turned her attention to Alek, fixing him with a determined stare. Alek squirmed under the two cousins' withering glares, fighting down the rising panic in his stomach.

'Guys, there's no point arguing about it.' Chris stepped forward, holding his hands out peacefully.

Benny spun, sparing Alek from having to answer his question, and focused his anger on the larger boy. 'Stay out of it, Christopher. No one asked you.'

'Hey!' Sarah snapped. 'Just because you're tired and scared of going through the Old Town doesn't mean you get to yell at him.'

Alek watched his two friends arguing as he weighed the pros and cons of cutting through the abandoned buildings below them. It was quicker than walking around, and his tired legs really didn't feel like walking for another hour. However, it was dangerous. Everyone knew that. He wasn't so sure the risk was worth it just to save time on the long walk home. No one knew what happened to those police officers that vanished; their bodies had never been found.

Alek was abruptly snapped out of his thoughts as he heard Sarah gasp loudly. Looking up, he saw Benny stepping up to the edge of the ravine leading into the Old Town.

'Don't call me scared,' Benny said angrily before he turned and disappeared over the edge.

Alek sighed; the decision had been made for him. Shooting an exasperated look at Sarah and Chris, he said, 'He is going to be the death of us all.' He started walking to the edge of the path. 'Come on. We can't let him go alone.'

Alek shuddered, holding his breath as he stepped off the boardwalk, stumbling slightly at the steep slope under his feet. Darkness swallowed the city lights behind him as he picked his way slowly down the side of the crater. Goosebumps erupted across Alek's skin as the chill air around him thickened, settling over him like a blanket and pulling him further into the night. If it weren't for the muffled sounds of Sarah and Chris breathing beside him, he would have felt utterly alone.

The side of the crater was steep. Loose rocks tumbled down from his feet, echoing loudly in the clinging silence. Alek had no way of telling how far he and his friends had descended and he had lost track of time, focusing instead on placing one foot in front of the other so he didn't lose his balance and break a leg, or worse.

Eventually, the ground levelled out, and Alek stumbled forward a step, his eyes finally adjusting to the darkness. Benny appeared in the shadows before him, his face set in an irritated scowl. Alek rolled his eyes; he knew that expression well. There was no point reasoning with his friend when he was in a mood like this. You just had to wait for it to blow over. Benny's brown eyes locked onto Alek's, and he saw his own fear echoed in his friend's gaze, re-iterating the danger they'd placed themselves in. Taking a deep breath, they stepped forward together, instantly sinking into calf-deep muddy water.

'Oh, lovely!' Sarah muttered sarcastically from behind them as she stumbled blindly into the same stagnant puddle.

'You wanted to come down here,' Benny muttered, stomping forward through the swampy slush.

'Come on.' Alek rolled his eyes. 'It looks drier up ahead.'

The group slogged their way through the water on the outskirts of the town. Alek wrinkled his nose at the rotten stench that rose from the still liquid. For the first time, he was thankful for the darkness around them. He wasn't so sure he wanted to see what the water looked like if it smelt this bad. The ground eventually levelled out and gave way to cracked, overgrown concrete. Alek grimaced as his wet feet squelched in his shoes with every step, the cold seeping into his bones. He wished they had stayed up in the city, where it was dry.

Imposing brick buildings loomed ahead as the friends cautiously followed a narrow pathway that led them steadily away from the crater wall and into the murky darkness. Alek's shoulders tensed as he noticed broken bottles littered around the path and graffiti scrawled across the rough walls closing in around them. His ears strained to pick out any signs of danger, but the only sound he could hear was Chris's heavy breathing behind him.

Though he would never admit it, having the larger boy at his back was comforting. *At least if someone does try to sneak up on us, they'll get Chris first!* he selfishly thought to himself with a pang of guilt.

The thought of a stranger chasing them down from behind made Alek turn, his eyes peering into the blanketing darkness behind them. No matter how hard he stared into the shadows, he could make out no movement. Chris suddenly clasped a hand onto his shoulder, making him jump violently. Forcing out a cough to hide the squeak of alarm that had escaped his lips, Alek tilted his head to see the boy grinning at him.

'We'll be fine, bro. We just go in a straight line and try not to make any unnecessary noise, right?'

Alek nodded, feigning confidence as he turned back around, continuing down the path. He appreciated Chris's comfort, but he hadn't been oblivious to the slight quiver in the other boy's voice or the wary look in his eyes.

Benny led the group onwards, Alek quickly becoming more claustrophobic as the tall buildings pressed in around them, threatening to trap them in the silent shadows forever. He and his friends rounded a corner and the path opened up around them, making way for what once must have been the main street.

Abandoned shopfronts and apartment buildings huddled together on either side of the strip of cracked bitumen. The windows were shattered, the inky black interiors threatening to suck Alek into their depths the more he stared into the glassless panes. A chill breeze blew down the street, rattling empty beer cans across the cracked concrete footpaths that bordered the road. Beside him, Sarah jumped violently at the sudden noise as the can skittered erratically through the otherwise motionless town.

Alek noticed many of the buildings were brick and imagined they would have been quite pretty once upon a time. Dead trees lined either side of the road, long since devoid of their leaves, which once would have rustled cheerily in the wind as shoppers perused the many storefronts. The contrast from the bustling city far above them atop the crater was mind-blowing. Alek and his friends had left behind a world of energy and life and instead descended into a pit of decay and ominous silence. Unease prickled in Alek's belly as he continued to scan the buildings for signs of life, feeling exposed out in the street.

'This place gives me the creeps,' Benny muttered. 'It's so dark. Who knows what's hiding in the shadows, watching us?'

'I know what you mean,' Sarah said darkly. 'How could the government let people live like this? It isn't right, leaving people down here to rot. They should pay for doing something so cruel. It just isn't fair.'

'We better keep moving, guys,' Alek said quietly, ignoring Sarah's grim words. 'The last thing we need is to run into trouble down here.'

Chris led the way across the main road and into an alley on the opposite side, Alek bringing up the rear of the group. He paused as he heard a slight rattle in the distance. His eyes desperately peered into the shadows around them, trying to make out the source of the noise.

'Alek, come on!' Benny hissed from further down the alley.

Desperately trying to ignore his rising panic, Alek hurried over to his friend as they continued deeper into Old Town. Putrid water collected in puddles on the muddy ground as they left the main street behind them, and Alek carefully picked his way around the rancid liquid as he hastily tried to block out the eye-watering stench.

The side alley Chris had led them down ended in a tall fence made of rotting timber boards. The old brick apartment buildings towered on either side of the friends, offering them some shelter from any prying eyes.

Suddenly, Chris lashed out with his foot, knocking off the bottom of the boards with a loud crack. Alek winced, the sound echoing around them in the eerie silence. One by one Alek watched his friends slip through the hole in the fence, impatience clawing at him as he ignored the need to glance over his shoulder.

Finally, it was his turn. He dived forward, hissing as his knees slammed into the ground while he scurried forward. He heard Benny swear violently from ahead of him and he looked up, his mouth going dry.

They were in another alley, this one filled with piles of discarded food wrappers and empty beer cans. Standing at the opposite end of the row of buildings was a group of older teens, staring at the friends in shock. Alek stifled his rising panic as he watched the opposing group's shocked expressions morph into dreadful grins. They didn't look much older than him; however, life in Old Town had not been kind.

They were pale, their faces pockmarked and bruised. Many were missing teeth, which was visible as they grinned savagely at the group of terrified friends. There were a few small clicks, and Alek's eyes widened as he saw an assortment of switchblades flick open, the metal glinting menacingly in the dim light.

'Well, look who we have here.' A large guy stepped forward. His nose was crooked, and scars covered his knuckles and arms. 'Some trespassers—rats from the city, by the looks of it.'

Chris shuffled forward, half stepping in front of Sarah and Benny as the gang moved slowly closer to the friends.

Alek's heart thudded in his chest, drowning out any coherent thoughts.

'We're going to have to teach you a lesson for trespassing on our turf.' The gang leader smiled, revealing his chipped and broken teeth. Alek watched through wide eyes as he picked up a metal bar from the ground, giving it a few practice swings.

Benny's elbow abruptly dug into Alek's side as he murmured, 'Alek, fire escape to our left.'

Alek tore his gaze away from the gang in front of them and glanced to the left, seeing a rusted metal ladder attached to the brick wall beside him. He hesitated. The ladder looked like it was barely holding together. Alek wasn't sure it would even hold their weight if they attempted to climb it. He closed his eyes and took a deep breath. What choice did they have?

'Fire escape on our left,' Alek muttered under his breath to Sarah and Chris, hoping they could hear him. 'Make a run for it on three. One. Two. Three!'

He spun on his heel, adrenaline flooding into his veins and his heart thundering in his ears as Sarah leapt past him, her hair whipping him in the face. She grabbed the ladder and hauled herself up it as fast as she could, her hands and feet a blur. Alek followed closely behind her, Benny and Chris on his heels.

He heard a howl from below, and an unfamiliar voice yelled, 'After them!'

Alek reached the top of the ladder and pounded up the stairs after Sarah, the metal rocking beneath him. She reached the top of the fire escape, gripped the edge of the roof, and vaulted herself up and over, landing lightly on her feet. Alek could not match her agility as he awkwardly hauled himself up and onto the roof, his arms shaking as he stumbled to his knees.

'Is there some way to get to another building?' he yelled to Sarah, climbing to his feet as Benny and Chris tumbled over the lip of the roof behind him.

'Over here!' she called back desperately.

Pounding footsteps rattled the metal fire escape behind Alek, jolting him into action as his friends raced ahead. He looked up to see Sarah reach the edge of the building and launch herself forward, sailing through the air and onto the roof of the next building over.

Alek swore as his footsteps slowed, watching the other two boys follow Sarah, catapulting themselves over the gap between the two buildings.

He glanced over his shoulder as the first gang member appeared, his eyes zeroing in on Alek with a savage grin. Steeling himself, Alek threw himself forward, pumping all his energy into his legs. He reached the edge of the building and hurled himself forwards.

Seconds seemed to stretch into minutes as his weightless body sailed over the gap between the two buildings. Alek wildly glanced below him and saw the hard concrete far below before the roof of the next building rose up to meet him, fast. He slammed into the roof hard, rolling head over heels across the rough surface, his shoulder barking in pain.

'Alek, hurry!' Benny's voice yelled in his ear as hands hauled him upright, shoving him forward.

Looking up, he saw Chris and Sarah hurtle through the cracked window of a taller building that butted up against the roof of the one he was now standing on. Summoning the last of his energy, he followed Benny as they sprinted towards the open window. Something whistled past Alek's ear and he flinched as a glass bottle shattered on the ground beside his feet, shards cutting into his legs.

Benny hurdled through the open window and Alek followed, hot on his heels just as the first gang members made the leap over to their building. Alek followed his friends as they slammed through the winding hallways, busting open doors and stumbling down rotted staircases. He quickly lost all sense of direction as fatigue took over his body, his footsteps becoming more and more clumsy.

Chris smashed open a pair of thick, wooden double doors and the friends rushed through, their breaths coming in ragged gasps. They were standing in a large glass atrium attached to the back of the old building. A small yard was visible on the other side of the glass walls, bordered by a tall brick fence. Soft moonlight filtered in through the transparent ceiling, illuminating the colossal willow tree that grew in the centre of the room, its branches rustling in the soft breeze. Plants of every shape and size filled the remainder of the space, vines clawing up walls, overgrown shrubs putting down roots wherever they could find soil.

Alek glanced around, his hands on his knees, trying to draw in as much oxygen as he could. The glass walls and roof left them completely exposed. If any of the gang members found their way outside and into the small yard, they would spot them instantly. Spinning around, Alek grasped the heavy wooden doors in his hands and heaved with all his strength. Slowly, the old hinges complied, screeching in protest as flakes of rust fluttered to the floor. Alek looked around frantically for a lock as his heart thundered in his chest, the sound of distant footsteps echoing through the building.

'Guys,' Alek gasped out between breaths. 'The door doesn't lock. We need to keep moving.'

Sarah had just opened her mouth to reply when the willow tree's branches suddenly parted and a strange woman stepped out.

The moonlight struck her silver hair, turning it bright white, bathing her in the glow. Her features were pale, her face angular as she quickly took in the four friends with her sharp eyes. She moved with an unnatural smoothness, causing the hair on the back of Alek's neck to stand on end. She felt dangerous, deadly. Some deep-rooted instinct in his body screamed at him to turn and flee, but his feet remained rooted to the floor.

Just as Alek was debating grabbing his friends and making a run for it, a strange feeling of peace bubbled into the air and his heartbeat began to calm, his breathing becoming more regular. He blinked, the wariness he had been feeling was quickly fading, breaking him out of his frozen state.

He stepped towards the woman, shaking his head to clear the last of his irrational fear. 'Who are you?'

The woman cocked her head to the side, her long silver hair rippling. 'I am Ash, and—' She broke off as there was a loud crash from behind the closed doors followed by angry yelling.

'You are in trouble?' Her intense eyes locked onto Alek's.

'Yes,' he replied, shivering as she stared at him.

'Come.' She pulled aside the flowing branches behind her. 'I can help.'

Alek took a hesitant step forward just as Sarah grabbed his arm, holding him back.

'Alek, I don't know about this,' she whispered in his ear, her voice strained. 'Something about her is off. Plus, she has a sword. Who the heck carries a sword with them?'

For the first time, Alek tore his eyes away from the woman's powerful gaze and inspected the sword hilt protruding above her left shoulder, the powerful arms that now beckoned to the friends and the strange skin-tight clothing she wore. A thick cloak hung from her shoulders, swaying around her ankles as she shifted her weight.

Loud thuds echoed on the other side of the door behind them, snapping Alek out of his thoughts. *What choice do we have?* he thought, panic threatening to overwhelm him. *Stay here and get beaten to death, or take our chances with this strange lady?* Weighing up his options, he quickly came to a decision.

'We go, now!' he ordered, forcing as much confidence into his voice as he could muster, striding towards the willow tree.

Surprisingly, he sensed Benny fall into step behind him, Sarah at his heels with Chris after a slight hesitation. One by one, the friends passed under the canopy of branches, the leafy tendrils caressing their skin just as the doors slammed open at the end of the room and gang members filed in.

Alek spun around, watching from between the branches as the group poured into the room, the leader's metal bar flashing threateningly in the moonlight. He heard Benny swear quietly behind him as he slowly backed towards the centre of the dense foliage, praying it would keep him and his friends out of view.

Alek continued to back further and further into the willow's thick embrace, feeling the thick fronds flow over him. His friends followed his lead on either side of him, their fear prickling the air around him. Alek noticed that the gang's voices became more and more muted until he could not hear or see them through the shimmering branches draped around him. An intense tingling feeling erupted under his skin and raced through his body from head to toe, causing him to break out in goosebumps. Alek shuddered, wrapping his arms around himself as he tried to make sense of the strange feeling as nausea threatened to overwhelm him.

Suddenly Sarah let loose a loud scream to his right and he spun on his heel, eyes widening in shock.

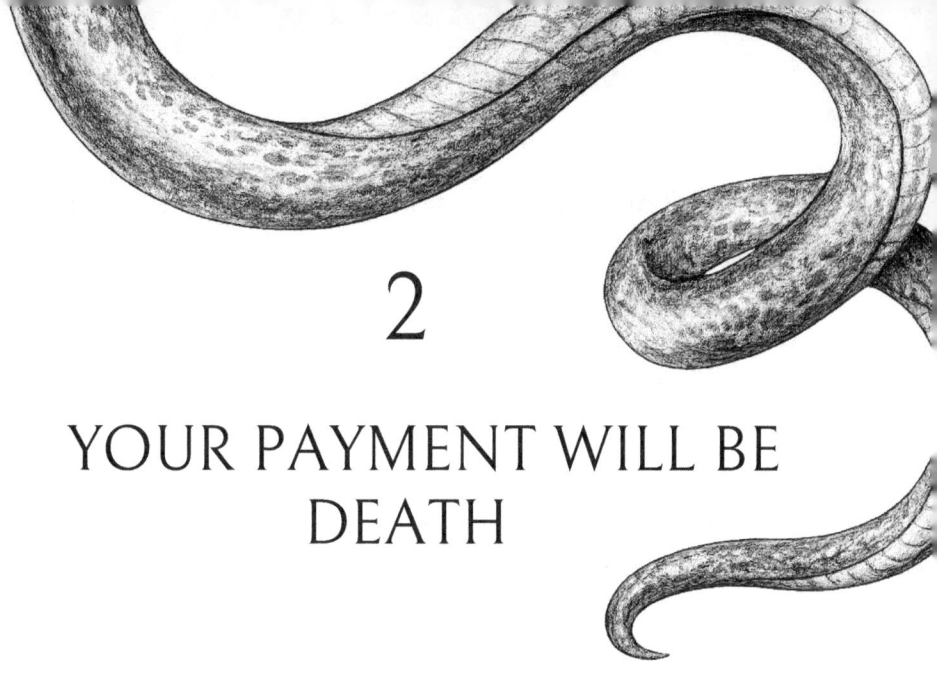

2

YOUR PAYMENT WILL BE DEATH

The first thing Alek took in was Sarah crouched on the ground. Ash's hand clamped over Sarah's mouth, whispering to her to be quiet. The second thing was how gloomy everything was.

Benny huddled beside him, looking around with awe plastered across his face. They were in what once would have been a lush forest. However, the skeletal remains of the woods around them spoke of death and violence. The dry grass beneath Alek's feet was grey with age, the fronds brittle and spiky. The ghostly trees rose ominously around the friends, their leafless branches clawing at the sullen, dreary sky. Mist churned around the base of the splintered trunks, concealing flickering shadows within its swirling depths. The large willow tree was to their left, its lush fronds full of green life in stark contrast to the surrounding decay.

Alek craned his neck to look past the bristling branches to the sky above, where brooding grey clouds offered no reprieve from the bleak woodlands below. Alek turned to look behind him and froze. Barely a metre from where he stood, the ground beneath him vanished. As if a giant had cleaved through it with a huge knife, one minute there was dead grass and broken trees, the next—nothing, save for more swirling mist, obscuring anything that may be lurking beyond the drop-off.

Alek jumped as Benny rounded on Ash. 'Where have you brought us?!' he snapped at her, his facing twisting in fury. 'What is this place, and who the hell are you?!'

Ash pressed her lips together, removing her hand from Sarah's mouth as she took a step closer to Benny. 'You would do well to be quiet.' Her voice was calm, although her eyes flicked warily to the trees around them.

'Quiet?!' Benny raged. 'Quiet? You want me to be quiet? We don't even know who you are, and you've brought us to god knows where, and—'

There was a loud slap and Benny staggered back, his hand rising to his face where Ash had struck him. 'I told you to be quiet,' she hissed, her hands trembling. 'You're going to get us killed.'

'Don't you dare touch him!' Sarah yelled, her hands balling into fists as she instantly reacted to the attack on her cousin.

She aimed a punch for Ash's face, but the woman was ready. She caught Sarah's arm in her hand and spun her around and onto the ground. Alek stood rooted to the spot in shock as Benny launched himself at Ash with a yell, the two of them tumbling to the ground.

There was a rumble in the air like thunder, and Alek noticed the mist around them darken ominously. The trees began to shake, the branches screeching threateningly through the thick air. The grass rippled towards them, the brittle fronds whispering as if they were alive.

'Uh, guys,' Alek said uncomfortably, shifting on his feet as the grass started to whip around them, despite there being no wind to cause it to move. 'Something's wrong.'

'Will you all just be quiet!' Ash's voice cut through the still air, 'before someone hears you?'

'I'm afraid it's far too late for that,' a sinister voice said behind them.

Alek spun around and saw the owner of the voice. He was tall, his eyes blazing like an orange inferno from behind thick lashes. The figure was partially obscured by the decaying trees and thick mist, but as he moved closer, horror seeped into Alek's bones. His face was angular, and as his mouth parted into a wicked smile, Alek glimpsed vampire-like fangs. Large, lethal looking horns protruded from the side of his skull, twisting slightly to a razor-sharp point.

His torso was unclothed and humanoid from the waist up. A brand depicting a circle with a cross in the middle was burned onto his chest. Thick, dark fur grew on his legs, which bent at the knees. Alek's eyes widened in shock as he realised that, instead of feet, the man had large, cloven hooves.

Alek heard a loud sob escape Sarah's throat and tore his gaze away from the creature's features, for the first time noticing what it was holding as it stepped out of the cloying mist. Chris was trapped. The creature's hand wrapped around the boy's neck, holding him just off the ground. Chris's feet scrabbled and kicked as he tried to escape the monster's grip.

'A satyr,' Ash whispered, fear lacing her words as her hand furiously fumbled inside one of her pockets.

'A what?' Alek and Benny asked together.

The satyr smiled evilly, showing his fangs as he reached behind his back with his free hand, drawing a massive, two sided axe.

'Wait!' Ash yelled, her voice strained, one arm outstretched towards the monster. 'I have—I have payment for safe passage!' Ash's hand trembled slightly as she withdrew a gold coin the size of her palm from her pocket. The satyr's head cocked to the side as his grip tightened on Chris's throat, causing the boy to gasp for breath.

Alek's heart pounded in his chest as sweat rolled down his back, the seconds seeming to stretch into hours as the beast studied the gold coin in Ash's outstretched hand.

'If I were a regular satyr charged with watching the gates, then maybe I would accept your offer. However ...' A low, guttural purr escaped the beast's throat as his shoulders shuddered. Panic shot through Alek's body as he realised the monster was laughing. 'I am not. Your payment will be death.'

With one swift movement, the satyr sliced with his axe, cleaving the blade across Chris's throat.

Alek barely had time to blink as the life drained out of his friend's eyes and Sarah began to scream. Bright ruby blood sprayed onto the dark grass, the colour stark against the misty landscape.

'I'm going to enjoy this!' The satyr smiled, dropping Chris's lifeless body to the ground. 'The first real fun I have had in over one hundred years!' He laughed maniacally.

The monster charged forward, his blade thrumming through the air in great horizontal strokes, aiming for Sarah, who was frozen in place, her eyes locked onto Chris's body. Ash leapt into the creature's path, her sword clashing with his axe with an ear-splitting scrape of metal on metal. The force of the blow knocked Ash back, and she struggled to regain her footing as the satyr advanced, carving the air around her with powerful strokes.

Sarah screamed and launched herself at the creature's exposed back, but long grass exploded from the ground and wrapped around her ankles, whipping her sideways and throwing her off balance. Alek watched in shock as she hit the ground hard, the breath knocked out of her. The force of her fall caused her to tumble back, straight towards the drop-off where the earth simply vanished. Sarah scrambled frantically for a handhold as she slipped over the edge with a shriek.

Benny yelled and dodged around the satyr's axe, leaping towards the drop-off and grabbing Sarah's hand just as she vanished over the precipice. Alek felt the earth begin to shake beneath him as his eyes flicked from Chris's lifeless body to Benny, who was now hauling a shaky Sarah back to the safety of solid ground.

Panic pumped through him, cold sweat trickling down his spine. He tried to force his legs to move, to help his friends, to do anything, but still, he stood rooted to the spot as the fight raged on around him.

Ash advanced on the satyr, her sword a blur as she spun and twisted, metal clanging loudly whenever the two opponents collided. Alek couldn't keep track of who was winning and who was losing.

Suddenly, the satyr reeled back, his hand reaching up to clutch his left eye. Ash stopped her mad onslaught, heavy breaths shaking her entire body. Black blood dripped down her blade, and as Alek flicked his eyes back to the satyr, he saw a long, deep gash across the creature's left eye.

The satyr snarled with rage as the grass whipping around the friends' feet latched itself onto Ash, throwing her off balance and causing her blade to fall from her hands, clattering towards Alek.

Before he could process his actions, Alek's frozen feet launched him forwards, his heart thundering in his chest. Energy pumped through his veins as he dived for the blade. Gripping it in his hands, he rose to his feet, facing the wounded satyr.

The sword was surprisingly light, and Alek took a second to marvel at the way the light glinted off the polished metal before the monster lunged forward, a murderous smile plastered across its face.

Alek lifted the sword up, meeting the satyr's slice with a loud *clang!* His arms jarred, and he felt as if every bone in his body broke as he stumbled backwards, ears ringing from the loud sound of metal on metal. If he could just get the satyr away from his friends, maybe they could escape.

The axe came at him from above this time. Alek's instincts took over and he dived sideways, hitting the ground and rolling head over heels, losing his grip on Ash's sword.

Alek barely had time to breathe before a heavy hoof collided with his side, knocking the wind out of him. Pain exploded through his stomach, his vision going black as he rolled onto his back, trying to force air into his lungs. He was dimly aware of Sarah screaming and Ash hacking at the grass around her ankles with a dagger.

The satyr's hand clamped around Alek's face, lifting his head and squeezing his skull until Alek screamed for him to stop. Through blurry vision, Alek saw the monster smile viciously, its fangs protruding beyond its lips. He had never felt pain like this before. His arms were still jarred from blocking the axe stroke earlier, and his core rippled with pain every time he forced a ragged breath into his lungs.

Through the satyr's fingers, Alek saw Benny and Sarah running towards them, determination written across their faces. Alek gasped as his neck was wrenched upright before the monster brutally slammed his skull back into the ground. White-hot pain pierced his brain, searing through his body before all coherent thought left his mind and the world went black.

3

A WHOLE NEW WORLD

A loud creak echoed through Alek's ears and he stirred, his deep slumber interrupted. But a soothing rocking slowly lulled him back to sleep, vivid dreams dancing behind his eyelids.

A handsome boy was standing in a pool of water before him. Soft blue light highlighted the curves of his muscles, accentuating his angular cheekbones and casting him in an ethereal radiance.

Tattoos spiralled up and down the boy's arms, spreading across his chest and abdomen and disappearing below his waist. He was clearly unclothed. As the boy stepped further into the water, his tattoos began to spark, lighting up with a fiery golden glow and illuminating the body they were etched upon. The boy smirked devilishly at Alek, reaching a waiting hand towards him.

Alek stepped forward, feeling power thrum through his body as he made contact with the water. He had never felt so alive. The tattooed boy's strong hand wrapped around Alek's, sending electricity coursing through Alek's veins. He glanced down, feeling blood rush to his cheeks as he saw his own nakedness. Warm heat radiated from the other boy as he pulled Alek close, his glowing tattoos so intricately designed that Alek wondered how many hours had been spent crafting them.

The boy's breath whispered around Alek's ear and down his neck as he felt the hard body press against his back, drawing them both further into the water. As the two sunk deeper into the pool, Alek arched his head back, his heavy-lidded eyes noticing the vast full moon floating above them. He reached an arm skyward as if he could touch it. Crystal clear droplets of water rippled across his skin, sparkling like diamonds in the glowing blue and gold light.

Gemstones spread out around the edge of the pool, emitting the soft blue glow that illuminated the crystal water. Alek twisted around, swirling effortlessly in the pool, the water supporting his every movement. His entire body tingled with electricity. His vision was clear, his breath light. He hooked a finger under the chin of the boy in front of him, wanting to look into his eyes.

Suddenly, loud thumping music erupted from his right and Alek spun around, no longer swimming in a pool of sparkling water. He was back at the house party. Power no longer flowed through his veins, his breath didn't come quite as easily, and his vision wasn't as sharp.

Flashing lights erupted from the windows, bathing the manicured yard in a rainbow of colours. He could see Sarah and Chris dancing and twirling inside, a huge smile plastered across Sarah's face. Both of them laughed as they took over the whole lounge with their spinning. Looking to the roof, he could see Benny, who had a panicked look on his face as he pointed behind Alek.

Alek spun around, seeing only the boy in his underwear from the party looking at him with a concerned expression.

'Woah, man, you okay?' he asked, once again hooking his thumb into his waistband.

Alek backed away a step, shaking his head. 'No, no, no. I don't want to go for a swim with you. It's not right.'

'What about me?' A stunning girl stepped forward out of the dark beside the other boy, long, raven-black hair cascading down her back. 'Do you want to go swimming with me?' She bit her lip slowly, her eyes flickering up and down Alek's body.

Alek stumbled backwards, his eyes darting from the boy to the girl and back again. 'No, no. I'm not doing anything with either of you.'

Panic overwhelmed him, his heart pounding and his skin turning clammy.

'Make a choice,' both the boy and the girl hissed in front of him, advancing a step. 'Make a choice.'

Both of their lips parted, revealing long, white fangs. Suddenly, they grasped hands, their bodies absorbing into each other and doubling in size. They took on a humanoid shape with burning orange eyes and long, wicked horns.

'Satyr,' Alek whispered, tripping and falling to the ground.

The giant satyr loomed over him, blocking out everything else as it filled Alek's entire field of vision. He scrabbled backwards, desperately trying to get away as thick, black blood splattered the ground around him, running freely from the slice across the creature's eye.

'Make your choice!' the creature roared, multiple voices echoing out of its gaping mouth.

Alek squeezed his eyes shut. 'Go away!' he yelled, his breath coming in short pants.

There was a loud rush of wind and then silence.

Alek inched open his eyes. Around him was only darkness. The giant satyr was gone. He scrambled to his feet, twisting to look over his shoulder, checking he was alone. Suddenly, shuffling footsteps hurried towards him from the dark. Alek froze to the spot as Chris emerged from the hazy blackness surrounding them. Only it wasn't Chris.

His head lolled from side to side, a bloody red gash separating his neck. Blood cascaded down the front of his clothes, splattering the ground. His skin was deathly white, lips a pale blue as they stretched into a mocking grin.

He launched forwards, hands outstretched as they clawed for Alek's face.

Alek screamed and shot upright in bed, his body shuddering from the nightmare.

His skin was clammy and his breath shallow as the recent events flooded his mind. The party, being chased in the Old Town, Ash, the satyr. Chris.

Poor, poor Chris, Alek thought to himself, his hands covering his face and rubbing his temples as he tried to piece together his jumbled memories. He remembered the fight with the satyr, then pain, and then nothing. He sighed, dropping his hands onto the thick blanket enveloping him, and for the first time, he took in his surroundings.

He was in a cosy, dimly lit room, the large bed taking up the majority of the space. Spread across one wall was a bookshelf with variously-shaped books and papers. On the opposite side of the room was a large window covered by a thick curtain.

What is going on? Alek wondered. *Where are Benny and Sarah? I hope they're okay. I need to find out what happened.*

Fighting down his rising panic, Alek eased himself out from under the soft blanket and swung his legs over the edge of the bed. The floor below his feet was wooden, much the same as all four walls and the vaulted ceiling above his head.

As his legs took the full weight of his body, Alek's head spun wildly, causing him to stumble sideways, grasping the mattress for support. A sharp pain exploded above his eyes and he gingerly reached up, inhaling sharply as his fingers made contact with a rather tender lump that had formed on his forehead. Gritting his teeth, Alek forced himself upright again, keeping his eyes squeezed tightly shut as he waited for the dizziness to subside.

When he felt it was safe to move again, Alek shuffled forward, moving for the window. As his hands clutched at the curtain, warmth seeped into his skin from the sun that bathed the material. With a grunt, Alek pulled the curtain aside, rays of warm sunlight cascading into the room around him from the floor-to-ceiling window. He closed his eyes, protecting them from the bright light as he welcomed the warm rays, letting them wrap around his body. The window was ajar and a pleasant breeze whispered against his skin, flicking through his hair and bringing with it a sweet scent of summer.

Alek breathed in deeply, feeling the warm air flood his lungs. He had never inhaled air so pure. Instantly, his head began to clear and his senses tingled, his body relishing the warm sun and the playful breeze tickling his skin. He took another deep breath and opened his eyes, his mouth dropping at the view before him.

An undulating ocean of tree branches filled the space outside of the window. The star-shaped leaves crowning the stems were a beautiful pattern. Sunlight filtered among the canopy, turning the emerald green fronds a brilliant, glowing gold in the late afternoon light.

He heard birds twittering in the branches around him, laughter and voices echoing from below. Tentatively, Alek placed a hand on the window before him, sliding it easily to his left, leaving a wide-open space for him to lean through. The pounding in his head returned as he peered through a gap in the surrounding foliage, seeing the ground far, far below. His vision twisted and Alek threw himself backwards into the cosy room, struggling to piece together his surroundings through the thumping in his head.

The leaves rustled gently as another breeze flowed around Alek, causing the room around him to rock slightly. Slowly, realisation dawned on Alek and his eyes widened, wonder taking over his fear of being so far from the ground. He was in a tree house.

Tentatively, Alek stepped back up to the wide-open window, being careful not to glance down at the long drop below. Staring out into the jungle of leaves, Alek made out another tree house nestled into the crook of two branches not far from his own room. As his eyes took in more detail, he noticed that more and more tree houses were nestled among the forest around him. They blended in with the foliage, seeming to grow out of the trees themselves.

Where am I? Alek wondered, gripping the window frame to steady himself as the tree house gently rocked back and forward again. *How is this real? How does this even exist?*

As he gazed around in awe, a figure stepped out of their tree house and onto the surrounding branches. They were too far away for him to make out any of their features, and the person gracefully slipped through the thick foliage, balancing easily on the rough wood, flitting from tree to tree and soon disappearing from view.

Alek shook his head, backing away from the window to perch on the edge of his bed. *This is unbelievable,* he thought to himself, his mind trying to comprehend the truth that was all around him. *I need to find Benny and Sarah. They must know what's happening and where we are.*

He looked down at himself. He was dressed in dark, skin-tight clothing, the material made out of something he had never felt before. It was light and breathable against his skin, flexing and stretching with his movements. He noticed a pair of boots by his feet and reached down, grasping one of the shoes in his hands.

The boots were made of dark leather, malleable but sturdy. He was surprised to see they were the correct size for him. *Maybe Benny told them what size I was?* Alek mused as he took a seat on the edge of the bed, slipping the boots on. As he laced the shoes up, tying a tight knot around his ankles, he wondered about the strange clothes he was wearing.

Where had Ash taken them? Were they safe? Maybe she had taken his friends hostage, and that's why they weren't with him. The clothes were strange, though. Why dress him in something new when his old clothes had been perfectly fine? One thing was for sure—Alek needed to find his friends to get some answers, and the only way to do that was to leave the tree house.

With a deep breath, Alek walked back to the window, the last barrier between himself and the unknown world outside. He gripped the ledge hard as he lowered himself gingerly onto a thick branch below him, his new boots easily finding grip on the rough bark. Breathing out slowly, Alek let his hand slip away, moving steadily into the maze of thick branches.

Alek slowly picked his way down through the foliage, the bark cutting into his hands as he gripped the trees too hard, trying to keep control of his unease at being so far from the ground. He was one wrong move from falling to his death.

After a few minutes of climbing steadily downwards, Alek still could not see the ground. The next branch below him was out of his reach, and he didn't fancy going back the way he had come to find another way down. Grumbling to himself, Alek lowered himself onto his stomach, slowly sliding over the edge of the branch until he was hanging by his fingertips.

He swore as his tired fingers lost their grip and he plummeted downwards, leaves whipping past his face and scratching at his exposed skin. His hands scrabbled wildly, latching onto a thin branch, the force wrenching his shoulders. He gasped in pain but gripped the branch as tightly as he could as it bent further and further down, bowing under his weight.

Alek desperately looked around, trying to find an escape route. There was a solid-looking branch to his right, so he desperately heaved his body, gathering momentum to swing himself across the gap. Just when he thought he would have enough force to launch himself over to safety, the branch above him gave out with a loud crack.

Alek flailed desperately for the safety of the thicker branch. His right leg slammed onto the bough, jack-knifing his body sideways and flipping him upside down and away from safety. He didn't even have time to scream as he fell through one last layer of thick canopy and thudded into a pile of soft dried-up leaves.

Alek lay surrounded by the golden and rust-coloured leaves, gazing up at the human-sized hole in the canopy above him. Barely comprehending the fact that he had survived the fall.

'Alek!' Soft hands wrapped under his arms, lifting him into a sitting position. 'Alek, oh my god, are you okay?'

Alek blinked as Sarah's face popped into view in front of him. She wore similar clothes to Alek's, and he noticed that her eyes were ringed with red; she had been crying.

'I—I think so?' Alek replied, rolling his shoulders and wincing as they barked in pain.

'We were so worried about you,' Sarah said quietly, her eyes taking on a haunted look. 'You've been out for hours. Ash told us to let you rest, and we've been with her for the last little while. But she's hardly answering any of our questions.

She just keeps saying we have to wait until you're with us. I'm sorry that you woke up and neither of us was there to make sure you were okay. You must've been scared!'

Alek's stomach filled with guilt as Chris's lifeless body flashed through his mind. He reached out, placing his hand on Sarah's shoulder.

'Don't worry about me. I'm fine.' Alek hesitated, contemplating how to continue. 'Sarah, about what happened with Chris …' He trailed off, not knowing the right words.

Sarah pulled away, blinking back tears. 'Don't,' she said softly. 'Just don't say anything.'

Alek's heart broke and he reached forward, gathering Sarah into him. His arms wrapped around her small frame as she shuddered, silent tears falling down her face. They stayed like that for an age, dappled sunlight filtering down from the sky above. The occasional leaf broke away from the foliage to fall peacefully to the ground, settling among the other withered greenery surrounding the two friends.

Once again, Alek was struck by the otherworldly beauty that surrounded him. The trees themselves were colossal, the lower trunks spattered with colourful mushrooms and thick vines. The only light came from far above, trickling down through the thick canopy.

The shadowy undergrowth wasn't sinister, however. The whole forest felt peaceful. Small paths wound through the thick grass, and tall piles of golden leaves pooled across the ground. Alek breathed in deep, once again relishing the sweet clear air and the scent of leaves and soil.

Eventually, Sarah pulled away, sniffling as she wiped a few last tears from her eyes. She climbed to her feet, offering a helping hand to Alek, who groaned as his joints protested at the sudden movement.

'So, where exactly are we?' Alek asked, glancing at the quiet girl beside him as they moved through the undergrowth, it was very unlike Sarah to be so silent. 'And where is Benny? Is he okay?'

Sarah rolled her eyes, looking a little more like her old self as she did so. 'My cousin,' she said critically, 'is fine. He thinks this is all some big grand adventure. As to where we are, let me show you.'

Before Alek could question her further, Sarah grabbed his hand and hauled him deeper into the undergrowth, leaving the narrow paths behind them. All around them, life flourished. Mice and squirrels foraged for food among the leaves, and birds were busy building nests within the branches that reached down around them. Baby birds squawked, their mouths open wide, ready for the next meal.

It's surreal, Alek thought as he was pulled along through a sea of bright green leaves and soft grass. They were in a living world of colour and life, the likes of which Alek had never seen before. The wind seemed to sing as it danced among the soft leaves, clutching and tugging at Sarah's long, brunette hair. The ground beneath their feet grew steeper as Sarah guided Alek further and further through the forest.

It grew steadily lighter the higher the two friends climbed up the side of the hill, leaving the depths of the foliage behind them. Alek noticed the temperature growing warmer as they left the deeper shadows below.

Sarah paused, turning to Alek. 'Are you ready?' A small spark had returned to her green eyes, almost masking the utter heartache that stirred not far from the surface.

'I guess so?' Alek said, not really knowing what to expect.

'This,' Sarah said, pushing aside the branches in front of them, 'is Aranasmin.'

What Alek saw took his breath away.

They were standing on a small hill. In the distance, the earth stretched up into a mighty mountain range. The tips of the craggy peaks vanished into light fluffy clouds, framed against the brilliant sapphire sky. The mountain range extended around them, sheltering them within a large valley that lay nestled among rocky crests.

Alek's eyes traced the mountain range, awe flowing through his body as he heard the distant roar of a torrential waterfall that flowed into a large lake at the opposite end of the gorge. Throughout the entire area, the colossal trees grew, forming a natural camouflage between the sky and the valley floor. Keeping the inhabitants safe from any prying eyes.

Near the edge of the lake, Alek noticed a large field where no trees grew, and beyond that, a cluster of stone structures nestled against the roots of the mountain. As his eyes picked over those small buildings, he noticed caves lining the lower edges of the mountains, dark shadows against the granite rock. A strong wind whipped up over the hill, wrapping around the two friends. Sarah sighed, closing her eyes and tilting her head to catch the rays of the sun.

'The air here is unbelievable,' she said quietly, inhaling deeply.

'This whole place is unbelievable!' Alek exclaimed, sweeping his hand in a mad gesture in front of him. 'Where — what is this place?'

'It's a school,' Sarah stated in a matter-of-fact tone.

'A school?' Alek echoed in disbelief. 'This valley, this forest … Aranasmin … is a school?'

Sarah nodded, grinning at his reaction.

'So we're not in any danger here?' Alek asked, not caring about how paranoid he sounded. 'We aren't prisoners of some sort?'

Sarah snorted. 'No, definitely not. Why? Do you feel like a prisoner?'

'No, I guess not,' Alek answered, his mind trying to keep up with what Sarah was telling him. 'I don't believe it.'

'Believe what you want, Alek. It's all right there in front of you. They take in all sorts of lost children—kids like us. They teach them to defend themselves, to survive, to fight. Apparently, Aranasmin means "hope" in an old language.'

As Sarah finished speaking, a low gong rang through the mountains. Alek watched in disbelief as the valley came to life. Kids of all ages swarmed among the trees and throughout the valley, all dressed similarly to Alek and Sarah. Some students headed for the lake, meeting up with others along the way; others headed for the grassy clearing. Alek continued to watch, hardly believing his own eyes as the kids on the grassy field began to fight, testing their skills against one another.

'Ash is the principal of this place,' Sarah continued. 'She gave me and Benny a brief rundown while some of the other teachers carried you to your room. We really wanted to stay by your side, but Ash convinced us that there wasn't much we could do while you were unconscious, so we went with her. She wouldn't really say much more to us while you were out of it, though, so I left Benny with her to come and check on you.'

'Okay, I believe you,' Alek said in awe. 'But ...' His voice trailed off.

Sarah turned to him, arching an eyebrow.

'Why are we here?' he asked.

Sarah sighed. 'That, I don't know.' Her shoulders closed in. 'If I could go back and change our decision to walk through the Old Town, I would.'

'Sarah, it's not your fault, what happened,' Alek said gently.

Alek gazed at his friend. The wind tugged incessantly at her long brown hair, her face drawn, mouth pressed into a hard line. He was used to her eyes sparkling with life and overflowing with laughter, but now they were hard, calculating, grim. Alek opened his mouth to ask if she truly was okay but closed it again, not finding the right words.

Surely his charismatic, smiling friend wasn't gone forever. She just needed time to process and grieve.

He turned his head to look back over the wonderous valley below and noticed a lone figure climbing the hill towards them. At first, he thought it was just another student from the school, until they looked up. Alek instantly recognised Benny's long, messy, dark hair and brown eyes.

'Ben!' Alek yelled, launching himself down the side of the hill. His feet slipped on some loose earth and he tumbled forwards, rolling head over heels until he collided with Benny's legs, sending them both sprawling across the grass. Clear laughter rang out from above them, and Alek sighed inwardly with relief at the sound of Sarah's voice.

Maybe she was going to be okay.

'That knock on your head in the Portal Realm must have ruined your balance!' gasped Benny as he swallowed down his own laughter.

'Wait, in the what?' Alek asked, frowning.

'The Portal Realm,' Benny said. 'That's the misty forest where Ash took us before we ended up here. I managed to weasel that tidbit of information out of her, at least.'

At the mention of the forest, Sarah's face darkened and her smile disappeared as she picked her way gracefully down the hill to her two friends.

'Anyway,' Benny said, climbing to his feet and offering Alek a helping hand, 'Ash wants to see us all. Apparently, she has a proposal for us.'

Alek grabbed the outstretched hand and hauled himself to his feet.

'Wait, a proposal?' Alek asked suspiciously, glancing between Sarah and Benny. 'Aren't either of you worried? We don't even know where we are or how far away from home we are! We're all dressed in weird clothes, and I just climbed out of a *tree house,* for god's sake!'

Benny rolled his eyes at Alek's outburst. 'Honestly, man, you are way too worried about the details. This is exciting! We're at a school that teaches you to fight, in a super cool valley. And don't complain about the tree houses! They're the best part.'

Alek gasped, his thoughts whirling. 'So you're telling me that you aren't worried about the fact that we were basically kidnapped by a crazy lady with a sword and now we don't even know where we are? What if we never get to go home?'

Benny shrugged. 'I guess it's all part of the adventure, right?'

Disbelief roiled in Alek's stomach as he struggled to understand his friend's nonchalance. He turned his head instead to Sarah, hoping she would be on his side.

'It couldn't hurt to hear Ash out, Alek,' she said calmly. 'She hasn't done anything but be kind to us.'

'She did slap me,' Benny quipped with a crooked grin, holding his hand up like he was asking a question in class. 'I didn't like that very much.'

'And I'm sure it won't be the last time you get slapped,' Alek muttered.

'Aw, come on, man!' Benny moaned. 'This is going to be fun! You'll see. Isn't this exactly what we were talking about at the party? A big adventure?'

'No, that's what *you* were talking about, Ben. I don't want that. I want to go home.' Alek cringed at the words falling from his tongue and how whiny they made him sound.

'Okay, this is getting us nowhere!' Sarah cried at the bickering boys, taking a deep breath through her nose. 'We're going to go hear what Ash has to say, and then we'll make a decision once we know what is happening.

'Benny,' Sarah snipped, glaring at her cousin, 'be nice to Alek. He's allowed to be worried. Now take us to Ash. I've already lost my bearings in these trees.'

'Lead on, Benjamin,' Alek said sarcastically, shoving his friend's shoulder as he fought down the anxiety flooding his body. What was this proposal? What did Ash want from them? Sarah rolled her eyes. 'You two are going to drive me insane.'

Benny wiggled his eyebrows, turning to lead the way into the trees surrounding them. 'You know, Sarah, most girls would love to be stuck in a magical world with two hot guys like me and Alek.'

Alek's gut clenched at Benny's words and Sarah snorted loudly, not even bothering to reply to her cousin as they headed into the valley.

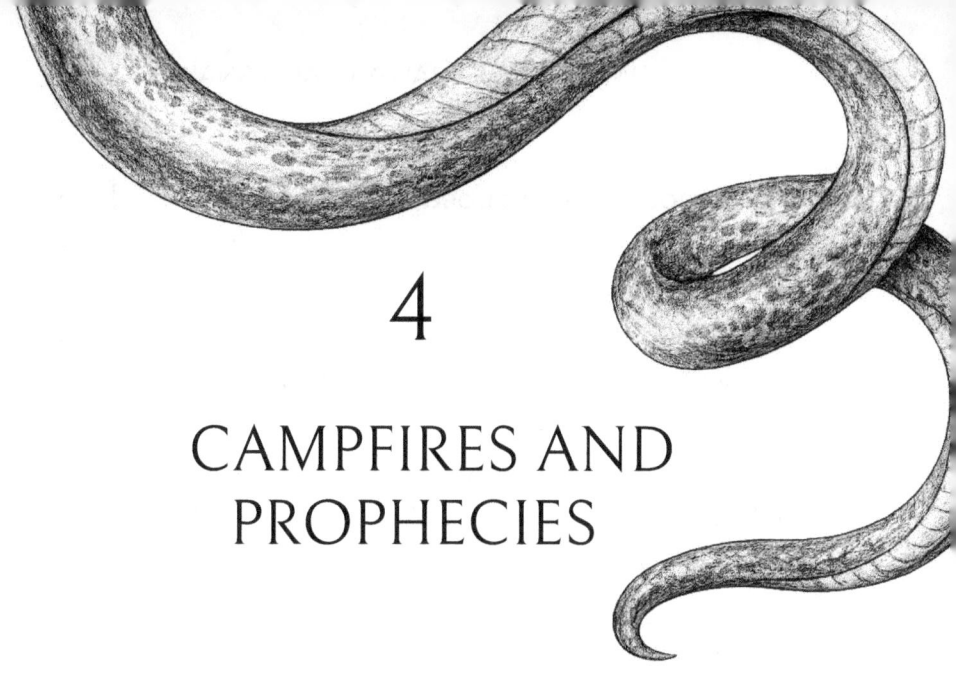

4

CAMPFIRES AND PROPHECIES

The three friends wound their way through the forest. The more they walked, the more Alek felt strength flowing back into his body. His breathing became easier, his steps smoother, and energy flowed through his veins. He pushed down his apprehensive thoughts and instead focused on the world around him, letting the new environment distract him from his worried mind. He smelled the fresh scent of broken leaves as his boots crushed them beneath his feet and the faint smell of smoke from a campfire somewhere in the valley ahead.

His ears picked out the rustling of tiny creatures who called the valley home above him. He marvelled at how magical the world around him seemed to be; everything was crisp and sharp, as if a veil had been lifted from his senses and he could finally see.

Benny led them to a thick grove of bamboo, and together the three slipped through the interlocked trunks.

The temperature dropped as they left the dappled sunlight behind them and were engulfed in the shade cast by the thick fronds above them.

As they emerged from the other side of the smooth wall of bamboo, Alek gaped, floored by the beauty that surrounded him.

They were in a private area, nestled up against the foothills of the mountain walls and screened off from the rest of the valley by the thick bamboo grove. Throughout the clearing, a multitude of small, crystal-clear streams flowed merrily, interconnecting and twisting around each other before disappearing into a small opening in the mountain rockface.

Above them, no giant trees towered, blocking out the sun. Rather, a dozen cherry blossoms grew among the streams, their branches in full bloom, casting the clearing in a brilliant pink haze. Sunlight danced on the rippling water, creating rainbows in the fine mist cast by the streams as they gurgled over smooth pebbles. The soft green grass was covered with fallen pink blossoms and more filled the air, drifting lazily on the warm breeze as they slowly spiralled to the ground, in no hurry to meet their final resting place.

Perched on stilts, sprawling throughout the cherry blossoms and above the trickling water, was a fascinating wooden building. Walkways arched over the streams and connected different rooms with open patios and large windows that opened into the sheltered clearing.

Beneath the twisted branches of one of the larger cherry blossoms, there was a carved, wooden bench. Perched upon the bench was Ash, her long silver hair tied back behind her, accentuating the harsh angles of her face. Her pale eyes glimmered with amusement at the friends' awestruck faces as she rose gracefully to her feet, picking her way across one of the streams using a path of steppingstones.

'Welcome,' she uttered, 'to my private home in the valley: the bamboo grove.' A wry smile tugged at her mouth, the only expression Alek had seen cross her impassive face.

'Thank you … I guess,' Benny stuttered, running a hand nervously down the back of his neck.

Ash gestured to the shade of the cherry blossom behind her. 'Come, sit with me.'

The three friends crossed over one of the small streams, using three steppingstones as a bridge. Alek marvelled at the crystal-clear water flowing beneath his boots. As he drew closer to Ash, a strange feeling of peace washed over him, soothing his tense muscles. Snapping his head up, Alek stared at the pale woman seated on the bench.

Is she doing that? he wondered dubiously. *It's exactly how I felt the last time I saw her. And I'm definitely not feeling that calm about all of this—at all.*

Shaking his head in an unsuccessful effort to dispel the strange, relaxed feeling in the grove, Alek settled down on the soft grass next to his friends, who seemed oblivious to the bizarre mood in the air. Annoyance pricked at his skin. Was he not even allowed to feel upset about being here?

'This valley, this school,' Ash began, 'is known as Aranasmin. I'm glad to see you all in good spirits. It's been a tough journey from your world to mine, and I must apologise for that. I never planned for events to turn out the way they did.' Her gaze lingered on Sarah's bowed head.

Frustration flooded Alek's body as he once again recalled Chris' recent death. Before he knew it, words were falling unbidden from his mouth.

'It's your fault Chris is dead,' he spat, his eyes narrowed.

Sarah flinched.

'Alek—' Benny said quietly, placing a warning hand on his friend's shoulder.

Alek roughly shrugged it off, his confusion and exasperation fuelling his harsh words. 'No, Ben. We don't know where we are, what's happening, why Chris had to die ...' His words grew increasingly more aggressive as he turned towards Ash. 'We don't even know who you are!'

'Alek!' Benny snapped, his nostrils flaring. 'You need to calm down!'

'No!' Alek raged. Tears stung the back of his eyes and he blinked rapidly, forcing them down. 'We would have all been fine if she didn't show up and portal us away to who knows where. Chris would still be alive!'

'You think I don't know that?!' Benny yelled back, the temper that was never far below the surface of his skin breaking free. 'You think I haven't thought about the fact that we all went into the stupid Old Town because I was dumb enough to take the first step?'

Alek flinched as sparks of flame exploded into the air around Benny and a wall of hot air buffeted against his face. Sarah's head snapped up in shock and Benny froze, his eyes wide as he looked at the singed grass around him. As quickly as the fire appeared, it flickered and disappeared.

'What … what just happened?' Benny whispered. His eyes darted from the burnt ground to Alek's stunned face. 'Alek, are you okay? Did I do that? I didn't mean to …' Alek watched as his friend looked down at his hands, inspecting the skin. 'I felt something just now, some sort of energy rushing through me. What was that?' He turned to face Ash, directing the last question at her.

The friends sat in tense silence as Ash took a breath, worry shining in her eyes. Her fingers absentmindedly twirled strands of her long silver hair into a small knot before she sighed, dropping her hands and letting the braid unravel.

'I truly am very sorry about Chris; I never meant for that to happen,' she began rather timidly, but her voice grew stronger as she continued. 'I have a tale to tell you. After I tell it, you will have a choice to make. You can choose to stay and help the people in this world, or you may return to your own world with the knowledge that this place exists and you chose to leave it and never return.'

Alek frowned, his sudden anger lost in the aftermath of Benny's outburst. Glancing at his friends out of the corner of his eyes, he noted the confusion plastered across Benny's face and Sarah's mouth set in a hard line, betraying no hint of her emotions. With a resigned sigh, he dipped his chin towards Ash. 'Tell us.'

Ash closed her eyes, leaning forward towards the friends she began to speak in a hushed voice.

'Long ago, the earth was young, and savage beasts ran untamed across a wild land. Dragons ruled the skies and the seas, and humans were hunted by all. Along came a stranger. A tall, elven maiden with long, golden hair that brushed the ground. She gave four people a gift. A gift to be passed on through generations. A gift to offer protection to the weak humans she had grown fond of.'

'Wait, wait, wait,' Alek interrupted abruptly, his thoughts spinning. 'Did you say elf? Like, little people with pointy ears?' Maybe he hadn't recovered as well as he had thought from the bump on his head.

Ash inclined her head with a small smile, the movement more animalistic than comforting. 'Yes. Although elves are not small, they do have pointed ears. They are ancient beings—one of the first to populate this land after the dragons.'

'Dragons?!' Alek scoffed. *This lady is crazy—maybe I'm still unconscious and this is all just some big messed up dream,* he thought, trying to justify the recent events.

'Alek, be quiet!' Benny shushed. 'This is so cool!'

Alek stared at his friend, flabbergasted at how invested he was in the strange tale, his guilt over Chris's death apparently forgotten as Ash continued.

'The elven maiden chose a young man with flaming red hair and took him to the fiery mountains where the dragons lived. The colossal beasts regarded humans with disdain but humoured the elf, granting her wish. From that day forward, fire burned through the man's blood, completely under his control and command.'

A chill rushed through Alek's veins as he pictured the flickering fire that had burned around Benny minutes before. His headache returned with a vengeance as he tried to rationalise the situation around him.

'Next, the elf took a dark-haired young woman,' Ash continued, reciting the words with practised ease. 'She took her to the bottomless depths of the ocean, to a place untouched by the sun where long, serpentine beasts dwelled amongst coral reefs. When the two surfaced, water flowed through the woman's body, its power at her fingertips.

'She then decided upon a young blonde boy, a pickpocket, who was quick and free-spirited. Together, they ventured onto the vast, mountainous plateaus to the east. When they returned, wind was completely under his control.'

Ash paused, moistening her lips as she gathered her thoughts. Next to Alek, Benny was completely transfixed by the tale unfolding before them. Glancing past Benny, Alek studied Sarah carefully, but her face was unreadable. It was impossible to tell what she was thinking.

How can they be so calm? Alek's mind head was spinning, and he could do nothing but listen as Ash continued the story.

'The last of the chosen four was a quiet man.

'"You are wise," the elven maiden said to the man, "unwavering." 'She took him into the ancient forests, and there he gained the element earth. For years, the human tribes lived in peace under the united forces of the four—until a scorching summer day brought a figure clad all in black to them. He befriended the villagers and all of the four except the fire warrior.

'One night, the man put the four under a spell that bound them to his every word.

Monsters made of shadows slithered from the darkness, trapping the humans. For he was a wicked man bent on destroying the four and taking the power for himself. But where he succeeded, he also failed, for the free-spirited fire bearer could not be controlled by anyone, just as fire cannot be controlled and tamed.'

'This story just gets crazier, and crazier,' Alek muttered under his breath, not meaning to speak the words out loud.

'Shhhh,' Benny hissed, motioning with his hands towards
Alek. 'It's just getting good.'

Alek rolled his eyes as Ash continued.

'As the man spent his power ensnaring the three others, the fire bearer, outraged at the man's actions, sought him out and banished him and his shadows from the land with the fury and strength of a fire dragon. The man fled beneath the onslaught of flames and vanished under the earth and into the darkness below. And as the man crossed the mountains, the spell was lifted

'The humans rejoiced, for they thought the man had died, and in ignorance, they feasted long into the night. But the wicked man was not dead, nor was he alone under the mountains. An ancient evil was awakened by his hasty retreat into the underbelly of the world. She began to whisper in his ear tales of revenge, of wealth, of power.

'The man created a mighty fortress under the mountain. And in the inky darkness, he grew a shadow army, biding his time, waiting for the world to be at its most vulnerable. It is then that those forces will strike, once again plunging the world into darkness.'

Alek blinked as Ash finished reciting the tale and looked at the friends expectantly.

'Ooookay,' he said sarcastically. 'And what exactly does this have to do with us?'

Ash tilted her head. 'Balathor—the world beyond these mountains,' she said, gesturing around them, 'is filled with towns, just like any other land. Great forests, rivers, and bustling cities where thousands of humans go about their lives, completely unaware that their home is once again in darkness. Evil is stirring, and with it, the shadows are whispering. Creatures that have not been seen for decades are crawling out of the earth. People are being attacked in their own homes by an evil force known as the Dark Warriors. This valley used to be almost empty, but now, with the violence outside of this school, we are rescuing more and more children whose homes have been destroyed and families murdered.'

She paused to gather her thoughts before continuing. 'The last time darkness covered the world and The Four were tricked by evil, they agreed to remove a large portion of their power and store it in an amulet so as to not become a danger to the people around them if they were to ever fall under the control of someone again. That amulet has remained hidden, here in Aranasmin, for hundreds of years. Until a week ago, when someone infiltrated our defences and stole it, murdering the principal in the same night.'

Tears formed in the corners of Ash's eyes and she blinked them away, tilting her head back to admire the bright streaks of colour in the sky as the sun began to set. 'You three are direct descendants of The Four,' she said. 'I have brought you here so you can fulfil your destiny and save us all.'

Alek snorted loudly, causing Benny to chuckle as he asked, 'What on earth makes you think we are the descendants of these four?'

'The principal before me and the one before him kept records of you and your ancestors' lives in case we ever needed to call on you once more.'

'This is crazy!' Alek exclaimed, climbing to his feet. 'Absolutely crazy! You expect us to believe all of this? And what exactly do you want us to do? Fight a war for you? In a world we know nothing about and people we don't care about?' 'Yes,' Ash answered simply.

Alek rolled his eyes, throwing his hands in the air. 'You've got the wrong people, lady.'

Ash shook her head. 'No, you are the descendants. The amulet called to you when it was stolen. The world shook, and green lightning tore through the sky with the power of its call. Can't you feel it? You've all sensed it from the moment you stepped foot in this world. You can feel the power flowing through you, feel yourselves waking up, becoming more alive with each breath you take. That's the magic in your blood stirring, ready to be awoken.'

Benny raised an eyebrow at Alek. 'That could explain the fire.' Alek hesitated. 'Whatever. Let's just say we choose to stay. What then?'

The silver-haired woman smiled. 'You will be enrolled as students, you will be trained as warriors, and you will learn how to harness your magic. And I hope, given time, you will understand how important you are for a lot of people in this world.' 'And if we choose to leave?' Alek asked.

'Then I will immediately return you home,' Ash said simply.

'I will not force you to stay here against your will.'

'Our families …' Alek turned pleading eyes to Benny. 'You know what happened to my brother, Benny. He vanished, just up and disappeared when I was a kid after dad died. My mum lost her husband and her eldest son in a matter of weeks; I was too young to do anything but watch her cry. You know it would kill her if I disappeared as well. She's barely been holding it together as it is.'

Benny avoided Alek's eyes as Ash softly cleared her throat and said, 'You will find that time works differently in this world. Years may pass here while seconds barely tick by in your world, so you will not be missed. Your mother will not even know you have left.'

Sarah raised her head, speaking in a quiet voice for the first time. 'I am staying.'

Alek's head whipped around, disbelief churning in his stomach. 'What?!'

'I'm staying,' she repeated, her mouth set in a determined line. 'Whatever you decide, I am staying.' 'Why?' Benny asked, frowning.

Sarah's eyes flickered and she bit her lip, dropping her gaze.

'Because it's the right thing to do.'

Alek stared at her; this couldn't be happening.

'Well, I guess that settles it, then,' Benny said slowly. 'I'm not leaving Sarah here, and Alek isn't leaving me here.' He turned to Ash with a grin. 'So you get your wish.'

Alek opened his mouth to argue and then frowned, realising Benny was right. He wouldn't leave his friends here alone—he couldn't. Nerves fluttered in his stomach as he wondered if they had actually had a choice, or had the decision been made for them, hundreds of years ago? He realised Ash was talking and tuned back in.

'Starting tomorrow, the three of you will partake in classes with the other students, as well as lessons with me on the subject of magic. Every night, we have dinner in the centre of the valley as a community.' She paused, glancing at the sky. 'Speaking of which, we are going to be late.'

As the friends gathered themselves, preparing to move out of the grove, Ash cleared her throat loudly. 'And one more thing. I must ask that you keep your identity—and your magic, once you learn how to harness it—a secret.'

Benny frowned, opening his mouth to argue, but Ash quickly continued, cutting him off, 'The legend of The Four is well known across the land. Many scoff at the tale and disregard it as a bedtime story for children, but there are those who believe the old tales. They still hold out hope that The Four will return when the world is at its darkest and save them all. If word gets out that you have been found and are, in fact, real, danger will come at you from every direction.'

Alek's heart skipped a beat, his mind replaying the prophecy in his head, painting vivid pictures of the evil man and his army of shadow monsters. His mouth went dry at the thought of facing down an enemy with a power such as that.

'We don't want that happening until you are ready,' the principal said matter-of-factly. 'Now come. It is time for dinner and time for you to meet the other students.'

Ash rose from her seat and led the way out of the bamboo grove, gesturing for the friends to follow her. Alek's head spun.

How is all of this happening? he thought to himself as they made their way through the ever-darkening valley, following Ash's lead. *Chris is dead, we're not even in our world anymore, and we're supposed to somehow save this one?* Anxiety flashed through his body, and he nervously chewed on his lip. What if Chris was just the first to die? What if Benny or Sarah are next? Despair rushed through him as he glanced at his friends, Benny looking around in wonder and Sarah stony-faced and determined. Once again, he narrowed his eyes as he stared at her.

Why on earth would she want to stay in this world where everything will remind her of what she's lost? Something's definitely off with her. She has a plan, and I'm not sure what it is.

The group rounded a clump of thick bushes and stepped into a large clearing. The canopy opened up above them, offering a breathtaking view of the twilight sky. A massive bonfire burned merrily in the centre of the glade. Alek marvelled at the way the firelight splashed across the bordering maple trees, painting their trunks in a golden glow and sparkling off the star-shaped leaves.

Throughout the clearing, students sat at wooden tables or in groups among the soft grass, talking and laughing in the dancing shadows cast by the flames.

Each student, male and female, was dressed in a uniform similar to Alek and his friends'. The same dark, tight clothing that sat like a second skin. He spotted a few students sporting cosy-looking jackets to ward off the evening chill. They looked comfortable, made from the same dark leather as his boots and lined with what looked to be pale fur on the inside. He made a mental note to ask Ash where he could get one for himself.

His ankle-length leather boots, laced up the front, seemed to be standard across the uniform.

A few faces turned to look at them curiously before they quickly lost interest and continued their conversations. Most of the students seemed to be a similar age to Alek, although he spotted a few younger children in the crowd, laughing together as they threw leaves and sticks into the crackling fire. On the outskirts of the clearing, less visible in the growing darkness, was a small knot of older people, some with grey streaking their hair.

Teachers, maybe? Alek thought to himself as he soaked in the beauty around him, trying to distract himself from the turmoil in his mind.

Anxiety began to knot in Alek's stomach the longer he stood awkwardly at the edge of the clearing, his heart beating fast as he tried to locate where he could get food from and where he should be sitting once he had it.

'Over there, buddy,' Benny said, pointing to the opposite side of the fire.

Alek looked through the flames and saw a massive buffet of food spread across a few tables. He exhaled the breath he hadn't even known he had been holding as Benny clapped him on the shoulder, leading the way through the crowded clearing to the food.

'You really should stop worrying, Alek,' Sarah said quietly.

'We're going to be fine.'

'How do you know?' he asked. 'Anything could happen.' 'I know,' Sarah said, selecting some food off the table. 'Because we have each other's backs. Nothing can hurt us if we stick together.' She elbowed Alek in the ribs. 'Although I am worried about my idiotic cousin!'

Alek followed her gaze and saw that Benny had drawn closer to the bonfire, which now seemed to be burning brighter and higher than it was earlier. He watched as Benny reached out a hand and the flames flared upwards, wrapping around his friend's fingers.

Alek lunged forwards, yanking Benny backwards. 'What the hell are you doing?!' he grabbed Benny's hand, twisting it around to see if he had been burnt.

'I have no idea,' Benny said shakily. 'I feel different. Like, I just felt energy flow through me as I got closer to the fire. And when it touched me ...' He shivered. 'I've never felt anything like it.' Alek shook his head, letting his friend's hand drop. 'You're an idiot.'

Benny frowned as he drifted over to the tables of food, following in Alek's footsteps.

The three friends piled their plates with an assortment of fresh fruit and a delicious-smelling broth. Alek's stomach growled as they settled onto the ground at the edge of the gathering students. He hadn't realised how hungry he was until he inhaled the smell of warm spices drifting up from his plate. As the three began to devour their food, the clearing went silent.

Alek looked up from his meal as a line of newcomers filed into the clearing, led by Ash. They were children of varying ages, boys and girls all sharing the same haunted, lost look. Unlike the rest of the students already halfway through their meals, these kids were not dressed in the black, skin-tight uniform everyone else was wearing.

'Who are they?' Sarah asked Alek.

Before Alek could answer, a boy to their left cut in and said, 'Newcomers. They're probably orphans from a town that was raided by the Dark Warriors. Most of us are. One of the valley's scouts would have seen them passing by an outpost and given them sanctuary here. Most of them will probably stay and become students.' The student turned and studied Alek and his friends. 'You're new here, too. Whereabouts are you from?'

Alek froze as his mind went blank. The boy stared at him curiously as Alek worked furiously to come up with a believable lie, but how could he? He didn't know anything about the world outside of this valley. The student was slightly tubby and maybe thirteen or so, with large brown eyes, a pallid complexion, and brown, short-cropped hair.

'We're from a small farm not far from here,' Sarah cut in, shooting Alek a sympathetic glance. 'Those Dark Warriors attacked us, too, killing our parents.'

Benny nodded along, plastering a sad expression across his face as the lies flowed easily from Sarah's lips.

The student shrugged. 'So the same story as the rest of us, then,' he replied with a sigh. 'And, more than likely, all these newcomers have the same fate. More and more kids have been appearing here in the last few months. It's horrible. It was exciting at first, having new people join us every week or so, but now it's just routine more than anything.' With that, the young boy turned away from the three friends, his interest in them gone.

Sadness tugged at Alek's gut as he looked over the new kids, taking in their ragged and well-worn clothing and the dirt covering their bodies. They must have travelled for miles. As he inspected the group, one last boy stepped into the clearing. He looked to be about Alek's age, and as he straightened, taking in his new surroundings, his eyes locked with Alek's.

Alek couldn't look away as the ice blue eyes bored into his own. He felt a shiver slide down his spine as the firelight flickered off the boy's handsome face, the shadows accentuating his angular jaw and full lips. The boy blinked, and the connection was broken as he turned to gather some food for himself.

The conversation around them grew again as the students lost interest in the newcomers. Alek only half-listened to Sarah and Benny debating what their lessons would be the following day as his eyes watched the strange boy move effortlessly through the crowd to a more secluded part of the clearing to eat his meal. Once again, their eyes met briefly, causing Alek to blush before the boy gazed at Benny and Sarah with a small frown and moved on to inspect the other students.

'Alek, come on!' Benny said, frustrated. 'Are you even listening to me?'

Alek jumped, startled out of his thoughts. 'I'm sorry, what?'

Benny groaned. 'If you were paying any attention at all, you would know we're leaving now. Ash is taking us back to our tree houses so we don't get lost.'

Alek looked around to see Ash and Sarah already on the opposite side of the fire. He quickly rose to his feet, following Benny as they wound through the crowd, heading into the shadows beyond the firelight. His neck prickled as he got the sense someone was watching him. He quickly spun his head around, his eyes darting around the clearing. But no one was paying him any attention, and the boy with the blue eyes was nowhere to be seen.

Slightly disappointed, Alek followed as Ash led the way through the dark valley.

Why the heck are you upset, you idiot? Alek berated himself. *Why would you care if someone was looking at you or not? You don't even know who he is. He probably just knew you didn't fit in—that's why he was looking at you.*

He spent the rest of the walk in silence, lost in the turmoil of his thoughts. Torches were mounted atop thin wooden poles at regular intervals throughout the dark forest, providing a safely lit path through the trees.

'Well, here we are,' Ash said, abruptly stopping at the base of one of the giant maples. 'You're all in this tree. I will see you tomorrow in the field to the north when the gong sounds at dawn.'

'I'm sorry, what?' Alek said, shocked. 'Dawn? You expect us to get out of bed ... at dawn?!'

Benny chuckled as Ash frowned. 'I expect you not to question me, yes,' she replied curtly, before turning on her heel and quickly disappearing into the darkness.

'Well, now is the perfect chance to say we've changed our minds and don't want to stay here,' Alek persuaded, glancing at both of his friends.

Sarah frowned. 'Alek … I'm sorry that you don't want to stay, I really am. But I have to. I just can't go back to my regular life after everything that's happened.'

'Yeah!' Benny jumped in, a wild excitement shining in his brown eyes. 'Besides, aren't you curious, man? We're in a whole new world! Look how big the trees are! And we have magic?! Who doesn't want to have magic? This is awesome!'

'No,' Alek pleaded, his heart sinking in his chest. 'Don't you get it, Benny? This place is dangerous! You heard Ash. We're supposed to fight off some sort of evil! And what about those Dark Warrior things … they're literally murdering entire families!'

Benny shrugged, glancing at Sarah. 'It can't be that bad, and we're going to learn how to fight, anyway. Alek, dude, this is a once in a lifetime adventure. I'd hate myself if I went home now, knowing this place existed and I didn't get a chance to explore.'

Alek stared at his two friends, utterly defeated. *How can they be so okay about staying here?*

Sarah glanced awkwardly at Alek, flicking her hair over her shoulder. 'Well, I guess I'll see you two at dawn.' With that, she leapt into the tree beside them, quickly swinging herself up through the branches and out of sight.

Benny wasn't far behind, grumbling to himself about sleep-ins and waking up before the sun. Despite his tumultuous thoughts, a smile tugged at the corner of Alek's mouth as he listened to his best friends moaning. Maybe he should give this place a chance. Besides, if he went home without his two friends, he knew he would be too worried about them to go about his day-to-day life anyway.

Someone's got to stay to keep them out of trouble and make sure they don't do anything stupid, I guess.

Alek slowly started his ascent, carefully picking which branches he would trust to support him. His whole world may have changed, but at least Benny and Sarah were with him.

Alek let loose a deep breath, and apprehension rolled off his shoulders. So long as he and his friends were in this together, they would be alright. Branches scratched at his hands as he hauled himself higher into the tree, his breath coming in ragged gasps by the time he pulled himself over the lip of his tree house and tumbled into the cosy room.

He crawled across the floor and dragged his body into bed, his eyes already closed as he pulled off his clothes and sunk into the soft mattress. The sounds of crickets chirping and leaves rustling around him slowly soothed him into a deep sleep as the moon rose high above the pristine valley.

5

MAGIC

A lek stretched luxuriously, a huge yawn escaping from him as the soft mattress below enveloped his body. He kept his eyes closed as he revelled in the warm sunlight that flooded his room and soaked into his bare chest, the heat making his skin tingle. He took a deep breath through his nose. The air was sweet and crisp and seemed to fill his body with energy every time he inhaled.

The cabin around him creaked, trembling slightly.

Hands clamped onto Alek's shoulders, shaking him roughly. Alek gasped and launched upright, his heart thundering as panic overtook him. His eyes flew open just in time for him to see Benny dodge out of his flailing arms' reach.

'Benny, what the hell are you doing?!' Alek hissed, taking deep gulps of air to try and calm his racing heart.

Benny snorted loudly, failing to hold back his laughter. 'More like what are *you* doing?' He gasped between chuckles. 'Do you attack everyone who wakes you up?'

'Yes.' Alek sniffed. 'Especially when they sneak into my room and grab me.' He collapsed back onto his mattress, rubbing his face with his hands.

'Come on,' Benny said, grasping Alek's blankets and ripping them off the bed. 'We're going to be late.'

Alek groaned, curling up into a ball as the crisp air bit into his exposed skin.

'Oh, good.' Benny smirked. 'I was hoping you had underwear on under there!'

Alek grabbed his pillow and threw it at Benny, who easily caught it and placed it on the bed between them.

'For real, man, we need to go,' Benny said, gathering up some clothes and throwing them at Alek. 'Sarah's waiting for us on the ground. She overheard some students talking, and apparently, we have to go for a run every morning.'

Alek had hauled himself to his feet by then, but he paused at Benny's words. 'I'm sorry, what?'

'Run.' Benny clasped a hand on his best friends' shoulder. 'That's right, buddy. You're about to go for a run.'

Alek groaned as he quickly dressed, stumbling as he pulled on his pants. Once he had his boots laced up, he followed Benny through the branches and onto the valley floor.

'What took you two so long!' Sarah exclaimed impatiently. 'We're going to be late on our first day!'

'Pretty boy here was enjoying his beauty sleep,' Benny said, jerking his thumb at Alek.

Alek rolled his eyes and followed his friends as they made their way quickly through the forest, joining a group of students who were headed in the same direction. The students made awkward eye contact with the three friends, and one of them offered a small smile before they increased their pace, moving ahead.

Well, at least everyone's friendly, Alek thought sarcastically.

A brisk walk took them through the winding tracks among the thick foliage. They stepped out onto a large, grassy field at the northern end of the valley.

Warm sunlight hit the friends as the world opened around them, leaving the cool, thick forest behind. A soft wind whispered around them, lifting Sarah's loose hair and blowing it lazily around her face. Before them, students were gathered in groups, stretching and talking among themselves.

Alek noticed Ash walking past, nodding to the three friends from a distance.

'We should get closer,' Alek said quietly, anxiety welling inside him as he wondered what exactly they were doing and where they should be standing.

As the friends shuffled through the crowd of other students, Ash's voice rang out in the morning air.

'Good morning, students.' She paused, making sure she had everyone's attention before she continued. 'For those who have joined us yesterday and the group that was rescued last night, every morning we go for a run around the perimeter of the valley. It keeps us fit and helps you understand your new home and how to navigate it.'

Alek balled his hands into fists. *Around the whole valley! I don't even want to run across this field.*

Alek tuned back in just as Ash turned and broke into a run, the other students springing into action and chasing after her. He groaned as he forced his legs to move, his friends beside him. *This isn't so bad. I feel stronger here. Fitter.*

Five minutes later, Benny and Sarah were nowhere to be seen and Alek had slipped right to the back of the group of students, gasping loudly and struggling to fill his lungs. Suddenly, he heard footsteps behind him and he quickly straightened, trying desperately to mask his heavy breathing as his unsteady feet continued.

He focused on the ground below his feet as a student fell into step beside him.

'You know,' a deep, enticing voice spoke, 'you need to focus more on your breathing. I can help with that if you'd like?'

Alek glanced to the left and choked on his breath, lost his footing, and fell face-first into the ground. Heat flooded his cheeks as he cursed his clumsiness, embarrassment washing over him. He waited for the laughter to begin, but none came.

Still struggling to draw in a full breath, Alek raised his head to look at the student next to him. It was the newcomer he had locked eyes with on the other side of the bonfire the previous night. The boy's icy eyes softened as he reached forward, offering a helping hand. Alek frowned as he saw that the boy was wearing gloves on both of his hands. Strange, considering it wasn't cold enough to warrant them. He ignored the gloved hand and hauled himself to his feet, giving up on hiding his rasping breaths as he forced air into his lungs.

The student cocked his head to the side. 'Are you okay?'

Alek nodded and continued at a slow pace along the path marked by the long-gone students before them.

'My name's Kai,' the boy said, falling into step beside Alek.

Alek glanced at Kai out of the corner of his eyes, taking in his perfectly-sculpted face, full lips, and the muscular body evident under his skin-tight clothing. His hair was dark, tousled, and windswept, a few wavy strands falling over his forehead as they walked among the trees.

'I saw you last night in the clearing with the fire,' Kai said pleasantly, attempting to make small talk. 'Have you been here long?'

Alek grunted. 'No. I got here yesterday, a few hours before you and your group.'

Kai frowned, seeming to contemplate something as they continued their slow walk.

'Why are you back here with me?' Alek asked abruptly, noticing how easily Kai glided through the undergrowth beside him. 'You're barely even sweating. You should be at the front of the group, not back here with a loser like me.'

Kai shrugged. 'I don't like people.' They walked on in silence for a few minutes before he spoke again. 'And you're not a loser. You just need to practise and focus on your breathing.'

'Is that right?' Alek asked, rolling his eyes.

'I could teach you,' Kai said softly, ducking under an overhanging branch. 'That is, if you want.'

Alek frowned. 'You want to teach me how to breathe?'

The other boy chuckled. 'If that's what you want to call it, yes. I want to teach you how to breathe.'

They walked in silence for a while longer, the rough mountains rising sharply into the sky on their left. Alek threw his head back, taking in long breaths of the clean morning air and trying to forgive himself for being so unfit.

Beside him, Kai continued talking. 'We can train on the shore of the lake at sunset. My tree house is near there. It's usually quiet at that time, and training on the sand will help make you stronger. I'm sure you'll need some help with combat training as well if you can't even jog around the valley.'

Irritation sparked through Alek and his head snapped around to glare at Kai. 'Excuse me? Am I a joke to you? Do you just assume that I'm hopeless at everything and you're going to make me your special project?'

Kai's eyes widened. 'No, not at all. I just—'

'I don't care what "you just",' Alek snapped, shoving past Kai. 'I don't want your pity or for you to look down at me.'

He winced inwardly at his harsh words as he glimpsed the slightly hurt expression on Kai's face. Using his frustration to fuel his tired limbs, Alek once again began to run through the valley, ignoring the sharp pain in his side and shaking legs from the unexpected exercise.

Over an hour later, Alek finally burst back onto the open field where the morning run had begun. His body was soaked in sweat and his breath came in ragged gasps as he looked around, noticing that there was only a small group of twelve or so students left on the field.

He heard his name being called from the group and saw Benny and Sarah waving for him to join them. As he grew closer, he noticed Kai at the back of the group, watching him with a blank expression on his face. Guilt stabbed through Alek's chest. *He was just trying to help,* he thought, avoiding eye contact with the boy. *He probably just wants a friend.*

'Where have you been?!' Benny said loudly as Alek drew nearer. 'You can't tell me it took that long for you to get around the valley. We've been waiting here for ages!'

'Drop it, Benny,' Alek muttered, resentment rolling through him.

'Finally,' a cocky voice drawled from behind Alek, 'you've decided to join us. I don't think I've ever seen anyone as unfit as you.'

Alek spun on his heel, anger flashing through him, only to come face to face with another, much larger student. His hair was shaved into a short buzz cut and his large, muscled body bulged against the skin-tight uniform as he crossed his arms and stared at Alek with a mean smirk. The long sleeves of his uniform were rolled up to his elbows so he could show off his bulging arms.

'Can I help you?' Alek snapped, frustration bubbling inside him as he felt blood flush his cheeks.

'Yeah, you could not keep everyone waiting just because you're a pudgy boy who can't even go on a small jog. How do you expect to survive here?' The boy had an ugly face with a bent nose.

'You watch your mouth!' Benny shouted, elbowing past Alek to stand between him and his tormentor.

'Benny, it's fine,' Alek said quietly, pulling his friend back.

'What, do you need your boyfriend to come and save you?' the boy asked mockingly.

Benny launched himself forward, landing a hard punch across the boy's jaw. The gathered students blinked in shock at the speed and force of Benny's sudden attack. Benny's eyes widened as he took a step back, realising what he had started and how much bigger the other boy was. Alek watched nervously as the other student shifted his weight, ready to lunge towards Benny, just as a voice rang across the clearing.

'Now, now, boys. Let's save the fighting for when we're actually training.' An older man walked briskly into the group of students. 'For those of us who are new, my name is Matthias, and I am your combat instructor. And I will not tolerate fighting outside of class time. Is that understood, Lucien?'

The aggressive student backed up a step, never breaking eye contact with Alek. 'Yes, sir,' he muttered quietly.

Alek shivered as Lucien continued to look him up and down, a sneer on his face.

'For today's lesson, you will all be divided up into pairs and we will be running through some basic self-defence so I can determine our newcomers' level of experience,' Matthias said, walking among the students with his hands behind his back.

He was middle-aged, his thinning brown hair tied back in a small bun. A large nose protruded from his face and small, green eyes peered out from behind bushy eyebrows. He wore the same uniform as everyone else, but a large cloak hung over his shoulders, rustling as he moved across the soft grass.

Alek groaned inwardly as he stood awkwardly at the back of the group, watching everyone else get paired up by the teacher.

He sighed with relief as Matthias paired him with a girl he had never met and not Lucien, who continued to cast threatening glares his way.

Less than two minutes later, Alek had been knocked onto his back for the second time by his opponent, a short girl with blonde hair around his own age. She glanced down at him apologetically as Matthias praised her form. Alek groaned and glanced around at the other students, the thick grass spiking into his legs as he refused to move from the ground.

Benny and Sarah weren't faring too much better than himself. Sarah managed to stay in the fight with her opponent the longest, gracefully outmanoeuvring most of the attacks aimed her way.

Alek quickly dared a look over at Kai, who was circling Lucien. Alek sat up straighter, arms hugging his knees as he watched the two students trade blows. Kai dodged and weaved, his feet constantly moving, his body controlled and tight, ready to strike at any moment.

Lucien lunged forward, and Kai quickly spun to the side, ducking and twisting up behind the much larger student, bringing Lucien's arm up at an awkward angle behind the boy's back. Lucien yelled loudly, and Alek couldn't help but feel some satisfaction from the boy's pain.

'Good, Kai!' Matthias praised the boy, slapping him on the back. 'Everyone, take notes. Just because your opponent is bigger than you, that doesn't mean they can beat you. Use your speed against them.' Matthias looked around, noticing Alek still sitting on the ground. 'Kai, pair up with Alek. Maybe some of your experience will rub off on him.'

Alek's heart sunk as the boy walked across the field towards him, every step measured and controlled. Alek remained on the ground, avoiding eye contact with Kai. As the other students around them regrouped and began the practice again, Alek heard shuffling beside him as Kai settled onto the grass.

'You know,' he began, 'this would be a lot easier if you just let me help you.'

Alek snorted, throwing his arms up and falling back onto the earth, gazing up at the brilliant blue sky.

'What's the point?' He sighed. 'I'm uncoordinated, unfit, in way over my head, and I hurt—everywhere.'

Kai chuckled, laying down on the ground next to Alek, his hands behind his head. 'You know everyone feels like that at some point, right?'

Alek snorted, glaring stubbornly at the sky. 'I feel like that every day.'

Kai turned his head to look at Alek. 'How long have you been here again?'

'One day,' Alek winced, repeating their previous conversation and realising how pathetic he sounded.

The other boy laughed again; the sound was startingly carefree in comparison to the carefully measured words that usually came out of his mouth.

Kai hauled himself to his feet. 'You just need time and practice. The only thing holding you back is yourself.'

'Yeah, says Mister Perfect over here,' Alek sneered sarcastically.

Hurt flashed through Kai's eyes as he glanced down at Alek before spinning on his heel and stalking away.

Alek closed his eyes and sucked in a deep breath, pushing his frustration down.

I don't belong here.

****

The sun rose higher in the sky as Alek stayed rooted to the ground, refusing to participate in any activities despite coaxing from Sarah and Benny. Eventually, the class dispersed, and Alek found himself following his friends into the cool shadows of the forest, heading towards Ash's bamboo grove.

'Welcome,' Ash greeted the three, her eyes sparkling as they wound their way through the many trickling streams. 'I trust you've had a good first day?'

Benny and Sarah nodded awkwardly, shooting sidelong looks at Alek.

'Good.' Ash clapped her hands, oblivious to the tension in the air. 'Now, every afternoon, you are going to study with me. We will be working closely on awakening the magic that each of you possesses.' Her gaze travelled over the friends and stopped on Benny. 'We've already seen you display some ability to project your specific gift. Now let's see if you can do it again.'

Benny nodded uncertainly. 'I don't know how I did that, though. I was just angry, and it just kind of burst out.'

Ash nodded. 'Magic is heightened with emotion. It becomes erratic, more difficult to control. So control your emotions, and you control your magic.'

'Is it going to be the same for all of us, though?' Sarah asked. 'If we each have a different element of magic, won't it all manifest differently?'

90

'Yes and no.' Ash cocked her head to the side. 'Magic all comes from the same place. From your core.' She raised a hand to her belly. 'Once you locate your centre, it's only a matter of letting your magic flow through your body and then pushing it beyond yourself. How it manifests once it leaves your body will then be different for each of you.'

Uncertainty flooded through Alek. *I don't feel like I have magic in me,* he thought. *I have felt different since I've been here, but not magical. Can I even do this?*

'Right,' Ash said briskly, bringing Alek back from his thoughts. He noticed he had been chewing nervously on his lip and he quickly stopped, focusing on what Ash was saying.

'I want you all to lie down on your backs,' Ash began as the friends shifted on the grass, their bodies facing the afternoon sky. 'Now focus on you and your surroundings. Watch how the cherry blossoms fall, drifting on the small currents of wind, spiralling to the ground. Notice the sound of the water trickling happily through the many streams, the grass rustling together softly. I want you to focus on your body and how it reacts to your surroundings. How the wind whispers against your skin, pulling at your hair. How your ears take in all the sounds around you. Now focus on your breathing. Steady breaths, in and out.'

Alek began to feel drowsy as the afternoon sun warmed his body and the gentle wind wrapped itself around him. He breathed in deeply and slowly let the breath out, feeling his body relax for the first time that day as his stress slowly melted away.

'Now close your eyes and delve into yourself,' Ash said softly, walking among the three friends. 'Your magic is there; you just need to reach deep enough to find it. Once you do, release it and let it flow through your veins.'

Alek closed his eyes, feeling stupid as he searched within his mind for some echo of magic. Instead, his thoughts swirled around inside him. *What did Kai want? Why is he being so nice to me? Why is everyone acting okay with being here? Is Sarah really okay after what happened to Chris? Why do I suck so much at everything I do? Am I really one of the people from Ash's prophecy?*

'Very good, Benny!' Ash said suddenly.

Alek squinted open his eyes and turned his head to the left, looking for his friend. Alek gasped as heat pulsed through the air around him, and he saw bright orange flames sparking down Benny's arms and out of his upturned palms. Benny sat upright, gazing down at the flames flickering between his fingers in wonder.

'How is this possible?' he whispered, holding his hand in front of him as sparks flew into the air.

'Does it hurt?' Alek asked, forgetting that he was supposed to be finding his own magic.

Benny shook his head, his gaze never breaking from the flickering flames. 'No. It's incredible. Like, my whole body feels amazing. I can't even describe it.'

Sarah suddenly gasped loudly and Benny's focus wavered, his flames vanishing. Alek watched as energy seemed to flow out of Benny's body, exhaustion replacing the look of wonder on his face.

Before Alek could comment, however, the wind picked up, viciously howling into the clearing, causing the falling cherry blossoms to spiral crazily into the currents. Sarah sat up straight, the air around her rippling visibly as power flowed from her body.

The sudden wind lasted barely a minute before Sarah expelled a loud breath and the spiralling air dispersed, energy draining out of Sarah as it did so.

'That was incredible,' Sarah whispered, turning to face Alek, tears pooling in the corner of her eyes. 'I've never felt so alive in my whole life. This whole place, this magic, just makes me feel … awake.' She seemed lost for words as she gazed at her two friends.

'Very good, Benny, Sarah,' Ash said approvingly. 'Now we just need to work on your stamina and control. Alek, your turn.'

Uneasiness welled inside Alek as he once again settled onto the ground. He was aware of his friends' eyes on him, adding to the pressure. He wasn't sure he liked the look on either of his friends' faces as their magic had erupted into the world. They had looked different. Powerful. Not like the friends he knew and loved.

'Just focus on your breathing, Alek,' Ash said.

Instantly, Alek's mind replayed his conversation from earlier in the day when Kai had told him a similar thing.

Focus on my breathing, he thought disdainfully, irritation flashing through him. *This is stupid. Everything is so easy for Benny and Sarah. Why can I not do anything? What does Kai want from me? What do I want from Kai? Why can't I get him and his stupid face out of my head?*

Alek lay there for what seemed like hours, struggling with his thoughts as he tried to search his conscious for some flicker of magic and found nothing.

'This is stupid!' he yelled, abruptly sitting upright. 'I can't do it.'

Ash's gaze softened. 'Yes, you can, Alek. You just need practice. Everyone learns at their own pace. Don't measure your success against anyone else's.'

Alek snorted. 'Whatever.'

'Now,' Ash said, ignoring Alek's negative attitude and rubbing her hands together. 'I'm sure you all have a million questions after the last day, and we have some spare time, so please, ask away.'

'I do have something,' Sarah said slowly, choosing her words carefully as she spoke. 'If my magic is wind and Benny's is fire, that makes Alek water or earth, right?'

Water or earth, Alek pondered dejectedly. *More like nothing.*

He sat in silence, wrapped up in his own miserable thoughts as Ash nodded, gesturing for Sarah to continue.

'But there are only three of us … so who is the fourth?' She took a deep breath, setting her jaw. 'Was it Chris?'

Alek stiffened as she spoke his name with the slightest quiver in her voice.

'No,' Ash murmured sympathetically. 'Chris was not a part of the prophecy. You were not supposed to be so close to the portal when I arrived. I had planned to collect you from your houses. Imagine my surprise when I exited the portal and found you all standing there before me.'

Benny grinned. 'You arrived just in time, too. Who knows what would have happened if those gang members found us.'

Ash inclined her head at Benny's words. 'Yes, fate works in mysterious ways.'

Despite Alek being intent on being miserable, his curiosity was piqued. 'You mentioned yesterday that you and the previous principals had kept tabs on our families for generations,' he said, allowing himself to be drawn into the conversation. 'So surely you know who the fourth person is?'

'Yeah!' Benny said enthusiastically. 'Do we have to go and find him?'

'Or her,' Sarah cut in, flicking her cousin on the shoulder.

Ash sighed. 'It's more complicated than that, I'm afraid.'

Alek watched the principal through narrowed eyes as she gathered her thoughts.

'Long ago,' she continued, 'our two worlds were more interwoven than they are now. The Portal Realm served as a bridge between the two worlds, welcoming travellers and providing safe passage.

'There were numerous doorways that opened from the Portal Realm to both of our worlds, and the satyrs were the gatekeepers. They accepted payment for passage through their realm and quite often would open new portals, or doorways, for those who paid the right price.

'After your ancestors placed part of their powers into the amulet, they vanished into the Portal Realm. Your world was safer for them. The only population was that of humans, who were not like the dangerous magical creatures that roam Balathor. In your world, they hid, and over time, knowledge of their power and the existence of Balathor vanished as they grew accustomed to life on earth.'

Ash paused, looking at them with a spark in her eyes. 'Many others chose to leave this world as well, years ago. Where do you think the fantastical tales of dragons and fairies and elves came from?'

'They were real stories of a world left behind,' Alek mused out loud, wonder in his voice as he recalled the joy he had felt growing up and listening to such tales. If only he had known the truth.

'Then a great war shook this land, extending to the Portal Realm,' the principal uttered, her strange pale eyes staring into the distance.

'Is that why all the trees in that place were dead?' Sarah asked.

Images of the misty, broken forest whispered in Alek's mind as he shivered slightly. Chris's body lying at the feet of the monstrous satyr was burned into his memories.

'Yes,' Ash continued. 'The war was known as the Dark Days, and the Portal Realm suffered heavily. The satyrs were sick of being abused for their power to open portals and they sided with evil, sealing off almost every single doorway into their realm as the battle raged around them, destroying their home.

'I believe that three of the four families stayed on earth, and by the time the Dark Days began, any memories of their family legacies had been forgotten.' The principal's gaze was clouded as she lost herself in the tale. 'However, one of the ancestors never stayed on earth. I'm sure they thought it foolish that all four families be together. So they stayed in Balathor.'

'Soooo they're here?' Benny asked uncertainly. 'In this world somewhere?'

Ash inclined her head. 'Yes, although I haven't the slightest clue where. Whoever the fourth's ancestors were, they did a remarkable job of hiding themselves and their family.'

Alek sighed, returning to reality as he felt the pressure of the prophecy pressing down on him. 'And how, exactly, are we supposed to find them?'

'I've sent out some of the older students to scour the land, searching for any rumours of a person possessing any form of magic,' Ash explained, knotting her pale hair around her fingers. 'Hopefully, by the time you finish your training, we will have located them.'

The friends sat in silence, absorbing the information that was presented before them. Alek's mind was whirling, every second he spent in this place created more unanswered questions in his mind.

'Okay, I think we're done for today,' Ash announced, glancing upwards at the fading afternoon light. 'Go and get yourselves some dinner and some rest. I'll see all of you bright and early tomorrow morning for the run.'

Alek's heart sank at the thought of enduring another day of failure. He trudged after his friends to the bonfire where they had dinner the previous night and briefly noticed Kai stand next to him as they waited in line for food, but he was too wrapped up in his own thoughts to pay much attention as he quietly sat next to his friends, barely tasting the food he put into his mouth.

'I'm going back to my tree house,' Alek said abruptly, standing up.

Benny and Sarah broke off mid-conversation, casting awkward looks at each other as they realised how left out Alek felt.

Benny began to climb to his feet. 'I'll come with you.'

'No.' Alek shook his head. 'I want to be alone.'

He turned and picked his way slowly through the clearing, his eyes briefly falling on the familiar icy blue gaze of Kai as he stalked into the undergrowth. Alek stumbled slightly. Had the boy been watching him from the other side of the fire the whole time? After a brief journey through the forest and slightly panicking when he thought he had gotten lost, Alek began to climb the rough branches that led to his tree house.

He winced as his sore muscles screamed in protest, and he hauled himself into his room, swinging around to perch on the edge of the solid floor. He glanced at the sky, admiring the bright pink and purple streaks spattered among the billowing clouds.

Sunsets are even more vivid here, he thought absentmindedly. Suddenly, he sat upright, remembering Kai's offer to train him at the lake at sunset. Maybe that's why he had been watching him at dinner? Alek tensed, leaning forward to climb off his ledge and back into the forest before he hesitated, biting his lip. In his mind, he pictured Kai waiting at the lake for him, hopeful he would turn up. The image alone was enough for him to climb to his feet.

Again, he hesitated, glancing back at the secluded comfort of his room. *Do I really want to go humiliate myself some more?*

Kai probably just wants to laugh at how hopeless I am, just like everyone else.

Alek spun away from the window, pushing down images of Kai waiting alone at the edge of the lake and instead walked over to his bed, leaving a trail of clothes behind him. He crawled onto the soft mattress, sighing contentedly as the comfortable blankets cocooned him, pulling him into a deep sleep.

6

ALONE

'Alek, wake up!' Benny's voice echoed around the small room. 'You're going to make us late again!'

Alek shuddered awake, the events of the previous day flooding through his mind. He rolled over, away from his friend.

'I'm not going,' he mumbled.

'What?' Benny gasped incredulously. 'What do you mean, you're not going? You have to!'

'Oh, so I don't have a choice now?' Alek snapped, pushing Benny away. 'You can't make me go, so I'm not going.'

'Alek—' Benny started, his tone softening.

'No, Benny,' Alek hissed, pulling the blankets over his head. 'I do not want to humiliate myself again. Leave me alone.'

Benny was silent for a few moments. Then Alek heard his footsteps walk across the room, a branch creaking as he left without saying goodbye. Alek sat upright, feeling guilty about the way he had spoken. Benny was his best friend, but he just didn't understand how hard it was for Alek to fit in here.

An hour passed and Alek stood in the middle of his room, at a loss for what he should do for the day and wondering if he would get in trouble for blowing off his classes. Deciding it was better to get out of his room, he quickly dressed and made his way down to the ground, absentmindedly walking among the trees.

He wandered aimlessly for most of the morning, enjoying the silence and his own company. Alek breathed in deep, feeling more refreshed now that he had a chance to explore the valley alone, without the constant talk of prophecies and magic. He heard a group of students chatting nearby, his ears pricking as he heard mention of their next class being in the library. Curiosity eating at him, Alek followed the students through the forest.

They emerged at the western edge of the valley, a place Alek briefly remembered from his jog yesterday. Before him, the mountains rose up in a brilliant smooth cliff face. Alek craned his neck back, trying and failing to see the top. Carved into the stone were two massive pillars bordering a large wooden door. Intricate designs spiralled around the colossal structures and spilled onto the cliff face itself.

Alek waited for the students to vanish through the wooden doorway before stepping up to the cliff face, taking in the images carved on and around the left pillar. He slowly ran his hand across the rough images etched into the rock's surface. He saw a large castle surrounded by a forest. Flying above the castle were massive dragons, each scale carved meticulously into the stone. Multitudes of animals and people swirled across the image, living together in harmony.

As he walked along the cliff face, trailing his hand across the surface and towards the wooden door, he saw the sculpted forest darken. Threatening mountains rose behind the treetops, and shadowy creatures lurked within its twisted branches.

He stopped as he reached the wooden door and paused. His hand reached out towards the brass handle, curiosity eating at him as he wondered what lay on the other side. However, the etchings on the stone to his right caught his eye and he quickly stepped closer, his eyes widening. This side of the engravings was almost a mirror image of the etchings he had just studied on the left side.

Except the castle was in ruin.

One massive dragon remained, perched atop the castle, spears sticking out of its scales.

Fire bloomed through the fields where the animals and humans had once frolicked, as depicted on the left side of the wooden door. As Alek's eyes analysed the carvings of the shadowy forest beneath the mountains, the only image he could see was a pair of large serpentine eyes staring back at him.

Sweat formed on the back of his neck as the shadows on the mural seemed to grow, reaching out towards him, the images swirling together until all that remained were the eyes. A colossal dark form seemed to slither through the forest, growing ever closer as the eyes held Alek captive. He panicked, trying desperately to break away from the wall in front of him. Fear reached into his throat, clutching at him, forcing him to watch as an enormous figure began to take shape before him.

'Alek!' a sharp voice cut through his mind, and Alek stumbled backwards from the cliff, panting heavily. Arms grasped him tightly and steadied him as he shook violently.

'Alek, are you okay?'

He recognised Ash's voice and looked up to see her gazing down at him with concern.

He pushed away from her and turned back to the carvings on the cliff, desperately searching the dark forest for the massive creature, but there was no trace of it. Not even the eyes remained. Just shadows.

'Alek,' Ash pressed, stepping up behind him. 'Are you okay?'

'What is this?' Alek whispered, ignoring Ash's question.

She frowned, looking at the wooden door beside them. 'The library?'

'No.' Alek shook his head. 'The carvings. What do they mean?'

'Oh, they tell the story of the downfall of the last King of Balathor. When humans, elves, dragons, and all manner of creatures co-existed in harmony, before the Dark Days ripped them apart and ended years of peace in the world. A war quickly followed, the same one we spoke about yesterday with Benny and Sarah, the result of which caused the extinction of the dragons and forced the elves into hiding. Not long after that, the rest of the magical creatures began to disappear.'

Ash shook her head. 'I do not know the full story, though, besides what I have already shared with you and your friends, and there are others that would tell it better than I. But we need to discuss your future here.'

Alek's heartbeat quickened as he noticed the stern look on Ash's face.

'I will not tolerate students skipping class. However, I understand what you have been through the last couple of days has been traumatic and life-altering, so I will give you time.' She paused, looking Alek up and down. 'You have one week. One week of no classes. Then you must decide whether to leave or stay.'

Alek gulped as Ash's stern eyes flickered to the doorway beside them. 'I would suggest you spend your time wisely, not just wandering aimlessly around the valley.'

With that, Ash spun on her heel and disappeared into the thick foliage of the surrounding forest. Alek shivered, turning back towards the library doors as he wondered once again whether he should stay, or whether it would be much easier to just go back home.

Shoving the thoughts aside, Alek steeled himself and pushed on the large wooden doors, wincing as they swung open with a loud groan. Nothing but shadows greeted him as he peered into the hollow mountain before him. Hesitating for a moment, he stepped forward, his footsteps echoing off the rough stone beneath his feet.

He heard his breathing quicken as the doors swung shut behind him, leaving him in utter darkness.

7

KNOWLEDGE IS POWER

Silence greeted Alek as he waited for his eyes to adjust to the dim light. Not eerie, unsettling darkness but warm, comforting. He took a deep breath, relishing the smell of old paper that rolled over him. He closed his eyes, savouring the comforting memories that unfurled from his mind at the smell.

Days spent curled up under a blanket by a window, soft rain pattering against the glass. Cosy light cast by the gloomy sky and a warm cup of hot chocolate next to him as he devoured page after page of his latest adventure. Not a care in the world as his mind took him to places his life could not allow.

As Alek opened his eyes, his mind still full of nostalgia, his jaw dropped open, wonder flashing through him as he beheld his surroundings.

The mountain before him was entirely hollow. Row after row of books sat nestled into alcoves carved into the stone walls around the inside of the cavern. Thick, plush rugs lay across the smooth stone floor, and tapestries depicting stunning landscapes hung haphazardly across the wall wherever space would allow.

Craning his head backwards, Alek's eyes traced the rows of books as they spiralled higher and higher, across multiple levels, until they disappeared into shadows. In the centre of the room before him, a cluster of gigantic, luminous crystals created the warm, glowing light that pervaded the interior of the mountain around him.

Alek stood rooted to the spot for what seemed like hours as his gaze roamed the inside of the mountain. He noted the narrower walkways connecting the higher levels far above him and the smaller, glowing crystals that speckled the cave walls throughout the rows of books.

Eventually, Alek forced his feet to move as he slowly crossed the cavernous room, passing the giant crystals in the centre and feeling a constant warmth rolling off them as he stepped close. Gazing around, he noticed for the first time a large desk set against the wall near the wooden door he had just entered through.

Hunched behind the desk was an old lady, sitting so still Alek thought for a second that she was a sculpture. Deep lines covered her face, and skin sagged off her bones as she reached forward. A bony hand appeared from the folds of her voluminous clothing and shakily turned the page of the book set on the desk in front of her. Alek shook his head at how frail the old woman seemed as he turned away from her, making his way further into the cavern.

The library was mostly deserted as he trudged up a ramp set against the stone wall, leading to a higher level. Only a handful of other students flitted among the multitudes of books.

As Alek climbed higher, his gaze picked out titles around him, piquing his curiosity. *The Origin of Elves, The Downfall of the Shifters,* and *Syrens: Tales From the Lighthouse.* Absentmindedly, Alek picked a book at random—*Sprites and Their Various Forms*—and began to flick through it. Illustrations of great, hulking beasts with long arms and terrible, gaping jaws lay etched onto the thick pages. A shiver went down Alek's spine as he tucked the book under his arm, hurrying deeper into the library.

There were books on history, on ancient legends, dragons, fairies, sprites, and creatures Alek had never heard of. Excitement took over him as he climbed higher and higher, grabbing books at random as he went. Eventually, he held too many books to continue.

Looking around, Alek saw he had only made it halfway up the inside of the mountain. He shook his head, resolving to come back every day until he had made it to the uppermost levels. Spotting a comfy-looking chair next to a handrail on the edge of his current level, he settled with a contented sigh, placing his stack of books onto a table next to him. Glancing over the railing beside him, Alek had the perfect view of the ground level, the towering crystals ending just below him and bathing him in comforting warmth.

He closed his eyes briefly as he settled back into the soft chair, feeling more at peace with himself than he had in a long time. Reaching forward, Alek picked up the first book on his pile, *Balathor: Its lands and peoples*. Letting go of all the anxiety that had been building up in his body, Alek flicked open the book and lost himself in the ancient text printed onto the pages.

****

Two days passed, and Alek had spent almost every waking hour at the library. He would only leave the comforting space for meals and sleep. His mind churned with all he was learning about the world he was suddenly a part of. The magic that once flowed wildly through every part of the world, the fantastic creatures that roamed outside of this valley, and also the many dangers that came with an unfamiliar land.

Today, however, he was distracted.

Alek was curled up in his regular chair a few levels above the entrance to the library, a large stack of books piled around him, but his mind was elsewhere. Every evening, he had been heading to the bonfire for dinner later and later to avoid the questioning glances other students gave him. However, one particular student was on his mind.

No matter what time he turned up to the fire, Kai was there. Often, the boy wouldn't talk to Alek; he just appeared, waiting in line for food. But Alek could feel the icy blue eyes staring at him whenever he wasn't looking, and he felt a pull of desire towards the other boy. He held his breath every time Kai appeared next to him, half-expecting Kai to be angry at him for deciding not to show up on the lake as they had discussed. However, Kai continued to say nothing; he was just there, gazing at him with an unreadable expression.

Alek groaned in his chair, sliding his booted feet off the footrest they had been perched upon and onto one of the many plush rugs that lay haphazardly across the library floor. Leaning forwards, Alek ran his hands through his wavy blonde hair, holding it tight against his skull as his mind spun.

Why did he feel such an inexplicable pull towards Kai? To have those wild eyes watching him, to hold the boy's attention … the thought thrilled him, sending a shiver through his body.

It's this place. Alek snorted, leaning back against his chair as his arms gripped the armrests. *It has to be. The magic in the air or something is making me crazy. That's why I can't stop thinking about this. I haven't felt the same since we've been here. Plus, he is the only other student who's really spoken to me, so that's probably why I feel some sort of connection to him.*

Alek groaned, rubbing his temples as his thoughts swam through his mind and grew increasingly jumbled as he tried to justify the way he felt. *Why does everything have to be so complicated for me? How come Benny and Sarah get it so easy?*

Alek was jolted out of his thoughts as the door to the mountain slammed open loudly. He glanced down over the balcony, irritation quickly giving way to curiosity as all thoughts of Kai faded to the back of his mind.

Sarah stood uncertainly in the entrance as the door slowly swung shut behind her. Alek had barely spoken to his two friends over the last few days; he still harboured some resentment for how easily they had fit into life here. He didn't want to hear how wonderful their training was going or how powerful their magic was getting.

Alek watched through narrow eyes as Sarah wandered over to the librarian, who was perched behind her large desk near the door. Alek had never once uttered a word to the ancient crone who ignored him every time he walked past. He had never seen her move from her seat or relax the heavy frown plastered across her wrinkled face.

Sarah leaned in close to the woman, gesturing with her hands as she spoke. Slowly, the librarian raised her hand and pointed to an alcove that disappeared off the main room below Alek. He blinked. How had he never noticed that room before? Sarah quickly turned on her heel and made her way into the alcove, hesitating slightly before she disappeared into the darkness.

What are you doing? Alek leaned back in his chair. He would investigate after Sarah was gone; he didn't want to awkwardly run into her. Especially when he had been avoiding her and Benny the last few days.

Hours passed as Alek waited impatiently. He tried reading, but every time he tried, his eyes would dart back to the alcove Sarah had disappeared down. He sighed, closing the book he was trying to read and leaned forward onto his elbows. Just as he did, Sarah at last emerged from the room below, a stack of books tucked under her arm. He watched as his friend hastily walked through the library and exited.

Instantly, Alek was on his feet, all but running down the stairs to the lower level as impatience flashed through him. Curiosity overwhelmed him as he lunged through the archway his friend had vanished into for hours. What was he going to find?

Alek blinked at what lay in front of him, disappointment showing on his face. More books.

Before him was what looked just like a small study nook. Cushions and soft rugs lined the floor, and small glowing crystals protruded from the walls around him. There were a few bookcases lining the walls, and that was it. A wave of foolishness washed over Alek. He didn't know what he had been expecting to find; it was a library, after all.

Alek exhaled loudly as he slowly dawdled over to the bookshelf in front of him and frowned as he saw one of the titles: *Pitfalls and Dangers of The Portal Realm*. Looking at the next few titles on the shelf, he realised that they were all related to the Portal Realm.

What is she up to? He turned and left the alcove, his mind churning. *Why would Sarah possibly want to know more about the place where her boyfriend died? Surely she isn't going to go back there.* A feeling of dread settled in his gut as he left the library to grab dinner.

After eating his meal, Alek found his mind still distracted by the thought of what he would do *if* Sarah was to go back to the Portal Realm. He couldn't protect her; she could die.

He suddenly wished he hadn't spent the last few days hiding in the library.

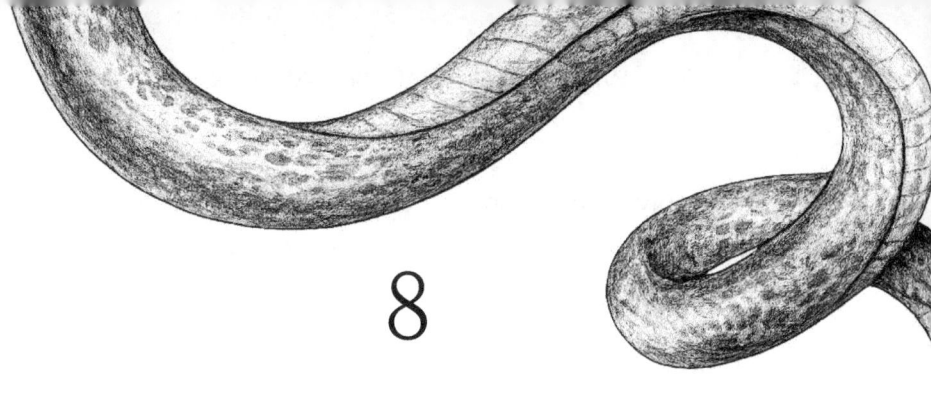

8

THE BOY WITH ICE IN HIS EYES

Alek didn't sleep that night. He tossed and turned, imagining Sarah disappearing back into that misty forest he and his friends had barely made it out of alive. He woke early, needing to do something.

Pacing back and forth across his room as the sun rose, Alek debated rejoining the students for their morning run and regular classes. But he hesitated. What would they think?

They probably all talk about me and make fun of me. He flung himself down on his bed. *The boy who couldn't even run around the valley and then disappeared to the library for days on end.*

The sun rose higher into the sky as Alek watched until the bright orange streaks of sunrise began to fade. It was too late for him to join in the day's activities. He groaned loudly, frustrated with himself as he ran his hands down his face.

Suddenly, he shot upright, remembering his conversation with Kai on that first morning.

He said he would train me! At sunset, by the lake! Excitement surged through him and he jumped up from the bed, only to realise that the sun had just come up and he had a full day to kill before sunset. *That is, if Kai is even at the lake.* Alek winced slightly. *He hasn't really said anything to me the last few days when we've seen each other ... but at least he doesn't seem angry, so that's a start. Hopefully, he will still want to help me.*

He set his jaw determinedly. He had to try. If Sarah really was studying the Portal Realm with the intention of venturing back in, the least Alek could do was have her back.

****

The air was sharp and crisp as Alek walked uneasily towards the lake. His stomach churned as he wondered whether or not Kai would be there. For the millionth time, he craned his head up, seeking out the pink sky between the dense branches criss-crossing above him. It was definitely sunset. *This is stupid,* he thought to himself, gritting his mouth in a thin line. *There is no way he'll still be waiting for me after he made the offer days ago.*

Footsteps sounded behind him and Alek stopped, spinning around as Ash stepped out of the undergrowth with a friendly smile on her face.

'I went looking for you at the library, Alek,' the principal said, stepping closer to the boy. 'Imagine my surprise when you weren't there!'

Alek's cheeks reddened as he realised how pathetic he must seem, hiding in the library.

'Yeah, I, uh, thought that maybe it was time to do something with my time here,' Alek muttered, rocking back and forwards on his feet awkwardly.

Ash's smile stayed plastered across her face but her eyes narrowed slightly, worry swirling in their depths. 'Have you thought about what we spoke about? Have you made your choice?'

'Yes,' Alek said softly. Visions of his friends in danger and him not being there to help flashed through his mind. 'I have decided to stay.'

Relief flooded Ash's face, and her body relaxed as she let out a long breath. 'I'm glad to hear it, Alek. it will be good to have you back in classes.' She reached forward, clapping Alek on the shoulder in delight.

'About that,' Alek said slowly, shrugging Ash's hand off his shoulder. 'I want to learn combat from Kai, not with the other students, and I will not be joining your magic classes with Benny and Sarah. If I do happen to have some sort of magic, I will discover it on my own, not with the others.'

Indecision flashed across Ash's face as she contemplated Alek's proposal. 'Kai hasn't been here for very long, but he has excelled in all of his classes. Very well. I look forward to watching your progress under Kai's tutelage.'

Alek watched as Ash dipped her head, trying to hide the worry that was evident in her pale eyes before she turned, swiftly disappearing into the forest.

Alek let out a tense breath as he turned back towards the lake, anxiety settling like a stone in his chest. The decision had been made.

He was staying.

Whether he wanted to or not, his fate was now sealed. Thoughts of the Dark Warriors and shadow monsters threatened to overwhelm him, and he hurriedly pushed his fear down. Now was not the time. The prophecy was future Alek's problem. For now, he would train.

He just hoped Kai was waiting for him.

As Alek pushed his way through the last few branches and stepped onto soft sand, his eyes focused on the well-built boy by the water's edge. Relief washed over him as he watched the boy go through some sort of practice stances, his body stretching and curving as he flowed from one move to the next with ease.

Alek watched, transfixed as the lake behind Kai glittered a brilliant shade of pink, echoing the cloudless sky far above. A cool breeze ruffled Alek's blonde hair as he stepped further from the trees, clearing his throat awkwardly.

'So,' Kai said, without breaking his current stance. 'Look who's left their room.'

Alek frowned and was opening his mouth to snap back at Kai when the boy chuckled, the sound as smooth as the water lapping at the sandy shore. Kai straightened up, his eyes closed as he drew in a deep breath before he opened them, smirking at Alek's expression.

'Tell me why you're here,' Kai continued, eyes sparkling mischievously.

'Well, I, uh,' Alek stuttered, thrown by Kai's friendliness. *Is he not mad I've ignored him for the past few days?*

'You want my help?' Kai guessed.

Alek nodded, licking his lips as guilt bubbled under his skin. 'I know I wasn't the nicest to you, but I was embarrassed, and you just look so good, and you do everything so easily, and I was — I mean, I am struggling so much, and I just thought …' He trailed off as Kai raised his hand.

'You think I look good?' Kai grinned, barely holding back laughter.

'Wait, what? I did not say that!' Alek backtracked quickly. *How did this get so out of hand?*

Kai nodded wisely, moving closer to Alek. 'Yes, you sure did, just before — you said, "Kai, you look damn good."'

Alek snorted. 'Well, I definitely know I did not say that.'

'Mmhmm, you did. My ego distinctly remembers that.' Kai was now barely a step away from Alek.

Alek looked at the boy in front of him, taking in the wild eyes, dark, windswept hair, and perfectly sculpted body before he reached forward and shoved Kai with all his might.

Kai's eyes widened incredulously as he did not even budge.

'If that's the best you can do,' Kai whispered, leaning close to Alek's ear, 'you definitely need my help.'

Alek shuddered as goose bumps ran down his body from the other boy's proximity. Before he could think of a smart reply, Kai stepped back and walked briskly down to the water's edge. He gestured for Alek to follow, and Alek numbly wandered down to the water, his mind still replaying the feeling of Kai's breath tickling his ear.

'Now,' Kai's sharp voice cut into Alek's thoughts. 'Like I told you the other day — you need to focus on your breathing. And your general fitness.' He held up a hand as Alek opened his mouth to argue. 'And don't try to tell me you are fit, because I saw you running around the valley the other day.' Kai paused. 'And it wasn't a good look.'

'Okay, we're going to spend every sunset running around the lake on the sand to build up your resistance faster, and I'm going to teach you to fight.'

Alek nodded, anticipation building in his belly. After the last few days in the library, it felt good to be doing something, anything. Suddenly, Kai took off, sand spraying in his wake as he yelled at Alek to catch him.

Alek scowled, launching himself forward after the boy, the cold air searing his lungs as he pushed himself faster and faster. *I can do this.* He narrowed his eyes, focusing on Kai's back, shoving his doubts and fears into the dark corners of his mind.

I can do this.

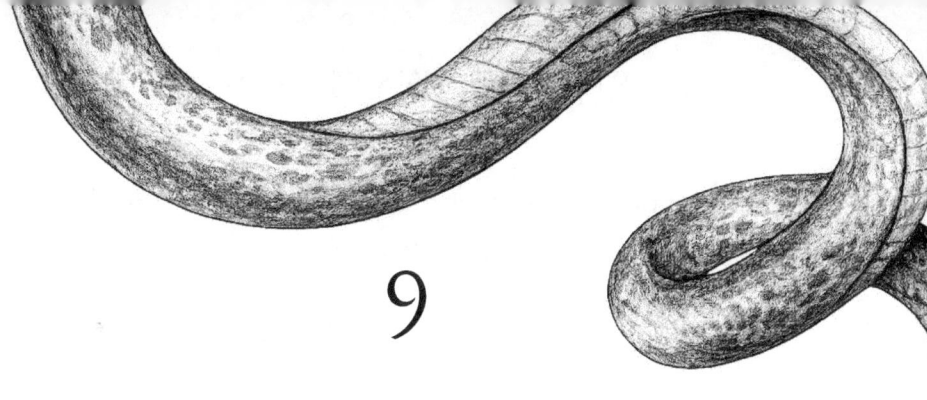

9

A VISITOR IN THE NIGHT

A loud thud woke Sarah with a start. Her eyes snapped open as she shot upright in bed, echoes of her nightmares flashing through her mind. Staring around her small tree house, her eyes strained, hunting for the source of the sudden thud in the near darkness. Her heart started to race as the images from her dreams blurred into reality.

Every creak from the surrounding branches grated across her skin, sounding suspiciously like someone sneaking ever closer. The rustling of the leaves caused her breath to quicken as she pictured him clawing through the canopy and into her room, eagerly searching for her in the darkness. The satyr that had prowled through the shadows of her mind, both waking and asleep.

Sarah pictured him now, his large shoulders filling the window to the surrounding forest as cloven hooves thudded threateningly onto the wooden floor. Lethal horns scraped against the wooden architraves as he ducked slightly to squeeze into the small space. Sarah's hands clenched the blankets around her as a cold sweat broke across her brow. Desperately, she squeezed her eyes shut, blocking out the vision in front of her.

It's not real, it's not real, it's not real, Sarah repeated to herself, chanting the words over and over in her mind. Shakily, she drew a deep breath in, holding it for a few seconds as it filled her lungs, then slowly releasing it.

When she opened her eyes again, the hulking figure of the satyr was gone. The swishing branches outside had lost their threatening aura as she separated reality from her dreams. The small room was empty, other than the pile of books that lay haphazardly on the floor beside her bed.

Sarah frowned, feeling her nose crinkle as she did so. Those books had been sitting atop her thick blankets as she'd drifted off to sleep. A small laugh escaped her lips as she realised the heavy tomes were the source of the thud. Collapsing back into bed, Sarah threw her hands over her face, wiping away the sweat that coated her brow.

The satyr had frequented her dreams for the last few nights since arriving in Aranasmin. If it wasn't her mind replaying Chris's death to her over and over like some sort of broken video, it was a haunting nightmare of the satyr climbing into her tree house to finish the job he had started in the Portal Realm.

The worst part, however, wasn't the imminent threat of the ghostly satyr. It was the fact that she never fought back. In every iteration of her nightmares, she was frozen, silently waiting for the monster to deal his fatal blow. Just like that dreadful day in the Portal Realm. She had stood, rooted to the spot as the life drained out of her boyfriend's body. Doing nothing.

Sarah shook her head, shoving down the guilt rising in her stomach as she crawled out of bed, her legs protesting slightly as they took her weight. The morning run around the valley was definitely doing its job; her muscles hadn't ever been this sore after any of her gymnastics practices. Quickly, she gathered the fallen books together and placed them back into a pile on her bed.

Sarah frowned at the assortment of worn covers. She had heard students talking about the school library yesterday and had immediately approached them, asking where it was located. In-between classes, she had sought out the hollow mountain and asked the ancient librarian where she could find information on the Portal Realm. The beginnings of a plan taking shape in her mind.

The librarian had pointed her in the direction of the small room stocked with books full of all sorts of information on the strange, in-between world. She had spent the good part of an hour picking through the different titles before she gave up, choosing a few of the books at random and bringing them back to her room to study further.

Sarah had stayed awake late the previous night skimming through them, searching for any information she could find about the satyr that had attacked them. She sighed. The books were doing nothing but fuelling her nightmares, she was sure of it.

Just as Sarah finished organising the pile of books and began to turn away, something caught her eye. A tuft of paper stuck out of one of the older-looking volumes. Holding her breath, she reached down, examining the leatherbound cover before her. It was plain; no title was printed across the front. The dark leather was worn, peeling away across the wrinkled spine.

Sarah quickly flicked the book open, the spare bit of paper floating free from the surrounding pages. Grasping the yellowed page in her hand, she stepped over to the window, where the pre-dawn light offered a reprieve from the surrounding shadows. What she saw splashed across the page made her gasp.

Inked upon the paper was an image: a rough circle with a cross through the centre. The same symbol that had been branded onto the satyr's chest. Sarah's hand trembled, causing the page to shake slightly as her eyes scanned the rough text beneath the symbol, her lips parting as she read it aloud.

'The closed gate. This ancient symbol is burned onto the chests of the high-ranking prison guards, proving their devotion to their role within the satyr's kingdom.'

Sarah turned the page over, revealing an infuriatingly blank page. She ground her teeth in frustration as she realised that was all the information she was going to get from the scrap of paper.

A prison guard, Sarah mused, carefully tucking the stray page into one of her pockets. *At least that's something. More information than I've gotten from any of the other books, at least! Now all I need is a map …*

Sarah stood with her hands on her hips, gazing absentmindedly out of her window. She would go back to the library after lunch. Ash had cancelled their regular magic classes that afternoon, saying she needed to hold a meeting with the other teachers. Maybe the librarian knew of a place where Sarah could get her hands on a map of the Portal Realm.

A beam of sunlight burst through the canopy outside Sarah's window, illuminating the girl and startling her from her thoughts. Quickly realising the time, she made short work of pulling on her uniform and lacing up her leather boots, pausing for a moment as she walked past the floor-length mirror in the corner of her room.

Her long, brown hair was wild from tossing and turning through the night, and she hurriedly ran her fingers through it, brushing out some of the knots. Chris had liked her hair like this, long and loose around her shoulders. Tears burned behind Sarah's eyes as she shook her head, spinning on her heel and stalking away from the mirror.

Now was not the time to dwell on the past. Sarah narrowed her eyes as she quickly began the descent through the trees from her room. She could see her path laid out before her, and she would not allow anything to get in her way.

Sarah reached the ground swiftly, finding Benny waiting for her amongst the thick leaf litter. He was leaning against the base of the tree, the size of the trunk dwarfing him as he stared absentmindedly into the distance.

'Still no Alek?' Sarah asked quietly, her voice betraying some of the guilt that churned in her stomach every time she thought of him.

'No.' Benny let out a long sigh, dragging his hands through his long, dark hair as the two friends began their walk through the shadowy forest. 'I'm really worried about him, Sarah. This is the longest we've gone without talking to each other.'

'I know,' Sarah said. 'But he'll come around. You know Alek. We just have to give him some time to get used to being here.' She winced at the sound of her own words, not even sure she believed them herself.

'Yeah,' Benny muttered. 'I guess so. It's just not the same doing this without him. He's missing out on so much. It just doesn't feel right.'

Sarah glanced at her cousin sympathetically, squeezing his shoulder as they stepped out of the shelter of the giant trees and into the large clearing where the morning jog began. They were early today, the sun barely beginning to light the sky. Glancing around, Sarah realised only a handful of students had crawled out of bed so far and were gathered in a small knot on the edge of the trees not too far away.

'What's going on?' she whispered, mainly to herself.

'What?' Benny asked, squinting in the direction of the other students. 'Oh, they were doing that the other morning, too. Did you not notice them?'

Sarah shook her head. She must've been too lost in her thoughts the previous days.

'A group of the older students that have been here a while get up early and have some sort of weird fight club every morning before the run,' Benny continued, lifting one leg behind him and giving it a good stretch. 'I honestly don't know why anyone would want to get up any earlier than they have to.' He snorted.

Her interest piqued, Sarah began to make her way around the edge of the field towards the throng of students. Benny called out to her, his voice exasperated, but she ignored him, moving quickly as the sky began to lighten around her.

As she drew closer to the group, a loud groan echoed through the air followed by quiet cheering from the knot of students. There were only about twenty kids, all gathered around a sandy pit on the very edge of the grassy clearing. Large branches hung low overhead, and Sarah's eyes widened as she took in the scene before her.

Two students brawled in the sand, mud covering them from the moist, dewy ground. These were not the carefully planned fighting stances they were being taught in class— this was an all-out tussle for victory. Sarah flinched as one of the contestants flipped her opponent over her shoulder and slammed him into the ground with a solid slap. The boy let out a loud hiss and threw his hands up in surrender.

The spectating students cheered, chanting a name repeatedly. 'Imani! Imani! Imani!'

Sarah watched as the girl drew herself to her feet, her breathing laboured as she grinned down at the boy lying by her feet, his face screwed up in pain. She was muscular, Sarah noticed, wearing only a tank top and what looked like bike shorts. Her deep brown skin glimmered with a layer of sweat as she offered a helping hand to her defeated opponent. Her other hand reached up, undoing the band holding her hair back in a tight braid.

Imani's hair was curly and wild, flaring around her head like a triumphant crown. Her wild smile caused the skin around her eyes to crinkle, accentuating the beauty of her features. The boy took her helping hand, wincing as he hauled himself to his feet, his shirtless torso covered in mud and sand.

'When will somebody beat you?' he asked ruefully, brushing the dirt off himself. 'I thought I had you that time.'

Imani threw her head back and laughed, her voice clear and loud. 'Boy, you didn't stand a chance.'

Sarah bit back a smirk as the confident girl patted the boy on the shoulder and stepped out of the pit of sand. As she did so, those dark eyes locked onto Sarah's, causing Imani to pause.

Sarah shifted uncomfortably as Imani bent down, scooping up a pile of clothing. As the students around them began to disperse, muttering amongst themselves, Imani stalked over the soft grass to stand before her. Dark eyes raked up and down, causing Sarah to shift uncomfortably in the silence.

'I've seen you before,' Imani stated matter-of-factly. 'You're new here, yet you've almost kept up with me on every morning run.'

Sarah nodded, unsure how to respond to the confident girl's statements. She glanced once more at the muddy pit behind them, and Imani smirked, watching her intently.

'You want to have a go?' Imani cocked her head, her expression unreadable.

Sarah shrugged, taking in a breath as she faced Imani, staring straight into her almond-shaped eyes. 'I don't know. I wouldn't want to upstage you at your own game.'

Imani's grin broadened and she threw her head back, a loud laugh booming from her chest. A few of the surrounding students glanced their way at the loud outburst. As she waited patiently for Imani to finish wiping the tears from her eyes, Sarah shifted her weight to one leg and placed a hand on her hip, projecting as much confidence as she could muster.

Imani paused, her shoulders still shaking slightly in silent laughter, taking in Sarah's defiant pose. 'Oh, you're serious?'

Sarah nodded, her back straight and shoulders tense. Imani clearly held some sort of respect amongst the other students. And she was skilled, so she had been training for a long time. This was someone Sarah wanted on her side, someone who could help her. She had a feeling she wasn't going to gain Imani's respect by submitting to her.

Imani reached forward, curling a tendril of Sarah's loose hair around her fingers. 'You'll never beat anyone looking like this, pretty girl. Whoever you're facing will grab a handful of your hair and gain the upper hand. That's why I had my hair tied up tight during the fight.' Imani gestured down to her dirt-stained body. 'Are you even prepared to get messy? I don't know if you have it in you.'

Sarah opened her mouth to argue, but before she could utter a word, Imani let go of her hair and stalked away.

'Now, if you'll excuse me,' said Imani, 'I need to get changed before the run.' She paused, turning back towards Sarah. 'Come and see me again when you're serious about getting into the ring. Until then, you can watch me from behind as you try to keep up every morning.'

Sarah blinked, a flash of adrenaline spiking through her veins at the challenge in Imani's voice. She balled her hands into fists as she spun, taking in the valley now full of gathering students.

'She was hot,' Benny suddenly said from beside her, making her jump.

'Ben!' Sarah gasped, digging her elbow painfully into his ribs, making him hiss in pain.

'What—it's true!' he exclaimed, taking a step away from his cousin in case she tried to attack him again.

Sarah ignored him as she played back Imani's fight in her mind again. The girl was skilled, her confidence backed up by her abilities. She narrowed her eyes as the wild-haired girl jogged out from the surrounding trees, clad in the same uniform as the rest of the students. Imani caught Sarah's eyes and winked at her, that confident grin once again breaking out across her face.

Sarah gritted her teeth, tucking her hair behind her ears as she watched the girl stalk to the front of the group of students preparing for the morning run. She was going to wipe that grin from Imani's face. Whether it took a week or a month, Sarah didn't care.

'Uh oh,' Benny muttered beside her.

'What do you mean, "Uh oh,"' Sarah replied absentmindedly, her eyes still watching Imani.

'I know that look on your face,' her cousin answered in a matter-of-fact tone. 'That's your *I know what I want and nothing's going to stop me look.*'

Sarah grinned; he was right. Nothing was going to stop her.

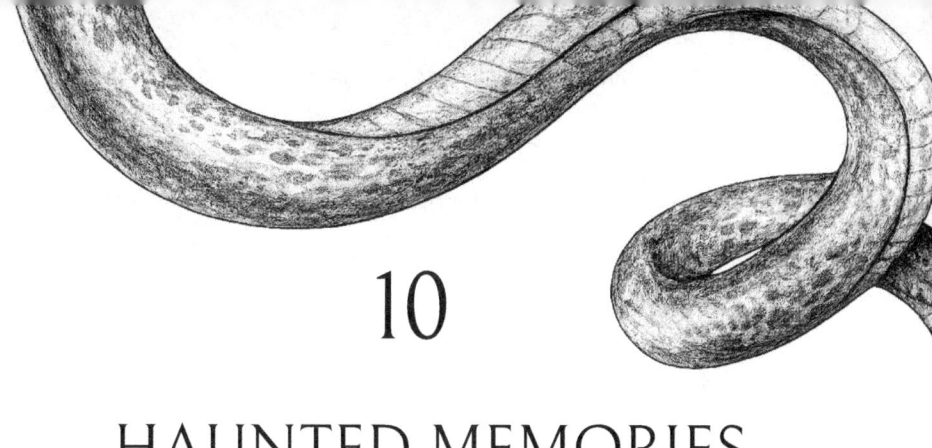

10

HAUNTED MEMORIES

Sarah eased open the old wooden doors and slipped into the shadowy mountain. She paused for a moment, giving her eyes time to adjust to the sudden darkness as the door swung shut behind her. Once she was accustomed to the dim interior of the library, she quickly walked across the lower level, heading straight for the librarian.

The day had passed quickly after the events of that morning. Imani had been infuriatingly right. Sarah had spent the entire morning run on her heels, watching Imani effortlessly move through the valley.

Sarah wrinkled her nose as she walked through the shadows, the warmth from the nearby giant crystals prickling her skin. She hated being trapped within the walls of stone. The air was musty and smelled of old books. No breeze wrapped comfortingly around her as she moved through the silent cavern. Her feet halted as she reached the librarian's desk and shivered involuntarily, imagining the years the old woman had spent tucked away in the stuffy library.

The desk was piled high with pens and paper, books stacked haphazardly on any spare space. More bookshelves lined the stone wall behind the desk, and a small wooden door stood slightly ajar behind the seated old woman.

Awkwardly, Sarah cleared her throat, shifting her weight from one foot to another. Ever-so-slowly, the librarian lifted her head, silently setting down the book she had been reading. Sarah studied the old woman for a moment, taking in the deep-set wrinkles across her face. The woman was ancient. Her hair was thin and grey with age, her movements frail and shaky as she laced her bony fingers together on the desk in front of her.

A gaudy ring flashed in the shadows on one of the crone's fingers, causing Sarah to frown. She hadn't noticed the jewellery the last time she had spoken to the librarian. The band was a plain silver design, but an obnoxious purple amethyst hung heavy atop her finger. The sparkling gem was a complete contrast to the bland layers of clothing the old woman draped herself in, and way too flashy for such an old lady.

'Do you want something, dearie?' The crone's voice was as quiet as the turning page of a book.

Sarah leaned closer to the lady, wrinkling her nose as the smell of dust and mothballs floated around her. *Maybe this is a bad idea. If the old witch realises what I'm planning, she might go to Ash. Then it would all be for nothing.* Sarah bit her bottom lip as she pondered her options, quickly concluding that she didn't have much of a choice.

'I need a map of the Portal Realm,' she blurted, keeping her voice hushed as she leaned in close to the lady on the other side of the desk.

The librarian's eyebrows rose so far up her face, Sarah worried that they would be permanently lost in a sea of wrinkles.

'You *need*, hmmm,' the old lady mused, fixing her startlingly clear brown eyes onto Sarah. 'Do you really need it, or is it that you want it?'

'Need,' Sarah stated matter-of-factly, shifting her weight from one leg to another. She was impatient to be done with the conversation and out of the stifling library and in the open air of the valley.

The librarian regarded her silently, the pause stretching for a millennia before she spoke again. 'And what would a pretty young thing like you be needing with a map of the world between worlds?'

Sarah licked her lips. Should she tell the truth? A version of the truth? Or make up some sort of lie? She really should have thought of this earlier.

'Don't you even think about telling me the lie you're concocting in that head of yours. The truth will get you what you seek, not a half-baked story.' The librarian snorted, disturbing the layer of dust atop her workstation, sending it spiralling into the air between them.

Sarah blinked, straightening to place some distance between her and the eddying dust. It was now or never.

'I need to find out how to get to the Portal Realms prison,' she blurted, the words strung together so quickly even Sarah wasn't sure she understood herself.

The librarian froze, regarding Sarah with an unblinking stare.

Quickly, before the old woman could tell her to leave, Sarah reached into her pocket, pulling out the small scrap of paper she had found earlier that morning. Feeling suddenly self-conscious at how crumpled the paper was, she quickly flattened it out on the librarian's desk, turning it to face the old lady.

'The closed gate,' Sarah read aloud. 'This is the symbol that was branded onto the chest of the satyr that murdered my boyfriend. It's the symbol of a high-ranking prison guard.'

The librarian pursed her withered lips. 'So you want a map of the Portal Realm so that you can make your way to the prison and then find this guard who supposedly killed this boyfriend of yours? That's what you've come to me for? To help you on your little revenge mission?' The crone betrayed no hint of emotion. 'What exactly do you plan on doing once you find him, pray tell? An eye for an eye? A knife through the heart?'

Sarah winced at the blunt question but balled her hands into fists by her side, her voice steady as she spoke a single word: 'Yes.'

The ancient woman on the other side of the desk began to wheeze suddenly, her shoulders convulsing within her voluminous robes. Sarah panicked, her hands raising uselessly in front of her as she wondered what was going on. Had her plan of revenge been too much for the old lady? Was she having a heart attack?

The strange noise continued to rise from the librarian's throat, and with a start, Sarah realised she was laughing. Frowning at the unexpected reaction, she watched as the old woman's chuckles began to subside and she sighed, wiping at the tears that had formed in her eyes.

'Oh, how you remind me of a younger me,' the librarian drawled, snickering as she slowly heaved herself off the chair she had been perched upon.

Sarah stepped aside, shocked at how quickly the old lady moved. Her back was hunched as she waddled through the cavernous library, layers of clothing dragging across the stone floor behind her.

The librarian glanced backwards and snorted at Sarah's surprised expression. 'What are you gawking at, hey? You've never seen an old lady walk before?'

Sarah shook her head in amusement as she followed the old crone through the first floor of the library and into the small room she had taken the books from previously. The small alcove looked the same as Sarah had remembered it; a few bookcases filled the space, and rugs lay scattered on the floor. Glowing crystals dotted the walls, growing from cracks in the stone.

The librarian paused before a huge tapestry that took up the majority of the far wall of the room. A familiar bleak landscape greeted her as she studied the intricately designed embroidery, a shiver running down her back. It was a depiction of the Portal Realm, the same dead, grey forest that haunted her dreams every night. She had somehow missed seeing it the first time she had entered the library, too engrossed in finding any information on the nightmarish in-between world.

'Like I was saying,' the librarian suddenly croaked, making Sarah jump, 'you remind me of myself. This little harebrained scheme of yours is precisely something I would have thought up many moons ago. Plus, you're beautiful like me, too.'

It was Sarah's turn to laugh, startled at the newfound gleam in the old woman's eyes.

'Revenge.' The librarian sighed, gazing into an unknown past. 'I used to live for it. Many thought I was crazy for obsessing over it, but I disagree. When someone takes something from you or wrongs you, there is no better feeling than watching them pay the price.'

A chill went down Sarah's spine. When the librarian put it like that, her plans for revenge almost made her seem sadistic, in a way. But as her eyes wandered once again over the tapestry hanging before them, resolve tightened in her stomach. This was the reason she had stayed in Aranasmin. This was why she had guiltily watched the hope drain from Alek's eyes as she told him she wasn't going home.

Humming merrily to herself, the librarian reached out one quivering finger and placed it against the woven threads of the mural before them. A white spark zipped into the air, startling Sarah, just as a wave of static electricity washed over her body, causing the hair on the back of her neck to stand on end.

The tapestry rustled as it came to life, the threads unwinding themselves from their tightly interlocked pattern. Sarah's jaw dropped as she watched the strands rearrange, threading themselves into a new image. The misty forest blurred and disappeared before her eyes and a new landscape appeared, becoming more distinct as the threads settled into place.

A huge ravine was depicted upon the tapestry where the forest had once been, illustrated by the magical strands. Spanning across the ravine were multiple rope bridges, each one descending lower and lower into the rocky chasm. Narrow landings and doorways were cut into the canyon on either side of the bridges, with no handrails to protect anyone from the deadly drop should they place one foot wrong.

Behind the rope bridges was what appeared to be a large wooden wall. Rivulets of water sparkled upon a brilliant silver thread, woven amongst the brown wood. Sarah frowned as she studied the image closely. *Some sort of dam wall ... maybe?*

At the bottom of the ravine was shadowy cave, the threads made of a dark, smoky grey. Cages hung from the stone ceiling, skeletal hands reaching out from behind the metal bars. Torches lined the edges of the dark cave, and Sarah's heart began to race as she made out the shadowy forms of satyrs. Their horns were honed to lethal points as they stood amongst the hanging cages, guarding their prisoners.

'This is the Portal Realms prison.'

Sarah jumped violently, tearing herself away from the intricately woven image before her and turning to look at the librarian. When she laid eyes on the librarian beside her, she frowned. New wrinkles seemed to line the old woman's face, deeper than they had been moments ago. Her brittle hair seemed thinner, her hunched back more pronounced as she shuffled backwards in the small room.

'Are you okay?' Sarah asked uncertainly, not wanting to offend the frail-looking woman.

'Ah,' the librarian scoffed, waving a hand in Sarah's direction. 'Don't you worry about me, love. This old lady is tougher than she looks. Besides, a zap like that always takes a little toll on the old body.'

'Was that … magic?' Sarah asked slowly, remembering the feeling of the electricity washing over her body.

The librarian's brown eyes twinkled. 'There is no known map of the Portal Realm,' the old lady's voice rasped as she completely ignored Sarah's question. 'I created this tapestry many, many years ago, showing the places I had seen on my adventure within the in-between world.'

'You've been there?!' Sarah gasped. 'To the prison?'

The librarian smiled sadly, haunted memories swimming in her eyes. 'Yes, and I promised myself I would never go back to that godforsaken place again. I lost someone very dear to me within those prison walls—someone I have not thought about in a long time.'

The old woman absentmindedly played with the amethyst perched upon her finger, twisting it around her bony knuckle as she gazed into memories only she could see. Sadness stabbed Sarah in the gut. What had happened to the librarian for her to want to isolate herself in the library? Alone with only the multitude of books to keep her company.

Sarah shivered; she could not imagine a worse fate.

'I'm sorry,' Sarah said gently, breaking the heavy silence, 'but how do I get there? To the prison?'

'Don't coddle me,' snapped the old woman, breaking out of her reverie and raking her eyes up and down Sarah. 'I didn't show you this for you to feel sad about some poor, old lady. I made my choice, and it's kept me alive all these years, tucked away in the comfort of my library.'

Sarah kept her mouth shut, not daring to speak another word, lest she upset the withering old woman.

'Now, before the Dark Days and the war that wiped out magical creatures and destroyed most of the Portal Realm and all that nonsense, many tried to map the strange in-between world,' the librarian began. 'However, we soon came to realise that the Portal Realm itself is ever-changing. That strange, misty forest is un-chartable. It has no north, no south. Many would swear they travelled in one direction for days, only to end up right back where they started. The very plants have a mind of their own. The grass would strangle you; the trees would claw at you, given the chance.' The librarian paused, letting her words sink in.

Sarah frowned, her forehead crinkling in confusion. 'So it's impossible to find the prison?'

'Did I say that?' snapped the old lady. 'You really need to step it up if you want to go into this prison and survive. It was discovered that the Portal Realm is constantly changing in the sense that it takes you wherever you wish to go. You want to go to earth? Keep that in the forefront of your mind, and the forest will lead you on a path to earth.'

'So what you're saying,' Sarah said slowly, 'is that all I need to do is walk into the forest and focus on going to the prison?'

The librarian nodded wisely. 'Precisely. The forest is alive. You let it know where you want to go, and it will take you there. When you reach your destination, there will be some sort of distinguishing feature to let you know you have arrived. A gate, a cave, a trapdoor.' The librarian paused, that same wild glimmer back in her eyes. 'A willow tree.'

Sarah started, remembering the long fronds of the willow tree draping around her as she had backed further and further towards its centre, only to find herself walking out the other side of its branches into a strange new world. Where death had waited, stalking through the shadows.

The librarian shuffled over to the wall beside the tapestry, and Sarah watched curiously as she grasped one of the golden crystals. With a huff, the old lady snapped the crystal from the wall, the glowing gem nestled into her palm.

'Here,' she said, waddling forwards to drop the rock into Sarah's outstretched hands. 'Take this with you when you feel the time is right for your adventure. Its light will never run out, and you never know when you might find yourself in darkness.'

Sarah had opened her mouth to say thank you for the librarian's kindness when a thought struck her. 'How do I get into the Portal Realm in the first place?'

The old lady chuckled, shuffling away from Sarah and into the main library. 'Think about it, girl. How did you end up here in Aranasmin? You had to exit the Portal Realm and enter the valley somewhere. Where was it?'

Sarah frowned. For the life of her, she couldn't remember. She had been numb with shock after Chris's death, and everything was murky in her mind from that point onwards. She shook her head to clear her thoughts; there was time to ponder that later.

Looking to where she had last seen the librarian, she watched as the last of the voluminous cloaks vanished into the door behind the librarian's large wooden desk.

'Wait!' Sarah shouted, earning a few dozen shh's from students studying high up on the mezzanines. She dashed across the cavernous room and paused before the shadowy doorway. 'What is your name?'

A chuckle echoed from the other side of the doorway. 'A name is a powerful weapon to have, dearie.'

Sarah frowned, trying to decipher the meaning behind the mysterious woman's words before her voice once again floated out from the darkness.

'My friends used to call me Zuri.'

And with that, the librarian's door clanged shut, a lock snapping into pace on the other side of the heavy wood.

A grin broke out across Sarah's face as she turned, walking quickly towards the exit of the library. As she stepped out of the clinging shadows and into the crisp air of the valley, she sighed, sucking in a deep breath of the fresh air.

Her head whirled with all the information the librarian had passed onto her. She needed time to absorb it all. Sighing again, she raised her face to the sky, allowing the wind to tangle in her long hair, playfully twirling among the brown strands. Opening her eyes, she frowned in surprise as she saw the beginnings of an orange sunset creeping into the blue sky.

She hadn't realised how long she had spent within the stone walls of the library, engrossed in the old librarian's tales.

And her magic! Sarah grinned ruefully, remembering how the old woman had brushed her off when she had tried to bring up the topic. *I suppose she's allowed to keep a few secrets!*

Sarah glanced down at her closed fist. Lifting it up, she opened it to reveal the small, golden crystal. It looked entirely unremarkable in the light of day, just like any other pale piece of rock. Carefully, Sarah tucked the small stone deep into her pocket, pondering librarian's words as she wandered through the valley, heading towards the bonfire.

Now I just need to remember where the entrance to the Portal Realm is. She thought to herself ruefully as she ducked into the shade of the surrounding maples. *I'll ask Benny. Surely he remembers.*

****

Sarah settled down next to her cousin on one of the wooden benches close to the cheery bonfire. Benny was already halfway through his meal, shovelling food into his mouth like there was no tomorrow.

Sarah shook her head, slightly put off from her own meal as she watched Benny inhale his food. She waited patiently for him to pause before she opened her mouth, planning to ask him about the location of the Portal Realm entrance. Before she could get a word out, however, a deep frown pulled Benny's eyebrows together as he stared over her shoulder.

'What is he doing with him?' Benny muttered irritably.

Confused, Sarah turned, following the direction of Benny's frown. Across the small clearing, in the flickering shadows at the edge of the surrounding trees, was Alek. Only, he was not alone. He was with another boy, one Sarah had noticed a few times before. She'd heard a lot of the girls giggling and gossiping amongst themselves about the handsome newcomer to Aranasmin. She vaguely remembered hearing his name: Kai.

She could understand why all the girls spoke in hushed whispers about him. He was handsome. Tall, muscular, his face was perfectly chiselled and dark hair curled over his forehead. Sarah blinked; he was almost too perfect, though. Not at all like the loud, goofy boy she had fallen in love with.

Chris had always made her smile, cracking jokes at inappropriate times and living his life with a childlike wonder. Kai was a mystery, his presence almost cold as he stared at the other students gathering around the bonfire. *How has Alek ended up with him?* she thought with a frown. It seemed like such an odd friendship.

'At least he's out of his room, I guess?' Sarah said, forcing as much positivity into her voice as she could muster.

Benny huffed. 'I've gone to check on him every day and stood outside his tree house, forcing myself not to go in and bother him.' Sadness cracked through Benny's voice, and Sarah turned away from Kai to look at her cousin in concern.

Benny waved his hand in Alek's direction. 'Yet all it took was for some random person to say hello, and out he comes. When I chose to stay here with you, I never imagined I'd be doing it without my best friend. I miss him, Sarah.'

'Ben, I'm sorry, but Alek will come around—I'm sure of it!' Sarah said reassuringly, watching her cousin through worried eyes. 'Like I said, we just have to give him time. If making a new friend is what it takes for him to feel more comfortable, is that really a bad thing?'

Jealously flashed through Benny's eyes as he stared into the flickering bonfire, his face painted scarlet by the flames. 'It's not like I have much of a choice in the matter, do I?'

'Don't be like that,' Sarah snapped, crossing her arms. 'He's out of his tree house. It's progress.'

Before Benny could retort, the clearing went quiet, a chill breeze twirling around Sarah's neck. She turned away from her cousin and noticed that Ash had stepped into the centre of the clearing, drawing the attention of the gathered students.

'Good evening, everyone,' the principal began, her pale features exaggerated harshly in the dim light. 'I hope you have all had a rewarding day today. And to our newcomers, I hope you are all settling into life within Aranasmin.'

Curiosity chewed away at Sarah; Ash had never spoken to the students collectively at dinner before. Did it have something to do with the cancelled lesson that afternoon? Glancing around the clearing, she saw that many of the students were leaning forwards, eager to hear what the principal had to say. Imani caught her eyes from the other side of the bonfire and winked at her, causing Sarah to roll her eyes as she focused back onto the principal.

'I won't take you away from your meals for long, but I do have an announcement to make,' Ash continued, gazing around the clearing. 'For the first time in this generation, sprites have been spotted within the valley.'

Murmurs broke out around the bonfire, and Sarah frowned at the unfamiliar word.

'What are sprites?' Benny whispered uncertainly.

'Nasty little creatures,' a girl behind them replied, overhearing Benny's question. 'They're tiny, barely as tall as your knees, and translucent-looking. They feed on blood and hunt in packs, although I thought they were extinct. No one has seen them for years; I'm surprised you've never heard of them. Where are you from?'

Panic at the sudden question rose in Sarah's chest as she spoke quickly. 'Oh, not far from here. Just the other side of the mountains. He must have just misunderstood Ash, right, Benny?'

'Totally.' Benny played along, nodding his head. 'I didn't hear her properly, that's all.'

Suspicion flashed in the students' eyes, but she didn't press the matter further as Ash continued to speak.

'As you are all aware, sprites hunt during the full moon. If sprites have returned to the land, then we have no idea what could be re-emerging from the shadows in the coming months.'

More voices broke the silence through the clearing as students began mumbling amongst themselves.

Ash cleared her throat, silencing the crowd. 'These are dark times, we all know that, and with darkness comes all manner of wicked creatures. Sprites may only be the beginning, so we will take precautions. From this moment on, no student is permitted to leave their rooms after dark.'

Cries of outrage rose from the gathered students, and Ash put her hand up to silence the outburst. 'It is only to keep you all safe, particularly on a full moon. The teachers will continue to watch over the valley throughout the night in shifts. If a student is caught out of their room, there will be consequences.'

Voices rang into the night as Ash stepped away from the centre of the crowd, moving to the outskirts of the forest where the teachers stood in a small circle, talking among themselves.

Sarah frowned. This valley was supposed to be a safe place, yet here they were, imposing a curfew to keep students safe from the monsters that crept through the night.

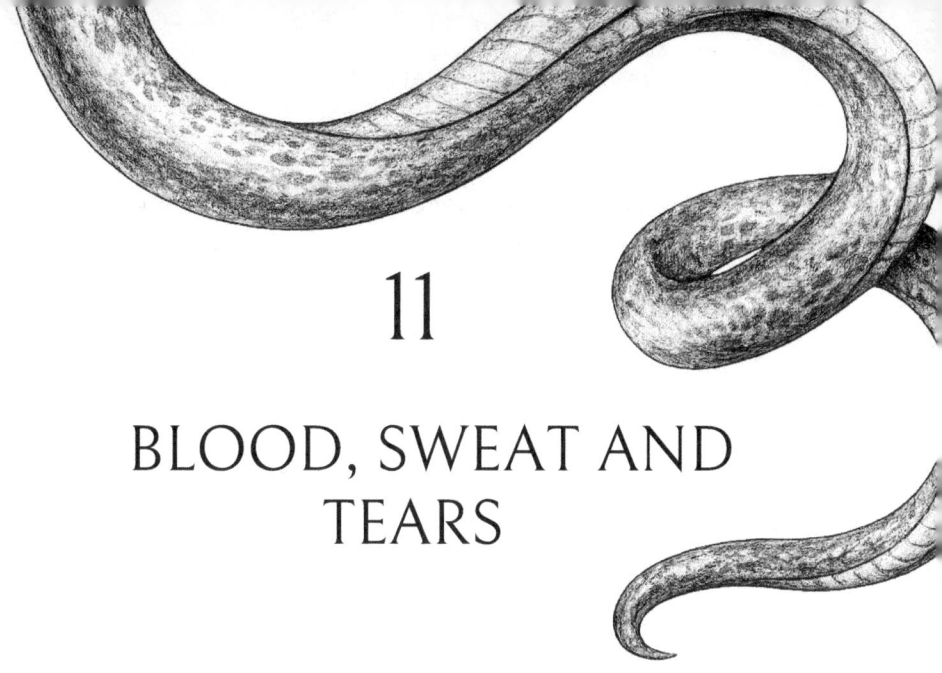

11

BLOOD, SWEAT AND TEARS

Sarah slept fitfully that night, her mind filled with magic tapestries and metal cages hanging in a dark cave. The satyr continued to haunt her mind, prowling through the blurry outskirts of her dreams, his cloven hoofs echoing forebodingly in her ears.

She woke well before dawn, crawling from her bed and stepping out of her room onto the surrounding branches. Inhaling the crisp morning air, she began to climb. The rough branches beneath her feet grew thinner the higher she clambered, bowing dangerously beneath her weight.

The cold air seared down her throat, filling her lungs with every breath. The air seemed to seep into every pore, every fibre of her being, causing energy to race through her body the higher she climbed. With one final push, Sarah's head burst through the canopy around her and into the open air. Wind whipped at her hair, pulling it into a halo above her head and tickling her skin.

Sarah tucked herself securely into a fork amongst the thin branches and threw her arms wide. She angled her face to the dark sky and closed her eyes, losing herself to the pre-dawn breeze. Her mind went blank as she felt the air around her, the currents gently brushing over her skin, tangling in her hair. A small pulse of warmth inside her chest reacted to the playful gust around her, growing steadily until her whole body was vibrating with power.

Sarah recognised the sensation of her magic and basked in it, allowing it to flow erratically through her veins and prickle under the surface of her skin. For the first time in a long time, she felt free. She was no longer head of the gymnastics team, no longer at the top of the social ladder at school.

No one in Aranasmin knew or cared who she was. She didn't have to worry about what anyone else thought or try to be the perfectly primped, pretty girl with the sporty boyfriend. She didn't have to attend all the parties, as fun as that may have been, and spend hours doing her hair and picking the perfect outfit.

That part of her had died with Chris.

She was in control, a new destiny laid out before her, and she was going to hit the ground running. Screwing her eyes shut, Sarah delved into the prickling power rushing through her body, yelling into the silent morning as she pushed the magic through her skin and into the air.

Wind buffeted her body, blasting her skywards in a chaotic swirl of leaves. Sarah gasped as the wild gale twisted and pulled at her, singing in her ears as it carried her towards the clouds. Opening her eyes, she caught a glimpse of the canopy below as she moved amongst the wind currents, whipping back and forth as her power merged with nature.

Wild energy thrummed through her body, pulsating around her and causing the air to ripple visibly as it held her aloft. But just as quickly as the explosion of magic had come, it began to dwindle, sucking energy from her body as it did so. Sarah felt gravity take hold of her as she drifted down to the treetops, gasping as she settled back amongst the branches.

Energy flooded from her, leaving an empty feeling inside her as the warm magic retreated to a tiny shell deep within her body. Uneasy breaths filled Sarah's lungs as she came to terms with what had just happened. She'd managed to summon a small amount of wind to her before, yes. But she'd never dreamed she would be able to fly!

Or at least float a bit! she thought with a shaky laugh.

Grinning to herself, Sarah quickly ducked back into the intertwined branches, moving swiftly back to her tree house and swinging into the room with the grace of a cat. She landed in front of the full-length mirror and straightened her shoulders, staring once again at her reflection.

Her sun-kissed face stared back at her, glowing in the early morning light. Her wavy brown hair was tangled chaotically around her shoulders, windswept and tangled with a few leaves. Laughing to herself, she quickly pulled the leaves out of her hair, turning and beginning to walk away from the mirror.

But she stopped, Imani's voice ringing in her ears from the day before. *'You'll never beat anyone looking like this, pretty girl. Whoever you're facing will grab a handful of your hair and gain the upper hand.'*

Sarah hesitated for a moment before she walked back into her room, rummaging through a drawer beside her bed until she found a hair tie. She quickly made short work of pulling her long hair back into a tight ponytail, stepping back to the mirror to examine her handiwork.

A new person stared back at her from the glass. The ponytail accentuated the angles of her face, making her look older, stronger. Her green eyes were hard, determination etched across her face.

Sarah watched a brief shadow of sadness flash through her eyes as she remembered Chris pulling her hair loose after every gymnastics competition, running the loose strands through his fingers. 'That's better,' he would say. 'Wild and free, like you.'

And yet here she was, her hair pulled tightly back, feeling freer than she ever had before. Her heart ached as the sound of Chris's voice echoed in her ears and she shook her head, dispelling the lingering memories as she left her tree house. It was all for him. She would rest once she had made it right, once she had taken her revenge.

It was still early, too early for Benny to be awake, so Sarah stalked through the forest alone, anticipation fluttering in her belly. Single-minded focus sharpened her senses as she moved amongst the maples, the green, star-shaped leaves rustling in the breeze. Stepping out onto the large training field, Sarah looked towards the fighting ring from the previous day, noticing a few students already gathering nearby.

Sarah's nerves fluttered, and she took a deep breath, clamping down on them as she marched across the field, catching the eye of Imani as she drew closer. That same confident smile split Imani's face as Sarah stopped before her, the small group of students watching the interaction with wide eyes.

Imani studied Sarah, her gaze lingering on the tight ponytail and determined expression. 'Well, well, well. Look who came to play.' Her voice was cocky, her white grin sparkling against the dark tone of her skin.

'I didn't come to play; I came to win,' Sarah shot back, surprising herself at the challenge behind her words.

Imani's smile broadened. 'Pulling your hair back into a ponytail doesn't make you a winner, pretty girl.'

Sarah winced at the term. She was sick of being called a pretty girl, sick of being the victim. It was time to fight back. 'Well, why don't we find out?' Sarah injected as much confidence as she could into her words, watching as Imani frowned, stepping backwards into the sandy ring.

'We have two rules,' Imani stated. 'One, no shoes. Two, if you surrender or ask to stop, then the fight ceases immediately, no matter what. Got it?'

Sarah swallowed hard, nodding as she reached down and unlaced her boots, slipping them off her feet, followed by her socks. Slowly, she stepped into the ring, wincing at the muddy sand that squelched around her toes. Her heartbeat thundered as she slowly circled Imani, the older girl's eyes unblinking as she studied Sarah's every movement. Like a predator stalking her prey.

'Fighters ready?' a student's voice broke through the tense silence from above.

Sarah nodded, watching Imani do the same.

'On the count of three! One, two, three!'

Blood roared in Sarah's ears as Imani struck, fast as a snake. Adrenaline spiked into Sarah's veins and she twisted, ducking to the left, sand spraying in her wake. As she quickly spun, searching for her opponent, a fist rose from the ground to slam painfully into her chin. Sarah's head snapped backwards and she hit the ground hard, pain stabbing through her skull as grains of sand embedded themselves in her skin.

Imani stepped over her, and Sarah reacted on instinct, lashing out with her feet, sweeping the legs out from beneath the other girl. Imani let out a shocked cry as she stumbled backwards, taken off guard at the sudden attack. Sarah managed to get her feet under her and lunged forwards, tackling the other girl into the sand, cold mud coating them as they tousled, both trying to gain the upper hand.

Imani's elbow slammed into Sarah's face, splitting open the skin above her eye. She gritted her teeth against the pain and dove back into the fray, managing to jam her knee deep into her opponent's ribs and knock the wind out of her.

The two girls separated, staggering to their feet. Blood dripped down Sarah's face from the cut above her eye, and dirt was smeared across the rest of her body. However, she barely felt the pain. Her body was singing with the adrenaline of the fight, and she grinned, thrilled to be taking control. Her magic began to re-awaken within her, roused by the blood pumping through her body.

'Sarah!' Benny's voice snapped her out of her thoughts. 'What the hell are you doing?! Get out of there!'

'No, Benny.' Her mouth twisted as she argued. 'I'm not done yet.'

Imani suddenly leapt forward, taking advantage of the distraction, her fist aimed for Sarah's face. Sarah blocked, wincing as her forearms absorbed the punch. She spun on her heel, lashing out with a vicious kick.

Imani caught Sarah's heel with ease, and too late, Sarah realised her mistake. Her opponent slammed her elbow into Sarah's knee and shoved her to the ground, sending her rolling into the sand.

Sarah groaned at the sudden pain that pulsed from her knee, and she rolled over onto her back, gasping as she saw Imani standing over her. A sheen of sweat coated the other girl's dark skin as she offered a hand to Sarah.

'Do you surrender?' she asked sweetly.

Sarah shuddered as she ignored the offered hand and hauled herself to her feet, shaking unsteadily as she put weight on her injured leg. Imani stood before her, hands on hips as she waited for Sarah's response.

Sarah dipped her head in acknowledgement. 'I surrender.'

Imani whooped, pumping her fist into the air as the crowd cheered. Sarah watched as the other girl turned her attention back to her. 'Good fight. I didn't expect you to make it so hard for me!'

Sarah blinked in surprise. 'Thanks … it actually felt kind of good,' she admitted with a small laugh.

Imani threw her head back, laughing loudly into the heavens. 'That, my friend, is why we do it.'

Sarah nodded slowly, allowing herself to feel the throbbing pain in her knee, the stinging cut above her eye, the multitude of bruises that were spread across her body. They hurt, yes, but they also felt good. Proof that she was *doing* something, anything, rather than just sitting by. 'So … same time tomorrow?' she asked, following Imani out of the sandy pit.

Imani glanced over her shoulder at Sarah. 'What, that wasn't enough for you?'

Sarah shrugged. 'I didn't win.'

Once again, Imani laughed loudly and Sarah grinned. The other girl's energy was contagious. 'It's Sarah, right? I like you.

You have guts.'

Sarah blinked. There she was again, speaking in her matter of-fact way, so sure of everything she said.

'Same time tomorrow, then.' Imani glanced down at Sarah's knee. 'Until then, you can enjoy watching me from behind on the morning run again, because there is no way you are beating me with that knee.'

With that, Imani stalked off into the gathering crowd to change out of her tank top and shorts. Looking down at her dirty body, Sarah wished she had had the wisdom to wear something similar. Instead, she looked like she'd just smeared herself head to toe with dirt, and she decided she didn't mind one bit.

'What the hell, Sarah?' Benny gasped, grabbing Sarah's arm and forcing her to look into his concerned eyes. 'What do you think you're doing? You could've been seriously hurt.'

Sarah rolled her eyes. 'Oh, calm down, Benny!' she exclaimed.

'I'm fine. And I can make my own choices.'

Benny frowned. 'I know, but—'

'No buts!' Sarah interrupted. 'If I want to fight Imani in the ring, no one is going to stop me, okay?'

Sarah stalked away without waiting for an answer, breaking into a jog as the students around her began to head out on the morning run. She winced as her knee barked in pain with every step, but she pushed through it, feeling the ache as she pushed herself harder, faster.

Soon, she was at the front of the group, her face set in determination as her knee threatened to give out with every stride. In front of her, Imani glanced over her shoulder, winking before she took off into the trees.

Sweat shone on Sarah's face, mingling with her blood as it dripped down her body. Despite the pain threatening to break her, she could feel strength bubbling below the surface of her skin. Feel the small kernel of magic ready to flood into her veins as soon as she willed it.

Sarah's stumbling stride smoothed as she focused, steadying her breaths. She was strong enough for this. She'd frozen when the satyr had attacked them and killed Chris; she'd been too afraid to fight back. Maybe if she had, Chris would still be alive.

I'll make it right, Chris, she thought as her feet pounded through the grass. *I'll get the revenge both of us deserve. Right after I beat Imani.*

A savage grin broke across Sarah's face as she pumped her legs, the wind tearing down her throat as she pushed herself faster, silent tears streaming from her eyes as the trees flashed past.

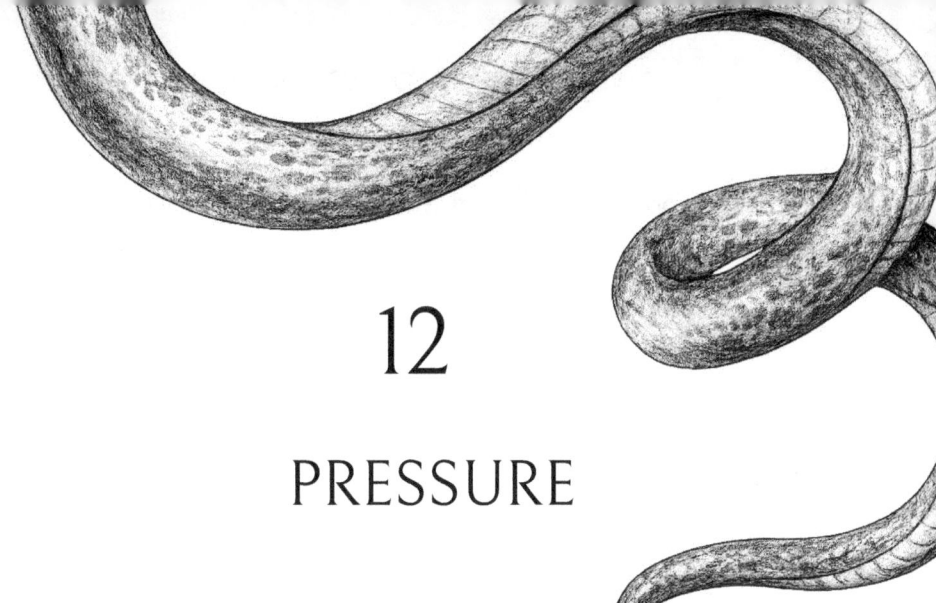

12

PRESSURE

Alek's legs shook as he balanced precariously on the balls of his feet, his body twisted into an unnatural position.

'You need to be unmovable,' Kai said, his blue eyes twinkling. 'When you are facing an enemy, you don't want to be caught off balance and risk being knocked over and made vulnerable.'

Alek huffed, rolling his eyes. Just over a week had passed since he had begun training with Kai, and the other boy was insufferable at times. He seemed to find joy in watching Alek fail at every task he set him, which only added to Alek's irritation.

Alek felt Kai's body close behind him, his muscular chest pressing against his back, causing his mind to go blank. Heat rose in Alek's cheeks as Kai's hands slid down his arms, correcting his form.

'Focus, Alek,' Kai said softly, his breath tickling Alek's ear as he leaned in closer.

Goosebumps exploded down Alek's skin, following the path Kai's hands had travelled. His mind spun wildly at Kai's touch as he struggled to focus on the movements Kai had shown him moments before. But those moments seemed like hours ago. Alek's heart beat faster as Kai dropped his hands to wrap around his waist, twisting his body to the side.

Alek swallowed, trying to clear the lump in his throat as Kai forcefully directed his body into the correct stance. *What the hell is wrong with me?* He wildly willed his body not to betray him to the other boy.

Alek felt Kai's body tense, and before he could react, his legs were swept out from underneath him in less than a second. Alek hit the ground hard, the sand by the shore softening his fall. Blood rushed to his face, painting it scarlet as Kai's laughter rang through the air. Alek stayed where he was, face down in the sand while he waited for his heartbeat to calm down and the lingering feeling of Kai's hands to vanish. Groaning to himself, he rolled onto his back, rising to a seated position and avoiding Kai's eyes.

'This is stupid,' he huffed irritably. 'I'm never going to get this right. You just keep knocking me over, day in and day out. I don't belong here, doing this.'

The sand shifted beside him, and he felt Kai settle down next to him. They sat in silence together, watching the tranquil lake change colours as it reflected the sunset sky far overhead. Alek felt himself begin to relax as he listened to the trickling water. Small waves caused by the large waterfall lapped on the sandy shore not far from his feet.

'Alek,' Kai began softly, pressing his shoulder comfortingly against Alek's. 'It's been a week. You need to give yourself a break.'

Alek sighed; Kai was right. But he couldn't shake the overwhelming dread that hung over him every time he thought about the reason Ash had brought him and his friends here. Who knew when the Dark Warriors were coming? *If* they were coming. He needed to be ready. How was he supposed to save the world and keep his friends safe when he couldn't even stay on his own two feet through a training session?

Pressure filled his mind as he felt a heavy weight pull down on his shoulders. Once everyone knew that he and his friends were part of the mysterious four, how could they not be disappointed? They were just a bunch of kids, and he didn't even know what his magic was yet.

While Kai sat blissfully beside him, Alek tunnelled down deep into his mind, searching for that small kernel of magic Ash had instructed him to find barely a week ago. He had witnessed the magic Sarah and Benny possessed, and jealousy flashed through him as he thought about his own failure.

Sweat formed on his brow as he gritted his teeth, searching for something, anything that would prove he had some sort of magical ability. Instead, all he found were images of tall, armoured warriors, plundering and burning villages, visions his mind had conjured of the Dark

Warriors. *Are they out there now? Searching for us?* Alek shivered at the thought, dread curling around his spine.

'What's wrong?' Kai asked, cutting into Alek's worried thoughts.

'Nothing,' Alek answered quickly, shrugging.

Maybe he should talk to Kai about it. The other boy seemed intent on helping him with everything for some unknown reason. Ash had warned them not to say anything about who they were to anyone, but what if she was wrong? What if the other students could help if they knew the truth?

'Have you ever seen a Dark Warrior?' he asked hesitantly, deciding not to reveal the truth about who he was supposed to be.

Kai frowned, turning to study Alek's face. 'What on earth makes you ask that?'

'I don't know. Curiosity, I guess?' Alek winced. His excuse sounded weak, even to him.

'I have,' Kai said slowly, his piercing eyes staring into Alek's.

Alek shivered. It felt as if Kai was reaching into his mind with those icy blue eyes, trying to find the truth behind his question. Blinking, he turned away from the other boy to gaze once again out over the lake, trying to ignore the prickling on his neck as Kai continued to stare at him.

'What ... what did they look like?' he asked. 'The Dark Warriors, I mean.'

Kai was quiet for a moment, and Alek waited in tense silence, wondering if he had offended him somehow.

Finally, after what seemed like an age, Kai spoke, his words slow and deliberate. 'They're tall. Dark armour covers their bodies, and most have war paint splashed across them. They're mindless. The only thing that drives them is violence and destruction.' Kai paused, seeming to struggle with his words as he continued. 'They're not human. I don't really know what they are. All I know is, when you kill one, they vanish in a cloud of black shadows.'

A chill crept down Alek's spine. Kai's description of the evil warriors sounded strikingly similar to the shadow monsters of Ash's prophecy. *Are they connected?* His mouth went dry. *Are the Dark Warriors made from the same dark magic as the monsters from the legend all those years ago?*

Ash had mentioned that creatures long since thought extinct had begun to return to Balathor, signifying the rise of the coming darkness. *And just a few days ago, she spoke about the sprites they found evidence of in the valley.* Alek squeezed his eyes shut. Everything was happening too fast for his liking. He felt the danger looming ahead like a dark storm cloud.

'Anyway,' Kai said, abruptly snapping Alek out of his anxious thoughts. 'You have a bigger problem to deal with than the Dark Warriors.'

'I do?' Alek questioned, wishing that was the case.

Kai nodded, amusement making him smirk. 'You need to go talk to your friends.'

'What? Why?' Alek gasped, his stomach tightening at the thought of how Benny and Sarah would react to him ditching them for the last few days.

'Because they're important, Alek,' Kai said, climbing to his feet and walking away from the lakeshore. 'You can't do this without them. Besides, it's time you stopped hiding out here with me all the time and re-joined some of the other classes with the other students. And you can't do that until you've spoken to your friends.'

Alek realised Kai was right. He groaned as he hauled himself to his feet. He'd done this to himself, running away from his problems. It was a good idea to face his friends sooner rather than later.

'Wait,' Alek huffed, catching up with the Kai as they left the lake behind and entered the thick forest. 'We'll still be training together, right? Just us?' He winced at how pathetic he sounded. *It's a wonder he wants to spend any time around me at all.*

Kai chuckled, wrapping an arm around Alek's shoulders. 'Of course! You still have a lot to learn, buddy!'

Kai's muscles flexed, and Alek suddenly felt himself sprawling into the undergrowth, shocked at the surprise attack.

'Hey!' he yelled, glaring up at the blue-eyed boy. Kai snickered, the sound washing over Alek and causing his heart to accelerate as he watched the other boy's body shake with laughter.

As Kai's eyes closed, Alek threw himself forwards, slamming into the taller boy. Kai's breath rushed out of him as he was caught off guard, the two boys tumbling into the surrounding bushes. Twigs scraped against Alek's face as he rolled over, pinning Kai to the ground underneath him.

Kai peered up at Alek, his full lips open in surprise. Goosebumps prickled across Alek's skin as he felt the hard body underneath him. Kai's dark, wavy hair was tousled from the fall and littered with twigs. Alek studied the boy's pale skin, lost in his thoughts.

Suddenly, Kai threw his weight upwards, his muscular body easily dislodging Alek and sending him once again sprawling into the leaf litter. Shaking his head, Alek crawled to his feet, taking note of Kai standing before him, his arms crossed across his chest and a begrudging smile painted on his face.

'Very good, Alek,' he said, his voice low. 'It's not often someone gets the drop on me.'

Alek shivered. There was something different in the other boy's gaze. His eyes darkened as he glanced up and down Alek's body. Suddenly self-conscious, Alek turned, heading back towards the path they had tumbled from.

'Get used to it,' he threw over his shoulder, feigning nonchalance. 'Maybe you're just not as good as you think you are.'

A snort echoed through the surrounding trees as Kai followed him. A deep breath escaped through Alek's teeth as he felt the other boy watching him from behind, boring into his back. The image of those darkened eyes flashed across his mind. What had Kai been thinking in that moment?

Alek shook his head. Now was not the time to worry about the mysterious boy's thoughts. He had bigger things to worry about, like facing his friends. He bit his lip as he strode through the undergrowth. What would they think after he had spent the last week actively avoiding them?

Maybe I'll do it tomorrow. No sense approaching them now, at the end of the day. Alek huffed to himself, heading towards the bonfire clearing.

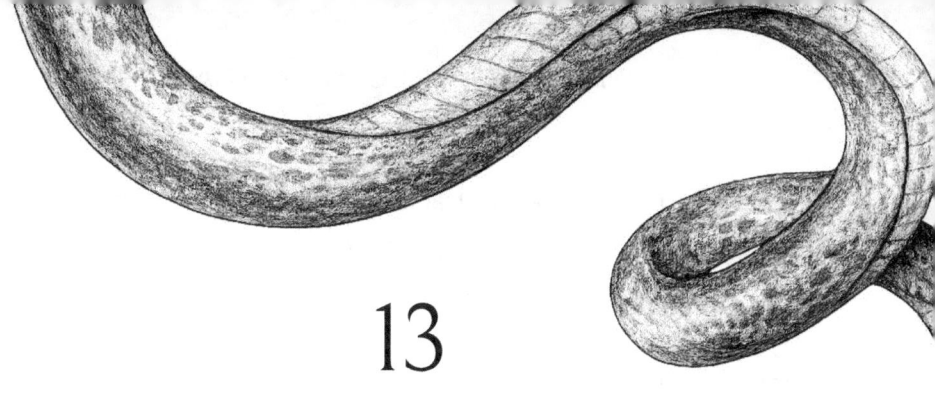

13

DON'T GET CAUGHT

Benny stared into the bonfire, lost in the dancing flames as he picked absentmindedly at his meal. The chatter of the surrounding students faded into a dull blur as he basked in the heat projected by the fire. His skin seemed to absorb the warmth, sucking it down into his core where it mingled with his own sweltering magic.

A fire churned in his belly as the events of the last half hour twisted through his mind. He had been wandering aimlessly through the valley, contemplating whether to seek out Alek and confront him about the distance between them, when he had unintentionally stumbled upon Alek. Only, he hadn't been alone; Kai had been with him.

The two of them had gotten into a playful brawl, rolling through the undergrowth as Benny watched with wide eyes. To his surprise, Alek had come out on top, pinning Kai down. But the look that the two boys had shared was enough to make Benny back away, feeling as though he was interrupting something private.

The forest had blurred around him as he hurriedly made his way to the bonfire clearing, jealousy baking in the depths of his stomach as he tried to block out the intensity that had filled the air between Kai and his best friend. His power had delighted in the intense resentment as it ignited inside him, warming him from the inside out.

The magic was always there, Benny had come to realise, burning just below the surface of his skin and waiting to be released. If he was being honest, it scared him a little, the way the newfound power simmered away in his core, a constant heat inside him. Whenever he tapped into the flames, they surged outwards, blazing through his body with the strength of a wildfire.

Benny shivered despite the warmth enveloping him. There had been a few moments when his emotions had gotten the better of him and he could feel the flames clawing up his throat and coating his tongue, threatening to burn whoever stood in his way. He usually relied on Alek to be his voice of reason and calm him down when his temper got the best of him.

However, he hadn't spoken to his best friend in over a week. Sadness pierced through his stomach as he shifted his weight, rolling his neck to ease the cramped muscles. When they had first arrived in Aranasmin, Benny could barely control his excitement. This was exactly the adventure he had been searching for. Plus, he would get to do it with his best friend by his side.

Visions of grand quests and secret missions had immediately grabbed his imagination as Ash told them the story of who they were. And the magic? It had all seemed too good to be true. And, in a way, it was. He couldn't help feeling as if he had traded his friendship with Alek for the thrilling adventure he had been longing for.

Benny sighed deeply, closing his eyes against the bright flames. Trying desperately to block out the images of Kai and Alek laughing together as they trained alone in the forest. Maybe Sarah had been wrong in saying they should give Alek space. He loved spending time with his cousin, but she was so obsessed with her training that she didn't have time for much else.

'Benny, my man!' a deep voice said from beside him, snapping Benny out of his reverie.

Tilting his head back, Benny took in the owner of the voice walking over to him—a tall, gangly boy with curly red hair. His name was Chad. They had been paired together that morning for a lesson on building a campfire. Benny had spent the entire class watching Chad's enthusiasm with a smirk on his face. Little did the other boy know, Benny would never need to build a campfire ever again. With a snap of his fingers, he had all the fire he needed.

Still, it had been nice to be in the company of someone other than Sarah—fun, even, as he laughed at Chad's poor efforts at creating a flame. The two boys had got to talking, and Benny had found out that Chad had been the valley for most of his life, not even remembering who his parents were or how he came to be an orphan.

When he was asked about his own reasons for being brought to Aranasmin, Benny had hesitated slightly before guiltily spinning the same lie he had told everyone. He, Alek, and Sarah had lived in a small village not far from here until the Dark Warriors attacked, killing their parents, and ransacking the town. Scouts from Aranasmin had seen them wandering by the mountains and offered them sanctuary.

Chad had nodded knowingly. It seemed to be a common story amongst the students who called the valley home. He hadn't pried any further or questioned Benny on where exactly his home had been located, much to Benny's relief.

'So, dude,' Chad began, settling on the soft grass next to Benny. 'Party tonight?'

Benny cocked an eyebrow, his interest piqued. 'You guys have parties?'

Chad nodded, his eyes playful. 'One of the older students is friends with the scouts; they smuggle in alcohol for them. Aaaaand they just got a fresh supply today, so you know what that means?'

Benny grinned at the other boy's excitement. 'Party time?'

'Yeah, bro! You in? Everyone will be there.'

Benny smiled. Parties had been a regular occurrence for him, Alek, and Sarah. *It might be a way for the three of us to get back to normal again,* he thought, excitement bubbling in his chest as the idea popped into his head. *I just need to find Alek and Sarah and convince them to come ...*

Benny's thoughts trailed off as he frowned. It had never just been the three of them at parties, though. Chris had always been there, looking out for them all.

Guilt replaced Benny's sudden excitement about the party as his mind began to spiral. Part of him wished he hadn't been so reckless and just stayed on the boardwalk that night and not led everyone down into Old Town. But another, larger part of him was so grateful he had. A whole new world was unfolding around him, ready for him to explore.

Shame ate away at him as he even entertained the idea of being happy that he had walked down into the shadowy Old Town. He couldn't shake the feeling that he was to blame for ripping apart Sarah's world and causing Chris's death. But he also wouldn't deny that part of him was more hopeful about the future here, in this world, than he had ever been back home. But was the price for that hope too high?

Benny pushed the thoughts deep down, into the dark crevices of his mind. Locking them away to deal with another day. He had no intention of wallowing in self-pity, and Sarah had never once said that she blamed him for what happened to Chris.

She's never said it out loud, anyway, he thought glumly. *She could be thinking it. Maybe that's why Alek is avoiding me; he's decided he's better off without me. Plus, Sarah has been spending less and less time with me, too, now that she's become friends with that Imani girl.*

Benny couldn't help the dark thoughts spiralling through his head as Chad chatted away beside him, not even realising that his words were going unheard. Even now, Benny could see Sarah sitting a couple of metres away, laughing and chatting with Imani.

Movement on the edge of the clearing caught Benny's eye and he turned, watching as a familiar blonde boy stumbled into the clearing. A small smile broke across Benny's face as he watched Alek take in the surrounding students with wide eyes. After hesitating slightly, Alek picked his way across the clearing towards the table piled with food.

Maybe I'll make the first move and go ask if he wants to come to this party, Benny pondered, gathering himself to stand up. *It might be too soon for Sarah. She'll have more fun with her new friend, rather than going to a party where she's sure to miss Chris.*

Just as Benny was about to rise, readying himself for the conversation with Alek, a tall figure cut through the clearing, heading straight for his friend. Jealousy reared up inside Benny as he watched Kai wrap an arm around Alek's shoulder, leaning in to whisper something in Alek's ear.

Alek threw his head back, laughter bubbling from his throat as he shoved Kai's shoulder playfully. The taller boy squeezed Alek tight, leading him to the outskirts of the clearing, a plate of food held in his spare hand.

Benny's frustration built, and a bitter taste filled his mouth. His skin flushed scarlet as heat raced through his blood, causing sweat to drip down his spine. So Alek couldn't spend time with him, his best friend, but he could spend all his time training and socialising with a complete stranger?

'Woah, dude, are you okay?' Chad's voice pierced through Benny's jealous haze. His temper bubbled just below the surface.

Benny swung his head away from where Alek and Kai had vanished into the shadows, his hands tearing at the grass by his sides. 'Where did you say this party was?'

****

'Now, remember, we're not supposed to be out in the valley once it's dark, so don't get caught,' Chad repeated for the millionth time, his voice tense as they slunk through the silent forest.

Benny rolled his eyes, sick of listening to Chad's non-stop chatter. The two had quickly left the bonfire clearing, heading steadily southwards through the ever-darkening twilight. The tall maples around Benny had become unfamiliar as they ventured further than he'd had the chance to explore yet.

Benny made no effort to be subtle, his booted feet stomping heavily through the densely-packed undergrowth as he tried to get out some of his frustration. The image of Kai and Alek kept relaying in his mind, regardless of how hard he tried to block it out. Jealousy coiled in the pit of his stomach like a snake, threatening to rear its ugly head with every passing second.

'How much further?' Benny huffed impatiently. 'I need a drink.'

Chad frowned as he glanced at the brooding boy next to him. 'We had to set it up far enough away that the chances of getting caught were low. No one usually comes to this part of the valley; there's nothing really down here.' Chad paused as the two boys ducked under some low-hanging branches, cautiously navigating the overgrown path around them.

'Alright, it should be just around here,' Chad mumbled to himself.

Benny rolled his eyes, wondering if he was being led in circles as they stepped into a small clearing. On the far side of the patch of grass was a grove of bamboo, similar to the shoots that surrounded Ash's sprawling home.

Benny hesitantly followed Chad's lead as the red-haired boy led them swiftly across the grass and into the bamboo. The trunks knocked together musically as they pushed their way through, the hollow sounds sending a shiver down Benny's spine. The long, thin trunks were smooth under his hands as he bent them aside, forcing his way further into the grove.

Suddenly, the dim chatter of voices reached his ears, barely audible through the densely-packed shafts. Jealous thoughts left behind, Benny forged onwards with renewed vigour, eager to see what awaited him on the other side. A few steps further, the bamboo in front of him abruptly ended as Benny stumbled forward, the buzz of many voices wrapping around him.

Benny glanced at Chad. 'No music?'

Chad shook his head ruefully. 'We don't want to risk getting caught, man. Music is too loud.'

Benny supposed that made sense and turned to study the area before him. Nestled in a small rocky ravine amongst the grove of bamboo was a burnt-out house. A frown pulled his brows down as he took in the ruined building. The wooden walls were charred, many of the planks fallen completely. The emerald green roof shone in the light cast by the crescent moon, marred by deep, black scorch marks. Large cranes perched stubbornly on each corner of the curved roof, clinging desperately to the ruined building.

Scattered throughout the clearing were candles, hundreds of them. They sat in clusters on the boulders surrounding the glade and were spread across the tumbledown building itself. Benny could make out more candles planted precariously in the empty windowsills of the structure, and small flames glimmered from the deep shadows swirling inside the wooden walls.

'What happened here?' Benny gasped, his eyes picking out the groups of students spread amongst the hollow, completely at ease with the ghostly house stooping over them.

'This was the old principal's house,' Chad explained as they walked further into the clearing.

Benny felt a strange sense of unease prickling his skin.

'It burnt down a little while ago, trapping him in inside,' Chad continued. 'Some sort of freak accident.'

Benny barely registered the fact that a bottle had been placed into his hand, the chilled liquid making his fingers numb. Ash had said the amulet had been here, in this very house. The thief had snuck in and stolen it before killing the principal and setting his home on fire.

His eyes were wide as he stepped closer to the brittle wooden walls. It had never even crossed his mind to come looking for the place the amulet had been. Yet here he was, and he could feel it. Some sort of presence floating through the heavy air around him, prodding at his own magic.

The power inside him flared in response to the touch of magic, sending heatwaves rushing through Benny's skin. He stepped up to one of the gaping entranceways; the wooden door hung sadly from its hinges. His eyes peered into the shadows, his mind lost to the magic burning in his veins. The darkness inside the building seemed to suck him in, pulling at him incessantly, urging him to enter its haunted depths.

'Uh, hello!' Chad said, waving his hand in front of Benny's face as his eyes flicked between the burnt house and the darkhaired boy. 'Come back to me, man!'

'Sorry,' Benny said quickly, tearing himself away from the whispering shadows and taking a sip of his drink. The liquid burned down his throat, causing tears to come to Benny's eyes as he tried not to cough.

'What the hell is this?' he gasped, earning a few snickers from the surrounding students.

Chad laughed, the tension leaving his body as he flicked his finger against his own glass bottle. 'It doesn't have a name. I don't even know where it comes from. All I know is that it does the job.'

Benny chuckled, taking a few more swigs from his bottle and trying not to shudder at the taste. The alcohol was much stronger than anything he had drunk before, so much so that he could already feel it going to his head, easing his tense thoughts.

Chad led him away from the derelict building and, much to Benny's relief, the strange presence that had called him towards the dark building faded as he moved further across the clearing. Benny took a large swig from his bottle, sighing as his worries faded away, the chill atmosphere of the party easing him into a relaxed state. He settled down next to Chad atop one of the larger boulders, joining a small group of other students.

Benny observed the kids gathered in the shadows of the destroyed building, dimly listening to Chad strike up a conversation with the group closest to them. It was the most laid back he had seen any of the students since he arrived in Aranasmin. There was a relaxed feeling in the air, despite the rules they were breaking to be out after dark.

The night air was cool and Benny took a deep breath, allowing it to seep deep into his lungs and ease the constant burn that simmered in his chest. Closing his eyes, he slid down the edge of the boulder, falling into the soft grass. Leaning his head back against the rough stone, Benny contentedly gazed up at the thin moon above him, sheltered in a shimmering sea of stars.

Raising his bottle to his lips once more, he poured the burning liquid down his throat, washing his troubles away. The chatter of the students around him blurred, becoming as indistinct as the wind rustling amongst the bamboo overhead.

A shadow fell over him and Benny frowned, looking up to see a large student standing before him. Irritation pierced through the blissful fog in his mind as his lips twisted in exasperation.

'Lucien,' he scowled, distaste coating his words. 'What the hell do you want?'

'Oh, nothing,' the ugly boy said, inspecting his fingers. 'Just wondering where your weirdo of a friend is—that blonde boy. Haven't really seen much of him lately.'

'It's none of your business,' Benny snarled, immediately defensive of Alek. 'You have no right to talk about him that way!'

He quickly climbed to his feet, facing down the bully in the flickering shadows cast by the candlelight. A hush settled over the grove as the gathered students turned to watch the confrontation, whispering amongst themselves.

Lucien sniffed, eyeing Benny dangerously from his beady eyes. 'Why do you care? He's never around, anyway. What? Did he dump you?'

'You watch your mouth!' Benny snapped, feeling a simmering heat burst into life beneath his skin as his magic reacted to his rising anger. 'Alek is my best friend. What he does is no concern of yours.'

As Benny spoke, flames burned in his belly, raging against the surface of his skin and begging to be released. Angrily, he shoved his magic down, struggling to stay in control of the powerful force.

'Watch my mouth?' Lucien sneered, grinning at the gathering crowd. 'Or what, huh? What are you going to do about it? You're all alone. I don't see anyone around to help you.'

'Benny, forget it. Let's go.' Chad placed a hand on Benny's shoulder and hissed in surprise, quickly removing it. 'Dude, are you okay? You're burning up!'

Benny ignored Chad, struggling to keep in control of the fire thrumming within him. Ash had warned them not to reveal their magic to the other students, but would it really be so bad if he used it on Lucien? A little bit of fire might make him back off a bit.

Rage burned in Benny's brown eyes as he squared up to the much larger boy, his nostrils flaring in anger. A few students gasped in shock as the candles around the clearing suddenly sparked, their flames spiralling into the air as Benny's magic spread across the clearing. Lucien's eyes widened as the blazing candles heated the air between them, a drop of sweat rolling down the side of his face.

'What's the matter?' Benny taunted, his breaths quickening as his magic fought for release. 'Scared of a little fire?'

Lucien quickly recovered from his shock, a cocky smirk tugging at his lips as a group of his friends stepped out of the shadows behind him, flanking the bully on either side. Benny's eyes flicked across the group facing him, a trickle of worry worming down his spine as he realised that he was drastically outnumbered.

'Who's scared now?' Lucien chuckled, cracking his neck as he stepped forward. 'You're outnumbered.'

Benny backed up a step, his heel hitting the boulder behind him as Lucien spread his arms wide, drawing in the surrounding audience. He gritted his teeth. There were too many for him to take on alone, but if he could remove one or two of Lucien's friends from the equation, he stood a chance. Could he risk using his magic? It would be worth it just to teach the bully a lesson.

The candles melted onto the stone behind him, the flames flashing chaotically into the night sky as he allowed a hint of his magic to escape, crackling into the air. But before he could commit to exposing himself and firing a shot at his antagonist, a figure suddenly stepped up to his side.

'Lucien, you and your idiot friends need to back off,' Sarah snarled, her eyes blazing in the flickering light.

Relief flashed through Benny as his cousin settled beside him, her expression fierce as she stared down the bullies in front of them. He didn't know how she had ended up at the party, and right now, he didn't care.

He wasn't alone.

Lucien threw his head back and laughed. 'You need a girl to save you? That's the best you can do?'

Benny felt Sarah tense next to him as Lucien continued mockingly, 'You're still outnumbered, and surprise, surprise, that loner boy of yours is nowhere to be seen. Why don't you tell us where he is, if you're so close?'

Benny growled deep in his throat, his vision turning red as fire boiled in his blood, but before he could make a move, a new voice rang throughout the clearing, startling the spectating students.

'I'm right here, Lucien!'

Benny blinked in shock as Alek stalked out of the shadows, the crowd parting around him as he moved to stand beside Sarah. He caught Benny's eye and dipped his chin, motioning his head back towards Lucien.

Smug satisfaction mingled in Benny's belly, mixing with the simmering rage. His two friends shifted next to him as Lucien's eyes flickered over the three of them. As they settled on Benny, Lucien raised his eyebrows tauntingly, rolling his shoulders.

'Looks like you were wrong, buddy,' Benny jeered. 'What's the matter? Now that I'm not alone, you don't think you can take us?'

The bully yelled loudly as chaos exploded in the clearing. Next to Benny, Sarah had bowled over one of the boys, grappling fiercely with him as they rolled through the grassy clearing. Pride settled over Benny as he watched Alek circle his own opponent, deftly blocking the deadly blows sent his way.

Benny grinned sardonically as he ducked under the fist Lucien threw at him, stepping to the side and ramming his shoulder into his opponent's chest. A thrill rushed over him as he followed up the attack with a savage kick, eliciting a howl of pain from Lucien as he clutched at his injured leg.

An elbow suddenly slammed into Benny's ribs and he dropped to the ground, grunting from the force of the blow as Lucien towered over him, his ugly face blocking out the stars. Benny felt his magic flare through his body, giving him strength as he slammed his fist upwards, connecting painfully with Lucien's chin in a hiss of smoke.

The other boy howled, his cries echoing through the night. Unease rippled through the spectating crowd as the fight paused, murmurs about loud noises passing amongst the surrounding students. Benny was dimly aware of the glade quickly emptying, the students scared of being caught out after dark due to the ruckus caused by the fight.

Alek stepped up next to Benny, blood dripping from a split lip. Sarah was a few steps in front of him, barely out of breath as she refused to take her eyes off Lucien and his cronies. 'Don't think this is over,' Lucien snarled as he backed away slowly. 'You're just lucky I don't want to be caught out here.' The last few students quickly disappeared around them.

'Yeah, yeah.' Benny snorted, adrenaline pumping through his veins. 'Until next time, big boy.'

Lucien's face twisted dangerously as he and his friends faded into the darkness, forcing their way through the bamboo and out of the clearing.

Once Benny was sure the bully was gone, he let out a whoop, pumping his fist into the air. 'Yes!' he crowed triumphantly. 'Did you see his face when you walked out, Alek? That was priceless!'

Alek grinned, shaking his head. 'Not gonna lie—that felt pretty good.'

Sarah rolled her eyes, gathering up three fresh bottles of alcohol and handing them out to her friends. 'You guys are idiots.'

'Oh, come on, cuzzy,' Benny whined. 'I know you enjoyed it just as much as we did. That guy is an asshole, and he was treating Alek like shit.'

'Oh, alright!' Sarah admitted, her eyes twinkling. 'It was kind of fun to watch his face as he realised it was a fair fight.'

Benny laughed, taking a swig out of his bottle. 'How did you guys even hear about the party anyway?'

Sarah rolled her eyes. 'Ha! This party was the worst kept secret ever. I'd be surprised if all the teachers didn't know it was happening.'

Benny chuckled as his two friends gazed around the clearing, sipping their drinks.

'Lucien had a point, though,' Alek said quietly, his voice uncertain. 'I haven't really been around lately. I—I'm sorry.'

Silence stretched between the three friends as the candles flickered around them, casting them in their comforting glow.

Benny tried to catch Alek's eye, but the blonde boy was staring into his drink, avoiding his two friends.

'Alek,' Sarah began softly, 'you don't need to apologise. I was so adamant about staying here, even though I knew it would hurt you. I'm sorry I made you feel like you couldn't be around us.'

Benny's eyes widened. 'Wait, wait, wait! You're all apologizing? It's my fault we're here in the first place! If I hadn't ran off down into the Old Town, none of this would have happened.'

Alek snorted as Sarah burst out laughing, much to Benny's chagrin. 'Ben, buddy, I love you, but this has nothing to do with you.' Alek wheezed, holding down his own laughter. 'Ash was coming to find us no matter what. We would have ended up here sooner or later.'

Benny frowned; he'd never thought about it that way before. He'd been so busy burying the guilt he had felt about dragging his friends to this world that he hadn't really stopped to think about the situation that had brought them here in the first place.

'Besides, it's neither of your faults,' Alek continued, twirling the bottle in his hands. 'I just needed time to adjust to everything changing.' He glanced quickly at Sarah. 'I only wish we'd had a smoother journey through the Portal Realm.'

Benny gazed at his cousin as she took a deep gulp from her drink, her face carefully guarded. Thoughts of Chris ran through his mind. He didn't want to admit that he missed the oaf that had followed Sarah around like a puppy for years, but he did miss the sarcastic banter the two had shared.

If only I hadn't been so loud in the Portal Realm, he thought to himself bitterly. *Maybe then the satyr wouldn't have shown up, and Chris would still be alive. No matter what the others say, he's still dead because of me.*

'I guess I just felt lost since the minute I woke up here,' Alek spoke, once again avoiding eye contact with his friends. 'Benny, you always wanted an adventure, and now you've got it. You seized the opportunity with both hands and ran with it. Sarah, you lost the most, and yet you're still so strong and decided to give this place a chance regardless of how much it's cost you. Then there's me.' Alek sighed.

'I was scared. I didn't understand why either of you wanted to stay. Ash made it sound so dangerous, and neither of you seemed phased by that. The whole thing is crazy. Magic, monsters, prophecies. This sort of thing just doesn't happen, yet here we are.' Alek swept his arms out around him, gesturing to Aranasmin nestled safely amongst the surrounding mountains.

'My family lost so much after my brother and dad left. You guys know that. It's just me and my mum, and God, I miss her. So it was hard to hear that you both wanted to stay when all I longed for was to go back to the comforts of home, but I couldn't leave you here alone. Then you both seemed to find everything so easy, your magic coming naturally to you.' Alek sighed. 'It was honestly hard to be around you when I felt so powerless, so … not special, I guess.'

The three friends sat in silence for a little while as Benny contemplated Alek's words. Despite his friend's comforting words and their refusal to lay blame around the cause of Chris's death, he couldn't help the spreading wave of guilt that threatened to overwhelm him. Added to that was the thought of how lost Alek must have felt, isolating himself from the only two people he knew in this world. And Benny had done nothing, too busy enjoying his time in Aranasmin to see how truly miserable his best friend had been.

'So you still don't know what your magic is?' Sarah asked quietly, kicking at some loose stones with her boot.

Alek shook his head. 'Nope. I've tried to work it out, but nothing I try seems to work. Maybe Ash got it wrong, and I'm not one of The Four.'

'She seemed pretty sure,' Benny said slowly, his tumultuous thoughts fading as the subject of conversation changed. 'Maybe you just need time to figure it out?'

Alek shrugged. 'Maybe, but hey, who cares? If I don't have magic, then I guess I just need to be okay with that, right?'

Sarah offered Alek a comforting smile as the sound of the gently clattering bamboo echoed around them. Benny looked between his two friends, a small smile tugging at the corner of his mouth. Maybe it was the alcohol in his system or the adrenaline from the brawl they had just been in, but he felt lighter than he had in days, his guilt dwindling in the company of his friends.

'What are you smiling at?' Sarah asked suspiciously, staring at her cousin.

'Nothing, nothing,' he replied quickly. 'I just missed this. Us.'

Alek grinned, his eyes shining in the candlelight. 'Yeah. Me, too.'

Sarah raised her glass towards the crescent moon. 'To us!'

The sound of clinking glass filled the empty clearing as the three friends sipped their drinks in peace. Their troubles melted away as the candles burned low around them, the soothing glow chasing away any doubts as they enjoyed each other's company.

14

JEALOUSY

'Benny, bro, you made it out of the party after all! Didn't get caught, hey?' Benny glanced up to see Chad walking past, grinning widely as his red hair glowed in the morning sun.

Beside him, Sarah shook her head, hiding her grin.

Benny had awoken that morning wondering if the events of the previous night had been a dream. It almost seemed too good to be true that the rift between him, Sarah, and Alek had been mended overnight.

But as he had stretched in the pre-dawn light, preparing for the regular run around the valley, Alek had stomped out of the surrounding forest, waving at his friend as he made his way across the field.

And much to Benny's surprise, Alek had kept pace with him as they completed the morning jog. Despite the pain in his knuckles from the fight the previous night, everything felt right for the first time, having his two best friends by his side.

Even now, as they trudged up the side of one of the southern-most mountains bordering the valley, he couldn't help the small thrill of happiness at having both his friends next to him. The morning's lesson had been kept a mystery as they were led through the valley, away from the large field where they usually trained.

Instead, they were climbing up a steep, rocky path cut treacherously into the side of the mountain. The wind howled in Benny's ears, making talking impossible as he focused on his feet, taking care not to slip and risk tumbling to his doom. Sarah and Alek were both ahead of him, moving cautiously on the narrow track.

They rounded a bend, the ground levelling out around them, and Benny gasped as they caught up to the other students, perched on the summit of the mountain. Behind them, the steep track they had just walked wound down into Aranasmin, bordered on all sides by the treacherous mountain peaks.

Benny could see the sparkling lake far in the distance at the northern end of the valley and the thick trees that blanketed the majority of the school. Turning his attention away from what lay behind him, he was floored.

On the other side of the mountains, a vast land stretched into the distance. Benny's eyes strained as he tried to take in as much of the landscape as possible, shifting to get a better view around the surrounding students. A long, winding river caught his eyes as the sun flashed off the body of water. Rolling green hills stretched into the distance, giving way to a great forest.

In the east, Benny could just make out a range of impossibly tall mountains, the peaks clawing at the sky. In the opposite direction, the undulating hills gave way to large plains, stretching out as far as the eye could see.

The immeasurable expanse of land stunned Benny. He had never given much thought to what awaited the friends outside the safety of the school, and the unknown world sent a shiver of excitement down his spine. Glancing directly down the side of the mountains below his feet, he could make out a small structure burrowed against the roots of the great mountain. The building was surrounded by a high wall, and a pale pink roof flashed in the sunlight.

That must be one of the outposts that the scouts occupy, Benny thought, quickly losing interest in the boring building.

Paper rustled in the chill wind as students passed around large sheets, murmuring amongst themselves. Benny grabbed the parchment from the student next to him, studying it briefly.

'It's just a map,' he groaned, rolling his eyes.

'*Just* a map?' Alek exclaimed. 'Benny, none of us know anything about the layout of the land beyond Aranasmin. This is so cool!'

'Whatever,' Benny grunted as he peered at the map in his hands, Alek and Sarah looking over his shoulder.

Scrawled in a rough text across the centre of the map was a large word: *Balathor.* Benny remembered Ash calling the land that on their first day in Aranasmin. He quickly moved on, studying the images inked onto the rest of the paper.

Balathor was oblong in shape, a large continent surrounded by oceans. A few islands lay scattered across the western coastline, close to what appeared to be a large city. Benny's eyes skimmed over the words, instead focusing on the pictures. A huge forest sprawled through the centre of the land, stretching from the southern point of Balathor, almost to the north.

The entire eastern half of the continent seemed to be made up entirely of mountain ranges, sheltering the rest of Balathor from the sea. Benny flicked his gaze upwards, studying the view spread out before him. *Those large mountains over there must be the range on the eastern side of the island,* he thought, proud of his map-reading abilities.

Pictured on the map at the foothill of said mountain range was a large castle. Benny's mind whirled with the amount of detail he was trying to absorb. A large desert stretched through the north-western part of Balathor, and small towns lay scattered amongst the mountains and forests.

Shaking his head, Benny passed the map into Alek's eager hands, content to just sit and enjoy the view before him. While his friends poured over the map, Benny allowed his excitement for the future to bubble up inside him.

He hadn't given too much thought to the magnitude of the prophecy Ash had shared with them. He had been too caught up in the excitement of having magic and power, not realising just how breathtakingly large Balathor would actually be. He had spent the last few weeks happily training in the valley, completely oblivious to the scale of the mission he and his friends had decided to undertake.

And we're meant to save all of it, everyone, from a shadow army before it's too late. Benny grinned, his magic flickering in his belly at the exhilaration that raced through him.

'Hey, Benny,' Sarah said nonchalantly, cutting into his daydreams. 'Do you remember where we entered Aranasmin after we came through the Portal Realm? I can't see it on this map.'

Benny shrugged absentmindedly, ignoring the suspicious look Alek shot in Sarah's direction. 'Kind of. I think it was in the northern end of the valley, near the mountains. I don't know, though; I wasn't really paying attention.'

Alek and Sarah went back to studying the map, discussing the different landmarks amongst themselves. Benny sighed to himself as time trickled by and the class ended. The students made their way back down the mountain path and into the thick forest. As the friends reached the valley floor and stepped back into the shelter of the trees, he couldn't help but wonder what grand adventures and dangers lay in wait for them outside the shelter of the valley. Glancing at the sky through the thick branches, he realised the day was halfway over, which meant it was time for their magic lessons with Ash.

Benny broke off from the rest of the students, heading for the bamboo grove with Sarah on his heels. The surrounding maples were now comfortingly familiar as he walked among the lush undergrowth.

'Alek, aren't you coming?' Sarah's voice cut through the chirping of the birds fluttering overhead.

Benny turned, a frown setting on his face as he saw Alek standing awkwardly a few metres away, rubbing the back of his neck.

'No, I'm, uh, still going to be training with Kai,' he said. 'I'm just joining you guys for the morning run and some of the other classes now.'

Fire flared through Benny's gut as a jealous fog settled over him. He'd just gotten his best friend back, and now he had to share him?

'I just don't really see much point in going to magic lessons just to watch you and Benny,' Alek continued, taking a step away from his friends. 'I'd just be sitting there, useless.'

Benny refused to say anything, feeling the anger bubbling under the surface of his skin as Alek turned and left, weaving quickly through the large trees.

Sarah sighed, oblivious to the jealous fire burning in the pit of Benny's stomach.

'Well, at least he's talking to us now, right?' she said with a small smile, continuing onwards through the forest.

Benny grunted, spinning on his heel as he stomped after his cousin, balling his hands into fists as flames flickered between his fingers.

****

Branches snagged at Benny's clothes as he pushed his way through the forest towards the lakeshore. He had been completely distracted during Ash's lesson, accidentally lighting some of the grass on fire in his absent-minded state.

He kept replaying the moment he had seen during Alek and Kai's training session the other day. The way the two boys had tousled amongst the undergrowth, each trying to gain the upper hand. Benny shook his head; he had never seen Alek be so competitive with anyone before.

Kai brought out something in his friend, and Benny tried desperately to ignore the pit of jealousy twisting his thoughts as he wished it was him training with his best friend. Not a random stranger. Still, he needed to apologise for how cold he had been when Alek had said he wasn't coming to Ash's lessons.

Laughter floated on the wind as Benny reached the last strip of forest separating him from the lakeshore. Benny paused, his eyes widening as he watched the two figures from the safety of the trees.

Kai and Alek circled each other, the shallow water of the lake lapping gently at the sandy shore. Benny frowned slightly as he noticed that Kai quickly darted backwards every time he drew too close to the shallow waves that circled Alek's ankles. Suddenly, Alek lunged forwards, spraying water in Kai's direction. Benny watched as Kai stumbled sideways, blinded by the sudden attack. Alek twirled impressively, stepping out of the water and gaining the higher ground as Kai quickly swiped the droplets from his eyes.

Alek grinned at his opponent, and Benny blinked in surprise. He had not seen Alek this happy in a long time. He was used to his friend being reserved, keeping his emotions close to his chest. Yet here he was, taunting the blue-eyed boy in front of him.

Benny's lip curled as he felt the twinge of jealousy once more, wishing it was him making Alek that happy.

Abruptly, Kai struck so fast he was just a blur. The sudden attack sent both boys sprawling across the shore with a loud thud. A cocky smirk crossed Kai's face as he rose triumphantly, pinning Alek down into the soft sand, the setting sun glimmering off the surface of the lake behind him.

Benny had seen enough; he could feel his fiery magic reacting to the growing jealousy in his veins. If he stayed any longer, he was afraid of what he might do or say. It had been a mistake to come here. Alek didn't need him anymore.

Benny turned, dejectedly leaving the two boys behind on the shore. So long as his friend was okay, that was all that really mattered. But he couldn't deny the twisting resentment that coiled within him as he pictured Alek's laughing face.

I just wish it was me that made him feel that way, Benny thought sadly as the sky darkened overhead.

When he had imagined his future, Alek had always been by his side, just as it had always been since they were kids. But now he was barely there, and Benny just had to get used to it and be happy for his friend.

15

THE DANGER OF SPRITES

Months passed. As Alek's legs carried him around the valley each morning, Benny by his side, he noticed the forest around him begin to change. The green, star-shaped leaves of the large maples began to brown, filling the valley with bright orange and yellow foliage.

The mornings became cooler as his body grew stronger, the run no longer causing him the severe anxiety it once had. Sarah was unreachable, always at the front of the group, racing against a few other students. Benny kept pace with Alek, and he enjoyed the company of his best friend as the now brittle leaves began to fall from the branches overhead. Gradually, autumn rolled into winter, and the struggle to get out of bed in the frigid mornings was almost unbearable.

But every day, without fail, Sarah and Benny were waiting for him on the ground beneath their tree houses, rubbing their hands together against the winter chill. Alek appreciated his friends' support and treasured the time spent with them.

Eventually, the clouds broke and the first snows began to fall, turning the once lush forest into an icy wonderland. The trees that had previously burst with colour were now grey, the leafless branches woven together tightly. Snow settled on the thick canopy, creating a natural ceiling above the valley floor. The morning run became more arduous as the slippery snow threatened to trip anyone who was unfocused.

His relationship with his friends mended as the seasons changed. They had long forgotten the days Alek isolated himself when they first arrived at the valley. The trials they had faced and the death of Chris on the journey to their new home had faded to a distant memory in Alek's mind.

Alek no longer resented his friends for their decision to stay in Aranasmin; they had all changed. Their senses had become heightened, their bodies much stronger in the past months they had spent training together. The only class Alek skipped was when Ash instructed them in magic. He had tried for many weeks to tap into his supposed power, with no luck.

Sarah and Benny continued to grow in their abilities, now able to control their magic for longer without becoming exhausted, while Alek had yet to find a single kernel of power inside him. Every day, he looked forward to the evening when he would train with Kai. He could almost hold his own against the other boy now, and it wouldn't be long before he matched him in fitness and strength.

His lack of magical ability bothered him more than it should, but he had buried the feelings, instead choosing to be proud of his two friends and resigning himself to learning everything he could from Kai, though he sometimes thought the other boy took it easy on him. Now was not one of those times.

Kai's fist sailed past Alek's head as he spun to the side, his feet easily moving through the thick sand. He gathered his weight and struck out with his right foot, sweeping it towards Kai's ankles. The other boy threw himself backwards, flipping through the air and landing lithely a few metres back before launching himself forward, the wooden sword they were practicing with whistling through the air towards Alek's exposed side.

He tensed his body and steadied his breathing, as Kai had taught him to do. Quickly, he snapped his own wooden sword up to deflect Kai's blow. Their swords met with a loud *crack*, jarring Alek's arms. A flash of white from the trees lining the shore distracted him for split second, and Alek could have sworn he felt Ash's gaze on him before she vanished, her white hair catching the light.

It wasn't the first time he had felt the principal's watchful eyes on him as she tracked his progress. She would often appear just out of sight and watch as he and Kai duelled. He noticed she had taken to watching him and his friends from afar in their other classes. Ash's appearance caused him to hesitate for only a second, but it was all Kai needed as he pushed against their locked swords with all his might.

Alek stumbled slightly, yielding a step and wincing as cold water splashed against his leg. He hadn't realised how close they were to the lake. Alek struggled against the force of Kai's sword pushing against his own. He took another step back, now knee-deep in water and holding of the full force of Kai's weight pushing down from above. The icy water soaked his skin through his clothes, and energy seemed to flood through his throbbing muscles. Gathering his strength, Alek planted his feet into the lakebed and pushed forward with all his might.

Kai's eyes widened as he was thrown off balance. Alek snapped into action, whipping to the side so fast Kai didn't even have time to react. Alek's sword whacked the other boy across the back as he moved lithely through the shallows, trying to circle his opponent and get the upper hand.

However, Kai was having none of it. He took Alek's blow as if he barely felt it and lunged backward, his shoulder driving into Alek's stomach, knocking the wind out of him. Alek gasped for air, doubling over as Kai spun around to face him, grinning as he thumped the pommel of his wooden sword into Alek's side, throwing him off balance.

Alek cartwheeled his arms, losing grip on his sword as it splashed harmlessly into the lake beside him. He desperately tried to keep his footing, but felt himself lose the fight and begin to fall. Suddenly, a strong hand grabbed his forearm, and he looked up to see Kai smirking at him with those brilliant blue eyes.

'You know, one of these days, you might actually beat me,' he mused before he released Alek's arm, letting him tumble into the icy cold lake.

Alek wheezed as the freezing water latched onto him, bubbles exploding from his mouth as he pushed himself back to the surface of the water. As he drew in a long breath of fresh air, he heard Kai laughing from a few feet away. Alek scowled and splashed water towards the other boy, who chuckled and danced lithely out of the water's path.

'Well, since I'm already soaked,' Alek said, returning to the shallow end and shivering as a chill wind stung his wet skin, 'I'm going to swim a few laps while you do your boring stretches.'

Kai cocked an eyebrow, shamelessly watching Alek as he peeled off his uniform down to his underwear. He kicked off his boots and threw the wet heap into a pile by the water's edge.

'You know,' Kai said, raking his eyes up and down Alek's body, 'you may be fitter now, but don't underestimate the importance of being flexible. It could save your life in a fight someday.'

'Yeah, yeah. So you keep saying.' Alek sniffed, feeling his heartbeat quicken as he felt Kai's eyes wander over his body.

With one last look at his leering friend, Alek turned and dived into the water, revelling in the cooling sensation that washed over him. The sweat and grime of the afternoon's training session fell away, replaced by a churning energy. He realised it was the same buzz he got every time he dived into the water.

He had discovered his love for swimming a few months ago in the heat of summer. Kicking powerfully through the water, he remembered complaining to Kai about how uncomfortable it was to train in their skin-tight uniforms.

'Don't you want to go for a swim to cool off? These uniforms are stifling.'

Kai's mood had immediately changed, his face becoming mask-like, and all he had said was no. When Alek pushed him on it, Kai said, 'Don't worry about me or what I'm wearing; we need to focus on your training.'

He had refused to go swimming every time Alek brought it up, and it had become something of a sensitive subject between them.

One evening, when they were both dripping with sweat, Alek had worked up enough courage to ask Kai whether he was self-conscious about his body. Instead of the angry retort Alek had expected, Kai's eyes had become shadowed, and his only reply was, 'Something like that.'

Alek reached the opposite side of the lake, the roar of the waterfall drowning out every other sound. He plummeted down into the depths of the water, feeling the current from the waterfall push him down deeper before he gracefully spun and kicked back towards the sandy shore. He swam strongly, lost in his thoughts.

It was obvious Kai had a great body. You could plainly see it from how he filled out his uniform, so why did he insist on wearing the head-to-toe clothing every time he left his room? *Come to think of it,* Alek mused as he sliced onwards through the water, *I've never even seen Kai's room. He said it was near the lake somewhere, but that's all I know.*

His mind began to wander as his legs propelled him powerfully through the icy water. What did Kai look like under his uniform? As the thought popped into Alek's mind, he felt his body instantly flush at the mental image, and his stroke became unsteady. Gritting his teeth, he pushed the thought from his mind.

What is wrong with me? he thought angrily. *Why can I not stop thinking about this?*

He noticed the lake shallowing around him and hauled himself to his feet, droplets cascading around him as he stomped through the shallows. Alek shook the water out of his hair and shivered as cold wind bit into his exposed skin. He glanced around, expecting to see Kai lost in his stretching exercises, but instead the boy stood, staring at him.

'What?' Alek asked, feeling awkward as he reached for his clothes to cover up.

'You just …' Kai seemed lost for words as he gazed at Alek.

'Ooookay,' Alek mumbled, struggling to pull on his wet clothes. 'Any day now, dude.'

'Alek, you just swam that whole way back without taking a single breath,' Kai said softly.

Alek shivered at the way his name rolled off the boy's tongue before he realised what Kai had said. 'Wait, what do you mean?' He turned to look at the sheer size of the lake. There was no way he swam that far on a single breath.

'You ... how did you do that?' Kai asked, his eyes wide.

'I don't know,' Alek said uncomfortably. 'I guess I was just lost in thought.'

'No.' Kai shook his head. 'That is not humanly possible.'

Alek stammered, unable to explain what had just happened. 'I—I don't know. You must have missed me coming up for air.'

'But I was watching you the whole time,' Kai pressed, stepping forward.

Uncomfortable with the sudden attention, and with no plausible explanation, Alek felt an overwhelming urge to end the training session. He knew he hadn't surfaced to take a breath, but how could he explain that to Kai?

Is this my magic? Alek thought dejectedly. *Benny gets fire and Sarah gets wind, but all I get to do is hold my breath for a long time? That sounds about right.*

'I need to go,' Alek grunted, picking up the last of his things before stalking into the forest.

Frustration rolled over him as he stalked through the trees. He was annoyed with himself, he realised, for the way his mind wouldn't stop playing back the way Kai had spoken his name and the way he couldn't focus when he was around the other boy. And annoyed that Kai didn't trust Alek enough to tell him why he wouldn't go swimming or why he was self-conscious.

Or whatever the heck it is that's wrong with him, Alek thought irritably, sighing deeply as he ducked under a low-hanging branch. *I'll have to confront him head-on about it next time I see him. Although, it probably won't make much of a difference with all the fuss he's making about keeping it a secret.*

'Alek!' Benny's voice rang through the trees as he jogged through the brittle undergrowth to meet him.

Alek slowed, allowing Benny to catch up to him. Benny had transformed the most out of the three friends as the seasons changed. He was practically glowing. His brown eyes were clear, he moved with an athletic confidence Alek could never match, and he had grown stronger and taller as the months rolled by, his face thinning and becoming more angular.

He certainly has the attention of half the girls in this valley! Alek thought jealously.

Alek suddenly realised that Benny was looking at him expectantly, and he hadn't a clue what his friend had just said. 'I'm sorry, what?' Alek winced as Benny rolled his eyes at him.

'Honestly, you're getting more and more distracted every time you train with that guy,' Benny moaned. 'You know I could train you just as well as he could.'

'Ha!' Alek snorted. 'You wish you were half as good as Kai is. He would kick your ass with his eyes closed.'

'Whatever, we just never seem to spend time together anymore,' Benny muttered. 'Don't forget tonight is the full moon, and it's already getting dark—you don't want to be out here once the moons out and risk getting picked apart by some sprites.'

Alek rolled his eyes as Benny continued, 'I'm serious, man. Ash was telling us about them today. Everyone thought they were wiped out in the Dark Days that destroyed all magical creatures, but somehow, they survived extinction. She thinks it's because they live underground. That's why you never see them; they burrow into the earth and disappear. No one's come across a sprite for over a hundred years. It's so random that they've suddenly decided to appear again.'

Benny paused, shivering slightly. 'They sound creepy. No one knows how many there are, but apparently they're popping up everywhere in the wild. Whatever hunted them and kept them in check was probably wiped out during the Dark Days, so now they live in giant hordes. It's good that they're enslaved by the moon, though. Their magic means that they're only strong enough to hunt and kill on a full moon or in strong moonlight.'

Alek's curiosity was piqued. 'What do you mean, "enslaved by the moon"?'

Benny rolled his eyes. 'I don't know. I was half-listening as Ash spoke, but she said if a sprite is caught outside of the moonlight and above ground, they're so weak you could step on one and kill it. Like a bug. They sound disturbing, though, the way she described them. They enjoy toying with their prey. Like a cat playing with a mouse it knows cannot escape before it tears it apart.'

Alek shrugged. 'Whatever. You really don't believe in something so stupid, do you? Have you ever even seen a sprite? I'm convinced they're just a bedtime story to stop us students wandering off at night.'

'What?' Benny snapped, his nostrils wide and fists clenched. 'Did Kai teach you that, too?'

Alek frowned at his friend as Benny turned and stalked away. 'Benny, wait!'

'It's the winter solstice in two weeks!' Benny yelled over his shoulder. 'Remember, we were supposed to be a team, you and I.' He paused. 'I think you should forget it and team up with Kai. He's the one you seem to want to spend all your time with.'

Alek stood, rooted to the spot, his mouth opening but no words coming out as Benny disappeared into the growing shadows. Alek frowned at Benny's words. He vaguely remembered Ash mentioning something about some sort of hunt that happened every winter solstice. But for the life of him, Alek could not remember anything specific, other than being annoyed at Sarah and Benny for being so excited about it.

Uncertain as to whether or not to follow after his friend, Alek shook his head and stomped through the forest, quickly scaling the large maple that held his tree house and entering his room.

****

A few hours later, thick clouds filled with snow hung heavy in the sky. Pale light from the huge full moon filtered through the leafy canopy, surrounding Alek as he sat on the precipice of his tree house. He was too agitated to sleep.

Kai was angry at him, Benny was angry at him, and he was angry at himself. He flinched as a large white owl swooped past him, landing on a branch on the next tree over. Frustrated, Alek ran his hands through his hair, glaring up at the moon. If he was going to get any sleep tonight, he needed to speak to someone. He didn't particularly feel like facing Benny's never-ending anger, and Sarah would most definitely take her cousin's side.

Kai it is. Alek sighed heavily, hauling himself to his feet and tugging on some boots, quickly tying up his laces.

He grabbed a thick jacket, threw it over his shoulders, and leapt off the edge of his tree house and onto a branch below. His sudden movement startled the owl as he climbed past. It let out a loud screech and flew quickly into the night sky.

Moments later, Alek dropped to the forest floor, landing silently among the leaf litter. Almost immediately, the clouds above him burst and snow cascaded into the air. Alek shivered, pulling his jacket closer around him as he trudged through the near darkness.

He had a vague idea where Kai's tree house would be. There was a small cluster of rooms in the maples that bordered the lakeshore.

Torches were placed at random intervals through the valley, the flames small and weak, sputtering against the increasing snow swirling through the air. A shadow moved through the darkness a few metres to Alek's left, and he quickly slunk behind a tree, barely breathing as one of the teachers stepped into view. He knew the valley had patrols constantly through the night, but he had never been out at this time to see them in action.

He vaguely recognised the older woman as she silently moved past his hiding place. Moonlight glimmered off multiple blades strapped across her body. Alek frowned. Was Ash really that worried about their wellbeing that a teacher would be so heavily armed?

She was training all the students in the valley at a breakneck pace. Did she expect an attack from the Dark Warriors? Was the world outside the valley really that tumultuous that war could arrive on their doorstep any day now?

We have been here a long while now, Alek thought as he waited impatiently for the teacher to move on, *and she warned us about the Dark Warriors when we first got here. Surely some sort of attack is imminent?* Alek went a little lightheaded at the thought of waking up one day and facing down an army of attackers. Was he ready for that? To face the danger he and his friends had been brought into this world to defeat?

As the teacher passed by, Alek eased out of his hiding place, the snow muffling his footsteps as he continued northward, shaking his head to clear his anxious thoughts.

A clearing opened before him. On the opposite side, Alek recognised the small strip of woods bordering the lakeshore.

His tree house should be around here somewhere, Alek thought to himself as he took a few steps into the moonlit clearing. Which would explain why he's always training at the lake.

'Alek!' a voice hissed through the silent night. 'What the hell do you think you're doing?!'

Alek jumped violently, recognising Kai's voice as the boy materialised in the shadows on the opposite side of the clearing.

'Looking for you, you idiot,' Alek said, rolling his eyes as he took another step forward and then halted, noticing the look of panic on Kai's face. 'Uh, Kai? What's going on?'

'Alek … It's a full moon, and you're standing right in the middle of the moonlight!' Kai's voice was tight with barely controlled emotion.

Alek relaxed, letting out a sharp bark of laughter. 'Oh, please. In the whole time we've been in Aranasmin, I've never caught a glimpse of a sprite; I'm starting to think they're not even real!'

Alek jumped loudly as a giggle split the night directly behind him. The hair on the back of his neck rose at the unearthly sound and energy thrashed inside of him as he spun on the spot, scattering snow across the clearing.

'Not real, are we?' a sinister voice hissed through the darkness. 'Not real?'

'Alek, you need to get out of there!' Kai yelled urgently from the safety of the forest shadows.

Alek yelped as tiny hands ripped into his legs, hauling him to the ground. Panic instantly overwhelmed him as his face was buried in the snow. Giggling echoed in his ears as more and more vicious claws ripped through his clothes and into his skin.

'You're a foolish boy,' a childlike voice whispered into his ear. 'Now do you believe we're real? Or will you only believe once we get to taste you?'

Alek froze as a tongue licked slowly down the side of his jaw, small teeth grazing his skin.

'We've tasted the magic in your friend's blood, and it was oh-so-sweet, the beautiful boy with the blue eyes,' the voice continued to whisper, as more tongues joined the first. 'But you, the magic is basically rolling off you. So much untapped power practically begging to be released.'

Alek screamed as sharp teeth ripped into his neck. He mustered all the force he had and surged upwards, sending the sprites flying. He stumbled forwards, his terrified eyes widening as the snow all around him shifted, revealing a swarm of tiny bodies surging towards him.

'Alek, run!' Kai yelled, still refusing to leave the safety of the shadows.

Desperately, Alek flung himself forwards, blindly sprinting towards the safety of the trees. But the sprites cut him off and Alek skidded to his knees, sending snow flying as he lunged to the side, hauling himself to his feet and launching himself into a sprint. Icy cold air ripped into his lungs as he thundered through the clearing towards the edge of the valley, the sprites laughing manically as they gave chase.

Alek's muscles spasmed in the cold as he reached the upward slope at the edge of the valley. He clambered over a boulder, ripping skin off his palms as he began to ascend the rocky mountain slope. He glanced behind him as he left the shelter of the trees far below, his heart skipping a beat as he saw the dark mass of sprites pushing and shoving against each other in order to reach him first.

His heart pounded in his chest as he scrambled up the steep rock face, angling towards the waterfall roaring to his left. If he could just get to the lake, he could dive in. Surely the sprites couldn't swim?

Glancing upwards, Alek spotted a shadow in the rockface ahead, concealed from below by boulders and weeds. Abruptly changing his direction, he leapt up over a boulder, scrabbling desperately as he misjudged the leap, landing awkwardly on the opposite side.

Instantly, a clawed hand scraped down his leg. Alek lashed out with all his might, hearing a scream as his boot connected with a hard body. Not pausing long enough to look behind, he clawed his way forward, throwing himself towards the shadows before him, relieved to see the entrance to a small cave.

Alek's hands hit the floor of the cave hard and slipped on the smooth rock below him, sending him sprawling. Glancing backwards, he saw his legs protruding out into the light. Quickly, he yanked them into the shadows just as the wave of sprites caught up to him.

They slid to a stop at the entrance to the cave, hissing at the shadows that now surrounded the boy. Alek stared in shock at the tiny creatures before him. The sprites were humanoid in shape, their skin a translucent blue that seemed to shine in the moonlight. Long, spindly fingers that reminded Alek of spiders' legs reached towards him, the tips razor-sharp.

The tiny creatures were barely the height of Alek's knees, yet they terrified him more than any predator he had ever encountered. Dark black eyes seemed to peer into his soul, their inky depths reflecting the moonlight. The sprites drew their lips back, revealing row after row of needle-sharp teeth as they giggled manically.

'You were lucky this time, boy,' the tiny creatures snarled at him.

Alek flinched away from the sprites' voices, moving further into the shadows and wincing at the stabbing pain in his wrists from his dive to safety. Suddenly, his hands slid backwards on slick stone, and his momentum sent him tumbling down a sharp incline. Alek yelled as he rolled head over heels before landing in a heap, pain flashing through his body as his head slammed into rock and everything went dark.

16

BROTHERS REUNITED

As Alek came to, he was aware of a soft glow illuminating the darkness around him. He groaned as he rolled onto his hands and knees, sharp pain exploding through his head. Giving his body time to adjust to the sudden movement, Alek slowly rose to his feet, squinting in the dim light around him.

He was in a narrow tunnel.

Luminescent veins of crystal spiderwebbed through the stone around him, casting a soft blue glow through the cave. Water trickled from the ceiling and the walls, sparkling like diamonds in the crystal light. The roar of a waterfall echoed from deeper ahead in the tunnel. Grimacing in pain, Alek limped forward, his hands trailing along the smooth wall, the ice-cold water slowly waking him up.

Alek glanced down at his ripped and ruined clothes. Blood smeared his legs and arms from a multitude of scratches across his body. He took a deep breath, forcing down his rising panic. He was lost. But he was also alive. And judging from the roaring growing ever louder before him, he was at least close to a stream that fed into the waterfall that flowed down the mountains and into the valley. Shivers racked his cold, wet body, and his teeth chattered as he wrapped his arms tight around his chest.

So maybe not entirely lost, Alek thought as he trudged onwards. *But I need to get warm—and fast.*

Alek lost track of time as he trekked through the winding tunnel, hoping that around each bend, there would be some sign to tell him he was going in the right direction. Instead, he just encountered the same wet tunnel. Eventually, the path began to slope upwards, and his legs burned with the effort of the steep climb, the water trickling around him soaked him to the bone.

I deserve this, he mused, his movements becoming increasingly clumsy as exhaustion tugged at him. *Why did I think I could fit in here? I have to try so much harder than everyone else. Now look at me, lost in a cave.*

He laughed to himself as he realised that he had been so frustrated with himself earlier that day, he had pushed all his friends away. *It'll probably take them a week to come looking for my body,* he thought with a snort.

Suddenly, Alek staggered around a corner and the cave opened up around him. He instantly panicked as moonlight cascaded over him. Stumbling backwards, Alek tripped over his own feet and slammed hard into the ground, wincing at the fresh pain to his body.

Cocking his head to the side, Alek listened out for the sound of sprites in the moonlight, but silence lay before him, save for the dull roar of water. Ever so carefully, Alek climbed to his feet and stepped into the soft light, gasping in shock at his surroundings.

The cave itself was shallow, barely a scoop out of the mountain face, but before him was a wide plateau. The stones around him were laced with the same luminescent blue crystal and water trickled down the rough walls, much like it had in the tunnel behind him. A small stream cut through the cave floor and flowed into a large, circular pool. Crystals bloomed among the soft green grass surrounding the pool, causing its rippling surface to sparkle like liquid diamond.

Alek blinked as he stepped forwards onto the grass. Warm heat spread through his body, so different from the bone numbing cold that he gasped out loud, almost laughing in shock. Revelling in the warmth flooding his veins, he glanced around, realising that although snow still fell outside the cave, it only gathered at the edge of the plateau, melting the closer it got to the pool.

Something prickled inside him as he gazed at the pool and a voice echoed in his head, urging him forward, willing him to sink into its depths. With great effort, Alek shook his head, wrenching his eyes away from the water. He looked at the wall on the opposite side of the cave and frowned, for the first time noticing markings etched into the stone.

Silently walking forward, his eyes devoured the carvings in front of him, watching as crystal water flowed through the designs in the rock. The images made no sense; they were a series of swirls and spirals. Flowing lines and rippling patterns. Alek reached out, his hand slowly meeting the smooth stone. As it did, power exploded into his body, sending a shockwave into the air around him.

Alek collapsed to his knees on the edge of the plateau, feeling wave after wave of electricity flow into the air around him. Snow spiralled through the air, and the trees in the valley below shook from the force of the power pulsing from the cave walls into Alek's body.

Thunder rumbled loudly as waves of sleet blanketed the landscape in a sea of white. He shook as energy flowed through him, his veins flooded with ice. He could feel every fibre of his being, every part of his body thrumming with power. His heartbeat echoed in his ears, every breath he took awakening that force, inviting it to pump through his body, to fill his blood.

Gradually the waves of power pulsing from the cave wall subsided, and the ebb and flow of energy coursing through Alek's body began to subside, slowly drawing deeper into his body. Dwindling to a dull pulse, reminding him of its presence.

Alek opened his eyes, feeling tears run down his cheeks as he blinked. His vision was sharper than it had ever been. He could clearly see individual leaves on the trees far below, even with the swirling snow. His nostrils flared, picking up the scent of stone and crisp air that had gone unnoticed before. Every sense he had was heightened. He looked down at his arms and marvelled as he saw that he had completely healed from his encounter with the sprites.

Suddenly, an achingly familiar voice echoed in his ears. 'Alek ...'

Alek spun around, shocking himself with the ease of his movements. His mouth went dry and his heart skipped a beat, for standing before him, his form slightly translucent, was his brother.

'Jaxtyn!' Alek shouted, tears streaming down his face. Memories of stories in bed, of days spent playing in the sun rushed over him, memories he had long since buried. Emotions swirled through Alek's body as his eyes drank in every inch of his brother's face, a sight he never thought he would see again.

Jaxtyn grinned as Alek unfroze and rushed to throw himself into his brother's arms; however, he met nothing but air as he reached his brother's glowing figure.

'I'm not actually here, buddy,' Jaxtyn said fondly, his crooked smile causing Alek's breath to catch. 'I mean, I was here, long ago. I left this memory of myself for you in case you were to ever find your way here.'

'You mean, you didn't leave me on purpose?' Alek gasped, his voice choked. 'When you vanished, it wasn't because you wanted to get away from me and Mum?'

Jaxtyn frowned, regret in his dark eyes. 'No, Alek, of course not. I love you! And I love Mum. I never meant to leave you forever. And my decision to leave had nothing to do with anything you or Mum did.'

Alek pressed his mouth into a thin line, exhaling loudly through his nose, feeling the power in him roil as anger formed in his chest.

'Then where were you?!' he shouted. 'Where were you, Jaxtyn? I needed you, and you weren't there! Mum needed you! I was so lost. I am lost. I need you!'

Overwhelmed with emotion, Alek threw his hands into the air, not even noticing the snow that lifted from the ground, spiralling angrily around him.

'Woah, Alek,' Jaxtyn said softly, holding his hands up in front of him. 'I am so, so sorry. Truly, I am. I didn't mean to hurt you, and like I said before, I never meant to leave you forever.'

Alek glared at his brother—or, rather, the ghostly form that was his brother. He noticed the wrinkles around Jaxtyn's eyes, the lines surrounding his mouth, the longer hair. This wasn't the teenage brother that had vanished into the night, leaving Alek alone and wandering what he did wrong. This was a mature version of his brother. Content with his decision to leave, and asking Alek to listen.

Alek sighed, stalking to the edge of the plateau and sinking to the ground, dangling his legs over the edge.

'Okay, so tell me,' Alek commanded. 'Why did you leave?'

'The same reason you did,' Jaxtyn said softly, walking over to sit next to his little brother. 'This world needed me, and I came.' Alek snorted. 'That's ridiculous. Ash never mentioned anyone else with supposed magic being called from our world in the last decade.'

'Alek,' Jaxtyn paused, searching for the right words. 'I'd been here for years myself when I found this cave and left my power here. And I don't even know how long it's been between that time and you finding this place.'

Jaxtyn gazed down at the valley below, making out the tree houses and small torches scattered throughout the forest. 'I'll tell you one thing—when I was last here, no one lived in that valley.'

Dread filled Alek's body. 'But … the students have lived in this valley for generations. You've barely been gone eleven years!'

Jaxtyn shrugged. 'Time works differently here, Alek.'

Alek shuddered, replaying his brother's words over in his head. 'Wait … you said you left your power here?'

Jaxtyn chuckled. 'Yes. I mean, part of it.' Alek's brother turned to look at him, emotion brimming in his eyes. 'I fell in love, Alek. That's why I stayed. I met a girl off the coast of Karithia, a town on the western shore of Balathor, and I fell head over heels.'

Alek searched his brother's face as his eyes looked into the distance, peering into memories Alek couldn't see.

'She was a handful, wanted nothing to do with me at first.' Jaxtyn smiled a dorky smile. 'But I won her over.' He turned to Alek, a sparkle in his eye. 'You're an uncle now. Twins. A boy and a girl.'

Alek gasped. 'Wait, what?'

Jaxtyn smiled, happiness radiating off him. 'Yep! The girl is Kylie, and the boy is named Alexander, after my brother who I left behind.'

Tears welled in the corner of Alek's eyes once more. 'I never thought … I mean, I thought you were dead.'

Jaxtyn smiled lovingly down at his brother. 'Like I said, I never meant to leave you. It's just that I found a new family here. One that I couldn't walk away from. And once my role here was fulfilled, I stored a portion of my power in this cave, along with this part of myself. Just in case, one day, a descendant of mine was called to protect this world again. I never dreamed it would be you.'

Alek drew his knees up to his chest. 'I don't know if I can do it.'

Jaxtyn frowned. 'Do what?'

'Any of it!' Alek exclaimed dramatically. 'I don't have any powers. I'm not brave like you. I'm never going to find a girl to fall in love with and live happily ever after.'

His brother pulled a face. 'Your magic issue is probably partly my fault. The key to our power is that it is passed down through generations, but I stored most of my power here, so here it has remained. Until you just claimed it.'

Alek shivered, remembering the surge of energy that had overwhelmed him when he touched the cave wall. In fact, he could still feel the power inside him, almost a tangible presence within his body.

Jaxtyn cocked his head, staring into his brother's eyes. 'And you're right, Alek. you aren't going to find a girl to fall in love with.'

'Excuse me?!' Alek snapped. 'I thought you were supposed to be helping me. Not making me more depressed.'

Jaxtyn smiled. 'You aren't going to find a girl to fall in love with because you are going to fall in love with a soul. It doesn't matter if it's a girl, a boy, an elf, or anything in between!' Jaxtyn paused, his eyes glimmering. 'I do have a hunch it's not going to be a girl, though.'

Alek's heart lurched and then skipped a beat. Heat pulsed through his skin as he awkwardly avoided eye contact with his older brother. 'I—I don't know what you're talking about,' he mumbled awkwardly.

Jaxtyn threw his head back and laughed. 'Alek, buddy, you're gay. I've known since you were little, whether you want to accept it or not. You want my advice? Don't live your life fighting it and being miserable. There's a whole world out there. Find yourself someone to love and be happy!' Jaxtyn narrowed his eyes at Alek. 'Unless you have already found someone, but you're refusing to admit you have.'

Alek winced as thoughts of Kai rose unbidden into his mind. 'Maybe.'

'Ha!' Jaxtyn said with a triumphant grin. 'I knew it. Don't fight it, little bro. Choose to be happy.'

'It's not just that!' Alek exclaimed, rising to his feet and balling his hands into his fists, 'I can't do it; I can't do any of it. It took me forever to learn to fight. I don't know how to use magic—'

'That's crap, Alek,' Jaxtyn said sternly, watching as his brother stalked back and forward across the plateau. 'I know you can feel the power flowing through you, and you absorbed my power when you touched the wall. Look around you, for crying out loud.'

Alek paused and glanced around, blinking in shock. The snow at his feet had risen into the air and floated, unmoving. Suspended by an invisible force in the air throughout the cave, glinting in the moonlight.

'I'm doing that?' Alek murmured disbelievingly.

Jaxtyn nodded. 'And there's a lot more you can do.'

He growled as the younger boy shook his head dubiously. 'What are you going to do, Alek? Wait for someone else to believe you can do it? Bullshit. *You* have to believe you can do it yourself. Otherwise, you're going to be in for a long and lonely road.'

Alek flinched at the harsh truth his brother spoke and looked up just in time to see his brother's image start to fade. 'Wait!' he gasped, his voice filled with panic. 'Don't leave me again!'

Jaxtyn smiled. 'I'm not really here, Alek. I've lived my adventure. It's time you embraced yours. Remember, trust in yourself. It doesn't matter if no one else does.'

Alek watched, tears rolling down his face as his brother's image slowly faded away into the moonlight. He took a deep breath and, for the first time in a long time, he felt whole. Indecision wasn't spiralling through his head; his mind was clear, and his future was laid out before him.

'Alek?' an uncertain voice echoed through the cave behind him.

Alek spun around just in time to see Kai move cautiously into the moonlight, gazing around in awe.

17

NAKED IN THE MOONLIGHT

Kai blinked, his wide eyes taking in as much of the cave as possible. Alek remained rooted to the spot, studying the other boy with his new, enhanced eyesight. He'd always noticed how achingly beautiful Kai was, but he hadn't appreciated it as much as he did right now, seeing him bathed in the moonlight.

Kai's face glowed. His pale blue eyes sparked a bright silver in the reflection of the snow outside. His dark hair curled deliciously around his temples; short stubble covered his chiselled jaw. Alek frowned in surprise as he realised that he could see exactly where the other boy had missed a bit of stubble shaving that morning, even from the distance they were standing apart.

'Alek, are you alright?' Kai asked worriedly, his full lips parting in concern as he moved further into the cave.

Alek still stood silent, watching as Kai's body flowed with liquid grace as he moved, barely disturbing the grass beneath his feet.

'What are you?' Alek whispered and winced, not meaning for the words to be spoken aloud.

Kai paused. 'Alek, are you okay? You look … different.' Alek frowned; Kai was avoiding his question.

'What are you?' Alek asked through clenched teeth.

Kai hesitated again, opening his mouth to speak, though nothing came out.

Minutes ticked by as the two boys stood on opposite sides of the cave, the pool reflecting the moon between them. Their bodies were motionless, Alek refusing to back down from his question.

His eyes slowly made their way up Kai's body and locked with the other boy's. Instantly, his heart beat faster and heat broke out across his cheeks, his mouth going dry. The other boy smirked as Alek licked his lips, refusing to be the first to break the silence.

Eventually, Kai sighed. 'You're definitely different. What the heck happened in here to do this to you?'

Alek shrugged, not backing down. 'Tell me who, or what, you are.'

Again, Kai hesitated, waging a silent war with himself. Alek waited patiently, silently drinking in the sight of the boy he had unknowingly grown so attached to over the past year.

'Okay, fine,' Kai said loudly, throwing his hands up in defeat. 'You really want to know why I wear this uniform all the damn time? Why I always have these stupid gloves on?' Kai blurted, raising one gloved hand in a rude gesture towards the other boy.

Alek cocked an eyebrow, a reluctant smile breaking over his face.

Suddenly, Kai grinned, narrowing his eyes. 'Why don't I show you? Turn around.'

Alek hesitated but remained silent, doing as he was told and turning around to gaze out over the valley. He suddenly heard a small splash and felt a ripple of energy brush against his skin.

Oh, now he gets into the water, Alek couldn't help but think with a soft huff. However, his sarcastic thoughts quickly gave way to curiosity and he turned back around, freezing to the spot as he tried to work out where to look first.

The first thing Alek noticed as he turned was the dark pile of clothes heaped among the glowing crystals. The second was Kai, standing in the pool, water lapping at his knees, clearly unclothed.

And at last, he finally understood the reasoning behind Kai's secrecy.

Alek's eyes roamed across the other boy's smooth skin. Soft blue light highlighted the curves of his muscles and his angular cheek bones. The rippling reflections from the water around his legs danced across his chiselled body.

What surprised Alek the most, however, was the dark ink spiralling across the boy's naked skin. A snake curved delicately around his arm, spiralling downwards, its diamond head resting on the back of Kai's hand. Alek followed the curves of the other boy's body, his eyes taking in every detail of the complex tattoos inked deftly onto his flesh.

He sensed Kai's gaze locked on him as his own eyes travelled down past Kai's stomach, pausing to take note of the other boy's growing excitement. Alek blushed, biting his lip as heat flooded his body, his thoughts becoming cloudy.

Slowly, Kai stepped further into the water. It now lapped irresistibly against his waist. As the water rose, Kai's tattoos began to spark, lighting up with a fiery golden glow, illuminating the body they were etched upon. Alek's skin prickled as he once again felt magic pulse against him, power radiating like heat from Kai's body, inviting him forward. Intoxicating him.

He closed his eyes and let it wash over him, feeling his newfound magic churning in his veins, adding to the fire already flooding through him. He breathed deeply through his nose and opened his eyes, marvelling at the golden light that now danced through the cave around him.

Kai smirked devilishly at Alek, reaching a waiting hand towards him. With a start, Alek's mind flashed back to his very first morning in this world. And his dream of the beautiful glowing boy, and the decision he had faced. Jaxtyn's words echoed in his head:

Choose to be happy.

Steeling himself, Alek released himself to the magic rolling off Kai in waves, enticing him into the pool. With a gasp, he felt his own power respond, surging out of his body as a wave of ecstasy washed over him. Through half-closed eyes, Alek realised Kai was still holding a hand towards him, waiting for him to make his choice. Not allowing himself to overthink, Alek made his decision.

Warm air washed over his skin as he stepped out of his clothes, glancing at Kai to see lust swimming in his eyes as he openly drank in every inch of Alek's body. Alek blushed, stepping into the pool and gasping as sheer energy washed over him, pulsing through him with every beat of his heart.

He had never felt so alive.

Kai's strong, tattooed hand wrapped around his own, sending electricity coursing through Alek's veins. He glanced down, feeling blood rush to his cheeks as he saw his own nakedness next to Kai's. An almost unbearable heat radiated from the other boy as he pulled Alek close, his glowing tattoos so intricately designed, Alek wondered how many hours had been spent crafting them.

Kai's breath whispered around his ear, his teeth grazing against the exposed skin, causing Alek to gasp softly. Alek felt Kai's hard body press against his back, holding him tight and drawing them both further into the pool. As they sank deeper into the water, Alek arched his head back, his heavy-lidded eyes noticing the vast full moon floating above them. He reached an arm skyward as if he could touch it. Crystal clear droplets of water rippled across his skin, sparkling like diamonds in the glowing blue and gold light.

Kai's lips continued to explore Alek's neck and shoulders as his hands lazily traced circles down the boy's abdomen. Alek gasped as Kai's tight grip wrapped around him, causing him to push back against the other boy, eliciting a sharp hiss in response.

Alek twisted, swirling effortlessly in the pool, the water supporting his every movement. His entire body tingled with electricity, his breathing heavy. He hooked a finger under the chin of the boy in front of him, wanting to look into his eyes.

Kai's sparkling blue stare locked with Alek's own and he paused, seeing for the first time in those eyes complete and open trust. No guarded secrets, no snarky comments. Just Kai.

Alek bent forward, and his breath hitched as his lips slowly brushed against the other boy's. He felt Kai stiffen against him as their lips locked, months of pent-up emotion finally being released.

Alek pulled back, opening his eyes in awe. Kai growled low in his throat and wrapped his arms tightly around Alek, holding their bodies tightly together as his lips crashed recklessly into the other boy's once more, passion exploding around them.

Letting the feeling carry him away, Alek tilted his head skywards as Kai's lips slowly moved down to his jaw, his tongue tracing spirals onto his skin. The kisses were soft but grew increasingly more deliberate as their bodies intertwined and Alek let go, losing himself in the moonlight.

****

Alek allowed Kai to gently pull him out of the warm water and onto the velvety grass surrounding the pool, softly brushing his lips against Alek's. He wrapped his arms around the boy and held him close, breathing quietly. Kai's glowing tattoos slowly faded back to black now that they had crawled out of the water, leaving behind only the soft blue light from the crystals around them.

Alek's magic dwindled, replaced by a tingling feeling throughout his body. He turned to look at Kai, a smile breaking across his face.

'What're you grinning about?' Kai chuckled, pushing blonde hair out of Alek's eyes.

'I feel happy,' Alek said, searching his mind for more words to describe how he felt. 'For the first time in a long time.' He broke into a laugh, his body shaking.

Kai chuckled, shaking his head as he pulled the boy closer into a tight hug.

Alek hummed, contentedly wrapped in the other boys' strong arms, laying side by side, their legs skimming the surface of the water. His fingers roamed Kai's body, slowly tracing a tattoo of a stag inked onto Kai's left thigh.

The craftmanship of the tattoo was impeccable. Alek could make out individual tufts of fur that covered the beast's body, from its hooved feet to the tip of its head. Elegant antlers sprouted from the deer's head, the right of which spread upwards above Kai's hips and onto the taut skin covering his abs, ending just below his belly button.

As Alek traced the antler, his fingers brushed dangerously close to Kai's waist, and he smirked as he saw the boy twitch and tense at the proximity of his wandering fingers.

'Tease,' Kai breathed softly, his arms tightening around Alek.

Alek chuckled. 'You know,' he began thoughtfully, 'you never answered my question. What are you?'

Alek tilted his head back to see shadows flicker through Kai's piercing eyes.

Kai frowned slightly, his face glowing in the soft, pre-dawn light. 'Let me show you.'

Kai unwrapped himself from Alek, sending droplets of crystal water showering onto the soft grass as he rose to his feet. Once again, Alek was shocked at his newfound senses, his eyes tracking Kai's every movement, watching his muscles tense and move beneath his pale skin.

Kai took a step back from Alek, the full extent of his tattoos on display, wrapping around his naked body from head to toe. 'Are you ready?' he asked, running his hand through his dark hair. Alek rolled his eyes. 'Get on with it and stop showing off.'

Kai snorted and closed his eyes, turning so his back faced the blonde boy, a deep breath causing his shoulders to rise and fall. Inked across the top of Kai's shoulders, wings outstretched, was an elaborately-crafted owl. Each individual feather lay highlighted against the boy's pale skin, and it was the only tattoo across Kai's muscular back. A pale scar shone just beneath the inked image, the blemish marring Kai's otherwise smooth, alabaster skin.

Alek felt the now-familiar sensation of magic pulsing against him as it poured out of Kai's body. He watched in fascination as the other boy gasped in pleasure, goose bumps erupting across his inked skin as magic coursed through his veins.

Alek's eyes widened in surprise as the owl etched upon the other boy's shoulders suddenly rippled, the ink coming alive as Kai rapidly shrunk, feathers erupting across his body. Within seconds, a large, white owl stood in Kai's place, flapping its wings as it turned and locked Alek in its intense yellow gaze.

Alek's jaw dropped as recognised the owl that had perched outside his cabin earlier that night.

'You … you can turn into animals?' Alek said slowly, the words feeling strange as they rolled off his tongue. He frowned. 'And you were spying on me earlier?'

The owl, Kai, blinked at him, ruffling its feathers in indignation.

Alek rolled his eyes. 'Okay, you've proven your point. I've seen what you can do, and I feel stupid talking to a bird, so you can change back now.'

Once again, Alek felt magic brush against him and watched in awe as the owl grew in size, its feathers growing flat and becoming skin. Moments later, the rush of magic subsided and Kai was once again standing in the rippling light, the owl tattoo settling into place on his shoulders.

'You can turn into animals?' Alek asked again as Kai settled down next to him, their shoulders brushing as he dangled his feet in the water.

Kai smiled crookedly. 'I'm a shifter. And I can't just turn into animals; I can only turn into the images I have tattooed on me.'

Alek's eyes roamed across Kai's body, this time taking in the multitude of animals inked onto his skin, from a moth on the back of his left hand to a tiger rippling down the side of his rib cage.

'You can turn into all of these?' Alek whispered, his eyes tracing the image of a bear that stretched down the front of Kai's leg.

Kai nodded. 'Only these animals, though.'

'How?' Alek asked quietly.

Kai hesitated, searching for the words. 'My people,' he began, stumbling slightly, 'were filled with magic. But we had no way of harnessing our magic, no way for it to manifest into something physical. But it was there, churning beneath our skin. I've heard stories of how it drove many of us mad, being unable to release the power, to have it building up inside of you.'

Alek nodded, his mind flashing back to what it had felt like to have his own magic roiling in his veins, begging for release. He couldn't imagine what it would be like to constantly live with that feeling beneath the surface of his skin.

'My elders communed with the ancient spirits of times past, begging for some sort of release,' Kai continued, his eyes far away, lost within a distant memory. 'And so, the elders were gifted with the ability to craft an outlet for the magic to manifest itself. Our tattoos. They started small— moths, snakes.' Kai smiled, holding up both his arms etched with those animals. 'And eventually moved on to bigger creatures. Animals we could use to defend ourselves against any enemies.'

Alek glanced down at the tiger on Kai's ribs, its jaws open in a vicious snarl. He shivered, imagining Kai's beautiful face shifting to bear those deadly fangs.

'The bigger animals take more energy, more power. Some animals are too big for us to shift into. Many died trying, searching for power ...' Kai trailed away softly.

Alek frowned. 'So where is your family? Your people?'

Kai visibly tensed beside Alek, drawing his knees up to his chest and wrapping his arms around himself. 'Gone,' he said quietly. 'Everyone magical was hunted down long ago, leaving behind an empty, broken world, devoid of power.'

Alek frowned. Sensing the bitterness in Kai's voice, he decided not to press the subject. The two sat in silence, watching as the sun began to rise, dull light filtering through swollen snow clouds.

'Now you know what I am,' Kai said suddenly, his sullen mood seemingly gone. 'What exactly are you?'

Alek snorted. 'I have no idea anymore. Ash told me, Sarah, and Benny that we were descendants of some sort of four magical people. That we can control the elements.'

Something dark flashed through Kai's eyes, and he hesitated before speaking, choosing his next words carefully. 'And do you believe her?'

'I'm not sure.' Alek frowned. 'I mean, part of me didn't until tonight. But now I think I do. I mean, I've seen Benny do some weird stuff with fire, and I did the snow thing before ... so maybe my magic is water?'

He turned to see Kai gazing into the distance, his shoulders tensed and a strange expression on his face.

'What's wrong?' Alek asked worriedly, wondering if he had said something wrong.

'Nothing,' Kai said quickly, his expression quickly becoming normal. 'Whatever you are, that blast of magic you sent out earlier tonight will be felt across this whole world.' He cocked his head to the side, dark hair flopping over his forehead. 'You and your friends must be very powerful if you can release that much energy into the sky and still be conscious.'

Alek shifted uncomfortably. 'I didn't know what I was doing, though.'

'All the more reason why you are more powerful than you think,' Kai muttered.

'More powerful than you?' Alek said teasingly, shoving Kai's shoulder.

The other boy barked with laughter. 'You wish. I've been one of the only magical people left in this world for years. Although, thanks to your blast of magic and the shadows whispering the past few months, I would say we are not alone anymore.'

Alek sighed. Although he was glad that he had magic, everything had just become more complicated. How was he going to tell his friends about his new abilities? He glanced at Kai out of the corner of his eye. Or tell them about the boy lying next to him, for that matter? Benny was not going to take it well. 'Could you train me?' Alek asked, searching Kai's face for reassurance. 'To use magic, I mean.'

'Of course,' Kai said, surprised. 'But don't you want to train with your friends?'

Alek shook his head. 'I don't trust Ash. There's something not entirely human about her.'

Kai laughed. 'And yet you trust the guy who can turn into animals.'

'Yes,' Alek replied indignantly. 'Yes, I do.'

Kai hesitated.

'What's wrong?' Alek asked.

'Nothing, nothing,' Kai said, forcing a smile onto his face. 'I would be honoured to teach you. We'll start with your breathing.' Kai winked at Alek, a smirk tugging at his full lips.

Alek rolled his eyes. 'Great. Can't wait.' He turned his attention away from Kai as the two boys settled into a comfortable silence.

Sunlight broke through the clouds above them, bathing the two boys in warm light. Kai turned his head upwards, sighing as he settled onto his back, relishing in the morning warmth.

'It's a miracle you found this place,' he murmured quietly, his eyes closed contentedly. 'Places of power like this used to exist all over the world when I was younger. I thought they had all been destroyed.'

Alek frowned. 'Is that why your tattoos glow in the water? Or why I can finally feel my magic?'

Kai squinted open an eye, glancing at Alek. 'Yeah, caves like this are a kind of convergence of magical energy. All sorts of rituals used to be performed at places much like this.'

'Rituals such as getting magical tattoos inked onto your skin?' Alek asked curiously.

Kai was quiet as he lay with his eyes closed, his words soft when he finally spoke. 'Yeah. Rituals like that.'

Sighing deeply, Kai settled deeper into the soft grass, his long body stretched out in the sun and his hands wrapped comfortably behind his head.

Alek, however, jumped to his feet, splashing Kai with water and causing him to curse in indignation. 'We're going to be late for training!'

Alek stepped to the edge of the cave and glanced down to the valley below, his heightened eyesight picking out the students already beginning their morning run. Suddenly, strong arms wrapped around him from behind and heat encased him as he felt Kai's skin press against his own, his lips brushing irresistibly against his neck.

'Don't worry about it,' Kai said slowly, his voice dripping with desire as his hands roamed across Alek's chest. 'It won't hurt us to skip a day of training. I can think of lots of other fun things we could be doing.'

Alek bit his lip as he felt his body reacting to Kai's touch. He spun around, gasping at the other boy's proximity.

Kai glanced down between their bodies, grinning. 'It looks like you want to stay here as much as I do.'

Alek shook his head. 'You're an idiot,' he said with a smile as he pushed Kai hard, sending both of them tumbling onto the soft grass.

18

PRACTICE MAKES PERFECT

Alek took a deep breath of the cold air as he strode confidently through the valley. The world around him felt new, full of crisp detail he had never noticed before. Every one of his senses had been heightened since his powers had awoken the night before last, the magic fusing with his body. He felt awake, as if a veil had been lifted from his senses, allowing him to see the world in startling clarity.

He could hear the tiny scratches overhead as squirrels raced through the tree branches. The smell of the rotting leaves buried underneath a thick layer of morning snow wafted upwards with every step he took. His eyesight was incredible, even now. As he focused on the fresh layer of snow blanketing the ground, he could make out the individual icy flakes glistening in the sunlight.

The first day had been almost overwhelming. The slightest noise that would have previously gone unnoticed caused him to jump, eliciting a string of laughter from Kai.

'Welcome to my life,' the shifter had said, grinning. 'This is what I see and hear every day.'

Alek rolled his eyes as he pushed through the last of the forest branches, shivering as cold snow shook loose from the foliage, running over his shoulders. Before him, the lake stretched to the foothills of the surrounding mountains, the huge waterfall roaring in the distance.

Peace washed over Alek as he took a moment to revel in the comfort the body of water had given him the last few months. Although he would never admit it to anyone, the lake had become a safe haven for him. The training sessions with Kai had been the one thing he looked forward to in those tumultuous first few weeks in Aranasmin. The water that gently lapped against the sandy shore had soothed his anxious thoughts, making his time in the valley bearable.

I probably liked being by the lake so much because some small, buried part of me knew that water was the centre of my magic, he thought with a start, recalling the time he swam the distance of the lake without taking a single breath.

Kai had been in shock, trying to bring it up with him, but he had been too wrapped up in his own thoughts to notice the signs that were right in front of him the whole time. Alek smiled at himself ruefully as he stepped onto the soft sand, noticing for the first time the lone figure waiting for him further along the shore.

Heat rushed to his face, painting his skin scarlet as his acute eyesight studied Kai from behind. Kai stood casually, his weight shifted to one side, but Alek knew that the stance was deceptive. Kai was ready to snap into action in a heartbeat. His dark, wavy hair was tousled from the night's sleep, curling around the nape of his neck.

Alek drank in the well-defined muscles of the boy's back, visible through his uniform. The image of Kai's tattoos flashed into his mind as he pictured the boy's body beneath his skin-tight clothes. His breath hitched as the memories of the previous day washed over him. The two boys had spent their entire day up in the mountains on the hidden plateau with the mystical pool.

The prospect of finally having magic and learning to harness it had been pushed to the back of his mind yesterday after the sudden evolution of the relationship between him and Kai. They had spent the day lounging together in the magical warmth cast by the pool, enjoying each other's company and pretending the valley below didn't exist.

But today, there was only one thing on Alek's mind: magic. He could finally feel it, a steady thrum deep inside his chest, almost like a second heartbeat. After months of being jealous of Sarah and Benny's abilities, his worries about being one of The Four were long gone. Ash had been right all along.

'Are you just going to stand there and stare at my butt all day?' Kai asked softly, not raising his voice despite the distance between them, knowing full well Alek would be able to hear him with his newly-developed senses.

Alek's jaw dropped open in indignation. 'I was *not* looking at your butt!' he gasped. However, his eyes had now subconsciously dipped down the boy's spine, making a liar out of him.

Kai smirked, turning around as the morning sun shone across his face. Alek tried to ignore how insanely handsome the shifter was as he quickly loped across the sand, pulling Kai in for a tight hug.

'Good morning,' Alek whispered, his face squished into Kai's chest.

The body beneath him shook as Kai chuckled, planting a tender kiss on Alek's forehead. 'Morning, water boy.'

Alek pulled back from the embrace, throwing Kai's arms down in exasperation. 'Water boy? Really?'

'Yup.' Kai nodded wisely, struggling to hide the smile that shone in his pale eyes. 'Now show me what you got,' he challenged, gesturing towards the lake beside them.

'Here?' Alek gulped, glancing around at the surrounding trees. 'Anyone could see, though!'

'Oh, please. Everyone's on the morning run and then in classes, and no one comes to the lake in the middle of winter anyway.' Kai crossed his arms smugly. 'Besides, you've barely used your magic. I don't think you're going to be making a giant spectacle of your abilities anytime soon, whether you want to or not.'

Alek grumbled to himself as he shoved past Kai, stepping up to the edge of the lake. Taking a deep breath, he closed his eyes, focusing on the gentle lapping of the waves around him. As the sound and smell of the water filled his senses, everything else faded away, the small kernel of power growing inside him.

Alek gasped as it burst into his veins, washing like a cooling swell under his skin. Pleasure rolled over him, making him shiver as goosebumps rippled down his spine. Gritting his teeth, Alek pushed past the intense feeling of bliss, reaching for the power flowing back and forth gently within him.

'Good, Alek,' Kai praised quietly. 'Now push that magic outward through your skin and into the air, focusing on what you want it to do once it's free.'

Alek's whole body tensed with effort as he grappled with the steady wave of magic that gently rolled from the tips of his toes to the top of his head and back again. A gasp escaped his mouth as the power suddenly swelled, bursting through his skin and into the crisp air around him.

Alek's entire body shook involuntarily as he desperately directed the invisible power towards the water in front of him, willing the liquid to rise into the air. His eyes widened in shock as ripples formed on the lake's surface, the water bubbling as his magic swirled into its depths. Clenching his teeth, Alek doubled his efforts, his arms reaching out towards the churning lake and commanding it to rise, envisioning a large wave.

To his chagrin, a small bubble of water suddenly shot skywards out of the agitated swell, making him jump in surprise. With a snap, Alek's magic rushed back into his body, shrinking in on itself as it settled once again at his core. His legs shook as energy rushed from his limbs, the toll for using his magic heavier than he had expected. A splash suddenly distracted him, and he winced as his small water bubble fell back from the sky, returning to the now still lake.

Kai whistled from behind him. 'Not quite the magnificent show of power you were expecting, hey, Alek?'

Embarrassment washed over him as he sank to his knees, wincing at the weariness that tugged on his eyelids. He'd known it would be hard learning to manipulate his magic, but he hadn't realised just how draining it would be as well.

And all I did was make a little splash, he thought dejectedly. *How is that supposed to be useful for anyone?*

Kai must have sensed his disappointment, because he continued in a much more reassuring tone, 'That was really quite good for your first time.'

'Not good enough, though,' Alek huffed. 'Sarah and Benny have been practising for months. How am I ever going to catch up to them?'

Kai was quiet for a moment as he stood patiently behind Alek, letting him wallow in his self-pity. Suddenly, strong hands wrapped under his arms, hauling him to his feet.

'Come with me,' Kai ordered. 'I have an idea.'

Alek turned with a frown, catching the twinkle in the other boy's icy eyes. 'This better be worth it,' he groaned, allowing himself to be led further along the lake shore.

'Shhh,' Kai reprimanded, shaking his head as he grabbed Alek's hand, tugging him quickly into the tree line. 'Just follow me.'

****

Half an hour later, the two boys stepped out of the narrow tunnel and onto the plateau where the magical pool sat, projecting its comforting warmth. Alek's blood churned as memories of the other night flashed through his mind, the feeling of Kai's skin on his as the full moon floated above them.

Stop it! he reprimanded himself. *You need to focus.*

'The pool magnifies your power, feeding your energy,' Kai explained, stepping onto the soft grass. 'You won't feel as drained if we practise here. Plus, you'll find it easier to actually manipulate your magic with the energy the pool gives.'

Alek stepped forward, moving past Kai as he gazed at the crystal-clear water sheltered amongst the grass and crystals. The pool seemed bottomless in its centre as he stared into the depths, the surface glassy and undisturbed. The crystals that sprouted within the soft grass glowed faintly in the morning sun, barely a ghost of how beautiful he knew they were once night fell.

With a start, he realised Kai was right. The magic that he'd had to force out of his body by the lake was now flowing around him uninhibited, called forth by the mystical water in front of him. He could feel the waves of power steadily surging around him, pleasure washing across his skin.

'Why is it so much easier here?' Alek asked in shock, the newfound strength flowing through him causing him to feel like a stranger in his own skin.

Kai shrugged, stepping closer to the pool. 'I don't really know. Places like this are special, but they should help you strengthen your connection to your magic faster. Can you feel it? Flowing around you?'

Alek nodded. His magic was almost tangible, rippling comfortingly across his skin, between his fingers.

'Good,' Kai grinned. Reaching down, he tugged off his boots.

Alek's heartbeat accelerated as Kai's shirt and pants soon followed, dropped in a messy pile on the grass, leaving little to Alek's imagination as the inked boy stood before him clad in only his underwear.

Alek greedily drank in Kai's toned body, the reflection of the pool rippling across his exposed skin. The tattoos were dark against the pale flesh, seeming to ripple over the defined muscles as Kai took a step forward.

An unfamiliar presence brushed against Alek's magic, sending a thrill down his spine as Kai stepped into the shallow water. He watched in awe as once again the dark ink began to glow a brilliant gold colour, spreading like a wave from where his feet touched the water. Within seconds, the shifter stood, illuminated before Alek, the glow magnifying Kai's already stunning features.

'Can you feel me?' Kai purred softly. 'My magic?'

With a start, realisation washed over Alek. The presence brushing against his own swirling magic was Kai. He had felt it briefly the other night but hadn't realised entirely what it was. It felt so different from his own steady, cooling power.

It was cold, powerful. It reminded him of ice and snow, of shadowy forests and crisp, early morning air. Kai's magic was dangerous and so much stronger than his. As it tangled with Alek's own swelling power, he felt insignificant in comparison.

Water splashed across Alek's face, making him gasp as he was snapped from his thoughts.

Kai was staring at him, an insufferable smirk tugging at his lips. 'Are you going to stand there all day or are you going to get in the water and train?' he asked innocently.

Alek's eyes narrowed as he saw Kai's abdominal muscles tense. An incessant nudge from Kai's magic urged Alek forwards and into the pool.

Rolling his eyes, Alek made short work of undressing, stepping into the soothing crystal water that was bathed in the golden glow from Kai's tattoos. Careful to stay in the shallower end of the pool, Alek paused when the water lapped around his waist, the magic swirling in the air around him making him slightly dizzy.

'Now.' Kai grinned widely. 'Make me wet.'

Alek snorted loudly, causing Kai's cheeky smile to grow as he stood in the shallows, crouched and ready.

Doing his best to ignore the half-naked boy before him, Alek closed his eyes, steadying his breathing as he focused on the power surging around him. Placing his hands on the glassy surface of the pool, he envisioned a wave rising up to smother Kai.

To his surprise, his magic responded instantly, the glowing water in front of him surging skywards in a stream, spearing towards the other boy. Kai deftly stepped sidewards, dodging the sudden attack. Alek watched, slightly disappointed as the spurt of water splashed harmlessly against the cave wall.

'See?' Kai declared. 'Wasn't that easier?'

Emboldened by the strength the magical pool had given him, Alek threw his arm forwards, revelling in the way his magic reacted, instantly doing his bidding. Water sprayed from the surface of the pool, splashing against the stones behind Kai as the shifter once again ducked and weaved with startling speed.

Frowning in frustration, Alek threw his hands upwards, pumping his energy into the air around him. He harnessed the magic swirling around him, arms shaking as every muscle in his body tensed. A roar filled the cave as a wall of water rose from the pool, blasting towards Kai.

Kai's eyes widened as the water pummelled him, the force washing him off his feet. Guilt instantly washed over Alek and he lost the connection to his magic, causing the wave to collapse onto the grass, dropping Kai along with it. Alek climbed out of the pool, rushing over to where Kai lay.

His heart beat faster in panic as he inspected the soaked boy, noticing the tattoos only glowing in small patches where droplets of the magical water ran in rivulets over his skin. Kai was lying face down, his face pressed against the grass. Desperately, Alek hauled him over, stretching the boy out on his back.

'Kai! Kai, are you okay?' He held the boy's face in his hands, searching for a sign the shifter could hear him.

Kai wheezed loudly, laughter bubbling from his lungs as his whole body shook. Alek frowned, dropping the boy's head back onto the soaked grass.

'You should have heard how panicked you were!' Kai gasped, forcing words out in between his laughter.

'That's not funny!' Alek pouted, punching Kai's shoulder. 'I thought I hurt you!'

'It's going to take a lot more than a little water to hurt me, Alek,' Kai chuckled, his laughter subsiding. 'Although you definitely made me wet!'

Alek groaned, climbing to his feet. 'You're an idiot. Let's go again.'

He quickly stepped back into the water, gasping involuntarily as his magic once again surged around him. Turning, he watched as Kai climbed to his feet, his tattoos once again sparking to life as he entered the pool with a mischievous glint in his eye.

'Go on,' Alek groaned, knowing he was going to regret his next words. 'Say it.'

Kai's white teeth glimmered as he smiled broadly. 'You didn't even offer me mouth-to-mouth?'

Alek rolled his eyes as Kai spread his arms wide, gesturing for him to step closer.

'It's the least you could do after trying to drown me,' Kai said.

With a scowl, Alek flicked his arm up, his magic surging forwards as water sprayed across the cave, the droplets pelting harshly into Kai's exposed skin. Alek grinned smugly as Kai shouted in indignation, examining the red marks that had appeared on his chest.

This was going to be more enjoyable than he thought.

19

BLOOD-STAINED SNOW

A week later, Alek was slowly woken from his sleep by soft snores coming from the bed next to him. The mattress shifted and a tattooed arm wrapped around his chest, pulling him close to the warm body buried within the blankets. His sleep-muddled thoughts swirled as Alek remembered training late last night with Kai and then suggesting that they sleep together in his tree house.

He was advancing quickly with his magic. He could easily manipulate water and ice now, and his stamina was growing exponentially by the day. It was a lot more challenging to use his magic outside the hidden cave above the waterfall, but he was quickly getting the hang of it.

Alek sighed, squirming slightly against the confining body beside him as his thoughts roamed. The last few days had been bliss. He woke every day with newfound energy and excitement for his training sessions with Kai.

The inked boy teased him mercilessly as he slowly grappled with the extent of his magic and the limits to which his power extended.

I still don't know why he bothers with me when he is clearly so much better than me in every way, Alek thought, closing his eyes and shifting to a more comfortable position. *I just don't get why he even has any interest in me.*

'Because,' a sleep-addled voice mumbled from the cocoon of blankets beside him, 'you challenge me.'

It took Alek a moment to realise that Kai wasn't just sleep talking and that Alek had said his thoughts out loud.

'At first, you intrigued me,' Kai continued, his voice dipping to a whisper as sleep threatened to drag him back into unconsciousness. 'You were obviously so competent and capable, yet you doubted yourself relentlessly. It made me want to know everything about you, to crawl inside your brain and understand why you couldn't see what I could.

'I think my magic sensed yours even though it was buried so far within you at first, and that pull was what first attracted me to you. Then I got to know you, in all your stubbornness and self-doubt. You're a leader, Alek. People listen to you when you talk. They like you and want to follow you. Regardless of how anxious and unsure you are on the inside. I want you to know that, to see yourself from my eyes.' Kai's arms tightened around Alek as he spoke.

'Plus,' Kai purred, his lips brushing against Alek's ear, 'you look ridiculously good naked.'

Alek snorted as his stomach twisted at the tattooed boy's words. He found it hard to fathom the faith Kai had in him and his abilities. Was he really that capable? *Maybe it's time to stop doubting and start believing,* Alek thought lazily as snores once again escaped from the blankets beside him. Alek's eyes grew heavy as his breathing deepened, giving way to a peaceful sleep, Kai's words echoing in his ears.

****

The golden morning light was flooding into the tree house, warming the air when he was abruptly torn from his dreams by Sarah's voice calling his name.

'Alek, are you awake? Can I come in?'

Alek immediately panicked, noticing the arm wrapped around his waist and the naked body glowing in the sunlight beside him.

Guilt rolled over him as he realised that he had barely spoken a word to either Sarah or Benny in the last week. All his time had been spent with Kai, either training or … Alek's thoughts trailed off, heat flooding his cheeks.

'Uhhhh, one second!' he yelled back, roughly shaking Kai's shoulder.

Kai mumbled something incoherently and shoved Alek away, pulling the pillow up over his wildly messy bed hair, burying his face. Alek hissed in exasperation and shoved Kai hard, sending him rolling off the side of the bed.

'Alek, what the hell!' Kai growled, climbing to his feet, the sun silhouetting his muscled body.

'Alek? Are you alone in there? Or is someone with you?' Sarah called again.

Kai froze, panic flashing across his face as he glanced down to see his tattooed skin exposed.

'Quick,' Alek hissed quietly. 'Get in the closet!'

'Excuse me?!' Kai said incredulously as Alek pushed and shoved the other boy into his wardrobe, slamming the doors closed behind him.

'It's you who needs to get *out* of the closet,' Kai mumbled grumpily from behind the closed doors.

Alek snorted, but apprehension rolled over him. Kai was right. He would have to come clean to his friends eventually. But not now. He wanted to enjoy this newfound happiness for as long as he could.

He just had time to tug on some underwear when Sarah grew tired with waiting and swung gracefully into the room, a small gust of wind blowing through Alek's hair as he stepped awkwardly in front of the closet.

'Hi, Sarah.' He forced a smile onto his face. 'What brings you here?'

Sarah frowned, looking around the room suspiciously. 'I could have sworn I heard someone else in here.'

'Nope.' Alek laughed nervously. 'Just me. Talking to myself.'

Sarah cocked an eyebrow at him before seating herself on his bed, her gaze observing Kai's clothes and boots strewn across the room. Alek winced, hoping she would presume they were his, even though his feet were clearly not that big.

'How are you, Alek?' Sarah asked uncertainly. 'I miss you. Benny misses you—even though he's too stubborn to admit it.'

'I'm fine,' Alek said, feeling guilty again. 'I've just been so busy training. I didn't mean to ignore you both.'

'I thought we moved past this after the party, Alek,' Sarah said sadly. 'You ignored us for so long when we got here. You were so upset about my decision to stay, and Benny and I felt so bad. But once you started training with Kai, you changed. You were more confident; you seemed happier.' She paused, looking at her friend. 'You seem happier now, and you look different, somehow.'

Alek hesitated. He should tell her about his powers, about Kai. But no. Not yet.

'I am happy, Sarah. I am. I mean it when I say that I didn't mean to become distant again. I just got so caught up with training. I'll find Benny and apologise to him. You're right; he's too stubborn to talk to me first.'

'Good,' Sarah said cheerfully, rising to her feet. 'Are you excited for The Hunt next week?'

'I don't really know what it's about, to be honest,' Alek said, feeling stupid.

Sarah rolled her eyes. 'Honestly, Alek, it's all anyone can talk about. It's on the night of the winter solstice and the new moon, so there is no danger of sprites.'

Alek shuddered as she mentioned the nasty creatures that had attacked him a week prior.

However, Sarah was too engrossed in her story to notice. 'There is a gold coin hidden somewhere in the valley by Ash, and the first student to retrieve the prize and bring it to her wins.' Her voice hitched slightly, and her eyes stared into the distance. 'The coin grants safe passage through the Portal Realm, allowing the winning student to travel anywhere in the world, going on an adventure. It's tradition, as the student that wins the gold coin is considered the best of the best and must go out and test their skills outside the safety of the valley.'

Alek studied his friend's face carefully as her lip trembled slightly, no doubt recalling the last time they had laid eyes on one of the golden coins.

Sarah closed her eyes and took a breath. When she opened them again, her face was set in a neutral expression and her eyes were dark. 'We all have a tag attached to our backs, and if a student attacks us and pulls off our tag, we're disqualified. No weapons allowed, just our own skills.' She looked at Alek expectantly.

'Yeah!' Alek said, feigning excitement. 'Sounds fun. I better see Benny, then. He wanted to be a team or something for it.'

'Yeah,' Sarah said, nodding. 'Apparently lots of students team up.'

'Why don't you team up with Benny and me then?' Alek asked.

Sarah hesitated. 'No, I think I want to do it alone.' Seeing Alek's confused look, she grinned. 'You boys will only slow me down.'

With that, she turned on her heel, stalking towards the cabin entrance. 'Oh, by the way, did you happen to feel the massive rush of magic that exploded through the valley the other night?'

'I, uh, what?' Alek stammered. 'I mean, no. No, I felt nothing.'

Sarah glanced over her shoulder, eyes narrowing as she looked at Alek and once again at the clothes strewn across the room. 'Whatever you say, Alek. Whatever you say.'

With a gust of wind, she turned and leapt gracefully onto a tree branch outside, quickly disappearing into the foliage.

Alek sighed and collapsed onto the bed with a groan, barely noticing as Kai opened the closet doors and walked over to sit next to him.

'Well, that wasn't awkward at all,' he said sarcastically as he started pulling on his clothes.

Alek didn't say anything, lost in his own thoughts.

'Come on,' Kai ordered, getting to his feet and offering a hand to Alek. 'We have a morning jog to get to, and you have to talk to Benjamin.'

'Great,' Alek muttered, allowing Kai to help him to his feet. He hurriedly dressed, and together, they left the tree house.

****

As Kai and Alek pushed their way out of the thick forest and onto the open field where the morning run began, they became aware of raised voices and a group of students bunched together. Alek recognised Benny's angry voice immediately and picked up his pace, his boots crunching through fresh snow.

'Why don't you prove it?' Lucien's nasty voice sneered as Alek pushed his way past the onlookers. What trouble was the bully stirring up now? For the most part, he had avoided Alek and his friends since their run-in at the party all those months ago.

Alek burst through the last line of students and stumbled into the middle of the argument. Benny and Lucien were staring each other down, barely controlled rage visible on both of their faces.

'Benny,' Alek began, positioning himself by his friends' side, 'what the hell is going on?'

Lucien let out a loud whistle. 'Look, your boyfriend's here to save you.'

'Enough!' Benny snarled, stepping forward. 'You have been nothing but mean to Alek since we came here. I'm sick of putting up with it, and I'm sick of listening to a brute like you continue to badmouth my friend in front of the whole school. I've kicked your butt once before, and I'm happy to do it again.'

Alek blinked, surprised that he was the cause of the argument.

'Benny,' he began in a placating tone, 'it's not worth it. Don't give him any of your attention; it doesn't matter.'

'No, Alek,' Benny hissed, heat rolling off him in waves. 'It matters to me.'

Alek began to panic as he felt a wave of wild magic brush against his own. He shivered. He was so used to the feel of his own magic, the calm pulsing as it rushed through his body—or the raw, icy power of Kai's magic. He had never felt Benny's before. It was untamed, lashing through the air around him, ready to explode at any second.

Lucien growled and took a step forward. As he did, Alek seized his chance. Letting loose a pulse of his own power, he turned the snow beneath Lucien's boot to hard ice. As the boy stepped forward, his foot hit the ice and slid awkwardly to the side. Lucien tumbled over with a strangled cry, hitting the ground hard.

Instantly, Alek felt Benny's power subside as amusement took over his roiling anger. Taking a breath to control the bit of magic he had let slip out, Alek looked up to see Kai nod at him from the crowd with a proud look on his face.

Lucien cursed loudly, hauling himself to his feet. 'You're dead! Both of you!' His eyes flashed between Alek and Benny.

'Is that right?' Alek said sarcastically, emboldened by his small victory over the bully. 'Not much of a threat coming from someone who can't even stand on their own two feet.'

Benny's eyes widened in surprise at Alek's confidence, and he placed a hand on his friend's shoulder in support.

'What is going on here?' Ash's commanding voice immediately disbanded the surrounding students, and her suspicious gaze washed over the three boys.

'Nothing, miss,' Lucien said politely, bowing his head. 'We just had a small disagreement, that's all.'

'Very well,' Ash sniffed, striding to the front of the group. 'Let's begin.'

As the students began to stretch, preparing for the jog, Lucien stalked past Alek and Benny.

'You're dead, both of you,' he sneered. 'You better watch your backs during The Hunt next week.'

Alek shivered as Lucien stomped away, joining a group of his friends on the other side of the field. He watched as the group of friends talked, stealing glances back at Alek and Benny. He needed to start watching his back if he was going to anger the other boy like that.

'Thank you,' Benny began awkwardly, avoiding eye contact with Alek. 'I know, it's been hard for you, being here, and you worry about your mum. I just don't want anyone else making it harder for you.'

'Ben,' Alek said softly. 'It's fine, man. You don't need to say anything. I'm good. We're good. I appreciate it.'

Benny nodded. 'I just feel like we've been distant again lately, and I don't want it to go back to how it was when we first got to Aranasmin. I know it's partly because of the magic thing, and you've found it difficult being here. But I miss you when you're not around, dude.'

Alek's heart dropped; he hadn't meant to make his friend feel so bad. Out of the corner of his eye, he noticed

Kai smile at him and turn and walk in the direction of the other students.

'I miss you too, Ben,' Alek began awkwardly. 'I'll work on it, I promise. Sometimes I just get a bit too caught up in my own head. I don't think about how I'm effecting everyone else.'

Benny smiled. 'What? Lost in your thoughts? That doesn't sound like you at all!'

Alek snorted, shoving his friend in the shoulder. 'You're an idiot. But that's why I like you. So next week for The Hunt, it's you and me. No one else. I got your back; you've got mine.'

'What about Kai?' Benny asked, a hint of snark in his voice.

Alek rolled his eyes. 'Kai's a big boy. He can look after himself.'

A blood-curdling scream broke across the valley. Alek winced as his sensitive ears rang from the noise. He sensed Kai's magic flare distantly in response to the screams and saw his head whip towards the forest behind them.

Alek followed Kai's gaze, and his heart skipped a beat. Splattered across the white snow in the shadows at the edge of the forest was bright crimson blood. Alek's eyes unwillingly trailed the gore further into the trees and he froze, his strengthened eyesight picking out the source of the blood.

Impaled on a snapped-off branch about a metre from the ground was a student. He was young, barely a teenager, with a messy shock of blonde hair. His throat was ripped open, the blood spattered down the front of his body. On her knees next to the body was a female student Alek didn't recognise. Her screams ripped from her throat, causing him to clench his teeth.

'What on earth—' Ash said, her voice cutting out as she saw the horror.

Alek began to shake, his vision blurring as his mind flashed back to Chris's death, replaying the moment the life drained from the boy's eyes. Hands roughly pulled him away from the bloody scene before them and he followed, lost in a haze of memories.

'Alek,' Kai's voice broke through his numb thoughts. 'Alek, are you okay?'

Shaking his head to clear his mind, Alek realised that the area was being cleared out by a handful of teachers. Sarah stood stiffly a few metres away, Benny holding her shoulders as he spoke to her softly.

'Do you want to go to them?' Kai asked quietly, following Alek's gaze.

Alek sighed. He should, but he would have nothing helpful to add. Sarah seemed to be okay. Her face was pale and her mouth was set slightly ajar, but she replied to whatever Benny was saying to her.

'No,' was Alek's answer. Kai relaxed him. He was being selfish. He should be with his friends to make sure they were okay, but the shock of the violent scene behind him was already fading as Kai wrapped a casual arm around his shoulders.

'Who would have done that?' Alek asked, breathing in the comforting smell of the boy next to him. It reminded him of wild places, of ice and power and paths untravelled.

'I think you'll find the question is what, not who, would have done that,' Kai said through gritted teeth.

Alek frowned, twisting his head to look at the other boy. 'You have an idea?'

Kai hesitated before answering, squeezing Alek's shoulders tighter. 'Maybe. I think your blast of magic the other night, along with you and your friends returning to this world, has awakened magic and creatures that have long remained dormant.'

The two walked in silence for a while longer before Alek asked. 'What do we do? I mean, if it's my fault he's dead …'

Kai froze, anger flashing in his eyes. 'It is definitely not your fault that boy is dead, Alek. You and your friends have powerful magic, and for that, you pose a threat. You're not safe. Your very being here threatens plans that have been in place for years and years, and you're all going to have targets on your backs. Besides, you can't control what your magic brings out of the shadows of the earth.'

'What the heck are you talking about?' Alek bit back, shocked at the other boy's sudden outburst. 'What plans?'

Kai sighed, pulling away from Alek and running a hand through his dark hair. 'I just mean with the Dark Warriors.' He hesitated, stumbling slightly over his words. 'I mean, they must have a plan, right? They're not just out burning towns and murdering people for no reason. They're looking for something.'

'So you're saying a Dark Warrior did this?' he asked uncertainly.

Kai let out a sharp bark of laughter. 'No, a Dark Warrior wouldn't have been so dramatic with a kill. I'm not sure what this is. But I'm going to find out.'

'What …?' Alek trailed off as Kai flashed him a grin and jogged off, the surrounding trees quickly swallowing him up.

With worry gnawing away at the back of his mind, Alek prepared to begin his morning run, hoping some exercise would clear his head.

'Alek, wait!' a voice called from behind him.

Alek groaned as he recognised the voice and he turned, slowing to a stop.

'Ash,' he said politely, dipping his head. 'Shouldn't you be dealing with … more important issues right now?' Alek watched as some of the other teachers in the valley carefully removed the dead student's body.

Ash hesitated, indecision flickering in her eyes as she opened her mouth to speak. 'I've been meaning to catch up with you for a few weeks now. How're you going? Your training seems to be paying off, judging from your results in your combat classes. You should be in good standing for The Hunt coming up.'

'Wait, wait, wait.' Alek's eyes widened. 'You're not actually going to go through with this hunt thing, are you? A student just got murdered and you don't even know how or why, and you're still going to allow everyone to run off in the middle of the night in search of a prize?'

Alek watched as the principal aggravatedly knotted and un-knotted a strand of her white hair around her finger, worry plastered across her face.

'Never has The Hunt been cancelled,' Ash said quietly, her voice shaky. 'Not once, Alek. I cannot be the first to break tradition. I can't fail.'

'Cancelling The Hunt wouldn't mean you've failed, though,' Alek replied reasonably. 'You'd be putting the safety of your students first.'

Ash sighed loudly, clenching her jaw as she continued to tug on her hair. 'Maybe you're right, and maybe you're wrong. All I know is that I will not risk destroying everything that the principals before me have built, and in order to succeed, I will do exactly as they have. I will not be the one weak link.'

Alek stared at her, dumbfounded at the reasoning behind the principal's decision-making.

'Yes,' Ash said, mainly to herself. 'I am making the right decision, aren't I?'

Alek shifted uncomfortably on his feet, clearing his throat.

Ash's head snapped up, and her worried expression turned into a pleasant smile. 'Anyway, I wanted to talk to you about your magic, Alek. How is it going? Did you feel the rush of power that flooded the valley a few nights ago?'

Alek's heart thudded in his chest at the mention of magic. He licked his lips nervously. How much should he reveal? The cave? Kai's abilities? The manifestation of his power?

'It's ...' Alek hesitated. 'It's going okay. I feel like I'm getting closer to finding my magic. It won't be too long now.' Sweat formed at his temples as the lies rolled off his tongue. 'And no, I don't know what you're talking about. What rush of power? Do you think it caused this?' Alek gestured to the blood-stained snow behind them.

Ash's eyes narrowed as Alek spoke, her expression unreadable as she listened to his lies. 'I do not know what has caused this death. I fear we may have a snake in our midst. And if that is the case, and someone is spying on us and feeding information to our enemies, then we are out of time ...' Ash trailed off quietly, casting her worried eyes to the cloud-filled sky above.

'The days are getting shorter, the storms are heavier, more frequent, and I am no closer to finding the fourth,' she muttered to herself, seemingly lost in her own thoughts. 'I thought our enemies would need more time to gather their forces, but I could be very wrong.'

Alek cleared his throat uncomfortably, and Ash's conflicted expression smoothed as she snapped back to reality. 'Whatever the case, I must be getting back to the other teachers,' Ash said curtly, beginning to turn away. 'Oh, and Alek? In the future, don't lie to me.'

Alek stood in shock as Ash hurried away, her long white hair as bright as the snow beneath their feet. *How much does she know if she knows I'm lying?* Alek thought. *Or is she just guessing that I lied?*

Shaking his head, Alek urged his feet to move, setting out into a run and allowing the steady thump of his steps to clear his anxious thoughts.

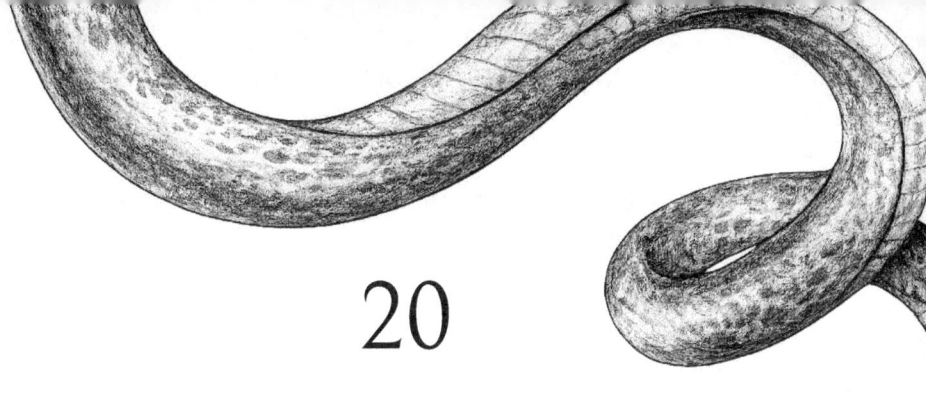

20

LET THE HUNT BEGIN

The night of The Hunt was here.

Alek was in Benny's room with Sarah. They were busy preparing, Sarah silently fastening a long white tag to a ring on the back of the boys' necks. If that tag was pulled off by another student during The Hunt, they were immediately disqualified from the game.

'As soon as the drums begin, The Hunt begins,' Sarah said, anticipation in her voice as she finished with the boys' tags.

'I'm surprised Ash is still allowing it to go ahead, what with all the deaths recently,' Benny said absentmindedly, helping Sarah with her own ring fastened to the back of her neck.

Butterflies fluttered in Alek's chest; three more students' bodies had been found over the last few nights. All the corpses were strung up in a similar fashion, impaled on a branch with their throats ripped out.

This was the ultimate test of everything he had learned over the last long months. Not only did he have to make his way through a valley filled with highly-skilled fighters, but whatever creature was killing students could be lurking around any corner.

Alek shook his head; he wasn't sure Ash was making the right choice in keeping to the tradition of The Hunt when there was so much danger in Aranasmin. *Not that she seemed so sure herself,* he thought with a snort. *She barely seems to know what she's doing, with how stressed she seemed the other day.*

'I wonder where the gold coin is exactly,' Benny continued as he tightened the laces on his boots for the fourth time that night.

Alek's mind flashed back to earlier that day when had been training with Kai. Over the last week, their training sessions had become increasingly short. The other boy had been sleeping through the morning run and turning up to classes with dark shadows under his eyes. Alek had a nagging suspicion that he was out all night trying to catch whatever monster was on a killing spree throughout the valley.

Alek had planned to sneak out and catch him in the act, but the thought of wandering through the dark valley alone at night with the risk of death had persuaded him to stay in his room. He felt a pang of guilt about his cowardice and the fact that Kai was possibly out risking his life every night, even if he could turn into a multitude of animals to protect himself.

That afternoon, the other boy had stated that he had shifted into his owl form and eavesdropped on Ash and the other teachers. The coin was at the northern end of the valley, among a small heap of neglected, overgrown buildings that had been constructed when the valley was first inhabited, before the tree houses.

'I've already told you,' Alek said, 'it has to be in those old buildings at the end of the valley. No one ever goes there, so it's the perfect hiding place.'

'Yeah, and we just have to get through an entire valley of students to reach that place,' Benny said snorting.

'That's why I'm going alone,' Sarah stated matter-of-factly. 'One person is a lot sneakier than two.'

'I still think—' Benny started but was immediately cut off as the booming of drums echoed into the silent night air.

The hair on the back of Alek's arms stood on end as anticipation surged through him. Benny climbed to his feet and Alek looked at each of his friends, taking note of how lethal each of them looked in their dark uniforms.

They all exuded an air of power, holding themselves with confidence they had not had months ago. Their bodies were stronger, leaner, more fluid. He noticed that both of his friends' features had changed slightly, their skin seeming to glow with energy in the night. Energy thrummed between them as they looked at each other.

'I guess it's now or never, right?' Benny broke the silence.

Sarah's face broke into a savage grin. 'I'll see you two losers later.'

With that, she turned and flipped out of the cabin, disappearing swiftly into the trees with a blast of wind.

Benny turned to look at Alek. 'You ready?'

Alek swallowed. 'As ready as I'll ever be.'

The two boys swiftly left the tree house, climbing through the foliage, heading towards the ground. As they moved through the branches, the drums continued to echo through the valley and flaming torches blinked into the night, illuminating the forest in a savage, wild glow.

Alek shivered; the night air seemed unnatural, dangerous. It was filled with energy, ready to burst into chaos at any moment.

The boys' feet hit the thick layer of leaf litter at the base of their tree, and they swiftly set off through the flickering darkness. The torches were scattered through the entire valley, creating an eerie pathway through the trees, with plenty of deep shadows to hide in.

Alek breathed in deeply as Benny ploughed forward, leading the way towards the northern end of the valley. Alek kept pace, a few steps behind his friend, his eyes flicking from left to right constantly as the dull beating of the drums echoed his own thudding heartbeat.

The two boys made their way onto a dried riverbed, the foliage around them thinning as they moved out of the depths of the forest. The soil beneath their feet gave way to fresh snow, the thinner canopy above their heads allowing the icy flakes to fall from the clouds.

The snow reflected the firelight around them, creating an otherworldly glow within the shadows. Suddenly, Alek heard rapid footsteps and two students leapt down on them from above, over the lip of the dried riverbed.

Alek reacted instantly, surprised at the fluidity of his movements. He threw himself backwards, twisting to keep his tag out of reach as one of the students descended on him.

Her fist flew towards his face with a speed he didn't expect and it connected painfully with his jaw, bright light bursting across his vision as he threw up a hand to block her next blow.

Without missing a beat, Alek bobbed and weaved, feeling the air around him whistle as the girl's blows barely missed him. Clenching his muscles, he threw his weight backwards, snapping his right leg out in a savage kick, his foot connecting roughly with the girl's stomach.

She doubled over in pain and he flipped forward, deftly tugging off the tag attached to her back. As he did so, he spun, crouching low and launching himself upwards at the boy attacking Benny.

The student gasped as his fist slammed into the underside of his jaw, sending him flying backwards into the snow.

Quickly, Benny reached over and snapped off the boy's tag, holding it up with a cocky grin. 'Looks like your hunt is over, guys.' He smirked, holding up the tag.

'Don't be mean, Benny,' Alek muttered as the two students' eyes flashed, and they disappeared together into the darkness.

'What?' Benny said defensively, turning and continuing along the riverbed. 'They lost, and we won.'

Alek snorted. 'Yeah, thanks to me.'

Benny rolled his eyes, pushing his long dark hair out of his face. 'Oh, whatever. I was doing fine. I didn't need your help.'

'Ha—I'll remember that next time,' Alek said sarcastically. 'Now come on.'

A few minutes later, the boys stood at the edge of the clearing separating them from the tumbled-down buildings clustered against the foothills of the northern mountains.

Benny sighed. 'Now what?'

Alek shrugged, his eyes darting left and right. 'As soon as we step out of these trees, everyone is going to see us and come running.'

The wind picked up around them, and Alek felt a tingling brush of magic against him. He spun around, searching for the source of the power. It seemed familiar, although he couldn't put his finger on why, exactly.

'We could go to the edge of the valley and climb along the mountain?' Benny continued, oblivious to the wind that now thrashed the trees around them, sending snow swirling chaotically into the air.

Alek ignored him, his eyes piercing the darkness as he spotted a small figure moving swiftly through the trees towards them. He frowned; the shadowy figure was moving way too fast to be human. Unease rose inside him as images of the dead students flashed into his mind. His body unconsciously slipped into a fighting stance, his muscles taut, ready to face whatever was heading for them.

Alek watched as the unknown shadow leapt from branch to branch, often swinging effortlessly across larger gaps and landing on impossibly narrow boughs.

'What on earth does she think she's doing?' Benny sighed, noticing the person rapidly approaching them in the trees above.

Alek frowned. 'She?'

With a start, Alek realised that the reason the magic had felt so familiar was because it was Sarah. The presence felt strange and powerful, but still had the essence of her. Of course, Benny had noticed right away; he had to be used to feeling her power in all the classes they had taken and trained together in.

Alek squinted as wind buffeted his face and watched in awe as Sarah passed overhead, a savage grin on her face and a wild look in her eyes. She reached the end of the forest and bunched her legs underneath her, launching herself up into the night sky. A pulse of magic battered Alek as the air rippled around Sarah, sending her rocketing towards the clouds.

Holding his breath, Alek tracked his friend across the sky as she sailed over the clearing, descending into the shadows on the opposite side.

'Show off,' Benny muttered, flexing his hands. 'Come on, Alek. We can't let her beat us!'

'Benny ... She just ... Sarah just flew!' Alek blinked, shocked at his friend's casual reaction.

'And?' Benny said, cocking his head. 'Her magic is wind, Alek. She controls the air around her. And I wouldn't call that flying. It was just a big jump.'

'I guess so,' Alek said, his voice trailing off. Jealousy flashed through him. He couldn't do anything like that!

'Come on, Alek, let's go!' Benny said, impatiently tugging on his arm. 'We can't just stand around here forever and let Sarah get all the glory.'

Alek was just turning to follow his friend when he noticed movement on the other side of the clearing. Disbelief washed over him as he cleared his throat.

'Uhhh, Benny?' he said. 'About Sarah beating us ...'

'What now?!' Benny huffed, the air heating around him as his frustration built.

Alek ignored the flicker of Benny's wild magic and pointed across the clearing.

Sarah was sprinting at full tilt onto the open plain, a group of students chasing her out of the shadows. Snow sprayed in her wake, launched from the ground by her speeding feet. Clutched in her hands was a small object, glinting in the firelight.

Benny swore. 'She already has it!'

He bunched his fists and stepped out onto the clearing, running to block Sarah's path.

'What are you doing?' Alek hissed from the trees, worried Benny's competitive spirit would cause him to attack Sarah and take the coin for himself.

He watched as Benny raced towards his cousin and launched himself towards her. Alek stopped breathing, disbelief stabbing through his body as he shifted from foot to foot. He was actually going to attack her, all so that he could win!

Just as Alek steeled himself to intervene, Benny sailed past Sarah, slamming into one of her pursuers, tackling him to the ground and sending them rolling through the snow, bowling over two more students.

Alek let out a relieved breath as Benny flipped upright, sweeping the feet out from another of the students just as two more descended on him in a ball of swinging fists.

Steeling himself, Alek raced out to help his friends, digging into his magic and letting it flood his veins with a surge of ecstasy. He gasped, power radiating off him as he slowed his pace, allowing Sarah to reach him. Her eyes were narrowed, determined, and she didn't hesitate as she swept past him.

With a breath, Alek turned and raced after her, throwing his magic out behind them. The snow beneath his feet hardened and cracked, ice spearing across the surface. The approaching students yelled as their feet connected with the solid surface, sending them tumbling to their knees.

Sarah slowed slightly, glancing back towards Alek with a shocked look on her face. He winked at her as he gave chase, following her into the trees, glancing back to see a student rip Benny's tag from his back while two others held him down. Alek winced; he would never hear the end of this.

He raced after Sarah as they rocketed through the forest, heading for the centre of the valley where the bonfire burned, awaiting the winner of The Hunt.

Suddenly, the drums that had been echoing through the valley in a steady rhythm faltered and stopped. The hair on the back of Alek's neck stood on end as an unearthly cry rumbled through the trees around them.

'Sarah,' he gasped. 'Something's wrong!'

Abruptly, the two friends burst into the clearing surrounding the bonfire and Alek skidded to a halt, horror filling him from head to toe.

The ground was a mess of churned-up leaves and debris, blood smeared across the forest floor around them, and a stench of death clung to the thick air. Bodies were strung up in a circle around the outskirts of the firelight, too many to count. Alek was speechless as his eyes stared into the faces of so many dead students, all with blood dripping from their mutilated throats.

Ash burst into the clearing behind them, a look of absolute disbelief across her face. Her searching eyes zeroed in on Alek and Sarah.

'What have you done?!' she demanded shrilly, her eyes wild.

'What?!' Sarah snapped. 'What have we done?! We just got here!' She stomped forward threateningly, shoving the gold coin into the principal's face. 'I was taking part in your stupid game, playing by your rules, living in your valley.'

Sarah angrily threw her arms around. 'Do you really think we killed these kids?'

Slowly, students flooded into the clearing, grief flashing across their faces as they took in the carnage around them. A student behind Alek vomited loudly as he saw the blood splashed across the earth.

Ash hesitated. 'I didn't mean that; I'm so sorry.' Her head bowed. 'I just don't know what to do,' she said, her voice barely a whisper.

The murmuring around them grew louder and louder as more students squeezed into the clearing, jostling others out of their way to get a better view of the scene in front of them.

As Alek was roughly pushed aside, he noticed Sarah glance quickly around before slipping out of the fire light. Alek frowned, shoving students out of his way as he hurriedly followed her, suspicion flooding through him.

Silently, Alek snuck through the shadows cast by the scattered torches amidst the trees. Sarah walked quickly, cutting a straight line through the forest towards her tree house. Alek relaxed slightly; she must just be going back to her room.

As she reached the base of the maple containing her tree house, she glanced around, her eyes darting to and fro. Alek quickly ducked into the bushes behind, crouching to peer through the vegetation.

Sarah hunched over, rummaging through the piles of frosty leaves at the base of the tree. Alek frowned as she pulled out a bag, brushing soil and debris off it. Quickly, she slung the bag over her shoulder and set off northward into the forest.

His heart beating faster, Alek eased out of his hiding place and uneasily followed his friend as she confidently stalked through the trees.

It wasn't long until they reached the clearing that Sarah had launched herself over earlier that night. She paused at the edge of the trees, glancing left and right, and then broke into a steady run across the unsheltered field.

Alek waited until she reached the other side, slipping between the abandoned buildings there before he stepped out of the shelter of his hiding place. He had taken barely three steps before a voice boomed into the night behind him.

'Well, well. What do we have here?'

Alek tensed, recognising the cocky drawl in an instant.

'Not now, Lucien,' he said through clenched teeth, turning to face the brute of a boy as he stepped into the clearing behind Alek.

'I told you I would find you during the hunt,' the bigger boy said aggressively, cracking his knuckles.

Alek hissed in frustration, glancing over his shoulder to the darkness where Sarah had disappeared. He was wasting time.

'I don't have time for this!' he snapped at Lucien.

'Now what gives you the right to speak to me like that?!' the bully snarled before launching himself forward.

Alek blinked in surprise at Lucien's speed as he quickly dodged the strike, snow spraying around them as he forced his tired legs into motion, quickly manoeuvring behind the other boy and slamming a fist into his side.

Lucien threw his body backwards, ramming into Alek with full force, sending him reeling as he lost his footing and fell into the snow. Distracted, Alek glanced past his attacker, impatience flaring through him. He was going to lose Sarah's trail!

Lucien loomed over him. 'Looks like you're all alone and all out of luck.'

Alek grinned. 'Not quite.'

As Lucien frowned, Alek dug his hands into the snow around him, power surging out of his fingertips. The snow exploded upwards around Lucien, spearing into the night and hardening to ice, trapping the boy in a frozen embrace.

'Now who's out of luck?' Alek asked as he climbed unsteadily to his feet, blinking at the loss of energy.

'What did you just do to me?!' Lucien howled, wriggling desperately against his icy confines.

'Now, now,' Alek said, his voice dripping with satisfaction. 'The ice will melt soon. Until then, you better hope that you haven't slowed me down too much.'

Grinning smugly, Alek spun on his feet and sprinted across the clearing, his sharp eyesight picking out Sarah's footsteps on the icy ground. Because it wouldn't be long before fresh snow-covered any trace of her tracks, gritting his teeth, Alek pushed himself harder, racing into the decrepit buildings on the opposite side of the clearing.

He slowed as the tumbled-down remains surrounded him.

During summer, the buildings were covered in brilliant green vines and shrubs, the ruined stone walls dotted with moss and wildflowers. Now, in the depths of winter, the only sign of life that remained were skeletons of the previous season's plants.

Brittle branches devoid of leaves clawed out of the snow around him, grating together in the slight breeze. The only other sound was Alek's footsteps crunching in the thick snow as he carefully picked his way around tumbled-down stones and grasping leafless branches.

Alek shivered; this place creeped him out. He had always felt uneasy whenever he had entered the small group of abandoned buildings. Deep shadows stretched behind gaping doorways, hiding secrets long since forgotten. His elation at finally getting the upper hand on Lucien drained out of him as he swiftly paced onwards, his keen eyes picking out Sarah's rapidly disappearing tracks.

A shadow flickered out of the corner of Alek's eyes and he spun around, adrenaline pumping into his body as his heartbeat spiked. His head darted left and right as he surveyed the barren land he had just crossed. The wind died down, and the temperature seemed to plummet.

Mist formed in the air in front of his mouth as his breathing became more rapid. Alek wrapped his arms around himself, frowning as he realised how quickly it had gotten cold. Seeing no reason to be alarmed, he swivelled on his heel and continued on his path, breathing easier as he stepped at last out of the opposite side of the abandoned buildings.

Unease still prickled the back of his neck as he strode into a large clump of winter-bare trees. Through the thin, bone-like branches, he could make out the edge of the valley and the mountain wall stretching far above him, disappearing into the thick clouds. Something moved in the shadows before him and he smiled slightly as he recognised Sarah. He had caught up with her.

Moving forward slowly to the edge of the trees, Alek crouched down, trying to determine what Sarah was doing. She had reached the cliff face and was slowly walking along; the snow was so deep against the mountain that it was tough going as she struggled forward. She ran her hand along the surface of the rock, stopping every metre or so to inspect the cliff face.

Alek frowned. What was she doing? The bag slung over her shoulders bulged with whatever she had concealed inside. Just as Alek was about to emerge from hiding and confront his friend, Sarah suddenly stopped in her tracks, turned towards the cliff wall, and vanished.

Alek blinked, standing up straight. His sudden movements disturbed the branches around him, causing snow to shower down on his head, sending a cold shiver down his back. He quickly stepped forward, following Sarah's path through the thick snow. As he reached the cliff face where her tracks ended, he turned, facing the rock before him.

Blinking in surprise, he realised there was a narrow fissure in the rockface, enough for a person to easily slip through. Swirls and patterns were etched into the stone on either side of the crack and Alek shuddered, remembering the murals carved into the stone beside the library doors. At least these carvings were staying put and not moving.

Something crunched loudly behind Alek and he spun around, heart caught in his throat. Snow twirled thickly around him, obscuring his view of the valley before him. A shadow moved in the direction he had come from. A large shadow.

His heartbeat quickened as visions of impaled students flashed through his mind once more. He wasn't safe out here alone, magic or no magic. Not wanting to find out what sort of monster was stalking him, Alek turned and ducked into the cave behind him.

21

REVENGE

The sound of the snowstorm outside faded dramatically as Alek stepped into the mountainside. Water dripped somewhere in the dark cave, and vines curled out of the rockface above him. Cautiously, Alek moved forward, keeping a steady hand on the wall beside him, unsure of his footing on the rough stone beneath his feet.

Light flickered ahead; Sarah must have brought a torch. Picking up his pace, Alek continued further into the cave, ignoring his rising claustrophobia as the tunnel began to slope downwards, into the depths of the mountain.

Where is she going? Alek groaned to himself as he narrowly avoided twisting his ankle on the slippery rocks below him.

Grumbling, the boy pressed on, intent on catching up with his friend.

As Alek rounded a corner, the ground beneath his feet smoothed into solid stone and the light flickering off the rock walls around him grew, lightning the tunnel. Frowning, Alek picked up his pace now that there was no risk of tripping over a pile of rough stones.

Suddenly, an intense wave of nausea coursed through his body and goose bumps erupted across his skin, causing a shiver to go down his spine as he tried not to gag.

The tunnel grew brighter and brighter around him until rough rock walls no longer pressed down on him from either side. Alek threw a hand up, shielding his eyes from the bright white light blinding him. He felt a warm rush as he left the feeling of the damp, chill cave behind.

Once his eyes adjusted to the sudden brightness, Alek lowered his hand and inspected his surroundings, squinting slightly. As the world around him swam into view, dread filled him.

He was standing in a familiar, decaying forest. Cloying mist pervaded the air around him, obscuring his view in every direction. Shadows stretched out towards him from the skeletal trees, and harsh light rained down through the mist from the sunless sky above.

Behind him was a large pile of rocks. A small cave entrance beckoned between the rough stone. To his right, the land fell away, disappearing into a sea of swirling vapour. A small river flowed through the surrounding trees, vanishing over the drop off with a dull roar.

They were in the Portal Realm.

'Alek, what the hell?!' Sarah's voice suddenly shouted in his ear.

He jumped, not realising she had been watching him as he looked around in shock.

'Why are you here?!' she asked.

Alek looked at her, taking in her tense shoulders, the way her mouth was set in a hard line. 'What do you mean?' he asked hesitantly. 'I saw you slip out of the valley and I followed you.'

'Why?!' she asked again, taking an angry step towards him. 'I don't want you here; it's too dangerous!'

Alek snorted. 'Well, then, it's lucky I am here if it's dangerous. And I followed you to make sure you were okay!'

The darkness around them flickered and the mist rolled in closer, blocking out more of the forest around them.

Panic flashed through Sarah's eyes as she quickly looked at Alek, stepping closer to him.

'Okay, okay,' she whispered. 'You're here now, and there's nothing we can do about that. Let's not make the woods angry.' She swallowed roughly. 'Like last time.'

Alek stared at her, his eyes narrowing as realisation dawned on him. 'That's why you're here? Revenge?'

Sarah tensed. 'Yes.'

Exhaling in disbelief, Alek rocked backwards, running a hand through his hair as shuffling footsteps suddenly echoed from the cracked trunks around them. Alek's hands turned clammy as Sarah spun around, carefully smoothing her face into a neutral expression.

The darkening forest around them seemed to hold its breath, silence falling over the two friends as a figure detached itself from the heavy mist, stepping into the small clearing.

Alek heard Sarah's breath catch as the satyr moved slowly forward, its hooved feet carefully stepping through the myriad of twisted tree roots jutting from the soil. This satyr was entirely different from the one that had attacked them the last time they had set foot in the Portal Realm.

It wore a flowing cloak over its naked torso. The fur covering its legs was wiry and grey with age, and the beast was hunched over as it moved forward. Its long horns fell down the side of its head, stretching almost to the ground, not spiralling to a lethal point like Alek remembered. Its eyes were not a fiery orange inferno but more of a dull, auburn glow as it stopped in front of the two friends, studying them silently.

'I have payment,' Sarah said, her voice a few octaves higher than normal as she stepped forwards, her hands shaking.

The satyr watched silently before slowly holding out its hand, palm upwards.

Sarah shuffled forwards, quickly depositing the gold coin from The Hunt into the beast's hand before she jumped backwards, her breathing shallow. Alek's heart thundered in his rib cage as the monster held the coin up to the light, inspecting it carefully. Ever-so-slowly, the glowing orange eyes moved from the coin to pass over the two friends before it dipped its head in acknowledgement.

Alek barely dared to breathe as the satyr turned and shuffled away, vanishing among the twisting trees.

Alek let out a long breath, his body shaking as he did so. He turned to his friend, taking note of her tense shoulders. The reality of what was happening came crashing down around him. *Revenge?* he thought, a shiver sliding down his spine. *All this time, she was preparing for this. To come back here.*

'Sarah, this is crazy! You don't know where the satyr that killed Chris is, or who he is, or anything! And what do you plan on doing once you find him?' Alek gasped, beginning to pace back and forth.

'You're wrong,' Sarah began, dropping her bag to the ground with a muffled clang. 'I know exactly where he is and who he is. The brand on his chest is the symbol of a high-ranking prison guard, so the prison is where I'll find him. That's *how* this forest works. You focus on where you want to go, and it takes you there. And when I find him, I'm going to slit his throat, just like he did to Chris.'

Alek flinched at his friend's harsh words but watched in silence as she unzipped her bag, revealing an assortment of blades glinting in the harsh light. Sarah quickly picked through the bag, strapping knives to her legs and a slender blade to her back. She glanced at Alek and sighed, tossing him a sword from the bag.

'Here, you'll probably need this,' she muttered, zipping the now empty bag up and kicking it aside. 'I've been practising wielding dual blades, but one will have to do. I can't have you running around weapon-less.'

Alek numbly buckled the sword to his back, taken aback slightly by the weight of the metal blade. He had only ever trained with the wooden practice swords Kai liked to use. The weapon strapped to him felt entirely different.

'Come,' Sarah said, spinning on her heel and stalking into the swirling mist around them.

Alek had no choice but to follow. He glanced around warily as he paced beside Sarah. A small pathway through the fog appeared before them and closed behind them, sealing them to whatever fate lay ahead.

The two of them walked in silence as Alek processed what was happening, how it was happening. His worst nightmares involved the horror he and his friends had faced in this inbetween world, and now here was, stuck in the middle of it yet again.

'Sarah,' he began softly. 'How long have you been planning this?'

She didn't slow or waver from her path as she contemplated Alek's question, her long brown ponytail drifting slightly in a small breeze. Alek began to wonder if she had even heard him as the minutes ticked by in silence. The only sound was the rustle of their boots moving through the long grass beneath them and the creaking of the trees in the mist around them.

'Since the day we got to Balathor,' Sarah suddenly said, causing Alek to jump. She turned slightly, raising an amused eyebrow at his jumpiness.

'That's why you said you were staying?' Alek asked, swallowing a lump in his throat. 'I always wondered why you were so quick to decide.'

Sarah nodded. 'I was angry, Alek. I am angry. That monster took Chris away from me, and he's going to die for it.'

Alek frowned. The Sarah he knew was not this violent. Being in this world had changed her, hardened her. 'Sarah ...' he started, but she cut him off.

'No, Alek. I don't want to hear it. Every single thing I have done over the last months has been to prepare me for this moment. From the second I woke up in this world, I have thought of nothing else but being here, in this moment, and taking the life of the monster that shattered mine.' Her hands balled into fists as she stalked ahead. 'I've trained harder than anyone else, pushed myself to breaking point, become the best I could possibly be, all for this. And I do not want to hear a single word against it, Alek. No one asked you to be here.'

'Sarah, I—'

Again, she cut him off before he could speak. 'You don't know what it's like, Alek, to have the person you love ripped away from you, murdered in front of your eyes. Especially right as you are thrust blindly into an entirely new world, right when you needed them the most.' She laughed harshly, wiping tears from her eyes. 'Why do I even bother justifying it to you? You've never even been in love. You don't know what it could possibly feel like.'

Alek winced at Sarah's ferocity, thoughts of Kai flashing through his mind. Should he tell her? Was now the time to come clean to at least one of his friends? Panic blossomed in his chest, and he pushed it down. No. Now was not the right time.

'I'm so sorry, Sarah. I should have been there. I should have made sure you were alright. You just seemed so strong, so in control all the time.'

Sarah glanced at him. 'Alek, you need to know, I lost the most by coming here. And today, I intend on taking back a piece of what was taken from me.'

'Are you sure this is even going to make you feel any better?' Alek asked. 'And how do you know about this prison?'

Sarah shrugged, avoiding Alek's first question. 'The library. I've been studying the Portal Realm all year, with help from the librarian. Whenever you enter this world, you start at the edge of the forest—hence the drop-off behind you. This path'— she gestured to the mist parting ahead of them—'takes me to wherever I desire, so long as I keep that thought at the forefront of my mind. When you reach the end of the path, there's usually some sort of entrance to the place you've been focusing on. Like the willow tree that brought us here.'

With a start, Alek remembered that very first week at Aranasmin, when he had hidden in the library every day. Sarah had come in then and disappeared for hours on end. Couple that with the intense training and her willingness to stay in Balathor, he should have seen it. Probably would have if he had not been so wrapped up in his own thoughts.

Alek shivered, trying to shake the feeling that the very trees looming overhead were watching him, listening to their quiet conversation. 'How is it light here when it was night when we left the valley?'

Sarah continued forward, picking her way lithely through the bleached trunks around them, careful to avoid touching the splintered bark. 'We're no longer in Balathor, or back home. This place is some sort of in-between realm, a place between places. There is no sun in this forest, no day or night, just this constant grey light.' Sarah cast a wary look at the forest around them.

She could feel it, too, Alek realised. The forest was very much alive, he decided, despite the death that seemed to surround them.

Alek was so focused on his own thoughts he didn't notice Sarah had stopped and he slammed into her, the sword strapped across her back digging painfully into his stomach.

'We're here,' she said simply, ignoring his clumsiness.

Alek glanced over her shoulder, noticing a metal grate in the ground.

'Where exactly is "here"?' he asked nervously, inspecting the looming trees around them.

'This is where the forest has led us. This is the way to the prison.'

Alek opened his mouth to reply as Sarah swung open the grate, revealing a thin, metal ladder descending into the earth. His mouth snapped shut as she glanced at him.

'Are you sure this isn't some sort of trap?' he asked warily, eyeing the dark hole in the ground apprehensively. 'How are we even going to find his satyr? Surely there's more than one prison guard.'

Sarah grinned savagely, swinging herself down onto the metal ladder in the ground. 'He shouldn't be that hard to find. Remember, Ash sliced open his left eye with her sword. So we just find the high-ranking prison guard with the cut-up eye, then I kill him.'

On that note, Sarah disappeared into the darkness below. Swearing to himself, Alek hauled himself down onto the ladder, quickly descending, the cold of the metal rungs biting into his hands.

As Alek steadily moved downward, the sound of rushing water grew louder and louder until it drowned out even the sound of his heavy breathing as his arms strained to hold his weight against the never-ending ladder. Glancing upwards, he saw that the grey light above him had faded to a distant pinprick in the darkness, and still, the ladder went on.

The air around him turned musty and humid the further he descended into the ground, and his damp hair clung to his forehead. Finally, as he reached his foot down to the next rung on the ladder, he instead struck solid rock. Groaning in relief, Alek shifted his weight to his feet, his hands shaking as the pressure was finally taken off them.

Light suddenly blinked into existence behind him, and he turned to see Sarah pulling a golden, glowing crystal out of her bag. He raised his eyebrows in her direction.

'Did you steal that from the library?' he asked incredulously.

She leaned in close, her words drowned out by the roaring water. 'Of course not,' she said with a grin. 'It was gifted to me.'

Alek shook his head, glancing around at their surroundings. They were in a man-made tunnel. Rough, rectangular bricks formed a circular dome around them, disappearing into darkness in either direction. Water rushed past them, flowing in a shallow channel in the centre of the passage.

Sarah grabbed Alek's shoulder, pulling him forward as she turned and followed the current of the water, trudging down the damp walkway. The only light they had was the golden glow from the crystal clenched in Sarah's hand. Alek glanced uneasily at the water beside them. The current was growing stronger, the water ferociously roaring past them.

Suddenly, a blood-curdling scream echoed throughout the tunnel and a pale body slammed into Sarah, sending her sprawling. The glowing crystal flew through the air, clattering onto the stone floor a few metres away.

Through the dim light, Alek watched in horror as Sarah rolled over on the floor, tussling with the screaming creature. It was human in shape. Rags of clothing clung to its bony frame, and large, pointed ears rose on either side of its bald head. Pale, pockmarked skin hung off its gangly body, and an awful stench that reminded Alek of rotting fish filled the narrow tunnel. It raised its head and screamed again, and Alek shuddered. Its eyes were milky white and bulged grotesquely from its skull.

Sarah slammed her fist into the side of the creature's ghostly head, knocking its skull backwards. As it recoiled, she managed to get her hands around its neck, her mouth curled in a viscous snarl as she twisted her arms, the creature's neck letting out a loud crack into the cavern.

Alek shuddered as the monster slumped backwards, slipping into the water and disappearing below the surface. Abruptly, another loud shriek echoed through the tunnel, and he ducked just as Sarah hurled one of her daggers. It whistled past his head and buried into another creature's chest behind him.

'What the hell, Sarah?!' Alek yelled, his heart thudding in his chest. 'What are they? This is stupid! We need to go back, or we're going to die.'

Sarah snorted, pacing over to the creature to pull out her dagger. 'Get a grip, Alek. They're just goblins. Nothing we can't handle.'

Alek stood still, lost for words as he watched his friend yank out her dagger from the dead goblin's body. He suddenly saw her in a new light. Not as the bubbly friend he'd known for years, who was always laughing and happy. No, this Sarah was a killer. She seemed totally unfazed by the two creatures she had just executed, and he watched as she quickly cleaned off her dagger as if nothing had happened.

Sarah's movements were precise, detached as she examined the corpse at her feet, not a hint of emotion on her face betraying her thoughts. The long brown hair that had once flowed long and loose around her shoulders when in Chris's company was now pulled back into a tight, no-nonsense ponytail. She deftly tucked the dagger into the side of her boot and straightened, rolling her shoulders as she stood. Silhouetted against the glowing light cast by the dropped crystal, Alek wasn't sure he recognised the warrior standing in front of him.

Turning to see Alek watching her, she sighed. 'What is it now, Alek? We need to keep moving; we have a job to do.'

Alek eyed her uneasily as she stalked ahead, stooping to pick up the glowing crystal she had dropped earlier. She marched onwards, not even looking back to see if he was following.

Losing Chris had changed her, and he hadn't noticed until now.

Another scream echoed down the tunnel, and Alek jumped, his heart pounding faster. Quickly, he hurried to catch up to Sarah, worried about what other horrors they would face once they reached the prison.

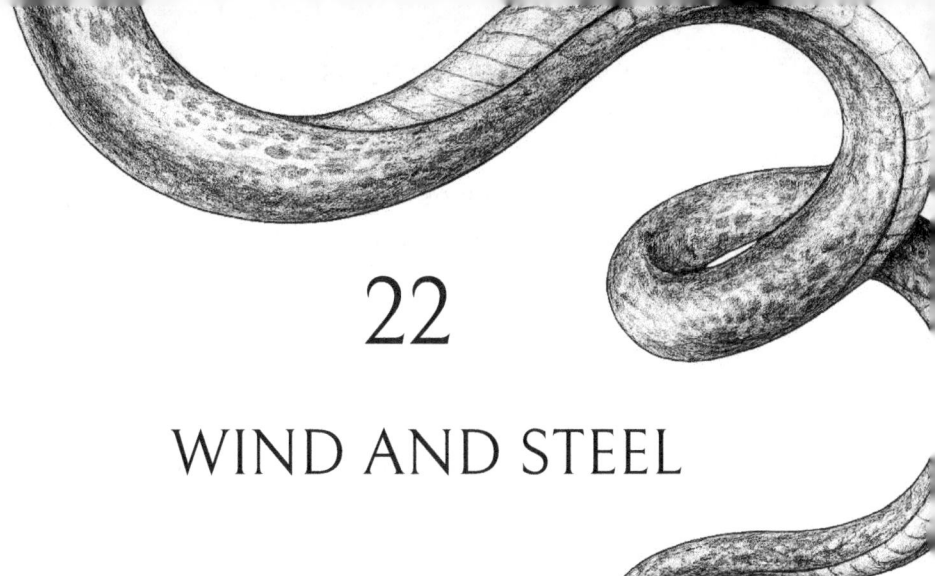

22

WIND AND STEEL

'We're here.'

Alek faltered; those were the first words Sarah had spoken since they were attacked by the goblins. An hour had easily passed as they trudged down the tunnel. Not long ago, the passage had finally gotten lighter, and Alek blinked as the two friends emerged from the darkness. A sapphire sky greeted them, two suns shimmering among billowing clouds.

Another part of the Portal Realm? Alek thought, surprised to see the shimmering blue sky and not the sullen grey light of the forest they had trekked through earlier.

The two friends were standing atop a dam at the end of a ravine. Multiple rope bridges at different levels spanned the length of the canyon, connecting one side to the other, where pathways and building facades were cut into the stone face. As Alek traced the cliffs downwards, he saw a variety of mezzanines and protruding buildings disappearing deep into the dark pit below.

He shivered as glowing orange eyes flashed in the shadowy depths of the gorge. Satyrs paced the entire area, most carrying a whip by their side. They moved casually among the multiple levels throughout the gorge, completely at ease as their cloven feet clacked across the unsteady rope bridges and vanished into the buildings carved out of the cliff faces.

As Alek watched, he saw one such satyr purchasing a variety of strange, multi-coloured fruit from a vendor about halfway down the cliff face. The vendor's stall was perched precariously on a narrow ledge, and the half-goat monsters crowded together on that particular level, seemingly eager to purchase the odd-looking fruit.

The water from the dam below them leaked down into the chasm, creating a damp mist that coated the satyrs and made the stones beneath their hooves slick with water. *It's a miracle they don't fall to their deaths*, Alek mused.

A ruckus emerged from the shadowy depths of the gorge, and a figure broke into view, hurtling along the cliff face and leaping up onto a rope bridge above. Alek's eyes widened as his sharp vision picked out the runner's features. He was slim, his skin a deep golden brown. He had a breathtakingly beautiful face, sparkling purple eyes accentuated by thick lashes and high cheek bones. He was dressed in pale rags that were ripped through and paper-thin.

He moved with a fluid grace that reminded Alek of Kai and the way he held himself. As the runner hauled himself up onto the rope bridge, his long dark hair fell to the side, revealing sharply pointed ears. Beside him, Sarah gasped.

'He's an elf!' she whispered.

Alek shifted as three more elves launched themselves out of the darkness and onto the rope bridge beside the original runner. Together, the group continued forward, sprinting dangerously fast along the narrow bridges and paths. Suddenly, a howl echoed up the gorge and time seemed to slow as, one by one, the satyrs at the fruit stall turned, their orange eyes focused on the four elves.

'The prisoners are escaping!' The shouted words echoed through the air, carrying easily through the narrow stone gorge.

Satyrs swarmed out of the buildings in the cliff face, hurling themselves into action. The elves glanced upwards at the force awaiting them but did not falter, continuing on their mad dash up and out of the shadows below.

Alek held his breath as the elves met the first wave of resistance: the satyrs on the level with the fruit vendor. The lead elf with the dark hair did not hesitate. He flipped himself onto the ledge and slammed shoulder-first into the closest monster, knocking over two others in the process.

His companions arrived shortly after him, and the landing erupted into a whirlwind of violence. The skirmish lasted only a few seconds before the group of elves stood victorious, picking a variety of weapons off the bodies of the fallen prison guards.

But the fight had lost them precious time. Only a few levels above them, the satyrs had organised themselves and formed a solid line of defence. Alek could clearly see hopeless desperation in the eyes of the elves as they glanced at each other. The dark-haired male straightened his shoulders and gritted his teeth before he nodded at his companions, moving forward once more.

'We have to help them!' Sarah hissed next to Alek.

He rounded on her, his eyes wide. 'Excuse me?! We don't even know them. What if we get caught?'

Sarah shook her head, her hands balled into fists. 'This is sick, Alek. Look at them! They look starved half to death, and those elves are kids. They're our age. We need to help them.'

'Sarah, there's two of us! We'll never get out alive.'

As he spoke, he felt her magic surge around him, the air crackling with energy.

'Sarah, no!' he yelled, lunging for her arm.

Wind ripped around him and he faltered as she launched herself out of their hiding place, dropping down towards the unsuspecting satyrs below. Alek chewed on his lip as his friend fell silently towards the gathered prison guards, the monsters unaware of the threat from above.

The air around Sarah rippled as she slammed onto the rock landing amidst the group of satyrs. A shockwave of wind rocketed out from her impact, launching her enemies into the air. Terrified screams echoed up towards Alek, and he watched in horror as his friend turned into a violent storm of death.

Most of the guards around Sarah had been blasted off the ledge and fallen screaming to the bottom of the gorge, and those that had managed to survive now met her blade. She was a blur. A nightmare of wind and steel.

Alek watched in disbelief as she carved her way along the landing, dodging, spinning, and hacking through the throngs of satyrs towards the elves below. Wind swirled through the gorge, howling along the rock face.

It churned around Sarah, making it impossible for anyone to even get close, let alone land a blow on her. Arrows fired towards her from a group of prison guards further down the ravine were knocked back by the wind before they even got close to their mark.

Suddenly, a fresh wave of satyrs swarmed out of one of the doorways just below Alek, cutting Sarah off from above. Cursing, Alek leaned out over the edge he stood on, searching for a way to climb down and help his friend. A narrow landing was cut into the stone face a few metres below him, where the recent group of guards had appeared.

Grumbling to himself about Sarah and her ability to jump down a dozen metres and be fine, Alek turned around and lay on his stomach, lowering himself over the edge. His fingers strained to hold him as he hung precariously on the cliff face. Glancing down, he saw the ledge was still a fair distance below his swinging legs. Cursing again, Alek steeled himself and dropped, landing awkwardly on the narrow landing.

His boots slipped on the water-slick stone, and he cartwheeled his arms, his heart in his throat as he imagined falling to his death. Regaining his balance, he stumbled forward, pressing himself against the rock wall and taking long, calming breaths as his heartbeat thudded in his chest.

A loud scream echoed up to him from below, and he cautiously peeked over the edge to see one of the escaping elves had fallen, deep red blood pooling around her body as she lay at an odd angle a few levels below the remaining elves. Taking one last breath to steady his nerves, Alek pulled out his sword, adjusting the grip in his sweaty palms.

But before he could so much as move, footsteps sounded on the stone behind him. He spun around, whipping his sword in a wild arc. It struck an oncoming satyr with a wet thud. Alek froze in shock as the force of the blow reverberated up his arms and he saw black blood pour from the wound he had inflicted. He looked up from his sword into the satyr's eyes and watched as the savage orange glow slowly faded and the creature slumped backwards, sliding off Alek's blade and into a pool of his own blood.

Numb, Alek stood frozen, staring at the empty eyes on the ground before him. He had just taken a life. Granted, the satyr probably deserved it, and he had been training for this for the past few months. But now he had done it. He was a killer. Alek took a step back, shaking his head, trying to get the image of those lifeless eyes out of his mind.

Before he had a chance to collect himself, pain flashed through his head and bright light burst behind his eyes. Groaning, he slumped forwards, his sword clattering out of his hand as another blow snapped his neck backwards and everything went black.

23

REVELATIONS

The sound of dripping water broke into Alek's dark mind as he slowly regained consciousness. Grimacing at the pain pounding in his head, he rolled onto his back, fighting down the waves of nausea that flooded over him.

'Alek?' a panicked voice spoke loudly into his ear. 'Alek, can you hear me? Are you okay?'

Slowly, he bought a finger up to his lips. 'Shhh,' he breathed, his throat dry.

'Oops, sorry!' the voice said, lowering dramatically in volume.

'But are you okay? Do you need anything?'

'Sarah.' Alek grimaced. 'I need you to shut up for two seconds.'

He heard her huff quietly beside him, and he swallowed down a chuckle. He twitched his fingers and toes, sensing if he was in any other pain besides the throbbing in his head. Breathing a sigh of relief as everything seemed to be in working order, Alek cracked open his eyes.

His surroundings were gloomy and damp. Metal bars enclosed him, and he realised suddenly that he was in a cage. He gritted his teeth and rose to a sitting position, the movement causing his head to swim. No, he realised, his head wasn't swimming.

The cage itself was swinging with his movements.

'What the ...' Alek muttered as he leaned forward, gripping the metal bars before him.

The ground was a couple of metres below him, covered in water. His cage was suspended from above, dangling over the dark liquid. He glanced up. He was in some sort of massive cave with light shining far above. As his eyes focused on the small sliver of light, he could make out interconnecting rope bridges and buildings. He swallowed a hard lump in his throat. He was at the bottom of the ravine.

This must be the prison.

He glanced around the cave, noticing dozens of other cages suspended from the ceiling throughout the murky cavern. One wall of the surrounding cave seemed to be made of wood, and Alek frowned, realizing it was the base of the dam.

Someone shifted behind him, and he turned around as the cage shrieked, swaying through the air. His confines were larger than he had initially thought. Sarah kneeled near him, her face pale and grimy, but otherwise unharmed. Behind her were three other female prisoners, all elves.

Two had deep, auburn hair, and the other was blonde. Alek was once again in awe of their beauty, even as they were covered in rags and filth. He noticed that one of the red-haired elves' eyes were swollen from crying.

'Who …?' he asked, his voice still dry.

'I am Krissy,' the blonde elf said, her voice was slightly lilting and foreign. 'This is Roselia and Lilly.'

'The dark-haired elf who led the escape earlier today was Roselia's husband,' Sarah explained quietly, her eyes flicking to the crying elf and back to Alek. 'Lilly is her sister. They were all supposed to escape together today, but they never managed to get free of this cage.'

'What happened to the other elves?' Alek asked, already knowing the answer.

Fresh tears fell down Roselia's face and fire burned in her eyes as she spoke, her voice fierce. 'They murdered them.' She jerked her head to the edge of the cave.

Alek followed her gaze and for the first time noticed the satyrs lining the perimeter of the cavern. They stood silently, their glowing eyes softly roaming through the gloomy cave as water dripped down the walls, splashing into the pool on the rock floor.

'We need to get out of here,' Alek whispered, half to himself as he wrapped his arms around his knees.

Roselia snorted as Krissy shot her a warning glance. 'We just tried that, boy. And now my husband is dead because this damn cage wouldn't open fast enough.'

Krissy sighed. 'We'd come up with an escape plan,' she explained. 'We've all been working in shifts to patch the dam wall for months now. Bran, Roselia's husband, attacked the guards when it was his shift and pulled the levers that lowered and opened our cages.' She pointed to a row of levers on the far wall, near a bridge that jutted over the water at the base of the cave.

'But our cage wouldn't open when we hit the ground. Bran tried, but there wasn't time. He had to go or the whole plan would have failed.'

Roselia let out a harsh laugh. 'Ha! It failed anyway!' she said loudly, her voice echoing around the cavern. 'All of you were too gutless to go with him! He died because you all preferred to stay in your cages.' Roselia stared wildly at the other cages suspended around them, each containing a handful of elves.

'Hush,' Krissy warned as the guards shifted around the edge of the cave, alerted by Roselia's raised voice.

'Three of them did go,' Lilly spoke for the first time, her voice was so quiet Alek had to strain his ears to hear her. The complete opposite of her sister.

Roselia snorted. 'And now they're all dead.' She crossed her arms, leaning her head against the cage bars as tears fell down her face.

'Get some rest,' Krissy said comfortingly to Sarah and Alek. 'They'll be coming for you two soon.' She stared pointedly at Sarah, her mouth curling into a smile.

'You caused quite a stir with your magic and how many guards you wiped out. I'm sure news of your abilities has travelled fast.'

Sarah blushed, wringing her hands. Alek frowned, noticing they were covered in black stains. Blood. How many satyrs had she killed? Dozens, probably. And he had almost vomited accidentally killing one.

Shame flooded through him, threatening to drown him. Maybe if he hadn't been so caught up in his feelings, he would have gotten to Sarah and Bran and the other elves, and they wouldn't be in this situation.

No. He shook his head, clearing his thoughts. He had to stop thinking like this and find a way to escape—a way to get him and Sarah and the elves home.

'What are you thinking about?' Sarah asked quietly, shifting to sit next to him, her warmth comforting.

'A way to get us out of here,' he muttered, a rueful grin spreading across his face. 'And how I always manage to get knocked out every time I'm in a fight.'

Sarah chuckled at his words, pressing her shoulder comfortingly against his.

Roselia huffed from the other side of the cage. 'Well, when you figure out an escape plan, let me know. I'll be right behind you, ready to murder those fuckers that killed my husband.' Sarah sighed and slumped sideways, resting her head on Alek's shoulder.

'How long have you been here?' he asked, turning towards Krissy. 'How did you end up here?'

She shrugged. 'Months, years? Who knows. It's hard to tell the time when you're always in this godforsaken cave. I haven't felt dry in what seems like forever, and I'm sick of patching up their stupid dam.

'The satyrs suddenly started appearing in Aladrial, our home, a few years ago, taking children one-by-one every few weeks. My people were going insane trying to work out why their offspring were vanishing.' Krissy paused, her eyes lost in a distant memory. 'Elf children are … rare. We live for so long that we don't feel the need to procreate as much as humans do. So to lose a child is … difficult. Once the children were gone, they started preying on adults, and that's how I ended up here.'

'But there are no children here that I can see,' Sarah said, looking through the darkness to the other cages.

Krissy shook her head. 'No, the children are in the castle, high up in the mountains. They serve the nobles and the lords of the Portal Realm. They're too special to slave away in the darkness like us.'

'Why elves, though?' Alek pondered curiously.

'My guess is the satyrs find it poetic, keeping elves as slaves,' Krissy whispered. 'My people used to treat them poorly, using their abilities to create portals without any form of regard for how the satyrs felt, long ago, before the Dark Days. I guess they never forgot, and this is their version of revenge …' Krissy sighed as her voice trailed off. 'We deserve it, in a way.'

Time ticked by, and the cave faded into silence. Only the trickling of water echoed through the air. Alek dozed on and off as hours slipped past, an aching chill settling in him as he leaned uncomfortably against the cage bars.

'I'm sorry for what I said earlier in the forest,' Sarah suddenly muttered beside him. 'About how you don't understand and you've never been in love and all that. It was unfair of me and insensitive. I'm sorry I dragged you into all of this.' She sniffed. 'I feel so bad. It's my fault you're stuck here with me. I was intent on revenge, so consumed by it. And look where it got me: locked in a cage.'

'Hey,' Alek said. 'No, it's not your fault. I chose to follow you. And besides ...' He hesitated slightly but then ploughed ahead, speaking before he could overthink. 'I am in love.'

'What?' Sarah gasped, twisting beside him to look at his face. 'With who? What's her name? Do I know her?'

Alek grimaced at the incorrect pronoun. 'He ... it's Kai. I love him.' He felt an enormous weight lift off his shoulders as he finally said the words out loud.

'Oh,' Sarah said, silence stretching between them as Alek waited apprehensively for her response.

'That explains the big boots in your room that morning I visited you!' she teased. 'What were you two up to before I walked in, hey?'

'None of your business!' Alek gasped, blood colouring his cheeks as Sarah giggled beside him.

Relief flooded through Alek at her response to his revelation. He wasn't sure what he had expected—shock or anger? But definitely not indifference. He felt a little lightheaded as he realised that his secret was no longer a secret. He had someone to confide in, a friend he didn't have to hide anything from.

Now he just had to face Benny. The thought made him cringe, and he quickly pushed it to the back of his mind. That was a problem for another day.

'And,' Sarah continued, 'you have magic now. I saw what you did with the ice during The Hunt.'

He nodded, smiling ruefully. 'That blast of magic in the valley the other night? That was me.' He paused only for a moment, not wanting to explain to Sarah about seeing a memory left by his brother. That was something personal between him and Jaxtyn.

'Kai's been helping me, teaching me to control it.'

Sarah frowned. 'What does Kai know about magic?'

Alek hesitated; Kai's secret wasn't his to tell … but it would be nice to have someone who knew everything about his relationship to talk to.

'Kai is a shape-shifter,' Alek began. Out of the corner of his eye, he saw Krissy's head whip around to face them.

'Seriously?' Sarah gasped. 'So he can turn into anything?'

Alek shook his head. 'No. Well, I mean, kind of. He has tattoos all over his body, and he can turn into whatever he has tattooed onto him.'

'I'd heard rumours about the last shifter,' Krissy murmured from the opposite corner of the cage. 'I had presumed they were just that—rumours.'

'Wait, the *last* shifter?' Sarah asked, frowning.

'Yeah, his people were wiped out with all of the other magical creatures when he was a child.' Alek sighed, running a hand through his hair. 'He doesn't like to talk about it, so I've never asked for details.'

'But Alek, magical creatures were wiped out hundreds of years ago,' Sarah said slowly. 'That would make Kai over one hundred years old.'

'What?!' Alek gasped. 'You're joking. He looks just as old as any of us!'

Krissy nodded from the shadows. 'She is right. He would have a long life, just like us elves. Most magical creatures do.' Alek sighed. What was one more secret to add to the tangled web of things Kai still hadn't told him about his past? Did the shifter not trust him? Had he done something to make Kai doubt his loyalty?

He would unravel all of the shifter's secrets one by one, eventually. Alek leaned his head back against the cage bars, the cold metal easing his headache. A realisation jolted through him, causing him to snort loudly and screw his nose up. He had slept with a one-hundred-year-old man. His mind whirled as he tried to fathom the idea of being alive for that length of time.

Why me? Alek thought, closing his eyes and pressing his hands onto the cold cage floor. *He's been alive for so many years, and somehow, he likes me. He must've had dozens of relationships before me. How can I possibly measure up to that?*

'So,' Sarah continued quietly, oblivious to Alek's tumultuous thoughts, 'my magic is Wind, yours is Water, and Benny's is Fire. We just need to find whoever has the power of Earth, then go steal back this amulet before everything erupts into chaos, and then save the world, right?'

Alek chuckled, pushing his thoughts aside and focusing on

Sarah's words. 'Right, no biggie.'

The cage swung as Krissy jumped violently at their words.

'Hang on, hang on, hang on,' she began, her eyes wild as she stared at the two friends. 'Your magic is elemental? You each wield one of the elements?'

Alek and Sarah nodded, exchanging an awkward glance as the red-haired elves' faces drained of colour.

'You can't be here!' Krissy exclaimed, urgency rolling from her lips, 'We need to get you out and back to Balathor. You're the only hope our world has of not falling into darkness.' She paused, choosing her next words carefully. 'My sister is the fourth. The one you've been looking for. Her magic is earth.' Silence fell throughout the cave as Alek and Sarah sat, shocked at Krissy's fierceness and her final revelation.

'Well,' Sarah began slowly, 'I guess now we just need an escape plan.'

Krissy spoke hesitantly. 'I think … I may have an idea.'

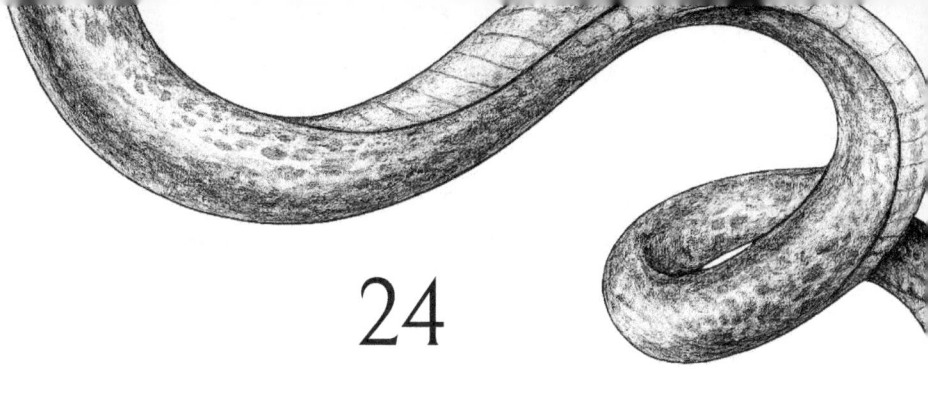

24

OF DEATH AND OF FURY

'**Y**ou can do it , Alek,' Sarah whispered beside him. 'Just breathe.'

He shot her an exasperated look. 'You know I'm getting real sick of people telling me to breathe,' he muttered, ignoring her confused expression as he focused back on the water lining the cave floor.

Taking Sarah's advice, he closed his eyes, steadying his mind as he did so. Slowly breathing in and slowly exhaling, he gently prodded the ball of magic inside of him, awakening it. It flooded his system, bringing with it the familiar, tingling surge through his body, the rush of pleasure.

Alek gasped, energy crackling through his veins. All around the cave, elves shifted in their cages, mumbling to themselves as they felt his magic sizzling through the air.

Reaching down to the water far below them, Alek concentrated, willing it to do his bidding. The water responded instantly as a stream of clear liquid surged skywards, detaching itself from the surrounding pool.

Grunting with the effort, Alek manipulated the stream, wrapping the water around the large lock on the outside of their cage. Sweat trickled down his neck as he doubled his efforts, pushing more of his power against the water, bending it to his will.

The water hissed as it hardened, turning opaque. A few seconds passed and the water had crystallised into shimmering ice, coating the metal lock and making it brittle enough to blast open.

Alek rocked backwards, releasing the hold on his magic but not pushing it down. He let it remain, flowing just below the surface of his skin. He had a feeling it wouldn't be long before he would need it again.

'Yes, Alek!' Sarah hissed triumphantly, pushing in front of her friend. 'Now it's my turn.'

Alek felt his magic surge as Sarah's suddenly crackled into the air around him. Within seconds, a small blast of wind slammed into the frozen lock with a muffled clang. The lock snapped and plummeted towards the water below.

Panic flashed through Alek as he realised the splash from the falling lock would draw the attention of the surrounding guards. He lunged forwards, swinging his arm upwards. As he did so, another stream of water rose from the surrounding pool, catching the lock before it could pick up enough speed to make a loud splash. Calming his breaths, Alek slowly lowered the water, returning it and the lock back to the cave floor.

Sarah let out a long breath beside him. 'I didn't really think about that part,' she whispered, her voice slightly shaky. 'Well done, Alek.' She turned to look back at the three elves in their cage. 'Ready?'

They nodded silently, their faces taut.

Sarah turned back to the cage door, pushing it open. Taking a deep breath, Sarah stepped forward, wind rippling around her as she dropped over the edge of the cage and into the open air.

Alek held his breath as he watched his friend manipulate the air around her body and slowly lower herself to the waist-deep water on the cave floor. Beside him, the three elves lined up, ready to follow once Sarah gave the signal. As the cage emptied one by one, Alek forced himself to focus. He would not freeze this time. The elves needed him; Sarah needed him. He was just as strong as any of them, and he would prove it to himself.

Suddenly, it was his turn. Before he could overthink the impossible task ahead, Alek sucked a deep breath through his nose and stepped out of the cage. His stomach dropped uncomfortably as he became weightless and aware of the rippling air around him, supporting his fall. Within seconds, his legs plunged into icy water, the cold biting into his skin.

He stumbled slightly as the sense of weightlessness left him and gravity returned. He glanced at Sarah, and she nodded at him. Her face was pale, but she still managed a savage smile as she waded silently through the murky water. He frowned. Was she actually enjoying this? The thought of a fight breaking out was making him sick. A cold sweat trickled down his neck as he remembered the feeling of his sword impaling the satyr only a few hours ago. Of the life draining out of his eyes.

No.

He shook his head, narrowing his eyes and pushing all thoughts from his mind. Now was not the time to think; that would come later. He would ensure everyone got out of here alive. No more elves were going to die today.

Sarah silently climbed onto the wooden bridge that spanned the length of the cavern floor, swiftly running through the shadows for the closest guard. Before the satyr had a chance to react, a blast of wind slammed into his neck, snapping it at an impossible angle. Sarah caught the body as it slumped, silently lowering it to the ground before moving onwards into the darkness.

Alek continued through the water, his power thrumming through his body as the cold liquid wrapped around him, caressing his skin. He heard a muffled gasp from behind him in the shadows, and he hoped the three elves were alright. They should be silently taking out the guards on the far side of the cavern.

Rocks rose up before him as he reached the edge of the cave and heard hooves shuffling not far above his head. Taking a step backwards, he narrowed his eyes, peering upwards through the darkness. A figure moved barely a metre above him, orange eyes flashing in the shadows.

Taking one last moment to steady his nerves, Alek threw his arm upwards, focusing his mind.

Water speared into the sky, crystalizing into ice as it plunged into the satyr's chest. Black blood sprayed across the cave wall as the figure slumped sideways. Alek withdrew his hand and the icy spear melted into water, running harmlessly back down the rock face.

Grasping the sharp rocks in front of him, Alek hauled himself up and onto the narrow ledge the creature had been standing on. Careful to avoid the slick blood pooling below his feet, Alek continued cautiously along the path, heading for the dam wall and thankful for the darkness obscuring the dead satyr behind him.

The next few minutes passed in a blur. Five bodies lay in Alek's wake as he continued through the shadows, anxiety prickling at him. Everything was going as planned; not a single alarm had been raised. Krissy and the others should be reaching the levers that lowered the cages shortly, and then it was just a matter of getting the captive elves out of the cave.

Roselia had said there was a tunnel that hollowed through the mountains, leading out into the misty forest that occupied the centre of the Portal Realm. Alek's role was to explode the dam. He would force the water being held at bay behind the weakened wall to flood the cave, ensuring that the prison was destroyed so no more elves could be forced to work in the murky darkness.

Alek had just sliced the neck of one of the guards when another dark figure rounded the corner, barrelling right into him. They both shouted in shock as they were thrown off the ledge towards the murky water below.

Icy cold enveloped Alek as shouting and firelight broke out above him, muffled by the surrounding water. He cursed, hauling himself to his feet. As his head broke the surface, chaos exploded around him. The cages were still hanging from the ceiling and Alek looked around wildly, seeing the three elves barely metres away from the levers. A line of fire flared around the cave, burning in a hollow alcove that circled the rock walls.

Satyrs shouted from above, and the sound of footsteps echoed through the damp air. Suddenly, a body slammed into Alek from the water beside him, knocking them both backwards. He threw his arm sideways as he hit the water and a strong current rocketed the satyr away from him. He pushed the current harder, slamming the guard into the rock wall, splitting open his skull.

Water splashed over him as he spun, his desperate eyes widening at the scene around him. Krissy was slumped against the cave wall, dark blood pooling from a blow to her head. Lilly was desperately defending her against a group of guards while Roselia thwarted attacks from the other direction. There was no sign of Sarah.

Gritting his teeth, Alek surged through the water, waves churning in his wake. He rapidly closed the distance between him and the captive elves before slamming to a stop, sending razor-sharp shards of ice flying into the air. The icicles shredded through the satyrs, their bodies collapsing at the elf's feet.

Energy drained from Alek's body as the water around him stilled. He rocked backwards on his heels as something whistled overhead and a sharp gasp echoed from above him. He glanced up to see Lilly's face drained of colour. Following her line of sight, he saw Roselia, her face pale with shock as an arrow stuck out of her stomach.

Deep crimson blood stained the front of her clothes, slowly spreading outwards. Lilly screamed, her voice ripping from her throat as she lunged for her sister. Alek watched as Roselia looked up, her eyes burning with rage. She pushed her sister away and spun on her heel, stooping to pick up a fallen guard's blade.

The elf then threw herself forward, slicing through the gathering satyrs as she made her way along the cave wall. Within seconds, she reached the levers, a pile of bodies in her wake. Without hesitating, she threw her weight into each of the large wooden handles, and chains rattled throughout the cave as cages crashed to the ground, doors springing open.

Alek blinked as another arrow appeared, buried in Roselia's shoulder. She threw her head back and howled, her fury echoing through the cavern. She turned to face the cave, her expression fierce even as her own blood splattered onto the rocks behind her. 'You!' a voice suddenly screamed above the echoing crashes.

Roselia's body jerked towards the sound and she hissed, baring her teeth. Fear washed over Alek at her savage expression. The elves may be stunningly beautiful, but they were equally as deadly. With another snarl, the

331

red-haired elf threw herself into the air, leaping through the flickering shadows.

Alek watched her splash into the water and make her away towards the bridge at the centre of the cavern. Where was she going? He looked towards the middle of the cave and froze. Standing upon the waterlogged wood was Sarah. A long blade clasped in her hands as she stood defiantly in the flickering firelight. Facing her was a single satyr, a jagged scar across his eye and a red brand etched onto his chest.

The blood drained from Alek's face as time seemed to slow.

Sarah dropped her sword and threw both of her arms forward, screaming in rage as the satyr before her gasped, clawing at his throat. He dropped to his knees, his mouth opening and closing as he scrabbled desperately at the bridge below him.

'You killed him!' Sarah screamed, and her magic flooded the cave as a strong wind howled among the stone walls.

With a start, Alek realised she was choking the satyr. She was forcing the air out of his lungs, drowning him above water. All around, the cave guards were running towards the bridge, and Alek cast a terrified gaze towards his friend. But she focused only on the one satyr, a cruel smile rippling across her face as his struggles grew weaker.

Suddenly, Roselia hauled herself onto the bridge beside Sarah, picking up the fallen blade by her side. Sarah faltered at the sudden appearance of the elf, and her magic died. Roselia screamed, launching herself into the oncoming guards with the fury of a dragon. Her blades whispered through the shadows, carving down her enemies as if they were made of butter.

Sarah collapsed to her knees as energy flooded from her. Alek felt her magic vanish, sucked from the air like a vacuum. He hurried forward, hauling himself up onto the bridge as the wave of satyrs pushed Roselia back a step. Then another.

Her own blood ran freely down her arms, mingling with that of her enemies below her feet as she surrendered another step. She paused long enough to glance behind her, her eyes locking onto Alek's.

'Run!' she yelled before a sword impaled her chest.

Before Alek could react, a catastrophic boom echoed through the cave, followed by blinding light. Lightning flashed down from the mountains above, illuminating the devastation around the cave.

Closing his eyes against the brightness, Alek rocked backwards, his ears ringing from the echoing sound of thunder. Seconds ticked past until Alek dared open his eyes, blinking in shock at what lay in front of him.

Six figures were illuminated before him on the bridge.

They were each perched atop a pale white horse. The horses were ghostly, almost translucent, a faint glow surrounding them. Each rider had no saddle, sitting bareback on their mount. They all had pale skin, white hair. Their eyes were a deep grey, like molten silver. The very warmth seemed to vanish from the air, leaving behind icy cold as the leader swung herself off her horse, landing silently on the wooden bridge.

Her hair was long, grazing the back of her knees. An intangible breeze floated among her and her riders, causing their hair to flow like running water. The now riderless horse snorted, pawing at the ground as its rider strode across the bridge towards the fallen Roselia.

Alek watched as the rider knelt beside the still elf; even in death, her flaming hair was so alive compared to the pale glow emanating from the silent woman. Electricity flashed through the air as the strange woman reached down, caressing the fallen elf's face. Light sparked from her touch and Roselia's body shuddered, letting out one final breath. As the breath fell from the elf's lips, it became a pale mist, growing in size and taking on a pale form. Within moments, a ghostly image of the fallen elf stood, gazing down upon her body.

The pale woman straightened, holding out a hand to the ethereal Roselia. The elf stood upright, taking the woman's hand, allowing herself to be led away from her fallen body.

'No!' a strangled voice called out.

Alek tore his eyes away from the scene unfolding in front of him and realised the satyr whom Sarah had been choking was climbing to his feet.

'Take your hands off my prisoner, death-dealer,' he spat, his voice hoarse.

The death-dealer slowly turned, power radiating from her as she glared down at the satyr.

'She is no longer of this earth.' Her voice was eerie, like a whispering breeze in the darkest night. It spoke of death and of fury.

Alek shivered as he felt a chill strike his bones.

'But—' the satyr sputtered before he was cut off.

'You know the deal, Ozark!' she snapped, energy crackling as her voice sharpened. 'We harvest the souls of supernatural beings whom we deem worthy.' Her molten eyes rested on Alek's face as she continued. 'Once they come with us, they belong to the sky, to death. To me.'

Alek shuddered underneath the unblinking stare, but he found familiarity in the pale face. An image of Ash's features flashed unbidden into his mind. She had the same white hair, the same ethereal beauty. She moved in a similar way. But where Ash was comforting, kind, this woman was cold and dangerous.

'You're nothing more than witches,' Ozark sneered, the scar over his eye pulsing red with anger as blood rushed to his face.

The death-dealer froze, her eyes sliding back to the satyr, her bottom lip curling as disgust rolled off her.

'The witches of old worshipped us. They sacrificed themselves to have our power. Allow me to demonstrate what we are capable of.' She raised her hand and snapped her fingers.

A sigh passed through the room, and the dozen satyrs assembled on the wooden bridge collapsed to the floor, dead. Horror rolled off Alek as he witnessed the immense power the woman wielded. The gathered death-dealers sat in stony silence as their leader stalked back to her waiting horse, Roselia's ghostly form trailing behind her.

As she mounted, helping Roselia up behind her, the riders in her wake shifted, and Alek heard Sarah let out a strangled gasp as she stumbled forwards. He frowned, glancing back at the riders as cold fingers of dread wrapped around his heart, suffocating him.

Sitting astride a mighty horse at the back of the group was Chris. Sarah reached out, tears streaming down her face.

The leader looked down at Sarah, sneering in disgust. 'What do you want, girl?'

Sarah ignored the woman, her entire focus on the wraith-like boy at the back of the group. 'Chris?' she asked uncertainly.

His unfamiliar silver eyes briefly flickered to hers before passing over her head to stare into the distance.

'He doesn't know who you are, you stupid girl,' the woman scoffed, but Alek did not miss the suspicious look she shot in Chris's direction.

'No,' Sarah said, her voice shaking. 'No, I don't believe you.' The woman scoffed, her unblinking eyes full of contempt.

'You're testing my patience. Step aside or die.'

Sarah shook her head. 'No. Give him to me.'

'Uh, Sarah?' Alek said, feeling energy crackle through the cavern. 'I think you should listen to her.'

'No, I'm done being the victim,' Sarah hissed. 'I'm done being ordered around.'

If it weren't for Alek's keen eyesight, he would have entirely missed what happened next.

Magic flared around Sarah's body as she shot herself forwards, a dagger grasped in her hand. Her muscles bunched as she twisted, savagely hurling the blade across the cave, pouring her magic into the throw.

The pale woman's eyes widened at the sudden attack, her horse rearing as thunder boomed through the air. The deathdealer behind the woman yelled, steering his horse into the path of the dagger. There was a thud as the blade buried itself in the rider's spine, and he slumped forwards just as lightning flashed and the ghostly riders vanished.

Alek blinked. Barely a second of time had passed since Sarah's attack and the riders' exit. The cave was silent, electricity still crackling in the air from the death-dealers' magic.

Suddenly, Sarah began to scream, clutching at her arm as cries ripped out of her throat. Panic made Alek lunge towards her. What was happening? No one had even come close enough to hurt her!

He grabbed her shoulder, watching in horror as a white-hot brand appeared against her forearm. Her skin hissed as the mark materialised, red raw against the surrounding flesh. *A lightning bolt*, Alek realised.

On the arm she had used to slay a death-dealer.

Maniacal laughing echoed over Sarah's screams as the brand started to fade, no longer glowing white-hot across her skin. Alek looked up, watching as Ozark stumbled a step closer, his glowing eyes hooked on Sarah's arm.

'You've slaughtered a death-dealer!' he crowed, raising his arms dramatically. 'A feat only accomplished twice throughout history. Oh, they'll be coming for you now, girl. They'll be hunting you down with that brand on your arm until the day you die.'

Before Alek could retaliate, Krissy hurled herself across the bridge, a blade in hand, and collided with the satyr. The two rolled head over heels, grappling desperately with one another. The blonde elf reared back, slamming her knee roughly into the satyr's gut, causing him to howl in pain. As if a switch had been flipped, chaos broke out into the cave as the elves, now free of their cages, attacked the surrounding guards.

'Alek!' Krissy shouted, panting heavily as she grappled with a giant satyr. 'Flood the cave. We need to end this now!'

Alek nodded, gritting his teeth. He roughly grabbed Sarah's arm, hauling her off the bridge with him. Together, they splashed into the blood-filled water below. Alek grimaced as bodies nudged against his legs while he strode towards the dam wall, delving deep into his magic.

He reached the end of the cave and stopped, placing his hands on the wooden structure before him. He could feel the water pulsing on the other side, the sheer power being held back by the leaking timber. Alek craned his head back, his eyes following the wall up and out of sight above him.

His stomach dropped as the rope bridges stretching far above shook violently from side to side. Hundreds of satyrs were surging down the ravine, heading straight for them. Releasing the water contained on the other side of the dam would be devastating. He would kill hundreds, if not thousands.

Alek hesitated, looking around the cave. Elves fought desperately against their guards. He watched as Krissy and Ozark violently collided in a clash of steel upon the bridge. She had assured Alek earlier that the limited magic elves still possessed would protect them from the rush of water. It would only be the satyrs that would be smashed against the rocks.

Plus, breaking the dam would essentially render the prison useless, submerging it underwater so that the satyrs could no longer hold anyone captive in the gloomy cave.

Suddenly, Lilly was beside him, soaking wet and limping slightly. 'I'm here to help,' she said simply. 'Take my magic, add it to your own.'

'I don't know how!' Alek looked at her desperately. 'I don't know what I'm doing!'

Lilly cocked her head. 'Yes, you do. Stop doubting yourself.'

The elf gripped Alek's forearm, staring into his eyes. He gasped as energy surged between them, writhing through his body. Alek clenched his teeth, keeping himself from screaming as magic threatened to tear him apart. He was barely conscious of the cave around him, just the white-hot power flooding his veins.

'Roselia gave her life for me.' Alek barely heard Lilly whisper beside him. 'Now, I give my life to my people.'

One last wave of power thundered into Alek's body and he fell to his knees, the water around him whipping into the air, swirling wildly. His vision began to black out as the sheer power threatened to rip him apart. What was the plan? He felt as if his skin was splitting, peeling off layer by layer. The water droplets that fell on him did little to help ease the burning, pulsing in his bones.

Water.

The dam. He had to free the water.

Alek blinked open his eyes. Water swirled in a vortex around him as he slammed his hands into the wooden wall. He was dimly aware of Sarah beside him as she wrapped her arms around his shoulders.

He could feel the water, feel it thrumming against the wood, feel the power swelling on the other side. He pulled, urging the massive amount of liquid forwards, drawing it with his magic.

Power surged down his arms, and he screamed as the entire cave reverberated, a loud crack cutting through the air. Seconds of silence ticked by, and Alek pushed the magic down and out of his arms, snarling at the timber separating him from his prize.

Suddenly, the wall buckled, a stream of water spurting from a crack in its centre. Barely a second later, a thunderous roar filled the cave as the dam exploded forward. Alek spun, throwing his arms around Sarah and wrapping them in his magic as they were blown off their feet by the force of the wave.

The two friends were hurled through the darkness, safe in a pocket of Alek's power as the colossal wall of water obliterated the cave around them. They rode the current through a labyrinth of underground tunnels until, finally, light broke through the water around them.

Glimpses of misty trees and cloudy skies speared through the water as the two friends were tossed down the river by the current. Alek calmed his mind, struggling to keep the safe bubble of magic around him and Sarah as his energy bottomed out. Water started to cave in around him, bursting through his defences, threatening to drag Sarah to the bottom of the river. Alek focused on Aranasmin, the valley he now called home. Images of Kai flashed behind his eyes, of afternoons spent training with him. Of laughing with Benny and Sarah over dinner. How the cold dawn air would slice through his lungs every morning as he ran beside his friends. The magical pool of water, hidden high in the mountains where he had finally felt free.

Tingling erupted under his skin, queasiness rushing through his body as cave walls wrapped around the two friends and they were hurled forward through a dark passage. Alek's magic at last gave out as they erupted into icy cold air.

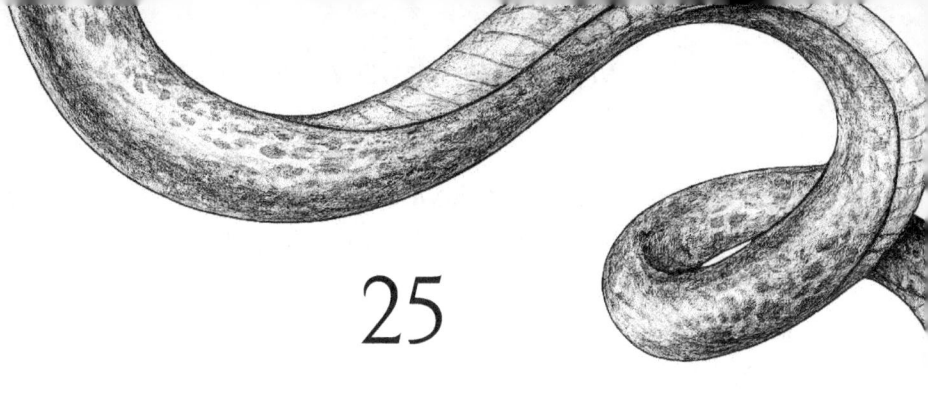

25

BELLY OF THE BEAST

Alek gasped as he was thrown from the cave mouth and into Aranasmin, water surging around him as he sprawled awkwardly onto the icy ground, his knees jarring from the impact. A few inches of snow coated the ground and the freezing cold ice soaked through his clothes, biting into his overheated skin. He gasped in deep breaths, his whole body spasming while he remained hunched on his hands and knees, trying to regain some of his expended energy.

His magic lashed around inside of him, swirling maniacally, and he clamped down on it, pushing it deep inside, quelling it. He gritted his teeth with effort. He had never had as much raw power flooding out of him as he had moments before, but he had to regain control.

Alek shivered; he hadn't realised how much power he had within him. How much he constantly pushed down and squashed, even without Lilly's added strength. He was afraid if he let it all out, it would consume him, kill him. As memories of his magic flooded his mind, the power surged within him again, the snow around his fists hardening into ice.

No! he yelled to himself. His arms tensed and, with one vicious push, his magic quieted, retreating to that silent place deep within him. He could still feel it roiling with power, but it was no longer out of control.

Letting a long breath out of his mouth, Alek dragged himself upright, slowly relaxing his tense body. He was okay, Sarah was okay, the elves had escaped—he hoped, wincing at the tremendous force of water he had unleashed on them. They had to be alive; Krissy had assured him their limited magic would protect them. Everything was going to be okay.

They were back at the northern end of the valley, the tumbledown ruins lying haphazardly in the night before them. A hand rested comfortingly on his shoulder, and he glanced sideways. Sarah stood beside him, her hair sopping wet and her eyes raw red, but otherwise unharmed.

'You did it, Alek,' she whispered, her voice cracking slightly. 'You saved us all.'

A dry laugh escaped Alek's mouth as he hauled himself to his feet, the cold night air drying the moisture on his skin.

'Barely,' he croaked, turning to look at his friend. 'Are … are you okay?'

Sarah bit her lip, breaking eye contact with Alek. 'He's alive. Alek, he's alive. This whole time, I've been so focused on finding that damn satyr, Ozark, and killing him, that I didn't stop to think of the possibility that Chris might still be alive.'

'Sarah, no,' Alek said gently, grabbing her hands. 'He isn't alive. He died; we watched him die. You know that. What we saw was a ghost of Chris, his soul or something. It's not him; he didn't even recognise us.'

Alek glanced down, looking at the shiny lightning bolt branded onto Sarah's arm, now faded to a bright white. If Ozark was right, they'd unknowingly made a very deadly enemy.

Sarah roughly pulled away from Alek, pacing back and forth through the snow. 'I've wasted all my energy on training and preparing for revenge when I should have been focusing my time on rescuing him!' she exclaimed, frustration flooding off of her.

Alek opened his mouth to answer—they had had no way of knowing Chris was alive—but he stopped. Something was wrong.

Alek spun around, his eyes flashing through the darkness, searching for the source of his unease. The wind had stilled. The rustling branches of the dead trees around them had stopped.

'Alek, what's going on?' Sarah said, stepping to his side.

'Do you feel it?' he whispered, the hair on the back of his neck standing on end.

She nodded, drawing her sword. 'There's something watching us.'

Alek groaned. What now? He didn't have the strength for much more after the fight they had just been through.

Just as he was thinking it must be nothing, a shadow detached itself from the rundown buildings before them, hauling itself over a small brick wall and landing with a solid thump on the snow.

Blood drained from Alek's face, and his mouth went dry. Before him was a creature straight out of a nightmare. The monster was easily ten feet tall, humanoid in shape. Its skin was dark, so black it seemed to be made of shadows. No light reflected off it as the thing stalked through the snow towards them. Its long arms dragged on the ground and its fingers lengthened into razor-sharp claws, clicking together menacingly as it moved ever closer.

Its head was elongated, the skull oval in shape. Huge, dark eyes took up the majority of its face, but the worst part was its mouth. It split the creature's head in two, stretching around half of the beast's skull. Hundreds of needle-sharp teeth poked out from behind the monster's lips, blood-stained and razor-sharp. A low gurgle escaped the creature's throat as its thin nostrils flared, taking in their scent. Alek frowned, momentarily distracted. Something about the creature was familiar. The noise it made sounded like something he had heard before.

Beside him, Sarah screamed, her voice splitting through the night, piercing his ears. Snapping out of his thoughts,

Alek looked up to see the monster launch itself at them, covering the space between them impossibly fast.

Before Alek could react, a blast of wind buffeted him and the monster was launched off its feet and slammed loudly into one of the old, crumbling buildings. It shrieked loudly, its roars echoing around the valley.

'Alek, move!' Sarah yelled, wind still rippling around her hands as she launched another concussive blast at the monster, buffeting it against the brick wall. It screamed in frustration, scrabbling against the snow as it fought against the powerful blast.

Alek snapped himself out of his thoughts and ran, forcing his tired legs into motion. His muscles shook and screamed at the effort. His energy was depleted after their escape from the Portal Realm; he didn't know how much strength he had left in him.

Footsteps thudded in the dark behind them as Sarah grabbed Alek's arm, dragging him forwards with her. Dead branches from the shrubs around them grasped at Alek's legs as the two friends struggled forwards. The monster's claws clicked together behind them, so close panic flooded through Alek and he threw himself forwards, his heart thudding in his chest.

The two friends stumbled into the clearing near the centre of the valley, Alek falling to his knees, gasping heavily.

'Alek, come on; you have to get up!' Sarah begged, desperately tugging on his arm.

Alek shook his head. His body was numb; he was spent.

Even his magic had grown cold, a small lump hidden deep within him. He turned his head as the monster erupted from the bushes behind them, sending branches flying into the air as it shrieked triumphantly, spotting its prey before it.

Gritting her teeth, Sarah adjusted her grip on the blade in her hand and stepped forward, her body covering Alek's. He felt her magic flare against his own as she prepared to unleash herself on their attacker.

The monster's eyes zeroed in on the girl, and it launched itself forwards, claws outstretched and grasping wildly. Sarah threw her arms up and another blast of wind slammed into the creature's side, sending it flying wildly across the field and crashing into the snow.

Without pausing, Sarah sprinted forward, moving so fast she was barely a blur. She reached the creature just as it rose from the ground, slicing its chest with her sword. Before the monster could retaliate, she launched herself skywards, sailing over the beast's head.

At the pinnacle of her jump, Alek watched in shock as she paused mid-air. Wind rippled around her and Sarah screamed as she pummelled the creature from above, blasting it with her magic. The monster was thrown into the ground with a resounding crack, forced deep into the snow by Sarah's steady blast of air.

Alek saw the energy drain from Sarah's face, and she fell from the sky, landing awkwardly in the snow. Pausing only long enough to draw in a deep breath, Sarah rose to her feet, determination on her face. With a snarl, she flung herself forward, snow spraying behind her as she rammed the monster.

Alek felt the power of her impact from where he was slowly hauling himself to his feet, and he watched as she collided with the monster, sword outstretched. The blade sliced across the creature's skin and then snapped, shattering into a thousand pieces.

Sarah blinked, staring numbly at the broken blade in her hands. The monster rose silently above the girl, dwarfing her with its size. The low gurgling noise tore from deep within its throat again, and Alek cocked his head to the side.

It almost sounded like …

Realisation flooded through him as his mind flashed back to his first day in the library and the book he had skimmed through—*Sprites and Their Various Forms.* The high-pitched giggling of the sprites that had attacked him weeks ago was etched into his mind, a sound he would never forget. This monster's gurgling was almost identical, only deeper and more menacing.

He remembered pausing briefly on a page within that book that talked about a magic-affected sprite, or a sprite that had consumed blood infused with magic. The book had described a horrifying creature, dark as night and monstrous in size.

It was a sprite.

Sarah's screaming snapped him back to reality as the sprite lunged towards her, its claws raised in a vicious strike. Before Alek could react, a pale figure exploded out of the trees at the edge of the clearing. He instantly recognised Kai, dim light reflecting off his pale skin, his tattoos rippling across his naked torso. A thin blade flashed in the shifter's fist as he quickly closed the distance between himself and Sarah.

Alek's heart thudded in his chest as Kai threw himself forwards, slamming into the sprite's body and sending them both tumbling backwards, gouging deep rivulets through the snowy ground. Kai was on his feet in an instant, his body moving with inhuman grace as he nimbly stabbed the monster's leg, black gore spewing onto the white snow.

The sprite's roar of pain reverberated through Alek's bones as it wildly swung its long arms, knocking Kai flying. The boy twisted in mid-air, landing deftly on all fours and instantly launching himself back towards the sprite with speed Alek had not seen before.

He blinked. He had thought he had seen the level of skill Kai possessed, the unnatural abilities being a shifter had gifted him with. But he had never seen him in the midst of battle, had never seen him unleash himself before. Alek watched the fight in awe as Sarah stumbled over to his side.

Kai was barely more than a blur; he was relentless. Always moving, twisting, dodging away from the sprite while darting in close and landing blow after blow upon the monster. However, every bit of damage Kai inflicted on the sprite was superficial. The creature was barely weakening; if anything, the wounds it had collected were making it more enraged.

'Alek, what do we do?' Sarah hissed, suddenly by his side. 'We're barely hurting it. We don't even know what it is!'

'It's a sprite,' Alek said distractedly, tensing as he watched Kai trade blows with the beast.

Sarah frowned. 'A sprite? But I thought sprites were tiny and can only come out in the moonlight?'

Shaking his head, Alek couldn't pull his gaze away from the fight before him. Kai was losing, only really buying them some time. 'It's a magic-affected sprite. It's either been exposed to magic or drank blood from someone who possesses magic.'

Sarah hissed. 'Your blast of magic that you released into the valley, Alek. That must have been what caused it to turn into this!'

Alek flinched, momentarily distracted. If he had caused the sprite to transform, then he was the one responsible for the massacre of the students in the valley. Dread washed over him as he realised that had caused the murder of innocent children.

'Alek!' Sarah said, roughly shaking him by the shoulders. 'How do we kill it?!'

Alek frowned, forcing his mind back to that first day in the library. 'I'm—I'm not sure. The sprite's weaknesses become their strengths when they transform. That's why it's appeared after dark, not during the moonlight.'

'So ... light becomes its weakness!' Sarah yelled, glancing around wildly.

'Sarah! Alek!'

The two friends jumped as a new voice echoed through the clearing behind them.

Alek spun to see Benny running through the night, his hair tousled and wild from sleeping. He paused before his friends and his eyes widened as he looked past them, taking in the carnage in the snow. Kai was circling the monster now, his breaths heavy, sweat shining across his chest as he focused on the beast, his eyes narrowed.

'What on earth is going on?!' Benny gasped, fear shining in his eyes.

'Benny!' Sarah hissed, her expression wild as she gripped her cousin's arm. 'We need fire, lots of fire!'

Alek blinked, surprised by Sarah's quick thinking. Fire would create light, which would weaken the sprite!

'Yes!' Alek yelled, his eyes shining urgently as he heard Kai roar in pain. 'You need to light up this clearing, Benny! It's the only way to end this.'

'But what—' Benny began to ask before Alek cut him off.

'We'll explain later!' he yelled desperately. 'Do it, Benny! Do it now!'

Frowning, Benny nodded, stepping away from his friend. Alek watched impatiently as Benny took a deep breath and wild magic rippled across the field.

Kai faltered in his war with the sprite, his head swinging to look in Benny's direction, the source of the magic. That distraction was all the sprite needed as it lunged forward, slamming Kai's head into the ground, its teeth lunging for his throat.

'Benny, now!' Alek yelled desperately.

Unbearable heat cracked through the air, followed by a roar as a wall of flames exploded into the night. The snow beneath Alek and Sarah's feet melted instantly as fire poured across the clearing, the warmth causing Alek's eyes to water as he ducked back from the blistering heat.

An ungodly scream erupted from the sprite's throat as it stumbled backwards, flames lashing at its dark skin. Kai struggled to his feet, his muscles rippling beneath a layer of sweat and blood. Steadying himself, the tattooed boy charged forward, his sword swinging in a great arc as the sprite flailed uselessly in the sudden light. Kai's blade glowed red in the flames as he buried it in the monster's neck, gritting his teeth with the force of the blow.

Time seemed to slow as Alek watched the scene before him unfold in the flickering light. Kai's blade sliced clean through the sprite's neck, separating the monster's head from its body. Abruptly, the creature's screams stopped, and its body collapsed to the ground, twitching as it turned the snow around it black.

Kai fell to his knees, the blade he carried thudding into the snow beside him. The fire illuminated his body, as great shuddering breaths rippled through him. The boy threw his head backwards, his dark hair slick as he forced air into his lungs.

Benny gasped in shock at Kai's killing blow and his fire abruptly stopped, plunging the field into darkness once more.

Alek rushed across the field, the snow beneath his feet turned to slush from the intense flames. He reached Kai and skidded to a halt before him, his tongue tied as he realised for the first time just how deadly the shifter could be. Tremors rippled up and down the inked boy's body, and panic flashed through Alek.

'Kai, are you okay?' he whispered, his heartbeat pounding in his throat as worry flashed through him.

Kai chuckled. 'I'm fine, Alek.' He took a heaving breath. 'It's just been a long while since I've had to fight like that. It took more out of me than it should have.'

Kai took a deep breath and hauled himself to his feet, wobbling slightly. Alek raked his eyes across the boy's body, from his booted feet in the snow to the inked animals across his torso and up to the deep blue eyes sparkling with amusement. He was unharmed; if anything, he was pale from exhaustion.

'Did you find what you were looking for?' Kai asked teasingly.

Alek frowned, shoving him in the stomach. 'You almost died, you idiot!'

Kai winced slightly at the blow. 'Would you prefer I didn't save Sarah's life?'

Alek muttered under his breath and Kai laughed, wrapping his arms around Alek and pulling him in close. Instantly, peace washed over Alek and he breathed in deep, letting the icy, wild smell Kai radiated wash over him. The challenges he had faced in the Portal Realm faded to the back of his mind as a sense of security rushed through him. He'd had enough adventures for a while, too much to wrap his head around right now. There'd be plenty of time for that later.

Raising his head, he planted a kiss against the taller boy's lips, holding his body tightly.

'Um, what the hell, Alek?!' Benny's voice snapped Alek back to reality.

Alek's heart sunk in his chest, peeling away from his rib cage and leaving behind a hollow feeling. Numbly, he turned to see Benny staring at him with a shocked look on his face while Sarah awkwardly stood next to him, grinning slightly.

Kai cleared his throat as he wrapped his arms around his chest, uncomfortably looking away from the situation before him. Alek searched for the words to say as Benny's expression went from shocked, to hurt to anger.

'You're gay?!' he hissed through clenched teeth, smoke rising around his fists.

'Benny ...' Alek trailed off, glancing at Sarah for help.

She stepped forward, placing a hand on Benny's shoulder. 'Ben, you need to calm down. It doesn't matter.'

Benny spun around, glaring at both the friends. 'You knew! Everyone knew except for me?! Your best friend?'

Alek flinched as Benny's familiar eyes locked onto his own, hurt and rage swirling in their depths.

'I didn't know how to say it, how to tell you,' Alek said softly. 'I was scared, Benny.'

'Scared? You've barely spoken to me the last few months, and now I find out you've been lying to me for years!' Benny raged. 'I've been on your side the whole time since we got here. Defending you from Lucien, fighting for you, and for what? This is bullshit, Alek. Some best friend you are.'

'Benny, no, I'm sorry. I didn't know how to say it, and I didn't even know myself until a few weeks ago!' Alek exclaimed, stepping towards his friend and feeling the world spin around him as Benny turned away.

Sarah started to speak but was cut off as metal flashed through the night and a sword suddenly pressed against Kai's throat.

'You,' a voice hissed in the darkness.

26

THE SNAKE

Alek twisted around, his head swimming, to see Ash poised behind the group, her face a picture of rage as she glared unwaveringly at Kai.

'You killed him. The only man I could call a father. You murdered him in cold blood. And you have the nerve to come back here! To take advantage of my kindness and live here, right under my nose.' She hissed, her sword shaking as she barely controlled her anger.

'Woah, woah, woah!' Sarah exclaimed, throwing her hands in the air. 'What the hell is going on?'

Alek shook his head, his mind a whirlwind of emotion between Benny's anger at him, getting attacked by the sprite, and now this.

Confused, Alek stepped forward. 'Ash, what are you doing? Put down your sword. Kai hasn't hurt anyone.'

'Ha!' Ash spat. 'He's the whole reason you three are here. He is the very thing wrong with this world. You've been the one murdering all of my students, stringing them up in the trees to rub it into my face, to haunt me.'

Kai flinched at her harsh words, a trickle of blood appearing at his throat as the sword cut into his skin.

'Kai did not kill those students,' Alek spat venomously at the principal, his fists clenching. 'It was a sprite. It had been infected with magic, causing it to grow into a different form. It turned this valley into its hunting ground. That was what mutilated those students and strung them up in the trees, not Kai! It's how it was marking its territory!'

'No matter,' Ash hissed, dismissing Alek's words. 'There are many more lies to unravel surrounding young Kai here.' The principal roughly jerked her chin at the three friends. 'Tell them,' she ordered. 'Or shall I?'

Kai's mouth pressed into a thin line as he remained silent, his eyes never leaving Alek's, his expression guarded. Alek searched the boy's familiar face, but the eyes that usually sparked with life were cold, dark, and unreadable. Dread settled in Alek's stomach as he glanced between Ash and Kai, unsure of what to do.

Laughing sarcastically, Ash spoke again, barely-concealed pain echoing with every word. 'Your friend Kai here is the murderer that snuck into this valley and stole the amulet I told you about. He has been lying to you for the last year.' Her face twisted in an ugly sneer. 'I knew there was a snake in Aranasmin. Little did I know he was right under my nose. And what's more, his name isn't even Kai. It's Kisho.'

The tattooed boy flinched at Ash's words.

She chuckled. 'That's right, Kisho. It's not hard to find information on the last living shifter. Especially when that shifter is a particularly high-ranking member of the Dark Warriors. Tell me …' She narrowed her eyes. 'How many people did you murder? How many villages did you burn before you found your way here? To the amulet? Hmm? And where have you hidden it? What have you done with it?!'

Alek was numb, his mind blank as he searched Kai's face for the truth. Surely this wasn't happening. At Ash's mention of snakes, his eyes had involuntarily traced the coiling tattoo down the shifter's arm.

'Kai …' he began, but Ash cut him off.

'His name is not Kai!' she snarled. 'Tell them!' She pushed the blade deeper into his neck.

Kai hesitated and then closed his eyes, surrendering. 'It's true,' he said simply. 'And as for the amulet, I gave it to *him*, to Azrael. The warlord now wears your precious amulet around his neck.'

With those few words, Alek felt the world close in around him, distantly noting the fear that shone clearly across Ash's pale face at the mention of the amulet's location. Numb with shock, he stumbled back a step, feeling Sarah wrap a comforting arm around his shoulders.

'Alek,' Kisho pleaded, his eyes wide. 'I didn't expect to meet you, to have this connection with you. I was sent back here to find The Four. We knew you would be called on once we took the amulet, so it was my task to find you and bring you all back as my prisoners. But once I saw you, I couldn't do it. Everything I feel for you is true … I love you.'

Alek flinched at his words as they echoed in his head. He turned them over in his mind, the words he had dreamed of hearing, and yet now they felt tainted, filled with nothing but lies and secrets. How could a hundred-year-old shape-shifter love him?

The last few months spent with Kai—Kisho—flashed through his mind: the training, the teasing. The magical pool hidden away in the mountains where everything had seemed to click into place. Everything had finally felt right. He had felt whole, happy. And now, in one fell swoop, that was being ripped right out from underneath him. Alek felt as though he was falling. His head was swimming.

Licking his lips, Alek opened his mouth to speak but was cut off as a horn echoed through the valley. Colour drained from Kisho's face as a loud howl boomed down from the mountains, followed by the clinking of metal.

Ash's eyes widened. 'Instead of taking them prisoner, you've led the Dark Warriors to us! You've been feeding information to them this whole time!'

Alarm flashed through Kisho's eyes. 'No! No, I didn't. I swear! They must have grown tired of waiting! And if they've brought the wolves, then it's just a hunting party!' He glanced back at Alek's blank face. 'And your blast of magic would have alerted them as to where you were hiding.'

'You will die for this!' Ash hissed, her arms tensing as she prepared to thrust her blade forwards.

'No!' Alek and Kisho shouted at the same time.

Ash hesitated, and Alek flinched as Kisho looked at him hopefully.

'We need him to slow the Dark Warriors down, to distract them so that we can escape,' Alek said, avoiding the shifter's gaze. 'It's the least he can do.'

'Alek,' Kisho began. 'You don't understand. I owe them—'

He trailed off as Alek turned away, looking to Ash. 'We need to leave. I know who the last of The Four is. But we have to get away from here first.'

Ash blanched, her mouth dropping open in shock. 'How … how do you know who the fourth is? I've searched for months and had no success.'

'She's an elf,' Alek replied, frowning as he saw a spark of surprise flash through Kisho's eyes. 'I don't have time to explain everything right now. Let him go so we can escape.'

Slowly, Ash lowered her sword, barely controlled anger flickering beneath her skin. Kisho stood frozen to the spot, his eyes never straying from Alek as the three friends turned and began to follow Ash out of the clearing.

As his companions disappeared into the shadowy forest before him, Alek hesitated, turning back towards the clearing. The once peaceful field was in ruins, echoing the pain that pulsed through his skin with every beat of his heart. His eyes burned as they locked onto Kisho's, seeing the same hurt mimicked in his blue gaze.

Thunder cracked loudly through the sky above them and lightning flashed, stabbing through the clouds. The brief flash of light illuminated the valley around them, revealing three large wolves stalking out of the forest at the opposite end of the clearing. Despite his hurt, fear flickered through Alek's chest as Kisho turned, rolling his neck and loosening his shoulders as the wolves paced across the field towards him.

Icy, wild magic crackled through the air and Alek watched as the shifter's body blurred, shredded clothing fluttering to the ground around him. The boy grew in size, thick brown fur exploding across his skin as long claws sprouted from saucer sized paws.

Lightning flashed again, and the large bear swung its massive head to look at Alek once more through familiar blue eyes. Alek blinked back tears and turned away just as the bear let out a defiant roar and the field broke into chaos.

27

CHAOS AND DARKNESS

As Alek hurried through the thick undergrowth to catch up with his friends, the heavens ripped open above him, sheets of rain pouring into the valley. His keen ears picked up the bone shattering thuds and snarls from the clearing he had left behind. From the boy he had left behind.

Alek stumbled after his friends, branches whipping his face as they raced through the narrow forest paths. Suddenly, the winding trail opened as he stepped into the bonfire clearing. The usual crackling flames in the centre of the space were reduced to dull embers by the pouring rain.

A shiver went down Alek's spine as images of the murdered students flashed through his mind. The bodies had been removed from the perimeter of the clearing, although dark stains marred the surrounding tree trunks where the bodies had been hung. Sarah and Benny huddled next to him as Ash stopped next to the remains of the bonfire.

The clearing was usually humming with life, the massive flames warding off the darkness with their warm glow. But now, the area seemed hollow and small as the violent storm battered the trees looming overhead. All around them, students appeared, awakened from their sleep by the sound of the horns, once distant but now alarmingly close.

'Imani,' Ash suddenly spoke, catching the attention of the girl as she emerged from the surrounding shadows. 'We are under attack. Alert the teachers, gather your classmates, and be prepared to fight.'

Imani's eyes grew wide as she nodded, glancing curiously at Sarah, who offered her a small smile.

'Go now!' Ash ordered, her voice rising to address the gathering students. 'Follow Imani. Defend our home.'

Alek barely registered the scared look on the students' faces as Imani led them into the night, his mind drifting back the field, wondering if the bear was still alive. Numbly, he realised Ash was leading his friends once more into the surrounding maples. Swiping rain from his eyes, Alek raced onwards, careful to keep up with the principal's fast pace.

Minutes later, the three friends were standing inside Ash's sprawling home nestled within the bamboo grove. Wild rain lashed against the roof above them, drowning out the sound of the approaching enemy. Ash rushed around the house frantically, piling clothes and belongings into three bags before thrusting them to each of the friends.

She hurriedly passed them each a sword and a thick, warm cloak. Alek numbly buckled the sword to his back and shrugged on the cloak, wrapping it tightly around himself as if it would protect him from not only the cold and blood that had been spilled that night but the truth.

'Alek!' Ash's harsh voice broke through his thoughts. 'Snap out of it. Your friends need you; the world needs you. It's time to focus. I'm sorry, but it's not about you right now.'

Alek blinked, clearing his head as he saw Sarah and Benny looking at him, fear shining in their eyes as they waited for him to make a move. He didn't say a word, just looked at Ash and nodded, noticing the relief wash across her face as he focused. 'We move quick,' she said through pursed lips. 'You do not stop—for anything or anyone. There is a tunnel behind the waterfall that will take you through the mountains. Continue on that path until you are far from here.'

She paused, her silver hair flashing as lightning clawed across the sky behind her. 'Azrael, leader of the Dark Warriors, now has the amulet.' Urgency laced her words as she continued, talking quickly, 'Which means our enemies now possess a weapon powerful enough to launch a war. You need to get to the fourth and stop the warlord before he reveals his hand. Do you understand?'

Alek dipped his head, slightly taken aback by the otherworldliness of Ash as she stood, illuminated against the raging storm behind her. Images of the death-dealers flashed through his mind as Ash turned towards the valley and drew her sword.

'Follow me, quickly.'

Taking a deep breath, Alek and his friends plunged into the storm, wind and rain instantly pummelling against them as they crossed the bamboo grove and snuck into the dark forest.

Beneath the deep foliage, the rain was just a trickle, the air still and silent. An occasional icy drop of water made its way through the dense canopy and dripped loudly onto the leaf litter around them. Alek took up the rear of the group as they swiftly navigated the shadowy forest.

A colossal roar reverberated through the air, shaking Alek to the core. The snarl was followed by loud shouts and a blasting horn. The Dark Warriors were in the valley, and Kisho had found them.

Ash picked up the pace, and before long, the friends were pelting through the forest at full sprint, panic clutching at Alek as the shouts of fighting students echoed through the trees around them. Suddenly, Ash was knocked flying off her feet, sprawling through the thick undergrowth around them.

Alek skidded to a halt, his heart beating faster as he took in the enemies stepping out of the shadows around them. They were tall. Easily over seven foot. They wore dark armour flecked with white war paint. Most of them had helmets covering their faces, fashioned with horns or protruding fangs.

One of the armoured men stepped forward, the top half of his face covered in a metal mask shaped like a skull. He grinned, brandishing a large sword.

'You're all going to lower your weapons and come with me.' Alek shuddered at his thick, rasping voice.

'I don't think so,' Sarah hissed before anyone else had a chance to speak.

Surprise flashed through Alek as Sarah drew her sword, narrowing her eyes dangerously. She had to be as exhausted as he was after everything they had been through, yet still, she stepped forward, ready to fight.

The Dark Warrior chuckled. 'This is going to be—'

His words ended in an abrupt gurgle as a dagger protruded from his neck. Alek spun around, seeing Ash palm another dagger from her belt. Before he had a chance to react, she had sent it flying, landing with a solid thud in the chest of another Dark Warrior.

As the two soldiers collapsed, their bodies disintegrated, collapsing in on themselves as they turned to dust. Chaos exploded around him as the enemies attacked.

His mind went blank as he ducked, feeling the wind as a sword hissed over his head. Stumbling backwards a step, he cursed himself for not drawing his own weapon sooner. His attacker pivoted, snapping his sword forward, stabbing for Alek's exposed stomach. With exhaustion clawing at his limbs, Alek whipped his sword up, blocking the stab and forcing the Dark Warrior to the left.

Using the momentum, Alek pressed onwards, raining down blow after blow on his opponent. The Dark Warrior flailed under the attack until the boy broke through his enemy's defence and felt his sword bite into his foe's neck. Seconds later, the body before him disintegrated, and Alek stumbled forward as his sword was freed from its grip.

He spun around just in time to see a Dark Warrior sneaking up behind Sarah. Without hesitating, Alek flung his sword forward before leaping after it himself. The sword embedded itself in the soldier's back and Alek followed, grasping the hilt just as the body below him crumbled away.

Fire suddenly flooded the air around him as Benny yelled, the scorching flames searing through two Dark Warriors, melting them away to nothing. As abruptly as the tongues of fire had appeared, they vanished in the night, leaving an out-of-breath Benny standing in a haze of smoke.

Adrenaline pumped through Alek's body as he glanced around. They were alive and unharmed—for now. The distant sound of metal clashing with metal resonated through the once peaceful valley, echoing the violent storm raging in the heavens above. Footsteps thudded through the trees around them, and the lightning flashing above them glinted off dark armour.

'You must go,' Ash said breathlessly, appearing at Alek's shoulder. 'I'll hold them off and draw them away.'

Figures began to emerge from the trees, surrounding the small group.

She turned her eyes to look at each of the three friends. 'You need to run. Now.'

With that, Ash launched herself into the fray, a whirlwind of steel as she began to cut down enemy after enemy.

Barely leaving any time to think, Alek roughly pushed Sarah and Benny. 'Run!' he yelled.

Without looking back, Alek led the way through the forest, flinching and ducking down low as an arrow whistled past his head, embedding itself into a tree trunk not far away. Gritting his teeth, he pushed his tired legs to move faster, stumbling over the rough ground.

Minutes later, the three friends broke out of the shelter of the trees and raced across the soft ground bordering the lake. Familiarity washed over Alek as his feet hit the sand he had spent countless hours training on. He glanced to his left, half expecting to see Kisho running beside him, a cocky smirk as he refused to let Alek beat him.

Instead, he saw a wall of dark bodies explode from the tree line, shouting as they gave chase.

'Hurry!' he huffed, looking at his friends' pale, strained faces.

They were all slowing down; the events of the night had drained their energy. The waterfall loomed before them, so close, yet they were not going to make it. Alek glanced behind them again, and his heart dropped as he saw the closest Dark Warrior barely metres behind him.

Desperately, he reached within himself, willing his magic to flood through his body one last time. His steps stumbled as his concentration slipped and rough hands gripped his shoulders, slamming him into the ground.

Light flashed behind his eyes and he gasped for air as he hit the ground hard, rolling through the sand. He heard Sarah shout his name as a heavy body slammed into him, pain flashing through his chest. The magic he had worked up faltered and sank back inside him, all but vanishing into his weary limbs.

Hands clasped around his throat, pressing down against his windpipe. Alek felt the earth shudder underneath him and he rolled his eyes to the side, his vision swimming as the ground vibrated beneath him again. Suddenly, the trees exploded across the shore and a huge bear violently ripped into the group of Dark Warriors.

'Kai,' Alek croaked, not caring if that wasn't the shifter's real name as he struggled to draw breath.

The bear's massive head swung in the direction of Alek's voice and he saw the blue eyes filled with rage and bloodlust focus on him, taking in the Dark Warrior holding him down. With a roar, the beast carved its way through the knot of warriors, blood running freely from a multitude of gashes down his muscled body.

Alek's fingers curled into the sand around him as he gasped wildly, his vision going dark until, finally, Kisho reached him, landing a devastating blow on the Dark Warrior holding him down. Sweet air rushed down his burning throat and filled up his lungs as Alek drank it in, sitting upright as the body above him disintegrated.

Hands gripped him and hauled him to his feet, pulling him away from Kisho and towards the roaring waterfall. Alek couldn't tear his eyes away from the bear as the shifter stood still, his great head watching as Alek was dragged beneath the thundering spray of water.

Moonlight broke free from the clouds above them, illuminating the colossal bear as it reared onto its hind legs, roaring in anguish. Alek's heart shattered at the mournful cry, and time seemed to slow as he cast one last look back into the valley.

He drank in the moonlit lake, the sandy shore on which he had wasted away the days with the boy he hadn't realised he had loved. The silver trees beyond concealing a valley that had never truly felt like home.

Water lapped against the soft sand as the bear's form shimmered, shrinking in on itself until the dark fur had transformed into alabaster skin. Alek watched as Kisho fell to his knees, his skin glowing under a layer of sweat. Pain stabbed into his chest like a knife as he realised this could be the last time that he saw the shifter. And all Kisho had ever done was fight for him, from the first day they met right up until this moment.

As if sensing Alek's gaze, Kisho turned and locked eyes with him. The shifter's face was pale, his eyes dull with grief. Alek watched as the boy slowly hauled himself to his feet and took an uncertain step towards him. Shaking his head, Alek backed away, and Kisho faltered, wrapping his arms around himself, his naked skin bathed in the moonlight.

The last shifter, his tattoos rippling across his body, stood alone as Alek tore his eyes away from the boy.

The effort of doing so shattered him. He allowed himself to be led behind the waterfall, the thundering water drowning out his thoughts as he pictured Kisho's bright blue eyes and the look of devastation that now filled them.

A wave of nausea threatened to overwhelm him as he felt tears running freely down his face. Alek's mind whirled as silent sobs racked his body, his shoulders shuddering as he struggled to hold his grief back.

Darkness closed in around the three friends as they entered a narrow tunnel carved into the mountainside. The air grew thick with moisture as they swiftly moved deeper into the earth, the sound of the ferocious storm slowly fading behind them.

Alek realised with a start that they were leaving behind the safety of the valley; on the other side of the mountains sprawled a wild, unfamiliar world. A world of whispering shadows and ancient enemies, of magic and danger. Taking a deep, shuddering breath, Alek stepped forward.

Into the unknown.

ABOUT THE AUTHOR

J.S. Burns is a YA fantasy author based in Brisbane, Australia, and the creator of the Whisper of Shadows Saga — a sweeping tale of YA Fantasy, Queer Romantasy, and Elemental Magic.

Blending heart-stopping adventure with slow-burn romance, J.S.Burns writes the kinds of stories he wished he had growing up — queer characters at the heart of epic fantasy journeys, discovering love, friendship, and power in a world that often underestimates them.

His goal is simple: to give readers books they'll stay up too late with, hiding under the covers long after the lights are supposed to be out, swept away into a story that feels dangerous, magical, and achingly real.

Away from the page, Jake can often be found in cafés and bars, quietly planning out new realms, weaving betrayals and forbidden romances, and plotting the twists that will one day trap his characters — and his readers — in stories they won't want to escape.

Contact the author

www.jsburnsauthor.com
www.instagram.com/j.s.burnss/

ACKNOWLEDGMENTS

First and foremost, a BIG thank you to my housemate and best friend Kylie, who put up with my whingeing and complaining as I set about writing this story in early 2019. You did a great job feigning interest and trying to remember all the characters' names until you were the first one to finally read it.

To Kara, you are the original fangirl. Your enthusiasm and excitement around the publishing process and genuine interest in making the story the best version it could be meant more than you can imagine. It was the first time someone had not just read my book but delved into the pages and grabbed the story with both hands. Those days at work where we would talk about the characters or possible plot ideas will stick with me forever.

To Sebastian, in a sense you made this story happen. Way back in 2008, you came to school and proudly stated that you were going to write a book. Me being me, I decided I too was going to do the same. But mine would be better. For over a year, I typed away on the family computer well into the night until I was done. Flash forward thirteen years, and here we are. This is, in essence, that book. Just a grown-up version, but still the same story I wrote when we were just fourteen. Thank you.

Mum and Dad. You encouraged my creativity, supported me in all my spontaneous endeavours, and taught me to never do things by half. Thank you for being the caring, supportive souls that you are. I couldn't have done this without you.

Granny, your delight at the fact that I was a bookworm was never a secret. Thank you for the excited way in which you would ask me what book I was currently reading whenever me and my brothers would come for a sleepover.

Nana, some of my fondest memories of you are when I would race into your room early in the morning to snuggle in bed and listen to you read me a story. *The Poky Little Puppy* being a personal favourite of mine. If this story gives that same sense of comfort and joy to just one person, somewhere in the world, I have done my job.

To Ocean, Jason, Kristy, Mikayla, Joshua, and everybody who worked tirelessly on making this book a reality at Ocean Reeve Publishing. I, quite literally, could not have done this without you. Your support and reassurance through the entire process has been nothing short of heroic. From answering all my questions and putting up with my indecisiveness when it came to formatting and cover design and everything in between. You guys are the real MVPs; you made my dream a reality. For that, I will be forever grateful.

To my boyfriend, Nic. You pushed me to step out of my comfort zone and approach Ocean Reeve Publishing with my little story, and look where we are now. I have dreamt of this day for so long, and all I needed was the push to make it happen. You will never begin to grasp how grateful I am to you for your unwavering support through this entire process as I stressed about every possible little thing. You've had my back from day one and allowed me to pursue this with everything that I have.

Lastly, Simba. People often say dogs are better than cats. But both are so different, how can one possibly compare the two? You sat next to me as I typed every single word of this story. You silently kept me company as I worked long into the night, giving up sleep to write just a little bit more. You listened as I discussed every aspect of the book with you, as I shared with you the hope that maybe, just maybe, my story might be published one day. Well, buddy, it's happened. You were with me through the editing, through the initial cover design concept, and always helped me with my decisions. Sadly, your time came too soon. You never got to see it, the finished product you so patiently helped me achieve. I'll never get to show you my physical book and say, 'Here it is'.

But you are here, in the words printed on every single page, just as you were there with me as I typed each letter. Fly high, little Simba, we did it.

The story continues …
Read on for an exclusive excerpt from Book 2 in The
Whisper of Shadows Saga…

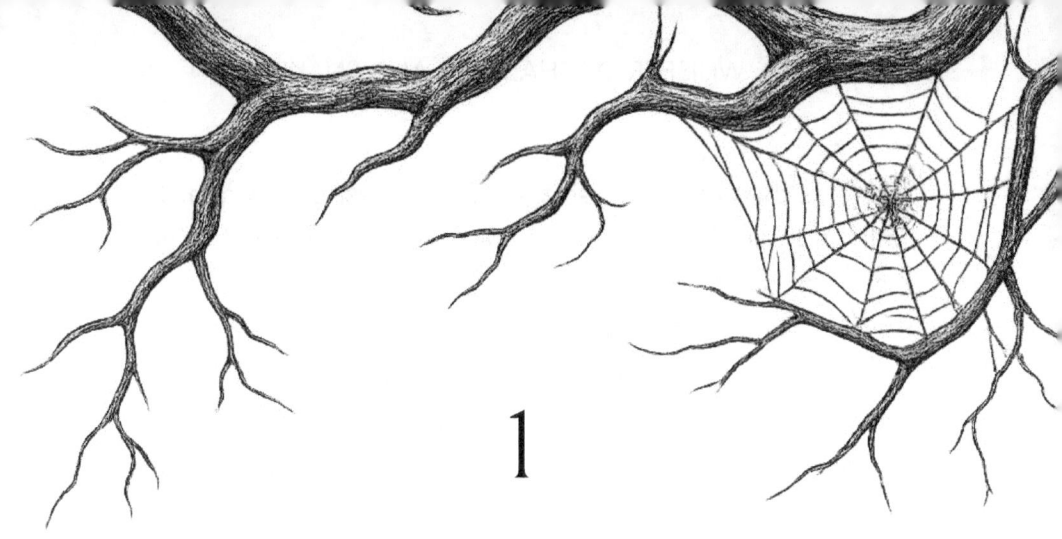

1

PUNISHMENT

'A pet bear?'

Kisho flinched as the sinister voice mused over the sentence. He carefully schooled his face into a neutral expression, keeping his eyes downcast as he knelt on the rough stone floor. The shifter had arrived in the kingdom under the mountain a few days prior to being summoned to the throne room.

Soon after Alek and his friends had escaped from Aranasmin, Kisho had shifted into his owl form and flown from the battle, careful to avoid detection from any of the remaining Dark Warriors.

Guilt washed over him as the scene once again played back in his mind—Alek's devastated face as he watched Kisho's body transform from the bear to his human self. The look of utter betrayal had turned into something far

381

worse as they locked eyes across the lakeshore. A guarded wall had slid into place behind the blonde boy's eyes. Kisho had been shut out, even as he made to run for the boy, to take him into his arms, protect him.

That expression had haunted him for the past few days, waking him in the middle of the night, making his stomach churn. He had kept to himself since he had returned to the mountain, taking to only leaving his room at night. Even then, he would sneak through the cavernous hallways, slinking through the flickering shadows to avoid this very moment.

To avoid him.

Hissing a long breath in through his teeth, Kisho rose to his feet, his eyes slowly lifting. He took note of his silent surroundings as more of the cavernous room swam into view. Giant stone pillars lined the space, stretching high into the vaulted ceiling far above. Fire burned within the columns of dark stone; the sputtering flames wrapped in lazy patterns carved into the surface of the rock.

The throne room was designed to be magnificent, the echoing space a symbol of grandeur for any visitors. But with no windows or doors to the outside world, the eerie silence caused the shadows to become oppressive, claustrophobic.

Kisho hated it here, locked within the ancient mountain's heart. His body begged him to turn away, to pass through the large metal door behind him and run. Up the winding stairs, down the countless hallways that zigzagged through the belly of the mountain range.

The kingdom was huge, filled with cavernous spaces and crawling passageways, many of which lay dormant. The secrets they held were long since forgotten by the army that now dwelled amongst the stone. Far above him, as high as you could get without leaving the mountain, Kisho's room called to him.

He had stumbled upon the room not long after arriving at this place of shadows and stone. He had been younger then, so much younger, spending most of his days exploring the sprawling kingdom. One day, he had stumbled down a dark hallway, one covered in dust and smelling of mould. His curiosity piqued, the young shifter had followed the dilapidated path as it wound up through the mountain, far above the heavily populated levels below. Pushing open an old wooden door at the end of the tunnel, Kisho's breath had been taken away.

A grand room had revealed itself before him, hewn into the grey stone of the mountain peak. A grated hearth was carved into one of the walls, and an imposing wooden bed sat proudly opposite it. A small archway led to a large private bathing area just off the main room, much better than the communal baths that were common on the lower levels where Kisho had been staying.

The feature that excited Kisho the most, however, was the wall he had not been able to take his eyes from the second he stepped into the room. The space opposite the doorway to his room consisted of a floor-to-ceiling window. Wrought iron cut through the glass in a swirling, leaf-like pattern, hiding the hinges that allowed for the windows to be thrown wide open.

Kisho vividly remembered the first time he had forced the rusty glass open, the metal groaning as if it had not moved in an age. The young shifter had instantly been buffeted by a wall of crisp wind, so different from the stuffy air beneath the mountain.

He had felt free.

A large plateau stretched outwards on the other side of the window, sheltered by the towering mountains. Kisho had taken two steps onto the plateau before his feet sent him rocketing towards the ledge and off, into space. He had whooped in exaltation as he fell through the sky, his magic overtaking him and his body blurring as he shifted into a snowy owl.

That night he had packed up his meagre belongings and moved himself up to the sanctuary at the top of the mountain, hoping that his troubles would not find him, tucked away in the mountain peaks.

The sound of someone roughly clearing their throat snapped Kisho out of his daydreams, and he nervously focused on the man before him.

Azrael, leader of the Dark Warriors.

He sat on a throne of dragon bones. The gleaming skeletons wrapped around the chair, the armrests consisting of two colossal skulls. The beasts had been captured by Azrael in the war that began the Dark Days. He had brought them back to his kingdom, chaining them to the massive columns in the throne room. Kisho now had only distant memories of the creatures and how their jewelled scales had glinted as if they were made of a thousand gemstones.

They had been young dragons, barely adult, and in that regard, Azrael had been lucky. There was no way any man would be able to chain down a fully grown dragon like a common animal. There were tapestries hung on the surrounding walls, depicting Azrael seated on his throne with the two hulking animals curled by his side. One shone gold, its scales blazing like the sun. The other, smaller beast, had a dazzling sapphire hide, glittering like an ocean of fallen stars.

The dragons had not survived long under the mountain. Chained to the ground and confined to the throne room, their scales had become dull, their bodies lethargic. When the beasts had passed, Azrael had butchered them. For three days and nights, the castle had run with blood, the smell of it heavy in the air.

Kisho remembered it well. The Dark Warriors who populated much of the kingdom under the mountain had seemed oblivious to the death of the two magnificent beats. But the young shifter had never forgotten that night. He had awoken abruptly, sensing the dragons' warm magic suddenly vanish. Cold had pressed in on Kisho from every side as he had raced through the mountain, stumbling over the rough stone as he skidded to a halt inside the throne room.

The air had been thick with blood, and by the flickering firelight, Kisho had watched in horror as Azrael cut open the dragons' chests. The man grinned savagely, blood pouring down his arms as he ripped the hearts from the beast's bodies. Kisho had turned and run, tears streaming down his face. The dragons had always been kind to him, their magic mixing with the shifter's own, making him feel less alone.

He had returned the kindness on occasion, risking everything to unchain the animals and lead them down into the catacombs within the mountain. Down to where ancient hot springs flowed through crystal caves.

He had held the dragon's chains so tightly his hands had bled; however, the two beasts never tried to escape— they simply frolicked in the heated pools, often disappearing below the water's surface for minutes on end as the young boy floated alongside them. He would marvel at the kaleidoscope of light that reflected off the dragon's scales, creating rainbows across the cave walls.

The dragons had been his only friends, and he had watched, too afraid to do anything, as the magnificent beasts slowly died. They had been trapped in a prison of shadows and stone, trophies for a twisted man, just like him.

Kisho's eyes rose past the skeletal throne to the man lounging atop the ivory bones. Azrael was tall, hulking. He had long dark hair tied back tight against his head, and a braided beard twisted from his chin. His skin was deeply tanned and battle-scarred, trophies from a lifetime of fighting. His eyes were dark, almost black.

There had been many times when Kisho had stared into their depths and felt as if his soul was being pulled from his body, ripped from his very skin by the man before him. A tattoo of an eye was etched onto his neck, the ink a deep red.

Rumours claimed that Azrael had slain hundreds of dragons over the years, consuming their hearts. This barbaric act had been said to grant him their power, prolonging his mortal life.

Azrael had once been human, of that Kisho was sure. He had never once sensed any kind of magic flickering beneath the man's dark gaze. However, whether by consuming the dragon's hearts or by other means of sorcery, the leader of the Dark Warriors was human no longer. What exactly he had become, Kisho did not know.

Glinting in the firelight around the man's neck was the stolen amulet.

Kisho had not seen the treasure leave Azrael's neck from the instant he had handed it over all those months ago. The constant thrum of the gem's power echoed through the mountain chambers, mixing with the shifter's own magic, a relentless reminder of what he had stolen.

Bones creaked as the leader of the Dark Warriors rose, making his way across the cavernous throne room. Hurriedly, Kisho dropped to his knees, bowing his head, avoiding eye contact with the powerful man. The hair on the back of the shifter's neck rose as the approaching footsteps grew louder and then stopped, the edge of Azrael's boots in Kisho's peripheral vision.

'So, let me get this straight.' The man's sinister tone cut through the air like a knife, causing Kisho's body to tense. 'I sent you back to Aranasmin to gather information and report anything back to me once the Four had been located.'

Kisho nodded, his eyes tracing the patterns in the stone beneath his bowed head as Azrael began to circle him, like a vulture hunting its prey.

'Week after week, month after month, I got generic messages. No news, no changes. No revelations. Nothing.' The footsteps paused behind Kisho, but the shifter did not dare raise his eyes.

'Now why is that, my precious shifter? Hmmm?' Azrael's voice was low, hissing between his bared teeth. 'How could my strongest child not notice that the prophesied were right under his nose? Or that the valley I once dwelled in now housed a very dangerous pet bear?'

'I-I don't know,' Kisho stuttered, words tumbling from his mouth as his brain tried to fabricate a believable lie.

'Did you not feel the Four's power calling to you? Their magic, mixing with your own?' Azrael purred, his mouth inches from the shifter's ears. 'I know you feel it now, boy. You feel the pull of the amulet thundering through your veins, singing to your soul, drawing your magic from within you.'

Sweat broke out across Kisho's brow as his body was overwhelmed with emotion. Azrael's words whispered across his skin, leaving goosebumps down his neck. Fear pumped through his body with every beat of his pounding heart, whilst at the same time, the shifter was acutely aware of the close presence of the amulet. The pendant sent magic thrumming through the air behind him, scattering his mind, causing his senses to writhe in chaos. There was only one person in the world Kisho feared.

And he was towering behind him, like a vengeful shadow.

'I don't know,' Kisho repeated, balling his hands into fists. 'Maybe I'm just so used to being the only person with magic, I didn't know what I was looking for.'

Weak! Kisho berated himself; his lies felt weak, even to himself. The shifter felt a sudden disturbance in the air before a fist slammed painfully into the back of his skull, sending him sprawling.

The rough stone floor rose up to meet him, violently slamming against his chin as the shifter tumbled to the ground. Kisho gritted his teeth through the pain, rolling onto his side to spit out a mouthful of blood.

'I wish you hadn't made me do that,' Azrael said, stalking across the throne room to haul the shifter to his feet. 'You know I don't like to hurt you,' the leader of the Dark Warriors continued, brushing dust off Kisho's shoulders. 'I raised you, boy. I pulled you out of the gutter when you had no-one. I stopped you from running, taught you to stop being a coward, to have some fucking *loyalty!*' Azrael's voice rose until he yelled the last word, sending it echoing through the throne room. 'Who saved you all those years ago? When the Dark Days were upon us and you were all alone and on the run? Who saved you from those that hunted you?'

Kisho's eyes unwillingly flicked to Azrael's left arm, where a pale white scar speared down his skin. A scar in the shape of a lightning bolt.

Fear surged through Kisho's body as memories he had long since buried threatened to bubble to the surface. Images of ghostly riders atop pale horses, of running, running until his feet bled. He took a deep breath, closing his eyes, forcing his emotions down. Pushing the violent memories away, burying them in the deepest crevices of his mind.

When Kisho opened his ice-blue eyes, they were clear, steady, betraying no hint of his inner turmoil. 'You did, sir. You saved me.'

Azrael nodded, approval in his dark gaze. 'Good. Very good, Kisho.'

The leader of the Dark Warriors turned, stalking across the echoing room to haul his body back onto the throne of bones. Kisho sighed, his muscles relaxing slightly now that there was distance between him and the wicked man.

'Now, we just have to discuss your punishment,' Azrael said, inspecting the fist he had used to strike down the shifter moments before.

Kisho's breath paused as Azrael continued, 'You will compete in the Pit. Show me that you are as skilled as I have trained you to be.'

Relief washed over the shifter; he'd endured far worse punishments than this.

'As you wish,' Kisho said, pain pounding through his skull as his jaw spoke the words.

Azrael merely waved his hand in dismissal. 'Go, prepare to prove your worth to me.'

Kisho bowed his head, hardly daring to breathe as he backed out of the throne room.

The Whisper of Shadows Saga, Book 2:

WHISPER OF SHADOWS AND STONE

Scared of getting lost,
Afraid of being found…

The shadows are shifting. Ancient monsters stir once
more… and Alek and his friends are being hunted.

With the stolen Amulet in enemy hands and the Dark
Warriors closing in, Alek, Sarah and Benny are thrust into a
treacherous race to stop a war that could destroy two
worlds. But secrets run deep, and trust is wearing thin.

Alek is torn between loyalty and love, haunted by
choices he can't undo. Sarah is unraveling the truth about
the Portal Realm. And Benny's heart burns with betrayal
that could shatter everything.

With every step forward, they're pulled deeper into a
world they don't understand.
And if the shadows don't break them, the truth just
might…

Old mountain fires still whisper of a boy
who did not cry when the world ended.

They say when the Death Dealers came,
the others burned.
They screamed.
They fought.

But one boy survived.

His eyes were like a winter grave.
His blood was brighter than gold.

And when the last flame died, he did not.

He walked out of the ashes alone.

www.ingramcontent.com/pod-product-compliance
Lightning Source LLC
Chambersburg PA
CBHW060808030726
47503CB00002B/388